ROSE
IN
CHAINS

OTHER BOOKS BY JULIE SOTO

Not Another Love Song
Forget Me Not

ROSE
IN
CHAINS

JULIE SOTO

FOREVER
NEW YORK   BOSTON

Forever
Hachette Book Group
1290 Avenue of the Americas, New York, NY 10104
read-forever.com

@readforeverpub

First Edition: July 2025

Forever is an imprint of Grand Central Publishing. The Forever name and logo are registered trademarks of Hachette Book Group, Inc.

The publisher is not responsible for websites (or their content) that are not owned by the publisher.

The Hachette Speakers Bureau provides a wide range of authors for speaking events. To find out more, go to hachettespeakersbureau.com or email HachetteSpeakers@hbgusa.com.

Forever books may be purchased in bulk for business, educational, or promotional use. For information, please contact your local bookseller or the Hachette Book Group Special Markets Department at special.markets@hbgusa.com.

Print book interior design by Taylor Navis
Family Tree by Taylor Navis

Library of Congress Cataloging-in-Publication Data has been applied for.

ISBNs: 978-1-5387-7122-8 (Hardcover: Deluxe limited edition); 978-1-5387-7586-8 (Hardcover: Deluxe limited signed edition); 978-1-5387-7534-9 (Hardcover: B&N deluxe limited signed edition); 978-1-5387-7585-1 (Hardcover: B&N Black Friday deluxe limited signed edition); 978-1-5387-7124-2 (ebook)

Printed in China

APS

10 9 8 7 6 5 4 3 2 1

For the Saturday Girls...

CONTENT WARNING

This work contains explicit sexual content, scenes with gore and violence, and sexual assault of a POV character. Non-consensual sex is referred to, and the buying and selling of human beings into captivity is a core theme of *Rose in Chains*. Forced sterilization, death of minor characters, and torture are present in this story. For a more detailed list of content warnings, please visit www.juliesotowrites.com

EVERMORE
ROSEWOOD FAMILY TREE

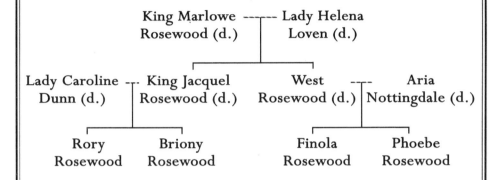

King Marlowe ------ Lady Helena
Rosewood (d.)   Loven (d.)

Lady Caroline --- King Jacquel   West ---- Aria
Dunn (d.)   Rosewood (d.)   Rosewood (d.) | Nottingdale (d.)

Rory   Briony   Finola   Phoebe
Rosewood   Rosewood   Rosewood   Rosewood

BOMARD
THE SEAT OF BOMARD – VERONIKA MALLOW

LINE TO THE SEAT

1st - Riann Cohle	succeeded by Del Burkin
2nd - Aron Carvin	succeeded by Lucille Piken
3rd - Genevieve Trow	succeeded by Canning Trow
4th - Hap Gains	succeeded by Stance Green
5th - Moira Locklin	succeeded by Rowan Locklin
6th - Caspar Quill	succeeded by Liam Quill
7th - Alba Twindle	succeeded by Collin Twindle
8th - Orion Hearst	succeeded by Toven Hearst
9th - Florence Kleve	succeeded by Ryden Kleve
10th - Cal Gidrey	succeeded by Evelyn Gidrey

ROSE
IN
CHAINS

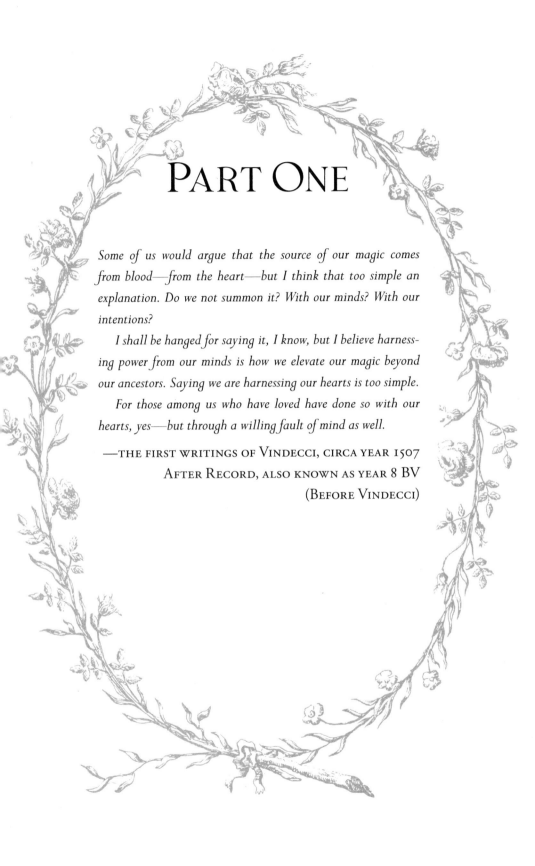

PART ONE

Some of us would argue that the source of our magic comes from blood—from the heart—but I think that too simple an explanation. Do we not summon it? With our minds? With our intentions?

I shall be hanged for saying it, I know, but I believe harnessing power from our minds is how we elevate our magic beyond our ancestors. Saying we are harnessing our hearts is too simple.

For those among us who have loved have done so with our hearts, yes—but through a willing fault of mind as well.

—THE FIRST WRITINGS OF VINDECCI, CIRCA YEAR 1507
AFTER RECORD, ALSO KNOWN AS YEAR 8 BV
(BEFORE VINDECCI)

CHAPTER 1

BRIONY THOUGHT IT WAS STRANGE that she didn't feel it when her brother died. The crack of the boundary evaporating rattled her ribs, and the rock scraped under her fingertips as she gripped the ledge looking out over what was left of the country of Evermore—but she felt nothing in her soul when Rory died.

As his twin, she'd tugged on the thread that ran between them many times—when he was injured, when he needed help. Briony reached for that thread now, seeking out the vein of magic in her chest that was reserved for Rory only. Dark silence was the only response. She supposed she'd had no premonition, either, when her father had fallen four years ago, and her mother had been dead already when they'd cut Briony out of her.

But when the dust billowed up like a cloud on a summer's afternoon just under half a mile away, and the calm that had curled around her and Cordelia collapsed into rumbling chaos, Briony knew that Rory was dead.

His protection boundary around the castle had fallen. He was dead.

And yet her soul didn't wrench in half.

Briony watched the moon move away from the sun, the eclipse ending as soon as it had begun.

How strange, she thought numbly.

"No . . ." Cordelia whispered.

Briony looked to her right and found her friend's pale fingertips almost translucent against her lips. The wind whipped Cordelia's auburn hair around her eyes, as if trying to spare her from the sight. On the other side of Cordelia, Anna stepped forward to the balcony ledge as if in a trance, her mouth open. The sunlight reflected off the purple rose crest on her armor.

Briony looked back to the cloud of dust and ash that blossomed higher and higher to cover the moon and the sun in their dance. She saw the reflection of it to her left in the water of the lake.

The last dragon flapped her spindly wings and soared away from the mess of humans on the battlefield, returning north.

"Stay here," Anna said, running quickly toward the balcony stairs. She pivoted, changing her mind. "No . . . You should go inside. Get somewhere safe and wait."

Briony stared at her. Cordelia choked on a sob.

Anna gazed back, and Briony watched her guard's mind twirl through her plans and strategies. Anna was supposed to stay by her side; she had held her as a baby and promised her father to give her life for Briony's.

Before she could overthink, Anna darted down the stairs.

Briony turned back to the dust cloud, wondering if parts of her brother were inside of it. Her brother who was supposed to be the one to end this war. Her brother who had been foretold.

She gasped then, as if the idea of the failed prophecy was the slap she'd needed.

Rory was gone. Tears filled her eyes on a shuddering inhale, and she imagined what the front would be like. A thousand soldiers realizing that their long-held hope, their Heir Twice Over, was just a man after all.

She shrugged off her cape. It wouldn't help her run. Neither would her slippers or draped silk gown, but she didn't have time to change.

She had one foot on the stairs when Cordelia grabbed her wrist, tugging her back. "Where are you going?" The panic pinched her voice. "We have to hide!"

Briony laid her hand on her friend's wrist. "If we hide, we'll be the last ones left," she said, her voice flat.

Cordelia's blue eyes widened. The moment Cordelia's grip relaxed, Briony spun and raced down the stairs, her friend's light footsteps chasing behind her.

CHAPTER 2

Six Hours Earlier

RIONY SAT AT THE DESK IN HER BEDROOM, gaze focused on the steam curling from her teacup like dancing flames. With a distracted twitch of her fingers, she imagined her favorite willow at the edge of the lake and watched as the steam did her bidding, rising up to form a trunk and falling down into hundreds of reedy branches kissing the water.

Sometimes it was easier to manipulate something unimportant when she couldn't find the spell she needed to make the world right. Steam from her cup could make a pretty picture, even if the picture outside the castle walls wasn't as pretty.

She grasped the humming thread of magic between her eyes. The translucent mist of the hot tea billowed out to show the lake next to it, and her mind supplied the silhouette of a boy with a lithe body sitting at the base of the tree. She had just conjured the book in his hands when her bedroom door opened. Briony startled, and the willow disappeared, steam curling like normal again.

She swung around, feeling caught in the act of something, and Rory was there in her doorway.

"Is it time already?" she asked, checking the clock.

"No, I'm just . . . visiting."

Briony pulled a face. "Don't do that."

"Do what?"

"Don't say goodbye."

"All right, I won't."

"Good."

His lips twitched. As twins, they shared the same curved mouth, the same brown eyes, the same chestnut hair color. His nose was broader like Father's, and her hair was wavy like their mother's, but the differences in their appearances were subtle.

Rory hooked his thumbs into the tailored trousers he'd had made for battle. "But I should warn you that Didion wants to say goodbye. Wants to probably say more than goodbye—"

Briony groaned and tilted her face back to the high ceiling. "This is your fault," she said. "If you hadn't proposed to Cordelia, then Didion never would have gotten these ideas."

Rory plopped onto her bed. "Actually, I'd say he got the idea when you started taking walks after midnight with him—"

She gasped. "Who told you about that? That was a year ago, and walking was all we did!"

Rory leveled his gaze at her. "Couldn't find a better time of day to walk?"

Briony bit her lip. "All right, maybe we did a bit more—"

Rory covered his ears. "Stop."

"But I swear my virtue is intact."

He rolled on his back and squeezed his eyes closed. "Stop talking, I beg you."

Laughing, Briony dropped onto the other side of the bed. "Is there anyone *else* who wishes to say goodbye? Any other suitors I should know about?" She fluffed her flowing summer skirts around her legs.

Rory smiled, but then the curve of his mouth dripped like wax. "I don't know. Are there?" he asked quietly.

Her breath caught in her chest. "What do you mean?"

His eyes flickered between her own, seeking. "If it's not Didion, then who does have your attention?"

"No one." Her voice was high and rushed. "It's—it's *war*, Rory, in case you hadn't noticed. Why would anyone have time for any of that?"

"Well, some of us find the time quite easily. Anyway, after today, things may be different." He sat up, and she watched his fingers as they played with the long leather cord he usually tucked under his shirts; the silver pendant at the end of it had belonged to their mother.

Rory was always so humble when the possibility of victory was brought up. As if he wasn't the one prophesied to be the victor. As if he didn't quite believe it himself.

"Yes. Today may change everything." She reached across the bed and grabbed his hand. "Do you want to go over it again?"

He looked up at her and nodded. It would always be like this with them, she realized.

On the first day of school, when Father had asked her to look out for Rory, she hadn't understood why she needed to take care of her sixteen-year-old twin brother. Shouldn't he be the one looking out for her?

"He may struggle in lessons you excel at," Father had said. "It would be nice if the Bomardi children didn't see the future King of Evermore bested by his sister."

Briony still didn't comprehend it until the results of the first exams came in and Father started asking her to switch entire assignments with Rory. Hours upon hours of work she did over the next five years were often given to her brother, and she had to gather what she could from his scraps.

She never forgave her father for that, not even in his death.

Briony took a deep breath and curled her fingers toward her palm, summoning a small vial filled with water into her hand. She held it up to Rory.

"This is water from the lake. It's the same water in the castle's well and the Eversun school's well." Briony swallowed, thinking of the thousands of Eversun families who were sheltering at the school across the lake until this war was done. "When you cast the protection, pour this onto your hands and place the last drop on your tongue. The lake, Claremore Castle, and the school will all link under one shield connected to you."

Rory took it from her, nodding. "General Meers doesn't like this plan, by the way."

"He doesn't understand it. He's not a Rosewood," Briony said.

Their Rosewood bloodline was strong with protection magic—shields, borders, and wards. It was one of the main reasons they were predestined to rule, according to Briony and Rory's father. He, their grandfather, and all the men behind them were celebrated peacetime rulers. Rory was the first Rosewood to know war in over five hundred years.

"The general values offensive magic. That's his job," Briony continued. "But it's your job as king and as a Rosewood to protect our people."

"What's left of them," said Rory, the exhaustion in his voice clear.

Over the past four years of war, they'd been beaten farther and farther south, losing their ground and losing people. It wasn't land that Bomard truly wanted. It wasn't the captives taken along the way—though that was always a plus for the power-hungry Bomardi. It was Rory. It was the end to the Heir Twice Over.

Briony placed her hand on his. "It will be over soon. Today is the day."

"What if it isn't?" Rory asked, the words tumbling out quickly. His eyes pleaded with her.

"It is." Briony's voice was stronger than she felt. She smiled reassuringly. "The eclipse. Everyone knows it's today. *When the sun shines at night, he who will bring an end to war—*"

Rory yanked his hand from her. "Don't quote the prophecy to me. Six-hundred-year-old nonsense."

He stood and went to the window overlooking her writing desk. Briony watched him lean forward on the ledge, like a child wishing he could play outside. She ran her fingers over the duvet, thinking of the old prophecy that had haunted Rory for four years now.

When the sun shines at night, he who will bring an end to war on this land shall be victorious. He shall be an heir, twice over, and a rightful sovereign over the continent.

The prophecy was from more than half a millennium ago. When it hadn't come true at the end of the Moreland civil war that split the continent into Evermore and Bomard, many had forgotten about it. But four years ago, at the outbreak of the new conflict, everyone began wondering if Rory was the one prophesied.

Briony's eyes drifted to the papers and correspondence on her desk—the letters she'd received back from the countries across the sea stating that they could not send aid, but that they would accept the Rosewoods and their court warmly in a retreat; the *Journal* page that updated daily with the news from the realm; the victory speech she'd written for Rory; the maps with all the locations of Eversun safe houses.

She cleared her throat. "You have to kill her," Briony said softly. "It has to end. Completely."

Briony hadn't even said Mallow's name, and yet a cold wind settled inside her chest.

Rory pressed his lips together. "I know."

"You'll have to use Heartstop if nothing else is working—"

"I know, Briony," he said harshly. He sniffed. "Sorry. I . . . I will. General Meers and I have been practicing on . . ."

His voice trailed off. Briony didn't want to know which small animals or birds around Claremore had been disappearing.

Heartstop was outlawed in Evermore. Of all the heart magic, Heartstop, the crushing of a heart within its owner's chest, took the heaviest toll on a magician. The first taking of a human life ripped one's own heart, and every subsequent kill sliced further and further. Rory had had to learn this complex magic from scratch, as only Bomardi used heart magic. Just as only Eversuns used mind magic.

It was this divide between the two countries that Veronika Mallow had seized upon. Bomard had been radicalized under her, believing that the Eversuns' mind magic was mind *control*, instead of what it simply was: a different source from which to pull magic. There were differences between the disciplines, too—certain mind magic spells could never be mastered by a heart magician, and vice versa, but the true difference was the source of power. Magic pulled from the mind did not exhaust the body, whereas magic from the heart took a greater physical toll. Heart magicians had always needed to rely on animal familiars to keep their strength for prolonged magic use.

Or worse.

Under Mallow's influence, some Bomardi had taken it all a step further. Why use an animal when you could use a person. Another magician's heart could give you much more power than an animal's, and creating a bond—a heartspring bond—would ensure that your own heart wasn't being exhausted.

There was a screech outside the window, and in tense silence, they both watched Mallow's familiar beat its black wings against the sky. The last dragon in the known world, the creature whose name had been lost to time, had begun circling at dawn.

There were times Briony didn't blame the Bomardi for following Mallow. She, too, might have put her faith in the mage able to bond with the last dragon. Not to mention the untold power Mallow received from that bond—the strength of magic and the access to skills that a heart magician could never acquire from a more common animal, or even a heartspring. Bonded to the dragon, Mallow might live two life-spans, like the last mage who'd bonded with it. The Dragon Lord, as he was called in the history books, had lived more than one hundred and fifty years. And it wasn't just a long life that Mallow had with the dragon bond. It was widely known that with the dragon's magic, Mallow could read thoughts, a trait heretofore only known among the most experi-enced *mind* magicians.

They watched the dragon sail until she disappeared over the ocean again.

Briony refocused her attention as Rory turned from the window. He looked at her with the same expression from when they were younger, like he needed the answer to a tutor's question.

"Do you believe the prophecy is about me? Really? In your heart, Briony?"

Briony was still as she answered without a waver in her voice, "Yes."

Rory watched her for hesitation, but she did not show it.

There was a knock on the door, and Briony jumped.

Rory sighed. "That'll be Didion, then."

Her lips pulled down into a frown.

Rory laughed. "Don't be mean to him!" he said. "He may die today, you know."

"Don't say such a thing."

"It's true!" Rory ran for the door and pulled it open. "Isn't it true, Did?"

Didion's lanky frame stood sheepishly in the doorway.

"Isn't what true?" he asked, peering at Briony and Rory from below messy dark hair.

"That you may die today," Rory said simply.

"Oh. Yes. Very sad."

Briony rolled her eyes and sat up tall on her featherbed. "Glad you two have a solid outlook on things."

Didion smiled and cleared his throat.

Rory clapped his hands together. "I have to find Cordelia. Is it all right if I leave you two unchaperoned?"

Briony parted her lips to protest, but Rory was already halfway out the door.

"We've been alone plenty of times," Didion said with a laugh.

Rory grabbed the doorframe and swung back inside. "You can die for *certain* today if you keep saying things like that."

Briony squawked, and a pink blush overtook Didion's olive skin.

"As if *you* aren't off to be *unchaperoned* yourself!" she yelled. Briony grabbed one of her pillows and threw it at her brother's head. With a flick of his wrist, he split the pillow apart in midair. Feathers floated everywhere, and Rory ran out, disappearing in the cloud of fluff.

Groaning, Briony twisted her palms toward her chest, gathering the feathers and floating them into the trash bin.

Once the place was clean again, she was alone with Didion for the first time in a year. He looked over her bedroom, searching her desk and the paintings that hung on her walls.

"Is it comfortable here for you?" he asked, raising his full eyebrows at her.

"I like it. I miss Biltmore Palace, but what can you do?" She shrugged. And immediately felt very awkward. "What can you do"—as if they'd lost the coastal palace in a coin toss instead of a siege.

His gaze focused on her teacup, next to her books. The same teacup whose steam she had been manipulating into the memory of a different boy only ten minutes ago. He hovered his index finger over the liquid and brought its temperature up again. The steam wisped upward as he held the teacup out to her.

"Here," he said with a shy smile.

Briony tried not to wince as she took the cup and he sat down next to her on her mattress.

"It's been a while since we've been properly alone together," Didion said.

Briony nodded. That had been her idea. When the stress of the tactical meetings and tension within the castle walls had become too much, she and Didion used to take walks together at night by the docks near Biltmore Palace, escaping prying eyes and inquisitive ears. He listened while she confided her frustrations about General Meers's strategies, and soon the walks began to end with soft kisses, like they'd shared in school. And then the kisses began to end with hands under fabrics.

Didion was gentle and patient. His hands seemed to spend hours fumbling to find just the right spot between her thighs, and once he found it, he quickly lost it, but Briony just smiled when he would ask if she enjoyed herself. Perhaps there was supposed to be more . . . enjoyment. Briony *hoped* at least. Perhaps when a bed was brought into it, things became easier, but she refused to let Didion into her bed. As the sister of the king, she'd already allowed Didion many liberties that only a husband should have.

It had been her idea to pause things between them after the retreat from Biltmore Palace, even though Didion was a comfortable choice. Safe. Kind. Her father would have been happy to see her married to Didion Winchester. Her brother, too. Briony often wondered why she didn't *want* comfortable, safe, kind.

"I was hoping to ask you for your favor today," he said, staring down at his hands.

Sipping to stall for time, Briony watched his thumbs circle each other. "Oh?"

"Perhaps I could wear your pin into the field today?"

Her fingers jumped for the silver brooch. "It's my mother's," she said quickly, ignoring her use of the present tense. "I've never taken it off. I can't part with it, I'm sorry."

"No, of course, right," he stuttered. "Not exactly your pin then. A lock of hair?"

"That's . . . also my mother's," she quipped awkwardly. All portraits of her mother had borne a striking resemblance to Briony as she'd aged to her twenty-five years—coincidentally, the same age at which her mother had died giving birth to Briony and Rory. "I don't . . ." Briony cleared her throat. "Is it necessary? Can't I just wish you well? You and my brother both?"

He nodded, blushing softly. "That's fine. I had only hoped . . . Well, if I could know that I had someone to come home to . . ."

"Come home?" She laughed. "You'll be hardly a mile away—"

"I'm trying to ask formally, and you're making it very hard." He ran a hand through his dark hair.

"There's nothing to ask," she said firmly. "Until this is over, we don't know if I'll need to be useful in some other way."

He looked at her sharply. "You mean a peace treaty betrothal? Rory wouldn't do that to you."

"He won't have a choice! He's thought of nothing but battle tactics for four years now, but after today, he'll need to start thinking like the King of Evermore." She set down her teacup, remembering the boy in the steam. "There have been plenty of marriages between Bomard and Evermore to sustain the treaty."

"Don't sound so excited," Didion mumbled.

Her head snapped to him. "What?"

He sighed and stood from her bed. "Briony, please just tell me that you'll be happy if I live through today. That's all I ask."

"Of course I'll be happy if you live through today—"

"Wonderful. Thank you," he said. And before she could form another sentence, he was out the door, closing it behind him with a soft click.

She groaned and fell back on her bed. She wasn't being purposefully evasive. Aside from two cousins, she was the only woman left in the Rosewood line who could be offered as a human sacrifice to a political marriage. Rory probably couldn't hold that thought in his head, but a political marriage would go a long way in restoring trust once today was over. There were many families in the Bomardi line of succession who weren't bloodthirsty vengeance seekers. A marriage between herself and a young Bomardi within the line wouldn't have to be a life of torture.

There were some with whom she'd attended school who looked down on the Eversuns but hadn't been so outwardly despicable. Finn Raquin with his dark skin and darker eyes was half Eversun himself; his parents had been one such convenient marriage. The Raquin patriarch was fourteenth in line for the highest position of power in Bomard—the Seat. Finn was a cad, but he wasn't evil.

On the other hand, evil had a face with Canning Trow. With wide-set eyes and pasty skin, Canning was terrible to look at, with a soul that was just as bleak. It had been common knowledge to steer clear of him in the dark corridors at school. The only reason he walked as if he owned the place was that he did. His mother was third in line for the Seat, and his father's family owned the entire mountain that the Bomardi school grounds were carved into.

There were several young men who were cruel only when it was convenient for them, like Lorne Vult and Liam Quill, though word was that Liam Quill was more interested in Lorne and Finn than extending his family line—sixth though his father was.

And then there was someone far harder to decipher. Icy cold most days, only to thaw at the oddest moments. With strong hands and opaque eyes, a wicked mouth and a silver tongue. Who inspired as much fear and uncertainty in her chest as he did yearning.

Briony shook her thoughts loose. It was useless to dwell on such things.

She glanced at her teacup. It was cold again. The steam gone on a sigh.

*　　*　　*

A few hours later, Briony stood in the castle courtyard, watching her brother kiss her best friend goodbye. Cordelia wrapped her arms around Rory's shoulders much more affectionately than was considered proper, but there weren't many people who cared about propriety in these dark days.

"Disgusting," said a voice on her left.

Briony grinned at her cousin Finola. She was tugging her gloves on and frowning playfully at Rory and Cordelia's display of affection.

Briony chuckled. "That will be you one day, you know."

"Not if I can help it," Finola said, winking at her. She flipped her honey-blond braid over her shoulder. "I'll see you when this is over, yeah?"

Briony nodded. Finola ran for the corner of the courtyard, the only location in the castle one could portal out of. Briony longed to ask where Finola was off to, but she wasn't given access to that kind of information, much to her disappointment.

Off to her right, General Billium Meers spoke softly to Anna Wevin, Briony's personal guard. Anna was, in fact, the only woman aside from Finola whom Briony had ever seen General Meers give any respect to. Certainly not Briony, when she used to sit in on strategy meetings, which always seemed to devolve into arguments. The general prioritized aggression in their attacks, to the point of callous risk-taking, and Briony was always quick to remind Rory about defense, shields, and protecting their people. At some point in the past two years, General Meers had convinced Rory that, out of caution and efficiency, military strategy meetings should involve essential advisers only, and then Briony was barred. Rory briefed her in private now. He could have named her an adviser, but he hadn't, and she wouldn't suggest such a thing.

Anna saluted the general and came to stand three paces behind Briony, as she had her entire life. General Meers gave Briony a cursory nod, which she returned with a glare.

The general's son, on the other hand, could not have been more opposite from his father.

Sammy Meers with his russet-brown hair, rosy skin, and cheery blue eyes came to a stop in front of Briony. He swept the ground in a deep bow and grabbed her hand before she could pull it back.

"Miss Briony Rosewood," he said loudly, "though you offer me your favor today, I cannot accept it."

Briony tugged her hand back. "*Stop* it!" she hissed, cheeks flushing as she caught Didion rolling his eyes at Sammy's theatrics.

"I know you want me to propose upon my return," Sammy continued, yelling for the entire courtyard, "but my heart belongs to another."

Sammy turned lovesick eyes over Briony's shoulder to Anna, who was twenty years his senior. He bowed deeply.

"Please back up from the princess," Anna said dryly.

"How I enjoy these little flirtations," Sammy said, batting his eyes. He winked at Briony and headed to join the line of troops outside the gates. He took up the Eversun flag, the purple rose, her family's crest, dominating the white background.

Briony looked over the courtyard at the easy faces and relaxed conversations. There was a buzzing in the air—the sense that this was the prophesied day, and that the long four years of warfare after the death of their father, King Jacquel, would soon be over. Rory's rule would extend over both kingdoms as he proved himself the heir mentioned in the prophecy.

Briony tried to feel the same ease, tried to relax in the same way. The moon inched closer to the sun, as prophesied. A dragon's cry pierced the sky. And everyone continued chatting and hugging and drinking one last toast.

When it was time for the troops to leave, Rory approached her for a hug.

"No," she said. "No need."

He dropped his arms and frowned at her. "Briony."

"I'll see you in a few hours," she said firmly. "Anything else we say to each other is unnecessary."

He touched his forehead to hers. "See you soon, Biney."

"I'll have a feast ready for us, Worry."

He winked at the sound of his childhood nickname and pivoted to his horse, ready to take his men out of the courtyard.

Didion glanced back at her once before following.

Anna stepped up to Briony's side. "You couldn't give that Didion boy a scrap, could you?"

Cordelia snorted.

Briony huffed. "Like I said, no need," she said, crossing her arms. "They'll be home by dark."

The castle gates closed behind the soldiers, and Briony turned to lead them up to the balcony to watch and wait.

The world went dark for a moment as something blocked the sun. Briony turned to see if the eclipse had begun.

A black dragon beat her wings above the castle, unable to touch them because of Rory's protection boundary.

The creature screeched, and Briony felt it in her marrow.

CHAPTER 3

Briony's heart was going to explode out of her chest. She pounded down the stairs from the outdoor balcony, too fast for her to wonder if silence was key. Cordelia's thick breath was only three paces behind her as they came to the fourth-floor open arcade.

She flew past an archway and stopped at the next, looking out to the lake. The cloud of dust and bone had started floating away on a tilt, and the moon had left the sun behind with a kiss. The dragon was nowhere in sight on the horizon. She looked down into the courtyard, and her blood froze in her veins.

A river of deep-blue coats ran through the gates, spreading out like tributaries.

Mallow's men were inside.

Cordelia gasped at the sight. Some of the Bomardi were engaging with the meager number of guards and servants left behind, but some were running straight inside as if their directive were as simple as capture the flag.

From a hundred feet up, Briony saw a man in a blue coat slash at the air with his fingers, and a maid grabbed for her throat, her blood spraying wide as she fell.

Briony wondered if that was Sofia, her own handmaid.

There was a wall inside her mind. As Cordelia choked on panicked sobs next to her, Briony felt a barricade between her brain and her eyes, not allowing her to cry yet. Perhaps it was a dam in her throat, refusing to let her body and her brain interact.

She watched that same man come at one of the footmen, and Briony leaned over the windowsill, reaching her arm toward a statue of Vindecci, the father of mind magic, on the tallest tower. She slashed her arm, letting the magic follow her command, and watched as the sainted philosopher slid off its post at a slant. As it fell, she pounded her palms together. The marble statue exploded. She guided a large chunk toward the man just as he reached up to slice the footman's neck. The stone slammed into his shoulder. He yelled out and threw his head back in pain.

Briony recognized him. Reighven. One of Mallow's most vicious soldiers, who had taken a personal interest in Briony since the day the war began at the Bomardi school. His face haunted so many of her anxious nights.

The other stone pieces landed around him, some knocking into other blue coats. Men halted either in their attack on the staff or in their steady stream inside. And then fifty pairs of eyes turned upward.

Briony pulled Cordelia back a moment too late.

They knew where to find them.

She grabbed Cordelia's hand and ran. They had to get away from this floor, this side of the palace.

She twisted them through a maze of servants' quarters and passageways that she had hazy memories of. They ran up a half staircase, crossed over what she knew to be the kitchens below, and then ran back down into the lakeside corridor. There was a narrow staircase hidden somewhere here, meant for the servants to come and go quickly between floors. She needed to remember which wall it was behind. They flew past so many places she and Rory had galloped like horses and taught each other magic meant for older kids. That dam in her throat held fast as she thought of her brother.

Where was his body?

Why had the prophecy been wrong?

Why had she allowed him to think he was invincible?

There was a crash ahead of them, behind the door they were running for. The sound of exploding stone and splintering wood. Briony and Cordelia skidded to a halt. Something in her brain skipped a step. That was the direction they were going. That was the *one* direction she'd known to go.

And then it was Briony being dragged by Cordelia. She followed her friend's steps backward, ducking into an alcove and jumping into a linen closet.

Their breathing was too loud.

That's the only thing Briony could think of as the staircase doors banged open and the men who'd gotten into the castle first came barreling down the hallway.

She grasped the thread of magic in her mind and tugged, forcing her heart to slow. Taking Cordelia's wrist, she rubbed her thumb over the vein, slowing her heart as well.

Their breathing was quiet, and now all she could hear was the slap of boots on the stone.

"Take Gains and check every room. Round them up."

Briony swallowed at the voice. The rough crackle of it belonged to Caspar Quill. And she realized something terrible.

The Bomardi men who were in her father's castle—

The men who watched her brother die—

The men who were hunting Eversuns—

They were the men to whom she grew up curtsying, the men she greeted at state affairs, the men who shook her father's hand just weeks before Mallow took the Seat and struck him down.

She likely knew them all.

Liam Quill and Larissa Gains—two Bomardi she'd been in school with for five years. It was their fathers on the other side of the closet door.

And she wondered if they would have ever imagined their own children hiding from her father like this.

She listened as two pairs of footsteps receded down the hall. To the right, she could just make out the sounds of the room being torn apart. She thought it might have been the servants' sitting room—

A scream broke across her ears.

"No! Please! Please, I'm just a maid!"

Cordelia gasped, and Briony pressed her fingers against her wrist to maintain their heartbeats and quiet breathing.

The girl yelped, and there was a crash.

"They sl—sleep upstairs! Fifth floor!" she cried.

Briony bit her lip. A lie. All the main chambers were on the third.

"Maybe it's not their bedrooms we're looking for," a deep voice said, dripping with malicious intention. It was Gains. "Think we have a few minutes for a diversion?"

His partner said, "What's the point of sacking the place if we can't do any *sacking?*"

The maid yelled out. There was a sound of a body hitting a wall. Fabric tore.

And Briony was out of the cupboard before Cordelia could turn pleading eyes on her.

The closet door banged against the stone wall as she darted forward. She skidded into the corridor, turning to stare into the room.

The adrenaline shook Briony's body. Her breath rattled her chest as she saw a young woman thrown onto a small sofa, two men looming over her.

Briony reached with her magic toward the closet door that Cordelia was just stepping out of. She lunged with her whole body and tugged. The door popped off its hinges with a crack and flew toward her. The wood splintered, and she lifted her hands to direct two pieces to rise into the air. She shoved with the magic, and the sharp wood barreled into the sitting room.

There were two matching howls of pain as the wooden stakes pierced both men's thighs.

Cordelia twisted her wrists to levitate two more sharp pieces. The men's eyes were wide with recognition as Cordelia pushed, hurtling the wood toward their chests this time.

Gains batted the air, and the shard of wood changed path, but his partner got a stake to his shoulder. Before Gains could retaliate, the maid was off the sofa, swinging at his head with a thick candlestick holder from the side table. Gains stumbled, and Cordelia lifted the final piece of broken door into the air, sending it toward his stomach this time.

The squelch of penetrated organs was sure to haunt Briony's dreams.

The maid dashed from the room, grabbing Briony's and Cordelia's hands and tugging.

"We have a passage! You have to go!" Her accent was thick with vowels from another land.

"That's what I was trying to find," Briony said, glancing back to make sure the men were down. Gains was alive, rolling in pain, but at least it would slow him. The other one . . . she wasn't sure.

They followed the girl through a stone wall that disappeared when pressed upon, and suddenly Briony was tripping down wet stairs. Cordelia lit their path with a twitch of her fingers—a ball of light casting shadows over the back of the maid's strawberry-blond head.

Briony remembered her now, a tumble of thoughts that came one per stone step. She had been here for only a few months, just over from Shurtarth. She and her brother both. Her brother volunteered yesterday to join Rory's army, the only Shurtarthian non-magician willing to do so.

Her mind refocused as the staircase started to turn. The maid stopped at the door at the bottom.

"This is the third floor. There's another passage down to the second floor—"

"Behind the portrait of my mother. I remember now," Briony said. "We have to be quick."

The maid nodded, and Briony vanished the limestone door with a flick of her wrist. She looked both ways, and then stepped out.

They found no one in the large hall, but someone had set fire to the flag of Evermore. The fabric was falling to the floor in crackling pieces, her family's rose burned to ash. The maid led them on quick feet toward the portrait gallery, and in no time at all, Briony was peeling back the portrait of her mother—all dark eyes and a strong jaw that Briony hadn't inherited. She held the portrait frame open like a door, and the maid slipped in first, followed by Cordelia.

Briony turned to close the frame behind them, listening to the other women's footsteps descend the stairs and—

BOOM!

The explosion rattled the very stone under her feet. Briony braced herself between the two walls of the passage as Cordelia turned, a dozen steps below, her eyes white in the dark.

And then the ceiling caved in, erasing Cordelia from Briony's sight.

CHAPTER 4

BRIONY PUSHED OUT OF THE PASSAGE before she was crushed.

Her heart pounded as she fell to the floor. A cloud of dust and rubble billowed out behind her, and she thought of Rory. How he had been inside a similar gray cloud.

Was Cordelia inside this one?

She scrambled forward, reaching out with magic to lift and remove the stones.

"Cordelia!" she called, inhaling dust into her lungs.

Behind her, she could hear paintings tumbling off the walls, the explosion still shaking everything. The castle could no longer hold strong without Rory's cycle of magic protection. It was falling down around them as the magic in the stones leached away.

She didn't hear a response from the rubble, and just as she was about to cast to narrow her hearing to one area, the sound of heavy boots running reached her ears.

She was on the floor of the portrait gallery, in plain sight, with no exit in front of her.

Briony jumped to her feet and ran. She turned past the dining room, listening to a woman screaming from down the hall. She headed for the grand staircase, not knowing which other way to go.

She turned the corner and stumbled to a stop. Anna's body lay at a sideways angle across the top of the stairs, her eyes open but empty. Briony swallowed back the pain of it and tried to step around her to continue going down.

Another explosion rocked the walls, and she staggered, barely able to keep her balance as the ground shook. When she stabilized, she glanced back at Anna's body again.

Why was Anna coming from these stairs? She should have gone down the other side of the castle.

There was nothing this way but the bedrooms.

And like lightning cracking in her mind, Briony remembered the papers on her desk. The secret correspondence from the countries who would give them refuge. The list of safe houses throughout the continent where the general's spies would gather.

At the bottom of the staircase, there were four blue coats twisting upward. They hadn't seen her yet. She continued, dashing down the corridor to the right.

She flew along, her only plan to get to the papers. There was no other exit this direction. She'd have to check the exterior wall to see if scaling her way down was even an option.

She stumbled through her antechamber and into her bedroom, her magic slamming both doors closed behind her. She sparked her hands together, and the papers on her desk lit on fire.

A door banged open in the next room. She could hear it through the limestone walls.

Briony froze in place, just long enough to have the decision made for her—she could not leave the way she came.

She dashed to the window and looked down. There were five of Mallow's men patrolling the ground below. It would be possible to take them out before climbing down. She just needed to be smart about it.

She glanced around her chamber, needing a hiding place for now. The attached bathroom was frustratingly sparse. The chest at the foot of her bed would be the obvious place. She ran for the armoire, knowing it was foolish, but it would at least buy her time to cast.

A spell for blending was treacherously difficult, but she'd mastered it in the past four years while her brother went into battle. It took focused mind magic to deceive someone else's eye.

She stepped up into the armoire and shoved her clothing aside. She tugged the doors shut and closed her eyes, imagining the string of magic behind her forehead. She stretched her fingers, casting, and imagined herself invisible, blending into the colors of the closet. A cursory glance into the armoire would show nothing, as long as she could maintain her focus.

The bedroom door flew open, banging off the stone wall, and in the crack between the armoire doors, Briony watched a man run inside and stop in his tracks.

Her heart seized, and a gasp broke past her lips.

And her blending spell fell away.

He seemed taller. His long, pale limbs were thick with muscles under his black shirt and tailored vest, but his waist still tapered into his black trousers in that frustrating way that had pulled her eyes for so many years.

She watched him spin in a circle, eyes casting over every part of her bedroom—every part of her that she never thought he'd see.

And while he got his bearings, she refocused on the blending spell, holding tight to that thread between her eyes until her physical form fell away.

Between the crack in the doors, she watched as he approached the desk where the papers were curling into cinders. Without giving them a second glance, he ran for the bathroom. He returned quickly, then ripped open her trunk at the foot of her bed.

A small shiver of satisfaction rose in her. Exactly right—those *were* the two easiest places.

But then he ran for the armoire, and she focused her intent on the spell, holding her breath.

He flung the doors open, and then she was face-to-face with Toven Hearst.

The eyes she'd realized years ago weren't fully gray, but also speckled blue, stared directly into her.

She should have cast another spell to soften her heartbeat. He must hear it.

His hair fell across his forehead, fine and so pale that the gray was almost silver.

The last time she'd seen this man, he'd been hunting her through the woods and killed the people that got in his way.

She quivered with his nearness. She told herself it was fear.

He stepped forward, looking from side to side.

The height of the baseboard in the armoire made her taller so she was almost his height, and if he poked his head any farther in, he'd touch his lips to hers.

There was something in his eyes as he pulled back, like he was trying to recall something. He stared into the armoire again, reaching his hand out.

Briony shivered. This was the end of it.

And then his fingers trailed down the side of a green dress to her left. One she hadn't worn in many years.

"Toven."

They both jumped.

Toven spun away from her, his hand almost brushing her body.

Finn Raquin, his best friend, stood in the doorway.

"We have to go," Finn said. His chest was rising and falling fast. "Mallow knows you're here."

Toven pulled away from the armoire and moved to Briony's desk to look out the window.

"Toven," Finn repeated. He scrubbed a hand over his face. "Don't do this."

She watched Toven's pale fingers reach out and brush against something on her desk. The teacup from that morning.

"They haven't called it off yet," Toven said. His voice was a deep baritone that always rumbled low in her stomach whenever he spoke. "There's still time."

He bolted from the room, and Finn sighed, following behind.

Briony could scarcely think. She listened to their footsteps pounding, leading them away. She lifted the blending spell and took a deep cleansing breath.

Peppermint and spice hit her nose.

She stepped from the armoire and ran to the door of her room, peering out. Finn was disappearing down the far corridor, hot on Toven's heels.

There's still time. For what? He was clearly looking for something. She thought of the chest at the foot of her bed and the armoire. Looking for some*one*.

It was as if she had plunged into a cold bath.

He was looking for her.

Toven Hearst was hunting her again. Just like the rest of them.

She always knew she was worth less than dirt to him—that all of Evermore was—but she had hoped he wouldn't be on the front lines today.

Had he watched her brother die? Would he have gloated if he caught her?

Briony took a deep breath and turned to head toward the other end of the palace.

And smacked into a chest.

She gasped, and a hand wrapped around her throat. She had one second to recognize the victorious grin on Gains's face before he cast a spell. Her eyes closed, and everything was darkness.

CHAPTER 5

Eight Years Ago

I T SEEMED TO TAKE BRIONY LONGER than the others to acclimate to the cold of Bomard. When the young people of Evermore had arrived in the spring for their first year of shared education, Briony had assumed that spring meant warmth and breezes and crisp-smelling trees. That was what spring was in Evermore.

In Bomard, spring was merely the end of winter. Snow was still melting, and heavy furs were still worn. Outdoor activities were limited. Briony and Rory had visited Bomard with their father plenty of times on official state business, but never this far north. Here, carved into the side of the mountain range that protected Bomard from the realms across the sea, the Bomardi school was crystallized in snow.

Briony longed for the warm breezes in Evermore. She pulled her cloak more tightly closed and tapped her fingers across her face, encouraging her blood to magically warm under the surface.

"Careful," Rory said, moving behind her at their shared breakfast table. "I saw Simon Leatherby trying that last week, and he ended up giving himself a fever."

"I'm careful," she said, teeth chattering. She sent a yearning glance at the dying fire. "Do you think they're toying with us? Giving the Eversun heir only three logs per day?"

Rory sat across from her, wrapping his fingers around his warm cup of tea. "Yes. I think they're hoping to laugh at our weakness. Maybe they want us to beg for it."

Briony rolled her eyes. "Well, we'll just have to remember this next year when we're home. Perhaps we'll weld all their windows shut so they can just swelter."

Part of the treaty that had kept Evermore and Bomard peaceful for five hundred years was that the youth of both countries would be schooled together, in alternate countries, for the last five years of their magical education. Next year, the Bomardi would be schooled near Evermore's temperate lakes, but this year it was Bomard's turn to host.

While there was certainly a divide between those who practiced mind magic and those who practiced heart magic, the basic principles were very much the same. It was the source of the power and the connection to it that differed. For a heart magician, lifting a rock into the air started in the muscle. For a mind magician, it started at the source of movement—the brain. Heart magicians felt a pulsing vein of magic in their chest, while mind magicians felt a thread between the eyes, tying their mind to the outside world.

Briony had always been taught that the Eversun mind magic was an evolved technique: Mind magicians did not tire as quickly as heart magicians, and the Bomardi didn't have the patience for mind magic. Heart magicians could accidentally deplete their magic, yes, but it took less training to get strong results the first time. Consistency was the friend of the mind magician.

"Let's just be happy that there are private rooms assigned to the Rosewoods," Rory said.

"I don't know what good it does us. At least in the dormitories, there's more body heat." Briony reached for her teacup and heated the liquid to scalding. They'd been in Bomard for a month, and she was the last Eversun still shivering in the classrooms.

She stared at Rory from across the small table laid with fruit and bread as he shoveled food into his mouth. He was a full head taller than her now and had been eating twice as much. Now, a few months shy of seventeen, they were finally looking less alike. He had put on muscle during a winter of training with the infantry, and she had spent the season broadening in all the places she wished she wouldn't. It had taken only one glance at Larissa Gains's cinched waist and delicate wrists upon arriving in Bomard for Briony to realize that perhaps a winter spent reading and eating honeyed pastries wasn't doing her any favors.

"Shall we go?" Rory asked, popping one more biscuit into his mouth.

Briony swallowed down the last of her tea, letting it burn her tongue. She grabbed a wool scarf from her wardrobe, hating the cool weight of it across her neck before it acclimated to her warmth.

She followed Rory down to the grand hall on the first floor, where the year one students were taught every morning from nine till noon. The year twos were the floor above, and the year threes were the floor above that, and so on, with the dormitories above those. The private suite for the Eversun heir was at the very top, in a turret. Rory and Briony were ten minutes late to the first day of lessons, and the Bomardi tutors had been incredibly unpleasant about it. Father had sent a letter the next day instructing Briony to focus on her brother's timeliness.

On the seventh floor, they picked up Didion from the boys' dormitories, and on the sixth, Cordelia joined them.

"How many logs for the fire do they give your dormitory?" Briony asked Cordelia as they linked arms.

"Wait! I'm coming!" a voice called from behind them.

Briony and Cordelia groaned. They pasted on smiles and turned.

A girl with bright-green eyes and hair as yellow as straw stumbled to catch up.

"Good morning, Katrina," Briony said.

"It's starting to warm up, isn't it!" Katrina said, voice perpetually a bit too loud. Briony frowned, suppressing a chill. Katrina's eyes popped wide. "I forgot my notes!" She turned and ran back toward the dormitory door.

Briony glanced at Rory and Didion as they continued on, descending the next set of stairs already.

"I suppose we can't just leave her now," Cordelia said dryly.

Briony sighed in agreement. Her father had foisted a friendship with Katrina Cove upon Briony a year ago, despite the two of them having nothing in common. Katrina was the daughter of a peace treaty marriage. She'd been raised in Bomard for her first fifteen years, but after her mother's death, her father returned home to Evermore with her. There was nothing *wrong* with Katrina, strictly speaking, but she was loud, clumsy, and talked about how happy she was to be back in Bomard daily as Briony seethed and shivered.

Cordelia and Briony waited for her and watched the rest of the early risers leaving their rooms, starting to pack the stairwell.

Briony's bones shook as a draft seemed to breeze by them.

"Still cold, your grace?"

The air in her chest seemed to frost over. She didn't need to turn to see who had spoken. There were only a handful of people who felt the need to poke fun at the Rosewood royalty.

Toven Hearst and his pack of Bomardi boys were descending from the seventh-floor dormitories.

Briony had suffered more slights and humiliations in the past month at the hands of Toven and his friends than she had in her entire lifetime. They called her "princess" or "your grace." They threw purple roses at her in the hallways, the symbol of the Rosewood crest. They swept into low bows when she entered a room. For someone who'd spent the first sixteen years of her life instructed not to outshine her brother—to be plain and unnoticeable—it was mortifying. Briony had sobbed into her pillow for the first week, wondering if her own people thought she was as snobbish and condescending as the Bomardi claimed she was.

Briony tilted her chin up and waited for them to pass without a glance in their direction.

"Oh stones, the chill has gotten her hearing as well," said Liam Quill, a handsome dark-haired boy with copper skin whose arrogance ruined his looks.

"Hey, Princess!" a thick voice said. "I know what will warm you up."

Briony's nose scrunched, and she spun to face them as they howled in laughter. The lewd one was Canning Trow. He was three years older than them and had no business talking that way to a sixteen-year-old, in Briony's opinion.

She glared into his wide and leering face as they passed.

"No, haven't you heard?" A high-pitched voice came from the girls' dormitory. "Her brother keeps her warm enough. That's why they share a suite."

Larissa Gains glided toward the pack of boys. A flowery scent somehow preluded her arrival instead of following it, and her thick sheets of blond hair swayed hypnotically in time with her hips.

The boys' laughter rang from the stairwell as they descended. Toven Hearst hung back with a sharp smirk in her direction and waited for Larissa to grab his arm before following her down the stairs.

Briony had learned from a very young age that as a woman in the Rosewood line, the most valuable thing she could learn to do was smile when she'd rather scream.

Cordelia, on the other hand—

"What an absolutely depraved thing to say!" she yelled after Larissa. Briony grabbed her wrist, trying to shush her, but Cordelia continued. "And you can't even say it to her face!"

Larissa paused on the top step and called back, "I did say it to her face, I just find it so hideous to look at directly." She winced dramatically and flounced down the stairs.

Toven threw his head back and laughed deep in his throat. "You're so *bad*," he said, the sound disappearing with him as he followed.

Briony closed her eyes and took deep breaths. Cordelia grumbled next to her.

"Where the fuck is Katrina?" Briony hissed.

"Here! Sorry!" Katrina linked arms with both of them and dragged them to the stairs. "Did anyone else have troubles with the assignment?"

Briony let herself be dragged. There was a bottleneck in the circling stairwell, as there always was if the younger students waited too long. They quickly caught up behind Toven and Larissa, and Briony slowed Katrina down. As the stairs twisted, Toven looked up and smiled smugly at them. Briony frowned at her shoes. The draft was back in the stairwell again, and she had to focus everything in her to keep from full-body shivering.

"It's a shame we don't have royalty in Bomard," Larissa said to Liam Quill, loud enough for them to hear. "I'd have liked to be a princess."

"Our rulers follow a bloodline," Cordelia said briskly. "Yours follow wealth and power. Completely up to chance."

"Oh, I don't know," Toven said, his voice drifting up to her ears. "My father's the richest man in Bomard—actually the entire continent of Moreland—and he's only eighth in line for the Seat."

Liam scoffed. "Richest only if you count properties and holdings across the sea—"

"Which we do," Toven said patronizingly. "We all do."

There was only one more staircase to take, and then they'd be free of them. Briony squeezed Cordelia's elbow, begging her to hold her tongue a little while longer.

"Katrina, dear, I don't know how you survived leaving us," Larissa said. "You *must* prefer Bomard to Evermore."

Katrina looked between them all, unsure how best to respond without insulting anyone. "Well, I do miss it—"

"Of course you do. I prefer Bomard to Evermore any day," Larissa said. "At least in Bomard they abolished patriarchal succession. A woman could never be ruler of Evermore. Despite how high and mighty they may act . . ." Her eyes drifted up Briony's embroidered wool dress to her face.

"I'd be pretty full of myself, too, if I had gold running through my blood," Toven said.

Briony kept her expression blank, even though the energy around them crackled.

When they finally turned into the classroom, a long hall with tapestries on one side and large windows on the other, they found it unrecognizable. Three dozen towering pine trees lined the center of the room, seemingly sprouted up overnight. Needles littered the bases of the trunks as wide as a human chest.

Briony found Rory and Didion staring up at one tree and wandered over to join them.

"Are we . . . climbing the trees?" Didion asked.

"No, Mr. Winchester." The long-suffering voice of Tutor Amelia came from behind them as she walked to the front of the classroom. She was a brusque woman in her forties who didn't seem to enjoy teaching all that much.

Didion blushed and pulled out his notes.

As Briony smiled at Didion's embarrassment, a chill crested over her shoulders, and her breath shuddered in her chest. She burrowed further into her cloak and scarf.

Toven Hearst came to stand at the tree next to theirs, and Finn and Liam joined him.

"Positively balmy in here, wouldn't you say, Finn?" said Toven conversationally.

Briony frowned. So he'd seen her shiver.

"Makes me want to strip down," Finn said.

"Wish I had some of those Eversun fabrics about now," Toven said, shedding his cloak dramatically and tossing it to the side of the room. "The silks."

She sent a glare his way and found him rolling up the sleeves of his shirt as if it were a warm summer's day. The veins under his pale skin seemed to strain.

"Absolutely," Finn agreed. "And I'd do anything for an iced glass of fairy wine. So cold, it could crack the glass."

Briony turned back to the front, waiting for Tutor Amelia to begin. She tucked her chin into her scarf, blowing hot air into the fabric and letting it warm her lower face.

Rory frowned at her. "You're cold?"

"You're not?"

She felt that draft again. And suddenly it clicked.

Briony's neck snapped to look at Toven. He was rolling up his other sleeve, his mirthful eyes on her. The fingertips of the hand by his side were rotating in infinitesimal circles.

He was the one sending a breeze her way. She was cold because of Toven Hearst.

Briony's eyes lit on fire. She watched Toven's lips turn up in a smirk.

"Comfortable, your grace?"

She flushed in anger, but despite that, her body shivered without her permission.

She heard Finn cover a laugh with a cough.

Briony ripped off her scarf and followed Toven's lead, defiantly shucking off her cloak and tossing it to the corner of the room. The air hit her in a rush, breezing over her uncovered arms and shoulders, but she grasped the thread of magic between her eyes and began pulling on the heat in her blood with rotations of her fingertips, warming her against the chill.

Now that she knew what was affecting her, she could counteract it nicely.

Tutor Amelia called for attention. Briony faced forward, but she could still feel Toven's eyes on her.

"We are going to put last week's lesson into practical use today," Tutor Amelia said. "As we know, all magic is done with gesture. From your early schooling, you may have learned simple magic that brings objects to you or pushes them away, but that is rudimentary at best. Last week we identified the original eight magical gestures, which are—?"

A dozen hands shot into the air. Briony's stayed by her side, even as Rory's palm shyly lifted.

She knew the answer, but this was part of the deal with her father. She was allowed to receive good marks, but never better than Rory. She couldn't outshine him in class. If Rory was struggling, it was her duty to make sure he succeeded. No matter how.

"Mr. Rosewood." Tutor Amelia turned to the chalkboard.

"Push, pull, throw, smash, tear, lift, drag . . ." Rory cleared his throat and glanced down at his notes.

He was forgetting the one gesture that Briony (and Toven, actually) was currently using. Briony paused the circling of her fingers that gathered the warmth in her blood and tapped into the thread behind her eyes again. With a curl of her finger, she pulled the words on Rory's page into new shapes, new letters.

She watched him focus on the ink she was manipulating. "Gather," he said, finishing the list. Briony released the ink, allowing it to return to the form it was before. Rory sent her the briefest of smiles in gratitude.

"Very good." Tutor Amelia wrote the first eight on the chalkboard. "And Vindecci identified two more with the advent of mind magic. What are they, Miss Rosewood?"

"I don't know, Tutor Amelia."

The older woman dropped her arm from where she was adding the word *gather* to the bottom of the list on the chalkboard. She turned, and the classroom held its breath.

"Two gestures. Not on this list," she said, pointing to the board.

Briony felt her skin heat, and it had nothing to do with the warming charm she was employing. She shook her head and stared again at Rory's notes, knowing exactly what would happen next. She twitched her finger and dragged the ink around the page again.

"One of them, Miss Rosewood?"

The letters rearranged. *R*...*E*...

"Mr. Rosewood, can you assist your sister? She seems to have slept through last week's lessons," Tutor Amelia said disdainfully.

Rory looked down at his notes, following the letters she manipulated. Even in the early years of their education at home, she'd helped him in maths and history like this. When they were very young, he used to say that they were answering the questions *together*, as a team. This spirit of teamwork continued at school now.

"Reach," Rory said, looking up from the moving letters on his page.

"Mr. Hearst? The final gesture added?" Tutor Amelia turned back to the board.

Briony lifted her gaze, watching the word *reach* added to the list. The pause before Toven spoke caused Briony to look over at him.

He was leaning against the nearest tree trunk, arms crossed and eyes narrowed on her.

No. Not on her. On Rory's notes.

He glanced up at her with suspicion in his gray gaze and answered silkily, "Penetrate."

Briony tore her eyes away, cheeks burning.

"Excellent. Please take note, Miss Rosewood." Tutor Amelia clapped her hands. "Today we are giving a practical application to the gestures.

Step one will be carving words or designs into the wood from increasing distances. And the more advanced step is cutting the trunk down, as with an ax."

Cordelia grumbled, "Wasteful. These poor trees."

"They were destined to become your firewood, Miss Hardstark," said Tutor Amelia. "We in Bomard don't consider our warmth 'wasteful.'"

Cordelia pursed her lips against the laughing whispers of their Bomardi classmates.

"Now, four to a tree," Tutor Amelia instructed.

Briony inched closer to the tree to her right, but unfortunately, Rory, Didion, Katrina, Cordelia, and herself made five. They shuffled, looking around for an empty spot. When Briony turned backward, Toven Hearst, Liam Quill, and Finn Raquin were smirking at her from their tree.

"Oh, Briony, dear," Finn said in a sugary-sweet voice. "We have room for one here."

Briony sighed and resigned herself to separating from her friends.

"Begin by choosing which of the gestures best suits your task," Tutor Amelia said. "You are to draw your initials into the tree trunk. First from a close distance. Then from a farther one."

Briony stood two feet from her tree and frowned at the bark. Just beyond the trunk, she could see Toven Hearst doing the same. Finn was to her left, Liam to her right.

Push, pull, throw, smash, tear, lift, drag, gather, reach, penetrate. Which one?

"Once you've chosen a gesture, call upon your magic. The vein in your chest for heart mages. The thread in your mind for mind mages."

She imagined a knife in her mind's eye. She placed it against the bark and dragged. The first line of the *B* eased its way into the bark. It was faint, but it was there.

Briony smiled at her success on the first try. The joy was short-lived, as she glanced past the trunk and found Toven narrowing his eyes at her. She tilted her chin up and refocused on carving the curves of the *B*.

She'd just gotten the basic outlines of it and was beginning to go over the letters again when she heard Liam huff in exasperation to her right. She glanced at his side of the tree, finding not even the first line of the *L*.

Briony quickly searched behind her. There were no letters carved yet into the tree Rory, Didion, Cordelia, and Katrina were working on.

All around her, classmates were glaring at their tree trunks. Some of them even had veins popping out in their temples in their concentration.

Tutor Amelia was circling them, coming closer to Briony's tree.

Briony turned back and quickly pushed the bark back together, healing the tree and hiding her initial. Tutor Amelia approached them, standing over Toven's shoulder.

"Barely there, Mr. Hearst, but it *is* there. Very good," Tutor Amelia said. "Work on the *H* now."

Briony's brows rose. Of all of them, Toven was making progress? It shouldn't have been a surprise really. The Hearst family had an incredibly powerful bloodline. Every few generations, a Hearst would manifest a powerful gift—some strength or skill that others worked years to build. Toven's father, Orion, could split his casting. Normally, a magician could only cast one spell per hand, but Orion Hearst could split one magical gesture into two spells.

As Tutor Amelia came around the tree, tutting at Liam's lack of progress, Toven smirked proudly at Briony.

Maybe Toven Hearst would manifest a skill for chopping down trees, Briony thought petulantly. He'd make a fine lumberjack. She almost snorted at the image of Toven tasked with such menial work.

Her gaze flicked to his exposed forearms again before refocusing on the bare bark of the tree as Tutor Amelia came to stand beside her.

A heavy sigh came from their instructor. "Pay better attention in the theory lessons, Miss Rosewood, and perhaps you'll have progress."

"Yes, Tutor Amelia."

Briony stared at the spot in the bark where she'd hidden her *B*. As the older woman walked away, Briony's eyes were drawn to gray ones on the other side of the trunk. Toven had knit his brows together, staring at her as if she were a rock stuck in his boot.

"The first person to carve two even initials on their tree will receive the top marks for today's lesson *and* the month," Tutor Amelia announced. "Mr. Hearst is leagues ahead of everyone else so far."

The class groaned, but Toven was still watching her.

Briony looked away from him, turning to see how Rory was coming along. No progress. She sighed. Their father wouldn't be happy to hear that Rory was bested by a Bomardi for the first month's marks.

Briony faced forward, staring at her tree trunk but relaxing her gaze. There was a vein in her chest thumping with unused magic. She imagined a string between herself and Rory, connecting their hearts, connecting their magic.

It wasn't the first time she'd amplified him. He'd been unknowingly accepting a push of her magic for years—during lessons, when healing from injuries, in rare boyhood brawls. She couldn't remember how she'd done it the first time, and it wasn't like there were a lot of people in Evermore whom she could ask about this kind of magic. This had to be a kind of *heart* magic that she assumed came from a bond with her twin.

She pumped her magic on a string to Rory's heart. And waited.

She heard a gasp from behind her.

"Oh wow," Rory whispered. "I did it."

She glanced at his tree. She wasn't sure what gesture he was using, but there, in the bark, was a perfect *R*.

Didion craned his neck to see it. "Well, do it again!" he whispered excitedly.

Briony watched Rory concentrate, and now that she'd opened the connection, she felt him tug on it. The bark split apart. A matching *R* appeared next to the first.

She saw the corner of Rory's mouth turn up in an amazed grin. He didn't look to her in silent thanks this time. It was only the book studies and assignments that Rory thought he needed extra assistance in. Briony looked down at her shoes.

Didion raised his hand. "Tutor Amelia! Rory's done it!"

The entire class turned to look at Rory and Didion's tree. The entire class but one.

Toven Hearst's gaze was narrowed on her.

Tutor Amelia congratulated Rory and told him to try it from ten feet away. Briony watched as he backed up and refocused. Tutor Amelia stood at his side.

Now that Rory had felt the burst of power, even without knowing where it had come from, he knew how to draw it quickly.

R R appeared like a crack of a whip. The class gasped, and Rory's smile was so bright that Briony couldn't help but match it.

That morning, Rory carved an entire poem into his side of the tree while the others worked to get their initials. Overall, the Bomardi were faster at making the carvings, but the Eversuns had more precision. With practice and patience, mind magic was much more effective, but heart magic would always show strength first.

Even so, Liam Quill was the last to accomplish it. He had sweat rolling down his temples and his breath was shallow by the time he'd crossed the Q. Not for the first time, Briony was glad she pulled on magic from the mind instead of the heart. Liam wasn't the only heart magician who was looking the worse for wear.

"Mr. Quill," Tutor Amelia said. She placed a kind hand on his shoulder. "Excellent work, but you'll need to rest now. Your magic will be drained soon."

He shrugged off her comfort, a snarl on his face. "I'll do no such thing. I intend to cut down every one of these trees!"

Briony felt the shame and anger radiating off him in waves. She glanced at his friends and found Finn chewing on his cheek in concern and Toven rolling his eyes.

"You look far too close to husking, Liam," Toven said.

Husking was what happened to heart magicians who drained themselves. They were alive but a husk of themselves; the magic was used up. There was no such risk for mind magicians.

"This wouldn't be an issue if familiars were allowed in school," Liam grumbled.

"And have bears and wolves roaming the castle? No, thank you," Finn said.

Tutor Amelia called for them to turn to the task of cutting down the tree, striking at the trunk.

"Won't that mean there will be trees falling down in here?" Larissa said, looking pale with the drain on her magic.

"I will be very surprised if anyone can actually slice through a tree today, Miss Gains," Tutor Amelia said patronizingly. "This lesson will test your skill as well as your aim, so please be mindful of not casting at classmates."

Briony watched as Toven Hearst raised a hand and sliced through the air, as if an ax were in his hand. Their tree shivered.

"Excellent, Mr. Hearst."

Liam made the same motion, but it was sloppy.

"Watch it," Finn said. "Focus, or you'll end up slicing *me* in half."

Briony glanced at Rory, casting a tearing gesture with his hands, trying to separate the trunk from itself.

As he lifted his hands to try again, she pushed the pulse of her magic down the vein to him.

There was a mighty crack, and the room went silent. Everyone turned to stare at Rory's tree. It had split up the middle, two halves separating from the center of the trunk outward. The class screamed as the pieces fell sideways, but Tutor Amelia slowed their descent to a soft landing.

"Very well done, Mr. Rosewood. The rest of you, spread out to another tree."

Katrina quickly joined their tree, and Briony made room for her between herself and Liam.

"Stones, it's so much harder to use mind magic over heart magic," Katrina said, pushing her hair away from her face. "It's incredible to see how much power Rory has, though!"

Briony heard a huff of exasperation and turned to see Toven glaring at them. He swung his arm through the air, and their tree shivered again.

Liam turned to Toven and whispered, "Are you boosting?"

"You know that's not allowed in school," Toven replied. Then he turned his eyes on her. "Is it, Rosewood?"

Briony narrowed her eyes at the conversation. What was "boosting"? A heart magic technique?

"I'm not letting every Eversun outrank me," Liam said under his breath.

He checked to make sure Tutor Amelia's gaze was elsewhere, and his left hand twitched toward Katrina.

"Liam," Finn said sternly.

Briony watched in confusion as Katrina gasped, her hand going to her chest. Before Briony could figure out what was happening, Liam sliced his right arm at the tree, and a mark like the chop of an ax appeared in the bark.

Katrina stumbled, and Briony helped her stay upright.

"What happened?" Briony asked her.

Katrina looked at Liam, fear in her eyes as he smirked back at her.

"Nothing," Katrina said. "Just a pain in my . . . stomach."

Briony was about to ask why her hand had been at her chest and not her stomach when Tutor Amelia came over.

"Miss Cove? I thought you were focusing your education on mind magic, not heart magic. There is no reason for your body to be exhausted."

"I . . . yes, Tutor Amelia. I should be using mind magic instead, my apologies."

"Husking is a very real thing," Tutor Amelia said. "Go rest."

Katrina retreated to the side of the room, and Briony looked from Liam to Toven and Finn, trying to figure out what Liam had done to Katrina. She caught Larissa's smug eyes at the tree in the center, then watched her left hand stretch toward the person at her side, an Eversun girl.

The girl gasped, and then Larissa sliced at the tree in one solid motion, the crack of breaking bark drawing everyone's attention. Larissa smiled at the progress she'd made, and the Eversun girl coughed, catching her breath.

"Come on, Toven," Liam said. "It's only against the rules if you get caught."

Liam glanced at Briony, and she saw his hand reach for her. She waited for the shock. The pain. Anything.

Liam's brow furrowed. Briony glanced at Toven, who showed no surprise at the lack of results. He was still watching her, almost disapprovingly.

Liam tried again.

"Hey!" They turned to see Rory looking furiously at Liam. "Are you boosting?" Rory hissed. "From the daughter of the king!"

"That's rich, coming from you," Toven said.

Rory turned his glare on him. "What are you talking about?"

Toven looked to Briony again, as if waiting for her to explain.

Was she boosting him? Was that what it was when she sent him her magic? But it didn't exhaust or pain her to send her magic to Rory, like it had done to Katrina when taken from her.

"I'm hearing talk of boosting over here," Tutor Amelia said as she arrived. "I hope we all know that the use of boosting from a human is grounds for expulsion for the Bomardi, not to mention *illegal* for the Eversuns."

Briony blinked at her, shock creeping over her skin. She looked down at her boots, worrying her lip between her teeth.

The Bomardi boys muttered excuses, but as a group they seemed to stop whatever it was they had been doing. As class ended, with no one but Rory able to fully cut down a tree, Briony stayed behind with Katrina, who was almost back to full strength again.

"Katrina, what is boosting? I've never heard of it."

Katrina sighed. "It's a quick boost of heart magic, only without permission."

Briony frowned at her, waiting for more.

Katrina continued. "Heart magic can be shared, like when a couple marries and decides to share their magic. They become heartsprings with each other in a ceremony that's usually incorporated into the marriage vows." Katrina reached for her words. "Kind of like combining your gold when you combine your families, the heart magic gets combined, making each person better, stronger. Since heart magicians grow weaker faster, it's like an alternative to bonding to an animal familiar. Or an addition, really, as you can have both."

"I've heard of spouses sharing heart magic, but that's a mutual cycle of power, I thought," Briony said as they reached the stairs. "Liam *took* something from you, didn't he?"

Katrina winced. Her hand rubbed her chest, almost unconsciously.

"Yeah. It feels like a zap, like a sizzle of lightning. Boosting feels like that when the magic is taken from you. If he'd asked permission, or if I'd given my magic freely, it wouldn't be painful."

Briony's skin tingled. She gave her magic to Rory all the time. She'd never thought of it as something that could be taken from her, only shared.

"So you can give or take heart magic without being bonded as heart . . . heart—"

"Heartsprings, yes. The official bond keeps the magic flowing at all times. It's usually tied to jewelry. My parents . . ." Katrina swallowed. "Even though my father didn't use heart magic as an Eversun, he still gave it freely to my mother through their wedding rings."

Briony glanced at her. Katrina's face was pale with the effort of climbing the stairs, and her eyes were watery as she spoke of her parents. A pang went through Briony as she thought of what it would have been like to lose a mother that she'd known for fifteen years instead of one she'd never known at all. She supposed she and Katrina might have some things in common after all.

"It sounds like the heartspring bond is synonymous with love, in a way," Briony said with a smile. "We don't have anything like it in Evermore. It's lovely."

"It's not always tied to love." Katrina checked the hall to make sure there were no eavesdroppers before lowering her voice. "There are some people in Bomard—in the woods or far from the cities—who, like Liam, don't ask permission. There are betrothals in the deep country that occur just for the dowry of the person's magic. There's no cycle of magic between the spouses, just excess for one. It's becoming more and more common, too. There are even people kept as servants, their magic weakened by the daily drain."

They stopped in between staircases so Katrina could rest.

Briony's mind was whirring. "How is this allowed in Bomard? Why isn't it illegal everywhere?" she asked.

Katrina's brows shot up. "I mean, what do you think caused our countries to split apart six hundred years ago? We were one happy country on this continent for so long—"

"Until Vindecci discovered mind magic, and the Bomardi refused to learn it," Briony said, reciting the history.

Katrina's nose wrinkled. "That's the history they taught you? Truly? Daughter of the king?"

A boiling fury rose in Briony's chest. She hated when she was made to feel uninformed. She pushed it down and focused on the here and now. ˙

"I don't understand. Does my father know what's happening in Bomard?" Briony asked.

"I'm sure he does. But why start another war over it?" Katrina shrugged and started to move up the stairs again. "It's really nice of you to wait for me, by the way."

Briony pasted on a weak smile and nodded.

She had so many questions now, but what worried her the most was she now knew she had been "boosting" Rory throughout their lives. And not only was it illegal in her country and prohibited at school . . . but now, Toven Hearst knew about it.

CHAPTER 6

BRIONY GASPED INTO CONSCIOUSNESS. Her body shot upright, and she blinked her eyes open into a dark room. It was moving, undulating, writhing.

And then Cordelia was in front of her, holding her face between two cold hands.

"Briony, it's me!"

Sound slammed into her ears. The room was shifting and slithering toward her.

No. It was bodies. The room was full of bodies. People. She wasn't alone.

"Are you all right?"

"What does she remember?"

"Is she injured?"

Briony shoved Cordelia away and gasped for air, feeling suffocated by the darkness.

"Water!" Cordelia shouted.

Briony's eyes adjusted, and a silhouette moved in the meager light. There was the sound of water being poured.

Briony held her hand over her chest, trying to slow her heartbeat. She was no longer at Claremore Castle.

"Where am I?"

"We don't know."

Briony turned to the dark-haired woman on her right. It was Phoebe, one of the cousins of the Rosewood family. Finola's younger sister.

Cordelia grabbed the water cup from someone and pushed it to her lips. Briony reached up to take it from her and found her hands shackled. She coughed, sputtering the water.

"What is this?" She tugged at her hands. The chains gave her only a few inches between her palms.

That might limit the spells she could cast—

"There's something special about the neckpiece," Cordelia said.

Briony spied a collar on Cordelia's neck. She reached for her own, a cool metal with no discernible lock. Every woman in matching collars and chains.

"It might be infused with the Gowarnus herb from Shurtarth, or it might be something entirely new, but whatever it is, it cuts off our magic."

Briony blinked at the collar, mind whirring. The Gowarnus herb worked to dampen and dissolve the connection between the magician and their magical thread. Briony had never experienced it firsthand, but her father had described his meeting in the Shurtarth region as unsettling. *I've never felt more vulnerable in my life than while that damned herb cut off my magic.*

She breathed deep, trying to find the string behind her eyes, the hum of her magic. But reaching for it was like trying to pull back a dream upon waking. It was gone.

Briony looked up at Cordelia and found her own devastation reflected back to her from blue eyes. What were they going to do with them?

She assessed the room. There must have been fifty people. All women, and most she recognized from her court. Katrina sat across the room with her arms around a girl who could be no older than sixteen.

"Where is everyone else? The men?"

Phoebe reached for her arm and said gently, "Rory isn't—"

"I know Rory is dead," Briony said sharply. She listened to the silence echo afterward. She cleared her throat. "Didion and Sammy? The generals?"

"They're holding them separately. We caught a glimpse of them a few days ago."

"Days?" Briony's eyes widened. "How long was I unconscious?"

Cordelia and Phoebe exchanged glances. "You were just dropped off today," Cordelia said.

Briony's jaw dropped. She scanned herself. No injuries. But there was something on her arm. Black ink that seemed to glisten gold when she twisted it under the moonlight.

Hap Gains. A tattoo of sorts. It was his signature.

The blood drained from her head.

"That's who captured you." Phoebe nodded at the tattoo. Briony's eyes drifted down to Phoebe's arm, where she saw *Lag Reighven*.

Cordelia cleared her throat. "What was the last thing you remember?"

Briony's mind flickered through images—Rory's boundary falling; Anna's body on the stairs; the maid who helped them; Toven Hearst's eyes inches from her own, the speckles of blue in them—

"The day of the battle. The boundary falling."

A collective gasp shivered through the room.

"Briony, that was *days* ago—"

"Three days? Maybe four?"

"Have you eaten at all?"

Phoebe hushed the room, jumping to her feet. "Let's get her some food." Her voice was authoritative, and Briony saw a glimpse of the older cousin who taught her defensive magic in the days following King Jacquel's assassination.

Briony's mind cleared. "Food?"

And suddenly a tray of fruit was pushed in front of her face. Grapes, apples, pears.

"They're feeding us?" Briony asked. "What in the name of the waters are they planning on doing with us?"

"Oh, someone just tell her. This is maddening." The voice rang out as clear as a bell, and Briony recoiled in recognition.

She leaned around Cordelia and Phoebe, and there—across the room, in a corner by herself, with no friends surrounding her for the first time—was Larissa Gains, collared and shackled like the rest of them.

Briony hadn't seen her in the four years since the war began, but it was clear she would recognize that perfectly symmetrical face underneath any amount of dirt and blood. Her hair was still lustrous in the minimal light, though limp. Larissa's cold eyes glinted at her.

Her mind tripped over the possible reasons Larissa was in this dungeon with them, but she refocused on the conversation first.

"Tell me what? Why are we being held here?"

Larissa smiled cruelly. "It's for the auction."

A shiver crested over her skin. She wished she could say, *What auction?* But memories bubbled up to the surface of her mind, and she was once again in the familiar hallways of the Bomardi school.

It had been just over six years ago, only a few weeks before the man on the Bomardi Seat was assassinated. Veronika Mallow's name was hot on every tongue in Bomard already, and that would have been the first clue that change was coming if only it didn't seem a completely preposterous idea. A Bomardi Seat hadn't been assassinated in ten generations.

But Veronika Mallow had found a way to speak to the hearts of the succession line. *We are the true magic,* she'd said. *Mind magic isn't an evolved magic. It is conniving and duplicitous. The Eversuns want to keep you weak, to take away your familiars, and to sever your heartspring bonds. But we are stronger than them, and they know it. We must do everything we can to keep them down.*

In their third year of study together, all the Bomardi were humming her words, threatening the Eversun students around every turn.

It had been Liam Quill who'd brought up the idea of an auction first.

"My father says it's only a matter of time before we chop off King Jacquel's head," he'd said loudly one day in late spring, when it was just warm enough for everyone to eat lunch outside. They were gathered in the farthest corner of the Bomardi school's courtyard, where the sun was strongest and the breeze nonexistent. He was reclined back on his tan elbows, chewing thoughtfully on an apple, shaking his raven hair out of his eyes every few moments. "And what do you think will become of you, Princess?"

Briony had been reading in a covered alcove. She'd been there first, and Liam, Finn, Toven, and a meaty, thick-headed, pale-skinned Bomardi named Collin Twindle had all sat down not ten feet from her. She turned a page instead of responding.

"We'll chop her head off, too," someone said.

"I have a few better ideas of what to do with her head——"

"You'll have to come into quite a bit of gold for those ideas, Collin," Toven had said, stretching catlike.

"Haven't you heard?" Liam said, more to her than to Collin Twindle. "We'll be selling them off to the highest bidder. Just like they used to do in Daward in ancient times."

Briony snapped her eyes up to find them all grinning at her. Toven's shirt had pulled free of his trousers, baring a sliver of pale skin as his arms reached over his head. Now at eighteen, he was becoming impossible to ignore in the hallways with his towering height and shock of white-gray hair that seemed to gleam silver. Her gaze landed on his stomach before looking away again. If she left, they'd win.

"Wouldn't mind having my own Eversun," Liam continued. "I'd make 'em clean my house *and* clean my cock."

Briony pressed her lips together as laughter reached her ears.

"You're missing the point, Liam," Toven said disapprovingly. "You're not buying a *whore*. You're buying power. A heartspring to keep all for yourself. A secondary supply of magic to pull from."

"I think *you're* missing the point, Tove," Collin said, chuckling. "You're forgetting about Sacral Magic."

"Yeah, *Tove*," said Liam. "That heartspring magic will be good, but Sacral Magic will only enhance——"

"——when freely given," Toven finished, correcting them. "Good luck getting your Eversun to beg you for it."

Briony snapped her book shut. "You're talking about people. Human beings."

"An Eversun isn't a human being, love," Liam said.

The only person who didn't laugh with him was Finn, who was peeling his apple with a knife. His mother was Eversun.

Briony shook her head of the memories, refocusing, readjusting to the dark of the cell.

Cordelia didn't even turn to Larissa. "Don't listen to her. If she knew what was going on, she wouldn't be in here."

"What *is* she doing here?" Briony asked, voice hoarse.

"She was dropped off when you were," Phoebe said.

Briony watched Larissa examine her nails as if there weren't dirt underneath them.

She turned back to Cordelia. "What happened to you?"

Cordelia blew out a breath. "The passageway collapsed, and that maid and I tried for a bit to get the rocks cleared. She finally ran when I said I wasn't leaving without you."

Briony closed her eyes, feeling tears blossom. "You should have gone."

"Too late to be helped now," Cordelia said, brushing Briony's hair away from her face.

Briony's fingers flew to her mother's brooch, hidden between the folds of her dress. She said a silent thank-you to the waters that she'd kept it with her.

Glancing to the only door, Briony said, "What do we know? How often do they drop people off?"

"In the beginning it was every hour, but now it's once a day." Phoebe sniffed and then wiped her nose with the backside of her pale wrist. "They bring a tray of food every morning. We're rationing."

Briony nodded. She stretched out her legs and brought herself up to standing. She was still in her flowing dress from the day of the battle, though it was covered in grime. Every eye in the room locked onto her movements.

"Has everyone tried their magic?"

The room of women looked around, nodding yes.

Briony ran through the possibilities. The Bomardi weren't going to kill them if they were feeding them. If there was to be an auction, there was only so much time until they were separated—until their strength in numbers was gone.

"Is anyone combat-trained? Hand-to-hand?" Briony asked the room.

Larissa laughed deep in her throat, and Briony glared at her.

"You want to kick and shove your way out of here?" Larissa said. "In these chains? You're absolutely mad."

"Why are you here?" Briony snapped. "To spy on us?"

Larissa rolled her eyes. "You're not important enough to spy on. Not anymore."

"So, you're a traitor then?" Cordelia said, joining Briony in standing. "I don't buy that."

"Believe what you want." Larissa dismissed them, glancing down at her nails again.

A woman stood up in the far corner of the room. She was tall and broad-shouldered with deep-bronze skin. She reminded Briony of Anna in the way she stood at attention. "Miss Rosewood, I'm Velicity Punt. I've served in the Eversun militia for the past seven years," she said. "Most of my training was with defensive and offensive magic, but I will gladly serve you as I served your brother and father before that."

Briony swallowed. She'd never received sworn allegiance from anyone but Anna. All allegiance was given to the king and his male heir in Evermore. Before she could tell Velicity it wasn't necessary, another woman stood.

"I only have one year with the militia, but if we're doing hand-to-hand, I want in." She had a black eye already and long raven hair that she kept in a braid.

Briony began weighing the options, wondering how many guards there were outside the cell.

"I'm really fast," said a young voice. It was the sixteen-year-old girl who Katrina was comforting. She had curly hair and a gap between her teeth. "Like, *really* fast. My brothers can never catch me."

Briony opened her mouth to tell her she needn't worry, that they wouldn't force her to fight.

Bang!

The room jumped and the women clung to one another. They faced the door where bolts were unlocking with a groan. When it opened, two men in blue coats stepped inside.

Lag Reighven was tall and thin, with thick black eyebrows and a twisted nose. He was at least fifteen years her elder, and every altercation she'd had with the man had given her nightmares. He had ties to the magical black market and was known to be in the business of buying and selling heartsprings—human familiars. The old Seat of Bomard used to regulate him, but Veronika Mallow gave him permission to do as he pleased as long as he served her. The use of humans as heartsprings in Bomard had exploded over the last four years, and it was well known that Reighven had both led the charge and profited handsomely from it.

The other man was Hap Gains, fourth in line to the Seat and the man who'd captured her on the day Rory died. Not to mention, he was also Larissa's father. Briony glanced at Larissa and found her looking down at the floor.

"Medical examinations today." Gains's voice was thick and low. He had a pink scar over one blond eyebrow that hadn't been there before.

Reighven was staring directly at Briony with a leering grin. "Look who's awake."

Briony raised her chin in response.

"You five," Gains said with a lazy point to a group that included Phoebe and Cordelia. "Come."

No one moved.

"I'll drag you if I need to."

Phoebe stepped forward slowly, volunteering to be first. Cordelia and the other three got into line, the chains between their hands clicking. There was a heavy thudding in Briony's heart as Cordelia glanced over her shoulder to Briony just before the door closed on them.

It was quiet in the room afterward.

"This is good," said Velocity. "They can tell us what to expect out there. And it will be two of them against two of us." She nodded at the black-haired woman.

"Three of us," the young curly-haired girl said, reminding them she was willing to fight. "I'm Eden." She introduced herself, trying to mimic the way Velocity had stood at attention in her greeting.

Briony didn't know how to pick and choose who would risk their lives today. She turned to Larissa.

"Larissa, can you help us at all? Do you know where we are?"

She was quiet, her eyes unfocused. Finally, she looked up at Briony. "I think it's the Trow estate. They have a dungeon."

Briony's heart thudded. "Can you tell us anything about this place? Is there a way out that you know of?"

Larissa sneered. "Oh, so you can skip out the door leaving me behind? No thank you."

"Who said I'd leave you behind?" Briony stared her down until Larissa looked away.

"I think . . ." Larissa cleared her throat. "I think we're five floors down. I think the main exit will be up four staircases."

Hope leached out of Briony a little. That was too many floors. "Thank you," she said. She glanced to the other women, all waiting with bated breath for Briony to tell them what to do.

"Is Rory really dead?"

Her head snapped to the left. A voice had come out of the mass of bodies. She couldn't tell who, but someone had spoken the question in her heart.

She swallowed. "I don't—"

"He is." Velicity looked at her and then away. "He is."

"But how?" a woman asked. "What about the prophecy?"

Briony wondered the same. Six hundred years ago, at the outbreak of the civil war, one of the seers had delivered a prophecy: *When the sun shines at night, he who will bring an end to war on this land shall be victorious. He shall be an heir, twice over, and a rightful sovereign over the continent.*

But one hundred years later, when Briony's ancestor sat down with the first Seat of Bomard to accept the secession of Bomard from Evermore and sign the Spring Treaty, no "heir twice over" brokered its terms or played any role at all in its making. The prophecy had been forgotten, as most unfulfilled prophecies would be.

Until this mess with Mallow. Until Rory.

As her father's only male child, Rory had been the heir to Evermore. Ten years ago, their father had quelled a dispute on the largest of the three southern islands, winning the self-governed island's allegiance. Rory became the heir presumptive to the island as well.

This made him an heir, twice over, just as the prophecy had stated.

"It was an old prophecy," Briony said softly to the women. "It wasn't accurate the first time the Moreland continent went to war, either."

It tasted like ash in her mouth, like betrayal. How many times had she told Rory he was the one. How many times had she promised her people that the war would stop on the day of the eclipse and that Rory would bring them together in peace?

She reached for him on that vein in her chest, aching to feel his magic respond. But nothing. Briony took a deep breath and locked Rory away in her heart.

The air was thick as they waited for the first group to come back. Only the sound of one woman sobbing cut through their silence.

When the *bang* of the door unlocking came again, everyone jumped and turned their eyes on the entrance. Cordelia, Phoebe, and the others returned freshly bathed, looking no worse for wear. Gains and Reighven took five more women and left them alone. Once the door was locked again and the footsteps receded, Phoebe turned her attention to the dusty floor and began drawing a map from memory with her shoe.

"Showers first," Cordelia said, pointing as the map took shape. "Then medics. Showers are two floors up. You'll have to strip down while they watch." Her voice broke, but she continued. "They keep the chains on you the whole time. Medics on the same floor. They tested us for pregnancies first, which was . . . unexpected."

Briony swallowed thickly. Phoebe dropped to her knees and reached for the grapes and berries to mark where the guards were.

"And Reighven confirmed it," Cordelia said. "There's to be an auction for heartsprings. They're going to use us." Her voice wobbled for the first time. "They're going to take our magic and use it for themselves."

Cordelia glanced at Briony with a sniff, then at Larissa—the only person who hadn't moved to watch the map be drawn.

"Is there nothing you can say to your father?" Cordelia snapped, her patience clearly worn thin.

Larissa glared back at her. "Is there anything you can say to yours?"

The room gasped collectively. Cordelia's father had been murdered a year earlier. The primary suspect was Hap Gains.

Cordelia stepped forward with a snarl on her face, but Phoebe jumped up and pushed a hand against her shoulder and said to the room, "Here's what we know."

Briony moved closer, standing at Phoebe's side. Velicity and the woman with the black eye joined her.

"There is a window on this floor and on the floor with the showers. I have no idea about the floor between—we didn't see it from the staircase."

"A window?" Briony turned to Larissa. "I thought we were five floors down in the dungeons?"

"The Trow property was built into the other side of the Tampet Mountains, just like the Bomardi school. We *are* in the dungeon, but every floor still has a view."

"How high is the property? How far up from the base of the mountain are we?" Briony asked.

Larissa pressed her lips together. "Hundreds of yards."

A muttering passed through the women. Hope was swirling down a drain. How could anyone get down a mountainside with their hands chained?

"All you'll have on your side is the element of surprise," Phoebe said quietly to Briony. "Don't waste it." She turned to Velicity. "Get Briony out. Don't come back for us."

Briony's head snapped to her. "What? No. We'll find the men, and we'll—"

Cordelia grabbed Briony's hand. "You have to go, Briony. You have to find whatever's left of Rory's forces. They need a Rosewood to rally behind."

"My line doesn't matter anymore," Briony whispered. "A woman cannot be ruler of Evermore."

Before Cordelia could argue, the first *bang* of the doors unlocking sounded.

Phoebe and a few others gathered the fruit from the floor. Velicity grabbed Briony's elbow and dragged her across the room to where Gains had been choosing women for the next round of medical exams. The woman with the braid and black eye joined them. Just before the second door unlocked, a figure dashed across the room, almost knocking into Briony in an effort to join the next group. It was Eden. Katrina was hot on her heels.

The door opened, and five women were readmitted into the cell. One of them was shaking so hard that she fell to her knees.

Gains gestured at the next five: Briony, Velicity, the black-haired woman, Katrina, and Eden.

Velicity stepped forward, volunteering to be first in line, and Briony suddenly realized that they had no plan. Just . . . fight? It wasn't enough. They had no signal. And what did *she* know about combat without magic?

Katrina moved in line next, then Briony. Eden and the black-haired woman fell into line behind her.

Reighven clicked his teeth at her as she passed him.

Her eyes flickered over every detail outside the dungeon as they stepped into a small antechamber of dark walls. The light was almost too bright after that darkness, and she had to squint against the torches. As Reighven locked the door to the cell with a twist of his hands, Gains opened the next one. Briony tried to remember the floor plan—the fruit against the dirty stones.

They followed Gains out of the second door and found a labyrinth of hallways. She had no idea how Phoebe had remembered it all. And a sudden fear struck her that she hadn't. What if she'd made mistakes? Two left turns should take them close enough to that window, but what if it didn't?

Reighven locked the second door with a heavy thunk, and Briony turned to watch what kind of locking gesture he used so she could replicate it once she got this collar off. He caught her looking and smiled with yellow teeth.

"Don't be smart now."

Briony hurried to follow Katrina's blond hair as she left the antechamber.

Gains led them around the two left corners, and there—

Briony could see the window. It was dawn.

They were ten paces from it when Velicity reared back and swung her chained hands at the back of Gains's skull. He fell sideways with the strength of it, smacking into the wall.

Briony spun as the black-haired woman delivered a hard punch to

Reighven's stomach, doubling him over in surprise. Eden darted the ten steps to the window and started working it open.

Gains recovered and shoved Velicity's body back with magic, pinning her against the stone wall. Briony moved to swing her chains at his head in the same way Velicity had, but she felt a hook around her waist, tugging her back on a string. She smacked into a hard chest, and Reighven's pale hand wrapped around her chest to hold her against him by her throat.

She kicked, trying to maneuver him into releasing her. He grunted and held firm, pinning the black-haired woman to the wall with magic. Katrina kicked Gains in the stomach, and Briony watched his hold on Velicity release.

Eden got the window open.

Reighven reached out, and Eden was yanked from the window by her hair. She screamed as she flew, landing hard on her back.

Briony curled forward as far as she could and then flung her chained hands over her head. The metal connected with Reighven's face with a crack, and he released her with an *oof!*

Eden scrambled back to the window, nimbly dodging every body part in the hallway and every spell cast. She *was* fast.

The raven-haired woman had her chains wrapped around Reighven's neck, choking him. Blood dripped down his head from the smack her shackles had given him. Eden was gesturing for Briony to run to the window, but Katrina and Velicity were struggling with Gains.

"Enough!" Gains bellowed. He reached out and contorted his arm. Velicity screamed and dropped to the floor. Her knee was angled wrong. He'd dislocated it.

Gains grabbed Katrina by the neck and slammed her head against the stone wall. Briony gasped as she crumpled.

Briony's heart pulsed with rage and fear. Without logic, she sliced her arm through the air, a magical instinct.

Something thrummed in her chest.

Gains gasped, grabbing for his sternum. Blood blossomed bright red against his blue coat.

Time seemed to stand still as Briony looked between Gains and her own hand. The hand that had just sliced his chest open with magic. Velocity's pained face was slack with awe.

Briony spun, finding Reighven standing over the black-haired woman, giving up on magic and kicking her in the ribs. She flicked her fingers, and her heart sent magic down her veins. Reighven's body flew from the ground, hitting the ceiling. She pinned him there.

Gains stared at her in shock as he started to heal himself, pulling his skin back together.

Velocity jumped at him, digging her fingers into the slice to tear him open again. Gains yelled in pain, and Velocity screamed, "Briony, go!"

Briony tugged on her magic—*heart* magic—and cast a shield around herself, the strength of the Rosewood bloodline. She ran to the window, feeling magic bouncing off her shield.

Briony joined Eden at the window, looking down. It was a steep drop onto jagged rocks.

There was a scream from next to her as Eden was yanked away from the window again. Briony whirled around and found Velocity on the floor barely conscious, Katrina out cold, the black-haired woman rolling in pain, and Reighven standing in the center of it all, Eden held against his chest like a shield.

One hand was holding her throat; the other was held out in front of him, palm up.

Briony's eyes widened as she recognized the beginning of the Heart-stop cast—the spell to crush a heart.

Gains was pale but healing his wound on the ground as Briony stared down Reighven.

"Playtime is over, Princess," Reighven growled. "Don't know how you're resisting the collar, but it's two of us against one of you. Step away from the window, and this one lives."

The black-haired woman came to her feet with unsteady movements and tried to rush at Reighven. He kicked his leg out, and his heavy boot caught her hip, sending her flying into the wall.

Briony watched his fingers begin to curl in toward his palm. Eden gasped, squirming as her heart began to collapse in her chest.

Eden's eyes begged her. Briony began to leave the ledge.

Velicity's voice stopped her. "Don't—"

Reighven crushed his fingers into a fist, and Briony screamed as Eden took one last breath—her heart crumpled, her eyes never leaving Briony's. Reighven let her body drop and began moving toward the window. Gains was just coming to his feet again.

Guards appeared at the opposite end of the hallway, and Briony took off to her left, up the stairs. She'd find the window on a higher floor, and maybe it would give the women a chance if they were separated.

She heard Reighven's heavy footfalls hot on her heels. She felt several of his spells rebound against her shield.

She spilled out onto an identical floor. A chunk of stone broke off a wall and slammed into Briony's side. She tumbled to the floor. Her shield was for magic, not physical force.

Her ribs burned in pain, but she rolled back to her feet. The balls of her feet slapped the stones as she ran down the hall, searching for the next staircase or the next window. She tried to find the thread of her mind magic, but it was still silent. It was her heart she was casting from.

Briony threw herself down a corridor and skidded to a stop. It was a dead end. She tried the two doors, but they wouldn't budge.

When she spun back around, Reighven was at the entrance of the corridor, panting and smiling at her.

"You're going to be fun to break," he said. He didn't bother moving down the hall. He had her cornered.

Briony reached her hand out, palm up. She tugged on the vein of magic in her chest, ready to rip her heart if it meant taking Reighven out of this world.

Reighven's eyes flew wide.

She'd never cast Heartstop before, but she thought the mechanics of it were clear enough.

Briony curled her fingers into a fist, concentrating on what it meant to kill him. To kill someone.

Reighven's body went still, and Briony waited. Even with the pulse of magic in her chest, nothing happened.

His yellow teeth smiled at her from under his twisted nose. "You have to really mean it, Princess. You'll get it next time," he mocked her.

His hand shot out, and magic as sharp as knives sank into every inch of her skin. She heard herself screaming through the tunnel of the pain. She dropped to her knees, trying to grasp onto any magic inside herself to make it stop.

A slim body with hair the color of straw crashed into Reighven, throwing them both out of sight. Katrina.

Briony's mind released the pain.

She pulled herself to her feet and ran toward them as Katrina screamed.

Reighven had Katrina by her hair, tugging her up to the same position Eden had been in when her heart had stopped in his hand.

"No—"

"Let's try this again, Miss Rosewood."

Gains was behind Reighven, gasping from running up the stairs.

"Hands above your heart, knees on the ground," Gains demanded.

Briony's mind raced as Katrina's ribs dragged in air.

"I already owe Caspar Quill and Riann Cohle a few thousand gold for this little stunt," Reighven said. He grinned. "Trow won't mind this one going to waste, too, I'm sure."

Eden was dead. Another one, too? Velicity or the black-haired woman? Katrina here, about to die. Fifty magicless women locked in a room two floors down.

The men were alive somewhere, but Rory was dead.

"On the floor, Rosewood," Gains bellowed.

He closed in on her as her eyes flicked between him and Reighven. Her hands were held out as far as the chains would allow, prepared to engage either of them.

She could kill them both. It might take some fighting, but she could do it.

And then what? Who was left?

"I'll kill this one, too, Princess."

She could try Heartstop again. Take out Gains. But not before Reighven ended Katrina.

She could kill Gains, then Reighven as Katrina's body dropped.

And then she'd be alone.

"It's okay, Briony." Katrina smiled at her. There was blood on her teeth.

Briony blinked at the friend she'd never been kind enough to.

Katrina nodded. "Don't think of me. Go."

Reighven snarled, starting to curl his fingers toward his fist. Katrina gasped but tried to smile through it.

"Go, Briony," Katrina wheezed.

She had to—She could—She—

Briony dropped to her knees and moved her chained hands above her head.

Katrina fell from Reighven's grip, gasping on the floor. Alive.

Gains grabbed Briony's chain and threw her onto her back. He put his boot on her chest, holding her down.

"Go tell Orion we need that Gowarnus elixir, after all," Gains ordered Reighven. "And clean this up."

Briony winced as Katrina coughed, clutching her chest. Had she done the right thing?

She didn't know why she had magic. Had this been her only chance? Had she wasted it?

Gains reached down for Briony's chain and dragged her down the hall on her back. Briony watched Katrina breathe, knowing the blonde would have done the same for her, tenfold.

She held on to that thought until she was dragged out of sight.

CHAPTER 7

T HEY PUT HER IN A CELL BY HERSELF. Gains strung her up against the cold stone wall, forcing her to stand with her arms above her head, her ankles shackled now, too. She was alone except for a black bird that watched her closely from a perch over the door. She recognized it as Reighven's familiar.

There were half a dozen heart magic spells she could do from this position, but all she could think of was the life draining from Eden's eyes. And the other two? Velocity and the black-haired woman whose name she didn't even know? What had become of them?

She thought about the Heartstop that she hadn't been able to complete. *You have to really mean it, Princess,* Reighven had said. She knew that to be true. To use the darker magics, one had to channel that darkness inside of oneself.

Reighven had killed Eden because she was nothing to him. The hate that burned in her heart now was enough to squeeze the life out of him. If she had the opportunity again, she wouldn't fail.

Standing upright with the feeling drifting out of her hands, Briony finally had a moment to think.

Why did she have her magic? No, not *her* magic. Her magic was mind magic. This magic was the thing she rarely tapped into, and then only when she needed to help Rory.

Did this collar only work on mind magic? No. Larissa was also wearing a collar, and she was a heart magician. Unless Larissa was there to deceive them . . .

Briony tugged on the magic in her chest. She twirled her fingertips and felt a breeze cast its way through the dark empty room. She felt the pulse of it in her chest, thick like honey.

It made her think of Rory.

Rory was dead. Her father was dead. There were no other Rosewood men that she knew of. The line was gone. Her entire realm was ended. Despite many other countries moving past patriarchal succession, though slowly, Evermore had never budged. There was only the king, and then his male heir. There would never be a queen. Any time in the past that Evermore had been left in a position like this, with no male heir, the women in the family had scrambled to produce one while the cabinet ruled as regent. Briony didn't even know how many cabinet advisers had survived. Any? Even so, it would take a male heir from Briony, Phoebe, or Phoebe's sister, Finola, to reinstate their line.

Where was Finola? She hadn't been in the dungeon with the other women. The last time Briony had seen her, she was portaling out of the Claremore courtyard, carrying out a mission. Could she hope that Finola hadn't been captured at all?

Briony created lists upon lists of questions that didn't have answers. She created lists of those who possibly survived. Sammy, Didion . . . Was Sammy's father still alive? She couldn't imagine letting someone like General Billium Meers live. Perhaps he was being tortured for all the realm's military information.

Briony tried to let her mind center on immediate problems, like the auction.

Would the Bomardi really sell them like animals?

But she didn't have to think on that long. She knew it to be true. The final year at the Bomardi school, before the attack, the Bomardi boys had whispered about it. She'd heard more than a few numbers thrown around when one of their prettier classmates walked by. Numbers they would pay to own her.

Briony shivered.

Perhaps she'd seen Toven Hearst talking numbers less than the others. Maybe she'd imagined it—the way he'd tell his friends to knock it off, the way he'd had to tell Collin Twindle to shut up about how much money he had to spend.

Maybe she just wanted it to be true.

Liam Quill had gotten into a fistfight with Didion in the final year at Bomard, and when they'd been separated—with Liam the worse off— Liam had given one parting shot: "When the walls come down in Evermore, you best not let me find you," he'd hissed. "I won't even sell you off. I'll keep you, chain you, bleed your magic dry"—he'd nodded at Briony in the crowd—"and make you watch as I fuck your girl every night."

Briony had scarcely known what Liam was talking about then, only that she was suddenly a part of the narrative.

Didion had bellowed at him, fighting off the tutors holding him back. Toven had stepped in, shoved Didion back with magic, and quick as lightning wrapped his hand around Liam's throat. He whispered something into Liam's face that had the boy snarling, and Briony had been swept into the retreating crowd as more tutors had appeared. All three boys had gotten demerits. Briony had thought a lot about Toven's reaction, both then and now. He hated vulgarity—always had. Toven's mother had been a socialite from across the sea, a dignitary's daughter. Briony thought perhaps Serena had raised Toven quite differently from the other Bomardi boys.

But of course, there were times he'd proved her wrong . . .

The black bird cawed, making Briony jump. The door opened with a creaking sound, and adrenaline flooded Briony's tired body. She stood upright, having started to sag.

Reighven slid into the cell with a coy grin, leaning against the door to close it. He crossed his arms, and it wasn't lost on Briony that she was alone with a dangerous, lecherous man.

"I appreciate your fight, Princess."

She said nothing, just watched him.

He sauntered closer, and Briony's eyes flicked to the crack in the door, begging someone to come in.

"I always have," he said, tilting his head. "Appreciated you, I mean. It's a shame you couldn't kill me back there. For you."

He stopped in front of her, and she had to press her back against the stones to keep from brushing him as she breathed. He lifted a hand, and her blood froze in her veins. He trailed a finger over the thin sleeve at her shoulder.

"Gains won't sell you to me privately. He thinks the Princess of Evermore will fetch a high price at auction." His fingertip slid down her dress, following the fabric. "But don't worry, pet. I've been saving for this for a long time. You'll be mine."

His hand passed over her ribs, over her hip.

"So I don't think there's a problem with an early taste."

The chains rattled as she shook. "Get your hands off me," she snarled, far braver than she felt.

He smirked at her, his rancid breath puffing against her face. "We're going to have so much fun together." His hand cupped her between the legs over her dress.

Briony gasped as every muscle in her body turned to ice.

"I wasn't aware Gains was open to negotiation," said a voice from the doorway. Reighven removed his hand and stepped back, and Briony's knees gave out in relief. Until she realized who it was.

Orion Hearst stood in the cell entry. Toven's father—and there was no doubt about it. He'd given his son that preternaturally silver-gray hair and his towering height. Orion was not only the richest man in all Bomard, but also the most ruthless. Over the four years that Evermore had warred with Bomard, Orion Hearst had been on every major front line. With an unheard-of skill to split his casting against multiple opponents, he was the most feared fighter in Bomard. And since Mallow had come to power, he had started increasing his power, now no longer feeling his heart rip with every kill. The price of Heartstop was something Orion Hearst no longer had to pay.

Rory once asked Briony why Orion Hearst was only eighth in line for the Seat. "With so much power and so much money, why is he so low on the succession line?"

"Self-preservation," Briony had guessed. "Any higher up and he'd be a target."

Rory hadn't understood that, but Briony, who'd hidden herself for years as something unremarkable, had a certain respect for someone who knew they deserved more but held themselves back for whatever reason. Briony's reason was Rory. She wondered what Orion's reason was.

Reighven frowned at Orion. "You got my message?"

Orion pulled a vial from his pocket, twitching it slightly. "The Gowarnus herb mixture." Orion stepped into the room, his form backlit from the hallway torches. "So good of you to keep her company, Reighven," he said silkily. "I'll be sure to let Gains know that his lot has a friend in you."

Lot. As in, a lot up for auction.

Reighven sneered and stepped away from her. "She'll be mine soon enough. I would have paid Gains the five thousand gold."

Briony's brows jumped at the sum.

"I'm sure," Orion hummed. He turned his eyes on Briony as he stopped directly in front of her. "Miss Rosewood. Lovely to see you again," he said mockingly. "I believe the last time we met was the day the Bomardi school fell." His brows lifted in fake realization. "Ah, no. I'm thinking of someone else entirely. Aren't I?"

Briony pressed her lips together. The other thing people said about Orion Hearst was that he liked to toy with his prey.

Briony met his gaze with more bravery than she felt. "Mr. Hearst. It's kind of you to call," she said, her voice steady even as her stomach turned to ice.

His eyes narrowed on her, and for a moment she felt examined, flayed open. He looked so much like his son, but where Toven lacked patience, Orion Hearst was nothing if not patient.

He uncorked the vial and tipped it to her lips. She pressed her mouth closed, shaking her head, but with barely a flick of his fingers, her mouth was magically wrenched open. She tried to close her throat, but she coughed on the sour elixir all the way down. Squeezing her eyes shut, she tried to hold on to the vein that channeled her heart magic, searching for the pulse in her chest. But with a final flutter, it was gone. There was nothing there—it was dormant now.

"Why didn't the collar work on her?" Reighven asked.

Orion lifted a pale finger and traced the metal around Briony's neck. A ring with a black gemstone glinted. "It could be any number of things. Rosewoods are known for their protective magic. She could have blocked the collar somehow." Orion glanced at Reighven. "It's a predicament for her future warden. For now, the Gowarnus elixir will render her innocuous."

"For how long?" Reighven asked.

Orion turned his eyes on Briony. "They all will need to be dosed every three days. Just to be certain." He capped the vial and tilted his head, speaking to her now. "Miss Eden Wincet is dead. Miss Velicity Punt is injured. Miss Katrina Cove is badly wounded as well. Why do you insist on hurting your own people, Miss Rosewood? What a waste of Eversun blood, one would say—if one cared for Eversuns, as you claim to."

Briony swallowed, knowing what mind game he was playing. "Eden Wincet was scarcely more than a child," she hissed. "And you—you proud and loyal Bomardi—were going to sell her off like livestock."

His brows furrowed in mock concentration. "No, no. I treat my cows far better than I'd treat an Eversun. Mark me."

Briony spat in his face.

Orion Hearst didn't blink.

He pulled a handkerchief out of his pocket and wiped her saliva without looking away from her.

She'd spat on his son once.

He'd had an entirely different reaction.

Orion looked down as he folded his handkerchief and put it back in his pocket. "I should have you killed for that." He looked up at her. "But I don't spend my money on slaves, and I'd hate to have to pay Gains thirty thousand just for slashing your throat." Briony sucked in a shaking breath, and Orion continued, raising his voice to address Reighven, "That's how men like me stay rich, you see. We don't need to waste money on magic heartsprings."

"Only one of the reasons I want her, but thank you for the tip," Reighven said venomously.

"Ah." Orion glanced at the other man. "Men like me don't pay for *that*, either." He sent Reighven a withering smile. "Now, Miss Rosewood. Someone would like to see you. I hope you'll pay them a bit more respect."

Briony's heart twisted. She looked up into Orion's eyes and only saw Toven, wondered if he was here, if he was coming to see her—

The door opened, and Veronika Mallow stepped inside.

Briony's muscles locked in terror.

"Briony. It's good to see you again." Mallow's voice was smooth and sinuous, as if it could wrap around a person and squeeze. She moved into the cell like a nymph through water, her long black robes flowing behind her. Gains followed her in, and then four of the most dangerous people in all Bomard were gazing upon Briony.

Adrenaline flooded her, and Briony swallowed around the fear in her throat.

Mallow tilted her head, catlike. She was thinner than Briony remembered. Her long black hair was pin-straight and fell like a sheet. She had a necklace of onyx stones and earrings to match. Her eyes traced down Briony's body, taking in her dirt- and bloodstained dress.

"The escape attempt happened before bathing, I presume."

This woman had killed her father, killed her brother, and still had the audacity to care about the grime on Briony's skin and clothing.

"We were on our way to the baths and the medics when she organized her little stunt," said Gains.

"She's feisty," said Reighven. "She got another killed—"

"Silence," Mallow all but whispered.

Briony noted the reaction—the immediate way the men quieted. The way their breaths caught in their chests, waiting for instruction.

Mallow's lips twitched. She stepped forward, and Briony could see the endless tunnels in her eyes.

"Isn't it fascinating to see that she bleeds just the same as we do?" she said to the others. She gripped Briony's jaw and turned her face, examining the bloodstains on her. "Not a speck of gold anywhere. Makes you wonder why there's such a fuss about the Rosewood bloodline after all."

Briony pulled her face out of Mallow's grip. It was a common legend that the king and his family bled gold. It was founded on nothing but the presumption that the king was predestined to rule by the nobility of his bloodline.

Mallow tilted her head. "Miss Rosewood, I am only letting you live because my followers have requested it. It seems you haven't kept from catching the eye of all the Bomardi men since the last time I saw you."

Briony shivered.

Mallow reached up a bony hand and traced one of Briony's curls.

"You still intend to put her up for bidding, Gains?" she asked.

"Yes, Mistress."

Briony's eyes flicked to him at the use of the title. Seats of Bomard went by "High Seat" or "Sir" or "Madame."

"All right," Mallow said. "We'll need to spay her."

Briony's stomach dropped. Her mouth opened. She couldn't mean—

"Wait." The words rushed out. "Please—"

"Do you wish to have Reighven's children, Briony?" Mallow said with a twist to her lips. "I hear he's the most likely to win you. And I think he'd find it hard to keep his hands off a . . . prize like you."

Briony swallowed, refusing to look at the man in question, who was probably smiling at her.

"He wouldn't—He could use protection," she mumbled.

She had always wanted children, always craved the creation of a family she hadn't had. But not like this.

And more than that, she wanted to believe that this wasn't the end of Evermore. That one day they would organize and rise from the ashes. That she would find a way to save her family's future.

Mallow stared at her, realizing Briony's deepest desires.

"Oh. No, Briony," she said softly. She ran her cold fingers down her cheek. "No, it's over, dear heart. I killed him. And I burned his body." She leaned in to Briony's ear and whispered, "There is no home to go back to."

Briony saw red. She lunged forward, reaching out with her teeth for Mallow's skin. There was bone under her grip, and she bit down as Mallow screamed.

Magic was flung at her from all directions. She was forced back against the stone, her head cracking. Her jaw was shoved wide, almost to the point of breaking.

Orion was at Mallow's side, but Mallow wrenched away from his protective arm. A perfect circle of teeth was impressed on the corner of her dainty jawline.

If Briony could smile with her mouth winched open, she would have.

The men spoke over one another, snarling threats, but Briony only had eyes for Mallow. *I'll kill you myself one day*, she thought, hoping the intention was clear.

Mallow stared at her in fascination, bringing her hands up to halt the men. The spells suddenly released her. Mallow narrowed her eyes and smiled. "You'll have your hands full, Reighven. I like her."

With a twist of Mallow's hand, Briony's mouth snapped shut, her teeth clicking loudly, and she was unable to separate them. She was muzzled.

Mallow stepped toward her again, only inches away. "Just so we're clear. I'm keeping you alive because you're interesting and because my men wish it." She shrugged. "I also happen to believe you're headed to a fate worse than death. But bear in mind that there are no promises kept for the other women. If you try to run again, I will kill every Eversun in that cell. And I will start with Cordelia Hardstark."

Briony's chest shook, but she refused to cry.

"Do you understand me?"

Briony nodded. "Yes," she said through her closed teeth.

"Good." Mallow tugged her fingers at the air, and Briony felt something heat in her throat. "That's the last word I want to hear from you."

She'd taken her voice.

CHAPTER 8

BRIONY WAS UNCHAINED FROM THE WALL and given to Reighven and Gains. She rubbed her sore wrists, finally free from the shackles. The collar stayed on. With a hand on each of her elbows, they led her up the stairs, past the blood-spattered windows, and to the floor with the baths.

They shoved her inside, and Reighven said, "You have two minutes."

The taps sprang to life, and scalding-hot water splashed down to the tub.

She glanced at the two of them, then to the door.

"Go on," Reighven said with a leer.

She swallowed, her jaw tight with the muzzling spell. They wouldn't give her privacy to disrobe.

Briony stared at the bath as it filled. The tub hadn't been cleaned in years, it seemed. Grime coated the sides, and there were numerous rings from the waterline.

She hiked up her dress and stepped into the hot water. It scalded her, turning her skin bright red. Lowering herself into the water, she let her dress cover her on the way down. She glanced at the two men and found Gains looking away, almost bored, but Reighven's eyes were glued to her chest as the water soaked her dress.

He approached her slowly, and Briony squeezed the sides of the tub. He produced a bar of soap and dropped it into the water with a splash.

"Make sure to scrub up *everywhere*," he said with a wink. "Or I'll do it for you."

Briony cast her eyes down to the bath. Her skin was burning, and the water was already tinted with dirt and blood. She dipped her hair back and ran the soap over her scalp and her skin as best she could. Reighven stood at the edge of the tub and lifted a furry black brow. She grabbed the soap and pushed it between her legs, ignoring the clicking of his teeth.

His arm reached, and her body froze in horror, afraid he would touch her. He grabbed at the wet dress at her shoulder, then pulled back with silver gleaming between his fingers.

Her mother's brooch. The last piece of her.

Reighven smiled as he pocketed it. Briony's heart cracked in two.

Gains tossed her a towel when it was time to get out, but they didn't dry her dress. Water dripped from her hem as they walked her down the hall to a different room.

When Gains knocked, a thickset older woman with deep umber skin opened the door. She was in a Bomardi medical uniform. When her eyes landed on Briony, they seemed to stay a bit too long.

"One last one for the exams," Gains said.

Briony shivered under her wet dress and wet hair as they shoved her forward. Another young female medic was in the corner. She had pale skin and bright-red hair and looked barely older than Briony. She blanched when she saw Briony. The older woman pointed for Briony to sit on a table.

Gains turned to Reighven. "Go check on the Meers kid."

Briony's head snapped to them. Sammy was nearby.

Reighven looked put out, but he obeyed, closing the door behind him.

They had her lie back and ran spells over her body, hovering their hands and waiting for light and heat to spark. One of them dried her hair and dress, muttering about hypothermia.

The younger medic placed both hands over Briony's stomach, pale fingers spreading wide. She looked up at Gains. "Not pregnant."

Briony swallowed, realizing she never would be.

The heavyset medic placed a plant bundle with branching white flowers over her belly, humming an old melody.

Briony knew this one. She always knew she'd have it performed one day before a wedding.

The woman's hands flew in circles, and the bundle caught fire against her dress before burning out just as quickly. The warmth and light stayed, but it lit up deep under her skin.

She stared at the ceiling with her jaw glued shut and voice stolen while the medic said to Gains, "Virgin."

Gains chuckled. "Five thousand more to me."

Briony's eyes squeezed shut. Was one night really worth five thousand gold? Was one moment? She supposed there were old rituals that could be performed with virgin's blood. Reighven would certainly know the black market of trade, but the way he talked to her—looked at her. She didn't think he wanted her just for the blood.

The medics were wrapping up when Gains said, "We're to sterilize her."

A tear slipped out of Briony's left eye.

It was quiet in the room for too long. She opened her eyes and turned her gaze on the younger medic who was staring at the older one.

"Is there a problem?" Gains asked.

"She's . . ." The redhead looked at the floor. "Isn't she the last of that line?"

"Evermore is gone," Gains said coldly as he stood from the wall he'd been leaning on. "Mistress Mallow has requested that all women and men who have ties to the Rosewood line be sterilized. You wouldn't be opposing Mistress Mallow's decision, would you?"

The redhead looked helplessly at the older medic, who didn't show any emotion.

Clearing her throat, the redhead lifted her chin up. "I won't do it."

Briony puffed out air, watching this woman in Bomardi-blue medical robes opposing Mallow. Maybe there was hope.

But Gains's hand shot out, his fingers curling into a fist as the woman grabbed for her heart, eyes wide. She sputtered and dropped to her knees.

"I'll do it," the older medic said, almost lazily. "Don't kill her. I need her."

Gains's fingers eased their grasp on the magic crushing the young woman's heart. She gasped, curling into a ball on the floor.

The older medic moved to Briony's side and brought her thumbs and index fingers over her pelvis in a triangle, closing her eyes. Briony prepared herself, listening to the redhead's gasping. There was a pinch and a burn on the left side of her belly, and Briony jerked. Her left fallopian tube had been cauterized.

As the medic moved around the table to her other side, Briony was glad that Gains's grinning face was out of her view. "How many others are you sterilizing?" the medic asked Gains conversationally.

Tears slipped out of Briony's eyes as the woman placed the triangle of her hands over her belly again, over her right side. She prepared herself for the sensation again.

"There's only one more here," Gains said.

"Well, we can't wait around all day," the older medic said.

And with her back to Gains, the woman pinched Briony's stomach with her nails as sharply as possible.

Briony jerked, kicking her legs. She gazed up at the medic in question, but she was already turning to Gains.

"It's done. Both fallopian tubes have been burned shut. She won't fall pregnant."

Briony tried to relax her face. The woman hadn't cauterized her right side.

And they both knew it.

Gains stepped forward. "Let's go," he said to Briony. "And you." He turned to the redhead who was still getting her breath back. "Do a good turn here, and I won't request your beheading when your services are no longer needed."

The redhead nodded, crying.

Briony got up off the table. The older medic had turned to her paperwork. As if nothing had happened.

Briony followed Gains out the door, her heart pounding. He put the chains back on her wrists, but her thoughts were focused elsewhere.

There were Bomardi out there who would help Evermore. She just needed to find them.

Her mind was spinning as Gains took her down two staircases, back to the cell with the women.

He didn't say a word to her as he opened the doors, and that was all right. She was too busy building hope in her chest like a palace of worship.

When she stepped into the cell, the women jumped up, running to her. Gains locked them in again, as questions were flung at her from every direction. Briony couldn't focus on any of them.

Cordelia stepped in front of her. "Briony?"

She tapped her fingers against her throat and shook her head. And then tapped her jaw and mimed a mouth closing with her hand.

But there was a fire burning inside her. She caught Velocity's eye across the room. She was chained to the wall with her arms above her head, much the way Briony had been, only there was dried blood all over her face. Katrina was next to her on the wall. One of the women was helping her drink water.

Briony cast her eyes around the room.

The women were looking to her, but she had no voice to tell them that they had support. That there were people out there who would still stand up for them—either loudly like the redhead or silently like the older medic.

Her gaze caught on the basket of food, and she remembered Phoebe placing fruit across the dirty floor.

Briony dropped to her knees, reaching for a bundle of grapes and making quick work of the vine.

"Briony?" someone asked, but she wasn't paying attention. She had to tell them.

She started spelling out what she couldn't say, the grapes laid quickly into letters. She reached for another vine of grapes while the women caught on and gathered behind Briony.

The first word formed, and she thought of that redhead almost dying for her. For *her*. An Eversun.

Someone started pulling the grapes for her and making a pile with them. Briony built the second word, working quickly to say so little.

But it would hopefully tell them what they needed to know about the older medic who defied Mallow right under Gains's nose.

Finally, there was one grape left, and she added it to the end. A period. A statement.

She stood and stepped back as the women gazed down at her handiwork.

Not alone.

CHAPTER 9

Seven and a Half Years Ago

BRIONY DESPISED STATE DINNERS, especially the ones that fell on the winter solstice. She'd learned by now—the winter between her first and second year—that spending time with the Bomardi students at school was enough for her. She didn't need to see them outside the school year as well.

She stood at the entrance to the grand ballroom with Rory and her father, welcoming in state officials from Bomard and Evermore and their families. The ballroom was decorated with fir trees that were native to Bomard's mountains, and a new tapestry had been hung, depicting a snowy morning in the Bomardi forest. All of it was so at odds with Biltmore Palace's open arcades, ornate porticoes, and reflective pools. They would mingle and dance until midnight, and then the feast would begin, going all night until dawn.

It had only been twenty minutes and she had already seen ten people she didn't care for.

And her dress was itchy.

"Briony, stop that," her father admonished when she adjusted her sleeves for the third time. "You are now seventeen. You have to start dressing like it."

"Are seventeen-year-olds itchy?" she grumbled. The dress was a green lace, the bodice tight from her waist up to her shoulders and laced down to her wrists. It was so unlike the flowing and loose wear that Eversuns favored, she really thought her father was trying too hard to welcome those frostbitten mutts. There was a place between her shoulder blades that she wanted to ask Rory to scratch for her, but she refrained.

Briony glanced at the Bomardi who had already entered. Was this the work of magic like that cold draft? Was one of them making her itch? No. Toven wasn't here yet.

When Finola and Phoebe came in, Briony hugged them tightly.

Finola leaned toward Rory and her. "Did you hear that the Vults brought their familiars?"

Briony glanced to where the Vult family was just now getting into the receiving line.

"Why?" Rory asked. "Do they expect a fight?"

"That's what I asked," Finola said with a laugh.

Briony glanced to see who was next: Hap Gains and his daughter, Larissa. Briony sighed.

It was custom for Evermore's king and his family to bow first as a sign of respect and welcome. And by the look on Larissa's face, this was clearly her favorite part of the entire state dinner.

Larissa stood directly in front of Briony with a calculated smile and watched her dip into a low curtsy.

"Welcome, Larissa," Briony said through clenched teeth. "How have you been since the end of the school year?"

"Fine, thank you, Briony. Absolutely *dreading* being in Evermore for the second year." She looked around at the decor—all the trouble Evermore had gone to—and added, "Evermore just isn't as comfortable. Far too warm and not enough to do."

Briony bit back a remark, and Larissa turned to Rory, indicating that he should bow next. Rory sighed and did so. Larissa bobbed the smallest, least respectful of curtsies to both in response and waved dismissively as the Gainses moved on.

Gin Pulvey, the Seat of Bomard, was next. He was a hearty man with a large mustache that took up most of his pink face. Seat Pulvey had a good relationship with King Jacquel, to many Bomardi's dismay. Behind him were Sammy and his father, Billium Meers, high general of the Eversun armies. Briony's father rose from his bow and pulled an exasperated face for General Meers in a rare moment of relaxed camaraderie.

"I think you should give me the first dance tonight, Briony," Sammy said as she straightened from her curtsy. His voice was bright with mischief.

"What?" She curled her lip. "Why?"

"Because I think it will bother Didion."

Rory snorted and brought a hand to his mouth to hide his smile. Briony looked between Sammy and Rory with a blush. Then she glanced over at where Didion was standing in the ballroom with Katrina and Cordelia, watching her. His eyes darted away.

"Well, of course I'll dance with you," Briony said, "but why first dance?" First dance was usually reserved for the king and his wife (only in this case, Jacquel refrained as he did not intend to remarry), the Seat and their spouse, and any young couples intending to make a splash in the spring season of courtship.

Sammy placed a dramatic hand on his chest. "I'll happily take second, third, and fourth as well, but I think they'll be taken rather quickly."

She blinked at him. "I don't understand."

Sammy laughed and grabbed her hand, bringing her knuckles to his lips. "I love that you don't know how smashing you look. If you were six years older, we'd be engaged already, love."

She snatched her hand back and pulled a face at him. Sammy laughed, and Rory made a gagging sound.

"You'll have to get used to it, Worry," Sammy said, using Briony's mispronounced childhood name for her brother. He pontificated, "It will only be a few short years before she's sold off to a Bomardi boy in the name of peace and unity."

"Sammy, that's enough," General Meers said kindly. He sent an apologetic smile to Jacquel. "Let's let the next group in the door."

Sammy saluted his father, winked at Briony, and said, "First dance." They walked on.

Briony rolled her shoulders back, dress still itching her. *Smashing*, Sammy had said. That was kind, but nothing more than that. She liked

Sammy like a brother, and she was sure his feelings were the same. But she didn't love the reminder that as the king's daughter, she might not be able to marry for love. She did envy the Bomardi a little. They didn't treat their women like pawns in a game. A woman could sit on the Seat of Bomard just as easily as a man.

When Briony turned back to the receiving line, she came face-to-face with the smirking countenance of Toven Hearst. More like face-to-chest. He was even taller than he had been at the end of the school year a month ago.

"First dance already taken?" he said coyly. "My, my, you don't waste any time, do you?"

Briony pulled herself together and glanced to the left. Orion Hearst stood in front of her father, and Serena Hearst in front of Rory. As one, the Rosewoods bowed and curtsied.

She rose, finding Toven's eyes glued to her, his teeth gleefully biting down on his bottom lip. "Welcome," she muttered.

Toven wore a gray suit the pale color of his hair. As her father exchanged stilted pleasantries with Orion, and Serena examined the ballroom with what must have been distaste, Briony stared up into Toven's face with thinly veiled hatred. He exuded arrogance, and Briony couldn't believe he had the audacity to look down on her in her own home.

"Meers is right, you know," Toven said in a jovial tone belied by his look of boredom. "Have you decided which son of Bomard you'll be attaching yourself to when you come of age? Like a leech."

She batted her lashes. "Well, I'm aiming for you, of course."

He smiled brightly. "Ah. Lovely. You'll make an excellent addition to my line of trophies. I'll hang you on the wall."

"Trophies? What for?" she asked innocently. "Couldn't be elixirs class. Didn't Rory take top marks in elixirs this last year?" She smiled simperingly at him.

Toven leveled a stare at her. "Did he?" His tone made it clear that he knew exactly how Rory kept getting top marks.

Briony's smile slipped, and she looked away toward the ballroom where her friends were gathered. He hadn't told on her for assisting Rory with his schoolwork and continuing to boost him, but he took opportunities like this to dig at her about it. Only a few more introductions and then she would be able to hide from the Bomardi until dinner at midnight.

"So who will claim the second dance with the princess," Toven said quietly as his parents continued to converse with Rory and her father. His eyes cast over the crowd. "Didion Winchester, I'd presume?"

"I have no intention of dancing the first or second dance—"

"But of course, all of this is up for debate," he said, ignoring her. He turned his pale-gray eyes on her. "Someone on the line takes precedence in these situations."

She narrowed her gaze at him. Why would anyone from Bomard ask Sammy to step aside for the first dance?

"What are you getting at?"

"I'm only stating tradition, of course," he said, melodically. "If someone in the Ten were to ask for the first dance or second dance, Meers and Winchester would have to step aside, wouldn't they?"

The Ten were the Bomardi in the first ten places in line. It gave them certain feelings of superiority. Among them were Orion Hearst, Canning Trow's mother, Hap Gains, and Liam Quill's father.

Briony felt like she was missing a piece to a very large puzzle, but before she could ask, Orion Hearst spoke loudly.

"Ah, here she is. Jacquel, allow me to introduce our guest. Veronika Mallow."

A tall woman with pale-white skin and straight black hair stepped forward. Her eyes were black as well, like bottomless pits, but they were close together, giving her a foxlike quality. She looked to be in her fifties, but then the light caught her at a different angle, and she could have been twenty years younger.

"Mrs. Mallow. Welc—"

"*Miss* Mallow," she corrected Briony's father, stopping him in an awkward half bow. "Unlike the Eversuns, Bomardi women don't need to be married to be introduced." Black eyes flicked toward Briony, and a chill crested her shoulders.

"Of course," King Jacquel said. "My apologies for the presumption." He continued to bow, and Rory and Briony did the same.

"What an odd tradition," Mallow said. "Bowing to a stranger in your own palace. Seems so antiquated." The curtsy she offered in return was much like Larissa's—barely a dip of her elegant head, and a shocking rudeness to the king.

Briony blinked. She saw Orion's lips twitch, suppressing a smile.

"I suppose that's why they call it a tradition," Rory offered kindly.

Serena smiled at him. No one else did.

Briony glanced at Toven and found his eyes flicking away, turning to the ballroom.

When the Hearsts and Veronika Mallow slipped away, Briony continued to watch Mallow as she took in the ballroom. She seemed deeply displeased.

"Who is that?" Briony asked her father.

"Mallow is the daughter of a soldier. That's all I know. She's fortieth in line, I believe."

Rory snorted. "She certainly acts like she's in the Ten."

"Fortieth in line, and she's invited to a state dinner?" Briony whispered.

"Briony, don't be elitist."

Her gaze snapped to her father's. "I'm not. I . . . I didn't mean to be."

Her face flushed, and she looked down. She pushed back embarrassed tears as the Raquins stepped forward.

Finn winked at her, and she glared at him. "I hope you'll save me a dance tonight, Miss Rosewood."

Briony smiled patronizingly. "I'd rather throw myself from the tallest tower."

"Briony." Her father's sharp voice caught her by surprise; the Raquins and her family had heard the exchange. "You forget yourself," he said cuttingly.

Toven had flustered her. Hot embarrassment rose in her cheeks. She was zero for two with her father tonight.

Finn looked downright giddy. "Your grace, it's nothing. We play like this at school all the time. Don't we, Briony?"

She nodded without speaking, not trusting her voice.

Briony and Rory said hello to Finn's mother, Ember, an Eversun woman with dark-brown skin and green eyes. She had been a friend to their mother before she and Rory were born and had been married to Finn's father, a Bomardi, in a peace treaty marriage. Supposedly, Ember had been the first person to hold Rory when he was born, as their mother slowly bled out with Briony still in her belly. They only saw her a few times a year at these state dinners. A similar future awaited Briony, she realized, when she would only return to Evermore for state dinners. Her heart fell.

Ember reached out to touch both Rory and Briony's cheeks with a kind smile.

"Is my son behaving himself at school?" she asked.

"Barely," both Rory and Briony said together.

Ember huffed in exasperation and sent a chastising look to her son. He batted his lashes at his mother, innocently. "What can I say? I'm incorrigible." He offered Ember his arm, and she took it, rolling her eyes at him.

Once the receiving line was done, Briony and Rory finally got to join Didion, Cordelia, and Katrina. Cordelia snuck her a glass of wine, and Briony turned to the wall, drinking almost all of it in one swallow. The herald announced that the dancing would begin in five minutes, and Briony stepped behind Cordelia, hoping Sammy had been offering the first dance in jest.

Didion cleared his throat from next to her, and she glanced at him as she took a final swig from her glass. "Briony, I was wondering if I could dance the first with you."

She blinked at him, cheeks puffed with wine, and focused on swallowing. Rory coughed a smile into his hand and turned to speak to someone else.

"I . . . Sammy asked me," she blurted. "Sorry, I mean to say, I would love to take the second dance with you, Didion."

His brows pulled together. "Sammy? He's six years older than you."

"As a friend, surely," Briony jumped to say.

"Not as a friend," Sammy's jovial voice boomed from behind her. She turned to him with a scowl. "As an avid admirer." He swooped into a low bow and winked at Didion.

Briony's lip curled. "Don't waste your time flirting with me, Sammy."

He grinned, but before he could spar with her, a deep baritone voice sounded from behind her.

"Your grace."

Briony turned to find Toven standing in front of her. His hands were behind his back in a strange imitation of civility, and Briony stared up at him, praying he wasn't here to do what she thought he was here to do.

"What?" she said shortly.

"Your first dance," he said. "As we discussed." He flashed a bright smile at her.

Every one of her friends was silent behind her.

She lifted her brows. "We didn't discuss anything. I'm dancing the first with Sammy."

Looking to Sammy for help, she extended her hand to him, waiting for him to take it. But he just glared at Toven.

"You're serious, Hearst?" Sammy said.

"Absolutely," Toven said. "I *am* accustomed to having the finest thing in the room, after all."

Briony snapped her eyes to him. He was trailing his gaze down the bodice of her dress, where the lace pulled tightly across her breasts and fitted to her waist.

Didion stepped forward. "All right. That's enough—"

"The first and the second dance," Toven said, looking past her shoulder at Didion, then flicking his eyes back to her. "Your grace."

Behind him, couples were entering the dance floor. They only had moments before the dance started.

"I am dancing the first with Sammy and the second with Didion," Briony said, voice flat and stony. "I do not accept your hand."

She started to walk past him, and his arm shot out and caught her elbow, pulling her into his side.

"And *I*," he said softly, "am exercising my right as eighth in line to cut in."

"Your father is eighth in line," Briony hissed. "Should he ask me, I'd be happy to accept these terms."

She glanced at Sammy, trying to encourage him to follow her to the dance floor. But he was standing with his hands in his pockets, looking resigned. "He's a member of the Ten, Briony," Sammy said.

"He's *not*! He *succeeds* eighth in line. He's sixteenth at best!"

Toven turned her to him gently, and horror filled her as he placed a hand on her cheek. His fingers were warm, and his eyes might have looked kind to anyone who didn't truly know him. Briony heard Katrina gasp.

She blinked rapidly up at him, not daring to move. If he kissed her at a state dinner, it would be as good as a declaration of courtship. But if she danced the first dance with him, was that not just as good an announcement?

"Don't try to make a fool of me in front of everyone here," he said.

"You'll do a fine job of it yourself. Get your hand off me."

"Or what?" he asked lightly. "Will you cause a scene? Don't look now, but everyone is watching us."

Her breath stuttered in her chest. The air in the room thickened, and she knew without looking that he was correct. There were eyes on them.

He smiled then and leaned toward her. She held her breath until he swerved at the last moment, moving his lips to her ear. "You'll come with me to the dance floor now, or I'll put in a formal request with your father for courtship. It's your decision."

Briony's eyes were wide. They met Katrina's over his shoulder. She was frozen still as well. Didion's jaw was clenched. Across the ballroom, she saw Canning Trow watching them calculatingly.

It didn't matter, she realized. He'd made a move on her publicly. If she danced with him first after this show, they would be assumed to be courting.

The music began for a waltz. Briony swallowed. She could do two dances and then be done with him until spring.

"Of course," she said, pulling back from him. "Toven, it would be my honor."

His grin seemed almost genuine, and for a moment, she remembered how shockingly handsome he was. He extended his hand to her with a flourish, opening his body to the room so it was clear to anyone watching that it was her choice to accept.

The dance floor was filling with couples, and she caught her father's eye as she took her place across from Toven. He tilted his head at her in question, and she shook hers quickly, hopefully signaling to him not to take this seriously.

She faced Toven on the dance floor, and there was a self-satisfied smirk on his face as the musicians counted them in.

The itching was back between her shoulder blades—and in most parts of her body—as he reached forward for her, slipping one hand around her waist and with the other picking up her hand from where she'd let it hang limply.

It wasn't until the moment she placed her other hand on his shoulder that she realized what dancing with Toven Hearst meant. It meant touching him. Breathing him in. Staring at his face from an arm's-length distance—or *not* staring at his face, as she decided to do. She looked past his ear instead.

"You must be excited to be schooled in Evermore for our second year," he said.

"We don't have to talk," she snapped.

A puff of air crested over her forehead, and she wondered if she possibly could have made him laugh.

As he twirled her, expertly shifting the pressure on her rib cage to guide her around the floor, Briony let her eyes move wildly over all the people who could see them.

Sammy, Katrina, and Didion were watching them from the corner, but Cordelia was missing. When Briony found a mane of auburn hair floating on the dance floor, she couldn't believe her eyes.

The waltz moved Cordelia and her partner toward them. She gaped at her brother with her best friend in his arms.

"What is this?" she said incredulously to Rory.

"What is *this*?" he returned, looking at Toven.

Cordelia's lips opened and closed.

Toven chuckled. "You didn't know?"

Briony looked up at him as they spun away. He was positively gleeful.

She glanced back at her brother. The king's heir choosing a partner for the first dance was just as impactful a statement as Briony's mess of a situation.

"Oh, that's rich," Toven sang. "They've been making moon eyes at each other for a year, and you didn't know?"

Briony snapped her mouth shut. He lifted his arm and spun her under it, then drew her back in.

"I'm sure they'll be sneaking around the school this year, finding all the private alcoves—"

"You're disgusting."

"Do you really think anyone keeps their hands to themselves in year two?" He laughed. "You'll need protection on the staircases now, Princess."

"And are you volunteering?" she said dryly. "Is that what this is about?"

His lips twitched as he looked past her. "Perhaps I'll come knocking on that private suite when your brother is occupied with Miss Hardstark."

"Perhaps I'll light you on fire if you try."

"I should ask your father for your presence at Hearst Hall during the summer solstice holiday, I think," he said, as if talking to himself. "No point in delaying the inevitable."

"Shall we get your mother's ring resized as well?" she snarked, playing along for her own sanity.

"Lovely idea, dearest," he said, twirling them. "Your hands aren't quite as dainty, are they?"

In her effort not to look at him, her gaze fell on Finn and Larissa at the edge of the dance floor. They were watching the two of them closely. And she realized—

"You're in a spat with Larissa, aren't you?" She almost sighed in relief. "By the waters!" she swore. "And you're using *me*? What an idiot plan!"

He stared down at her, and she couldn't help but notice the sharp angle of his jaw and the strands of gray that had fallen over his forehead. "What plan is that?"

"I haven't the faintest clue," she said. "But you're trying to make Larissa angry, and it's working."

She watched his eyes flick over to where the blonde stood at the edge of the dance floor, as if he hadn't thought of the idea until that moment.

"I assure you, your grace," he said, "I'm just trying to pay respect to this outstanding dress you're in."

"You don't have to call me that," she said, suddenly tired with the game. "I may be the daughter of the king, but my title doesn't have a formal address."

"Oh, but you do," he said, quickly. The dance slowed, and he twisted them once more. "You are *Eversun*, and that is formal enough, isn't it?"

Her brows drew together as the musicians ended and the crowd applauded. She dropped her hands and stepped back. "What do you mean?"

"Pulling magic from the mind," he said mockingly. "You think you're so much better than we are. Evolved, isn't that what you say?"

"It is evolved," she snapped back. "To pull magic from your own mind, without draining yourself dry—without needing a familiar to boost you, nor going against the laws and draining a heartspring, either."

The second dance started, and he drew her into his arms again. Closer, she thought.

"And yet blood is still important to you all, isn't it? One bloodline. One king."

She gazed up at him, their faces closer than before. This was a distinct misunderstanding between most Eversuns and Bomardi, she knew, but this seemed personal to him.

"You know as well as I do that I don't get much out of that bloodline. I'll just be passed on to one of you while my brother becomes king."

"Which is why I find it so fascinating when Eversun women get up in arms about it all." He stepped forward and she stepped back, following his lead. "Not all Bomardi drain other magicians for a boost."

She watched his eyes flicker over her face. "Not all Eversuns can pry into your thoughts."

His lips twitched. "No?" He lowered his head to come eye-to-eye with her. "You don't know what I'm thinking now?"

Her eyes were glued to his as their feet glided over the floor. He had specks of blue in the gray. She could feel his breath on her face.

"I never know what you're thinking," she whispered.

His gaze burned as he stared down at her.

There was a tap on her shoulder, and she jumped.

Liam Quill stood behind her, a smarmy grin on his boyish face.

"Toven," he said. "I thought perhaps I'd take Miss Rosewood for the second dance." His eyes glinted. "As sixth in line."

Briony stared at Liam in confusion, until Toven slipped his arms from her, sending daggers to Liam but stepping aside.

He had to defer to him.

Briony hated that she missed his arms and his sure step.

Liam smiled patronizingly down at her. "What a splash you're making, Briony."

"Yes, the boys of Bomard certainly are honoring me tonight," she said, sarcasm in her tone.

She took the opportunity to glance around the dance floor. Rory was still dancing with Cordelia, and her stomach twisted.

"What did Toven talk to you about?" Liam asked.

"I have no clue," she said. "All sorts of things."

Liam narrowed his eyes at her. She looked away from him, and her gaze caught on Larissa as she spoke with Toven, her expression harsh. He looked bored.

Briony must have been right. A lovers' quarrel.

When Liam tried to take the third dance with Briony after making almost no conversation with her, she was about to give an excuse when a thick hand dropped on Liam's shoulder.

Both of them looked up to see Canning Trow smirking down at her.

"Miss Rosewood."

His mother was third in line. She couldn't even beg off about needing to dance with Sammy or Didion.

Liam stepped aside, and Briony accepted Canning's hand. He pulled her in too close, and his hand rested about five inches lower on her back than what was appropriate.

Canning was entering his fourth year at school and acted as a bit of a ringleader for the Bomardi boys. He had a wide jaw, wide-set eyes, and a large nose, but he walked around like he was the waters' gift to women.

"You're quite lovely tonight," he said as the steps began.

She said nothing, tired already of this.

"Where on earth have you been hiding this body?"

Her eyes snapped up to him, and she sent him a hard look as he turned her. "Do you have to be so crass? Just dance with me."

They followed the steps, pulling away from each other and circling.

"I'll be in year four this spring, beginning my specialization in elixirs."

She could yawn, but refrained. "Oh?"

"But I'd be happy to escort you to class."

"I know how to walk down stairs, thank you."

He laughed and tugged her closer. There were more couples on the floor now, and they were hidden in the center of it. She could feel his hands getting bolder.

"My mother is third in line, you know."

"You never let us forget it," Briony said.

"And it would be a great match between us."

"You think so?" She gave him a closed-lip smile. "That's kind."

She saw Didion on the edge of the dance floor, still waiting to dance with her. She didn't know if she had the energy after all this.

"You really are so lovely." He gazed down at her breasts.

"So you've said."

"We've all been talking about it. How lovely you are." Canning shifted the hand on her low back even lower.

"Can you not?" Briony hissed.

He tugged her closer still. "It's an honor to be wanted by the third in line."

"Son of the third in line." She shoved his hands off her as the music came to a close. "Thank you for the dance."

She spun on her heel and moved quickly away from the dancers before anyone else could accost her.

She slipped to the edge of the dance floor, near the exit. She nodded at one of the guards, who slipped out to find Anna to escort her upstairs.

"It's so strange to me," said a voice to her left. Veronika Mallow stood in the corner, blending into the darkness.

Briony patted down her dress and smiled thinly. "What is, Miss Mallow?"

"You must have your pick of the boys in Evermore, but you insist on catching the attention of all the eligible Bomardi boys."

Mallow's eyes watched her, unblinkingly.

Briony was tired. Too tired for this.

"What can I say? I'm a catch."

Mallow lifted her chin at her, assessing her. "I find the arranged marriages between the realms so archaic."

Briony was inclined to agree but had a feeling they were talking about different things.

"What do you mean?" she asked.

Mallow took a sip of her wine, her eyes casting over the dance floor. "Well, if we were really two realms at peace, why must we hand over women as collateral? Or our young people, for that matter?"

Briony narrowed her eyes at her. "Collateral? You mean the alternating school years?"

Turning her dark gaze on Briony, Mallow replied, "Why, yes, of course. For what possible reason would we school our young people together if not in an eternal promise not to harm them." Mallow tilted her head at her. "Promises are only words after all. They can be broken."

Briony stared at her until Anna coughed lightly behind her, ready to take her to her rooms. She gave Mallow one last glance over her shoulder.

Three and a half years later, she would remember that conversation when the Bomardi attacked the school, looking for Eversuns to take captive. And she would know exactly whose idea it was.

CHAPTER 10

BRIONY SPENT THE NEXT DAY drinking water through her closed jaw and figuring out inventive ways to get softer fruit between her teeth. She still didn't have a voice, but that seemed inconsequential when she hadn't eaten in two days.

After Briony had been returned, they had taken Phoebe to be sterilized. She came back and curled up in a corner, sobbing through the night. Orion's elixir was given to everyone as a precaution, in case the reason for Briony's resistance to the collar was widespread.

No one checked on them that day, and some of the women had started to wonder if they would just let them wither and die in there. Briony couldn't keep her mind off Eden, who had been killed. But she started to look around the room, wondering . . .

Just before everyone began lying down for bed, Briony approached Velicity. She tried to use gestures to ask her a question, counting to five on her hand, asking, *Where is the fifth woman?*

Velicity nodded. "They told us she died. You didn't see them kill her?"

Briony shook her head. And Orion Hearst had said nothing about the raven-haired woman with the black eye when he'd listed off the casualties of her stupid decisions. Velicity's brows furrowed as she stared out over the room.

"The last I saw her, she was climbing out the window." She paused. "Maybe she fell."

Velicity and Briony shared a look. *Maybe she didn't.*

Reaching out with long fingers, Velicity plucked a grape from the bowl and popped it into her mouth with a grin, calling back to the words that Briony had spelled for them with those very grapes.

Briony agreed, silently. More reasons to believe they were not alone.

The next morning, they bathed the women again. When it was Briony's turn, they took her alone and removed her chains. And then Gains left her with Reighven in the bathroom.

He didn't give her a choice to keep her dress on this time.

"Take it off or I'll take it off for you. And trust me, Rosewood, I'll enjoy it."

Briony turned to face the tub. If she relaxed her eyes, she could imagine she was at the Biltmore Palace. Perhaps these stone walls were sandstone, perhaps the running water was the trickling of the streams throughout the entire palace, perhaps she was in her private suite.

She reached up for the straps at her shoulders and let them slide down her arms.

Perhaps Sofia would be in soon to tell her how long she had until dinner.

Briony stepped into the tub, imagining ornate taps and not a water ring in sight. The water burned her skin, and she focused on that.

Perhaps she could sink under and pretend she was a siren, like she had as a child—

"Don't take all day."

And with a rubber snap of her mind, she was in the Trow dungeon, with the first man to see her naked body.

Briony sank into the water, and as Reighven approached the tub and stared down at her in the water, she wondered if maybe this wasn't truly her skin. This wasn't truly her body. Maybe she was in her tub at the Biltmore after all.

"You need me to lather you up, love?"

She ignored him, reaching for the soap and cleaning herself as fast as possible.

When it was time to get out, he gestured to the towel he'd left near the door. Briony pulled herself from the water and forced her legs to carry her across the room.

There was a tent in his trousers by the time she'd dried off. She kept her eyes on the floor as she dressed.

When she was rechained and returned to the cell, Briony wanted to be alone, but she couldn't. As much as she wanted to take a break from these fifty women, she needed to stay stoic for them.

It became harder to find hope when she sat chained and muzzled, knowing exactly where she would end up.

A while later, a group of five came back from the baths with twittering energy. As soon as the door closed behind them, one of them burst out—

"We saw Sammy and Didion. They're still alive."

Briony felt something flutter in her chest before it fell back to sleep again. Her prevailing emotion was fatigue. It was hard to rejoice at a mere sighting of a familiar face—not when the life before them was one of servitude and magical draining, with no way out of this that anyone could see.

They learned that the auction was scheduled for the following evening, but about half of the women still found the energy for hope, including Cordelia.

"All right, we have to do something," Cordelia said. "We can try strength in numbers again. There's usually only two of them that come in at a time for us, so maybe it's fifty on two. Then we find the men and it's maybe double that." Cordelia glanced at her. "Briony?"

Briony felt fifty pairs of eyes turn on her. For some reason, Larissa Gains's gaze was the one she held.

Her blond hair was limp and oily, and she constantly picked at her nails, as if checking a manicure she'd just received. She stared back at Briony, lifting a brow.

Briony looked down and shrugged. She didn't know if Cordelia's plan was wise or worth trying. She was so tired.

Cordelia gaped at her. "Nothing? Just—" She imitated Briony's shrug with disbelieving eyes. "You're giving up?"

Briony pressed her lips together, still biting back words even without a voice. Cordelia hadn't watched Eden die. Cordelia hadn't had Reighven's eyes on her naked body or felt his hand reaching between her legs. Cordelia hadn't looked into Mallow's eyes as she told her it was over.

The only purpose they would have in this new world was to make a Bomardi's magic stronger. Briony would cease to be an Eversun, cease to be a Rosewood, and cease to be a human. She was starting to understand that, even if Cordelia wasn't ready.

"You can't give up on us," Cordelia hissed. "You worked for *four years* to keep Evermore safe—to keep faith when battles were lost . . . and *now* you give up? The prophecy wasn't true—so what?" Her throat swallowed thickly, and her eyes were unforgiving. "Rory's dead," she said, voice cracking. "So what? You're not."

Phoebe stood up. "All right, Cordelia. Let her rest a moment."

"No!" Cordelia threw off Phoebe's arm and their chains clinked together. "I want to know why she won't fight anymore. Because we *all* lost people, and I can't lose her—" Cordelia broke off in a choking gasp. Tears filled her eyes.

Briony came to her feet and dragged Cordelia into her chest, unable to hold her properly with the chains. Briony whispered soundless promises to fight, to find her, to build it back. Cordelia sobbed against her shoulder.

The first door opened with a *bang*, and they sprang apart. The women scurried into corners like rats in the light as the second door opened.

And Canning Trow stepped inside with a smirk on his wide face, eyes surveying the room.

Briony stepped back in surprise. To see someone they'd gone to school with, *gloating* at them . . . It brought back too many memories. It reminded her that just days ago, Toven Hearst and Finn Raquin had torn through her bedroom, hunting her.

"Ladies," he said jovially. "So many familiar faces." His gaze cast over the room, finally stopping at Briony. "Miss Rosewood, always a pleasure." He held a paper in his hands and looked down to consult it. "Ah. Of course not." His eyes flicked up to her again, sighing dramatically. "It would have been too good to be true."

Briony eyed the paper warily as Canning took a deep breath.

"Let's have Velicity step forward, Coral step forward, and . . ." His brows ticked up and his eyes cast over the room, searching. "Larissa Gains," he said gleefully. "Step forward."

"For what?" Larissa said, and his eyes finally found her in the corner she'd claimed.

"I have a new elixir to test out," Canning said, rocking on his toes like a child on winter solstice. "It's all a bit hush-hush for now, but I think it will be incredibly lucrative in this climate, to help . . . initiate Sacral Magic. They said I get my pick of anyone on this list, or else I'd owe someone five thousand gold."

Briony's heart thumped. It was something sexual then. He had a list of the non-virgins.

"So, step forward," he said darkly.

Velicity and a woman with short red hair obeyed. Larissa stayed put. Canning looked them over and consulted his list, clicking his tongue. Briony glanced at the open door behind him; she could just make out Reighven's profile though the crack in the door.

"Mm, Velicity, step back. Let's see . . . Oh, Jellica Reeve!" His eyes searched the room until they landed on a tall blond woman whom Briony recognized from school. She had been a few years older. "Jellica, dear, it's been ages." He grinned at her, baring his teeth. "Step forward, step forward."

Jellica moved on shaking legs. She had been beautiful at school as well, with large blue eyes and full lips. She stood in front of Canning with her chin tilted up.

Canning leaned in and whispered, "Do you remember when I kissed you in year five, and you slapped me across the face?" He laughed, his wide face grinning at her.

She didn't respond, just held her head high.

Faster than a bolt of lightning, Canning's palm shot out and slapped her, knocking her head to the side.

Briony jumped as others gasped. Velicity stepped forward before stopping cold.

Jellica slowly turned her face back to him, staring him down.

"I'll take these two," he said, gesturing to Coral and Jellica. "And we'll bring Larissa along in case anyone prefers a Bomardi girl." He winked at Larissa. "You know quite a few tricks, if I remember."

Larissa glared daggers at him, and it wasn't until Reighven tugged her forward with magic that she fell into line behind the others.

The doors locked behind them.

Cordelia turned to Katrina and asked quietly, "What did he mean? What's Sacral Magic?"

Katrina's voice shook. "It's—it's meant for love matches. It's a kind of . . . escalation of the heartspring bond. Much like boosting, in some ways," she said, glancing at Briony. "But in the same way that sharing a physical union strengthens your marriage in some cases, the heartspring magic grows stronger when you . . ." Her breath shuddered, and her eyes flitted as panic set in. "It's meant for love matches," she repeated.

"And when it's not a love match?" Cordelia asked, her voice tight. "When they chain our magic to them and drain us for power? What does Sacral Magic become then?"

Katrina swallowed thickly. "The power gained from a physical union . . . it only works when freely given. You can't—*force* someone to share Sacral Magic with you."

"But Canning thinks he's found a way?" Cordelia asked. "A way to benefit from Sacral Magic when it's not freely given?"

Phoebe, who had stood silently until that moment, turned to them with a flat voice. "I spent five years in school with Canning Trow. I'd bet anything that that elixir will do something to those women—something to make them 'give freely.'"

Briony chewed on her lip as Cordelia finally realized what Briony had known since the moment Reighven had put his hand on her: Regardless of the magical benefits of holding the Eversuns captive to be heartsprings, for some of them, they would still be a woman locked in a man's house. And Canning Trow had figured out how to make the most of it.

She could only hope that Canning's "hush-hush" comment meant that his elixir would not be widespread in Bomard. Briony knew her own future—Reighven had made that clear—but her friends might not have to suffer in the same way. Many Bomardi, primarily the women on the line, would find this in poor taste. She wondered at Canning's audacity in distributing such an elixir with a woman on the Seat.

"Why in the waters does it matter if some of us are virgins then?" Cordelia said, eyes wet and voice cracking. "Virgin's blood and and virgin's tears are important for obscure and dark elixirs, but why pay extra gold for a virgin if you're just going to—to—?"

Cordelia choked. Briony took her hand.

Katrina's voice was hollow when she spoke. "They used to tell us as young girls that our heartspring magic with our future husband would be stronger as virgins, but I had always assumed that was—"

"Utter bullshit," Phoebe finished for her. "A woman can be on the Seat or on the line in Bomard, but it's all the same shit as Evermore."

Briony watched Phoebe's fire burn hot as Cordelia's was extinguished.

Coral and Jellica were returned four hours later. They didn't speak to anyone, only lay in a corner, not wanting to be touched.

Larissa didn't come back.

*　　*　　*

Briony woke on the day of the auction to a quiet room, only the sound of muffled weeping. She pulled herself from sleep and opened her eyes.

Larissa Gains was sitting next to her, staring down at her face with an open expression, as if she'd fallen asleep with her eyelids open. When she saw Briony was awake, she closed herself up, painting on the familiar pout of her lips and arch of her brow.

Briony looked her over. She was still in her chains. She didn't know how long Larissa had been gone, and she longed to ask her what the elixir was, even if Larissa wouldn't tell her.

Larissa gazed down at her.

"I used to envy you," she said in a low voice.

Briony blinked up at her, not understanding. She waited for Larissa to laugh at her or mock her hair or her clothes. Something familiar.

"When I was nine, my father told me he wouldn't leave his position in line to a woman, so I'd better find a husband quick." She tossed her hair behind her shoulder and stared out over the room. There were bite marks on her neck. "I thought it was an odd thing to say to someone who hadn't started to bleed, but what did I know. He was furious to see all the Bomardi boys falling over themselves to dance with you at that state dinner between first and second year. He said that should have been me. He sent me to an evening woman to learn how to seduce men. I was seventeen."

Briony blinked up at her in astonishment.

Larissa sighed. "She was good, though." She smiled secretly. "*Really* good. The two weeks I had with her were . . ." Larissa nodded, laughing. "When I came back, it was time for year two to start. My father said good-bye to me and told me he wanted me engaged by the end of the summer. And if I wasn't, then I should be pregnant at the very least."

Briony's teeth ground together, anxiety swimming in her veins.

"But I said, 'Don't worry, Daddy. The Hearst boy is wrapped around my finger. I'll have him by the end of the year.'"

She chuckled darkly, like there were layers upon layers to the joke.

Briony stayed curled on the floor in her same sleeping position, not willing to break this dream—this dream of Larissa . . . sharing with her? Being open with her? She tried to think what could be so funny. How had Larissa and Toven ended that year? She struggled to remember.

Larissa bit her lip, still laughing to herself.

"And now here we are. At the end of the world. Standing in a line to be sold and drained of our magic, and some of us raped, too. And still, I can't sleep for envy of you. Of what your life will be."

Larissa's head leaned back on the wall, staring up at the ceiling. Briony wished she could speak, ask her what she meant.

Briony watched as Larissa turned to look at her lazily. She seemed to be taking in every inch of her face. Larissa's lips parted as she took a breath to speak again.

"Get away from her! What are you doing?" Cordelia jerked awake, pulling Briony away from Larissa.

The commotion woke several other women.

Larissa rolled her eyes and stood. "Nothing. Just a little girl talk. Calm down." She waltzed back over to her side of the room.

Cordelia asked Briony if she was all right. Briony watched Larissa as she stared at her nails and played with her split ends until the door opened hours later.

Larissa's father entered with an older gentleman with white hair and spectacles. He had a kind face and reminded Briony of her grandfather who'd died fifteen years earlier. His fuzzy white brows twitched as he took in the room of women. He cleared his throat and carefully avoided eye contact with any of the prisoners.

"Is this all of them?" he asked Gains.

"There's about twenty men down the hall."

The older man nodded and took off his glasses to clean them. "If you wish to start at eight tonight, perhaps we should start the appraisals with the men while the women are . . . prepared."

Gains nodded. "Trow will meet you upstairs with the first men in five minutes. Princess," he called out, gesturing for Briony. "Come with me."

The older man quickly left the room, while Gains waited for Briony to walk to him.

He led her out and toward the staircase. When they passed Reighven in the hall, standing guard, he smirked at Briony.

"Tell Trow to collect Meers for appraisal, then do the rest five at a time."

Briony's heart leapt. Sammy was just behind one of these doors.

Reighven nodded and whistled at Gains before they turned the corner. Gains looked back.

"Tell them to take it all," Reighven said lecherously. "I like 'em bare."

"Don't we all," Gains said flatly.

It wasn't until Briony was bathed and dressed in a robe with two beautiful women with accents from across the sea tending to her that she realized she was having her body hair removed, her skin buffed, and her hair styled. A lot was being done to her, and several of the other imprisoned women were coming and going in the time it took Briony's skin to look glossy. She had the distinct feeling that Gains was in charge of this demand.

When the women with sharp faces and patronizing smiles were done with her, Gains gave her clean undergarments and a chemise to wear, then brought her to the next set of stairs. She followed him curiously. No one had been up this flight. He brought her up through the kitchens, bustling with servants. In Bomard and Evermore, these were usually non-magicians from across the sea looking for work.

When they came to a large room, Briony was immediately aware that she was in her undergarments in the drawing room of Trow Castle. But more important, the Bomardi elite were across the room near the fireplace, smoking pipes and drinking amber alcohol.

As she was led toward a two-foot-tall dais at the center of the room, she counted them out.

Mallow was missing, but the man who stood as first in line for the Seat was there: Cohle. He was a brutish man who loved power more than leading, which was why Evermore had suspected he was allowed to keep his place in line when Seat Pulvey was assassinated. Canning's mother, Genevieve Trow (third in line), was chatting with two other women whom Briony recognized as fifth and seventh in line, respectively. Liam's father, Caspar Quill, who was sixth, laughed boisterously at something said by Gidrey—tenth. Florence Kleve, a woman in her seventies with deep-bronze skin, whispered to Carvin, second in line. And Orion Hearst, eighth in line, drank from a glass of amber liquid, eyes glued to her. With Gains, fourth in line, at her side, leading her to the platform, she deduced that the Ten were accounted for. It seemed the men and women here were getting an advance viewing of those to be auctioned.

The older man with the spectacles from earlier stepped forward. He seemed like he didn't want to make eye contact with her at all.

Briony shivered in the morning air as she reached the platform, some thirty feet away from the Ten.

Gains unchained her wrists, and to her astonishment, he opened her collar. She hardly had time to memorize the spell he'd used to unclick the bolts before the collar was off her. He grabbed her jaw and pushed her lips apart with his fingers on her cheeks. Her teeth were still snapped together, but he poured an elixir into her mouth, letting the liquid slosh into her throat. She choked, recognizing it as the magic-suppressing elixir that Orion had brought her.

Then she was shoved forcefully onto the platform, tripping over her feet and landing on her elbows. One of the women laughed as she brought herself up. They were talking among themselves, sitting in comfortable chairs, barely giving her a glance.

The older man tipped his glasses up his nose and said, "Name?"

Briony didn't have a voice, but Gains supplied it for her. The older man wrote it on a slip of paper. He glanced at the ink on the inside of her left elbow, and Briony watched him notate Gains's ownership.

"Age?"

"Twenty-five," Gains said.

"I see here that her medical bill is clean." The older man—the appraiser—glanced at Briony quickly, as if he'd rather not see her face, see her soul. He twitched his fingers, and a measuring tape jumped out of his bag. It quickly took in her height, then after an infinitesimal pause and a glare from Gains, it wrapped itself about Briony's hips, waist, and chest before returning to his bag.

The appraiser spread his arms in front of Briony and cast a spell she didn't recognize. A light glowed between his palms, steadily pulsing brighter.

A murmuring reached her from the Bomardi in leather chairs. Something about the pulsing light had caught their attention.

"That'll be the Rosewood blood," Genevieve Trow said, sipping from a glass. "Fascinating to see the strength of it like this."

"Is that a five, then?" Gains asked hungrily.

"From the *rudimentary* scale you've given me," the appraiser said, "yes. This is the closest grading to a five we've seen today."

It was a spell to measure her magic? Briony's eyes flickered to the men and women lounging and smoking cigars. Orion Hearst's gaze was on her, calculating.

The appraiser cleared his throat.

"Starting bid for Miss Rosewood should be no lower than seventy-five hundred gold based on your grading system." He pulled his glasses from his face. "But I've heard that Miss Hardstark and the Miss Rosewood will be starting at ten thousand, regardless."

Briony stared at him. Ten thousand. That was the same sum a magician would earn after a year's commitment to the king's army in Evermore.

"Apologies," he continued, squinting at his numbers again. "With the virginity, they will be starting at fifteen thousand."

Briony took a silent inhale through her clenched teeth.

"And what's your estimation?" Gains asked greedily.

The appraiser rubbed his forefinger and thumb over the bridge of his nose before turning to the room of Bomardi. He spoke loudly, possibly magically enhanced.

"Briony Rosewood. Estimating thirty thousand gold."

Briony felt like she was swallowing sand. That was enough to buy a farm with acreage to keep a family of four fed. That was enough for the fees at Heatherly, the school across the sea that taught the highest degree of magical healing.

She would not be killed. No one would be idiotic enough to buy her and then kill her off. No, it would be a slow death for her. Maybe years.

How on earth did Reighven think he could afford this?

The Bomardi chuckled, not surprised by the estimate, and she heard Genevieve Trow say, "Does Reighven even have that kind of gold?"

"He certainly thinks he does," Quill said. He raised his voice to Gains. "You're about to be a rich man, Hap!"

Gains had a bounce to his step as he led Briony back the way they came. As they descended the staircases into the bowels of the castle, a guard led a dark-haired man up the stairs past them.

"Briony! Briony!"

It was Didion. She didn't have the strength to struggle like he did and could do no more than watch dully as he thrashed in the guard's arms, calling her name as they dragged him up the stairs.

"It will be all right! I promise!"

Briony listened to his voice call out to her the entire way down. She could almost still hear the echo of it in the dungeon when she was dragged back into the cell with the women.

It was only a few short hours before every woman was cleaned and dressed for the evening. They were bound in new collars, but the chain between their hands was left off. Briony couldn't be sure in the darkness of the cell, but she thought the new collars were brightly metallic. Some of them were given white dresses in the Bomardi style, tight in the bodice and long flowing to the floor. Others were given black dresses. She could guess what the white meant. Then the Bomardi fighters came to collect their prizes.

When the first man entered the cell, he collected two women, placing his palm over the ink on their arms and then drawing a portal to step through, dragging the women with him.

Briony made a note of the skin contact.

There were a few scrappy commoners who came to collect three or four women, claiming they had a few men as well. They were hunters, looking to turn profit by capturing and selling as many Eversuns as possible.

When Reighven entered, he took Cordelia and three other women, most of them in white. And Briony began to have an idea of how he thought he would be able to afford her.

As the numbers dwindled, soon it was only Briony, Larissa, and Larissa's father.

Briony watched with bated breath as Hap Gains commanded Larissa to join them in the center of the room.

Larissa stood on shaking legs in her black dress, her whole body trembling.

"Come here," Gains repeated.

"Daddy . . ."

Briony watched in horror as Larissa started to cry, her body heaving with sobs.

"Daddy, don't do this."

Gains adjusted the cuff buttons on his wrists, ignoring her.

"I'm your only daughter—"

Gains snapped his head to look at her directly, the first time Briony had seen him do so in the past week.

"I don't have a daughter," he growled. "Not anymore."

Briony's eyes were wide as Larissa seemed to breathe into a deep place inside of her, calming her sobs with a last gulp before walking forward to join them for the portal.

Gains turned to Briony. With a twist of his fingers, her dress pulled tighter to her body. She gasped soundlessly as the fabric shivered on her, turning gold.

Gains smiled. "Our gold-blooded royal."

Briony glared up at him. He took Larissa's arm, then hers, and dragged them through the darkness.

CHAPTER 11

PORTALS ALWAYS FELT LIKE THEY FLATTENED YOU and pulled you apart at the same time. As Gains tugged her through behind him, with his flesh touching her tattoo, she wondered what would happen if he let go of her in the middle of the portal. Where would her body go?

When they broke through to their destination, Briony had two seconds to let her eyes adjust to the dark before she was forced onto a chair, arms dragged behind her. Two guards in Bomardi blue affixed her hands to the back of the chair with a simple spell that worked like glue.

Gains secured Larissa to a chair on her left, instructing the guards in low voices. Briony saw chairs with restrained people lining the entire room.

Was it a room? She looked up to a tall ceiling, maybe three stories, dizzyingly high. There were catwalks and ropes, but also strange things hanging from pulleys. The entire room was a circle.

The hum of hundreds of voices slithered down to them from above the ceiling.

She knew where they were. It was the Bomardi Circus. Her father had taken them when they were young, and the entertainers had given her purple roses for her hair.

And now she was below deck, like one of the animals that danced for applause.

She looked to her right and found Cordelia sitting several chairs away, eyes wet and cast down.

Briony glanced around. The chairs with prisoners continued in a broad circle, and she startled when she recognized Didion looking back at her.

His eyes were bruised black, and his lip was cut. To his left were more men looking much the same, many of them from Rory's army. She found Sammy, and when he nodded at her from across the circle, tears pricked her eyes.

Briony whipped her head around, trying to take in as much as she could. Exits, hiding places, weapons.

There were about seventy prisoners according to Gains's count yesterday. She counted fourteen Bomardi down below with them, and half of them were loudly planning to bid. They couldn't do that from down here. One guard was standing directly in front of Briony with his back to her. He scanned the room, looking for threats.

He was so young, though. He couldn't be older than twenty. He had pale skin and dark brows that made him look more menacing than his slight frame suggested.

"Parsons, right?" Larissa said to her left. Her gaze was on the back of the guard's neck. He gave her his profile in response. "Stones, you've grown up. How's your father?" she said conversationally.

Briony squinted at her. Was *now* really the time for catching up?

"He's fine," Parsons said shortly.

"I was sad to hear that the Trows wouldn't clear his gambling debts. Shame."

Larissa seemed to be sympathetic, but Briony couldn't believe she would poke a sore subject while restrained to a chair.

Before Parsons could respond, a man swept in through the stage door with Cohle trailing behind him. Briony recognized him instantly, but she didn't know his name. He was one of the most well-known Bomardi entertainers. In the cities, they drew his face on the sides of buildings, advertising his performances. He had probably been in the circus that day she'd been with Rory and her father, young and just starting out.

The man's piercing blue eyes traveled over the chairs, stopping briefly over her face. He knew her. He looked down at his shoes and fiddled with the papers in his hands.

"Bomard thanks you for your services, Mr. Vein," Cohle hissed, clapping him on the shoulder.

"Yes, Cohle. I am . . . glad to be of assistance." He shuffled the papers, and Briony recognized them as the notes the appraiser had taken.

She wanted to scream. Vein could stop this. He could try. He wasn't like the rest of them.

Vein looked down at one of the pages and turned to Cohle. "Is this an error? This number?"

Cohle smiled and nodded at Cordelia. "No error. The future Queen of Evermore. If you think that's good, take a look at the Eversun princess."

Vein flipped to the next page, and his face paled.

Briony frowned. The Hearsts had not come to collect Eversuns from the cell. Orion had said he wouldn't be buying heartsprings, but did that mean he had no one to sell? Would any of the Hearsts be out in the crowd tonight?

She looked to Larissa. Toven would be. Briony couldn't imagine a world in which Toven Hearst didn't come to claim Larissa Gains. They'd been close at school, and at one time their betrothal had been imminent. As for why they hadn't already been married in the years since, Briony could only assume that the uncertainty of war kept young Bomardi from creating unions, much in the same way Rory and Cordelia had put off marriage.

"We need to take our seats, Mr. Vein," Cohle announced, earning the attention of the other Bomardi. He offered his hand, and Vein took it. "The circus is yours."

Briony watched as Gains and the others followed Cohle out. Reighven made sure to sweep by her, trailing his fingertips across one shoulder, dipping below her collarbone and across. When she could bring her eyes off the floor, she looked up to see Parsons glancing away from her.

"Yes, *she's* been the center of attention all week," Larissa said to Parsons. "Everybody has their eye on her." Suddenly, Larissa leaned forward as far as her restrained arms would allow. "And did you hear how much she's estimated to go for?" she said in a loud whisper, as if she and Parsons had a secret. "Thirty thousand gold."

That caught Parsons's attention. Briony didn't know how Larissa had heard about her estimated price, but it didn't matter. Parsons turned to look over his shoulder, his lips parting at the number.

A bell chimed. Vein cleared his throat and moved to the center of the room. He seemed focused on ignoring the presence of the people whose sale he was about to facilitate. A circle in the ceiling opened, and a platform rose with Vein on it, lifting him to the audience.

A stage light hit him, igniting his smile and jaunty step. The theater roared, and Briony jumped with the pressure of it. Thousands of people.

The platform completed its lift, and the ceiling was closed again.

"Welcome!" Vein's amplified voice spun over the crowd, reaching below stage easily. "Welcome. Find your seats, ladies and gentlemen!"

Briony's heart thundered in time with the applause.

One of the women a few chairs away started to hyperventilate. She dipped her head between her knees, tears tracking down her cheeks, mouth open wide. One of the guards went to check on her, wrenching her up.

Vein began his opening remarks. "We are honored tonight by the presence of Mistress Mallow. May she reign forevermore."

Briony shivered. Mallow was up there. As she listened to the shouts and applause, Briony imagined the tunnels of Mallow's black eyes on her as Bomard sold her off to the highest bidder.

Vein launched into propaganda about the days to come, signaling Mallow's power and Bomard's right to rule over the entire Moreland continent.

Two of the guards stared up, listening to Vein. The others were hovering around the men across the room, as if waiting for trouble.

"And she's a virgin," Larissa said. Briony glared at her, wondering why she was still pushing this. Larissa relaxed in her chair and gazed at her. "I couldn't fathom what anyone would want *that* for in the bedroom, but the blood?" Larissa whistled.

Parsons's head was turned to listen.

"They've only asked for another five thousand for the virgins, but I would have gone higher. Imagine if you drain her blood once a week—not enough to kill her, of course, but a healthy amount of it. What does that go for on the black market here? Five hundred gold?" Larissa smiled. "I was never very good at maths, but do that once a week for a year? Two years?"

Briony stared at her. Where was she going with this?

Above them, Vein continued. "We have seventy-four lots for auction tonight," he announced magnanimously. The crowd erupted. Across the room, Didion pulled against his chair, fighting the spell that stuck his hands to it.

"Ladies and gentlemen, we'll bring each lot onstage, one at a time. I have here a measure of their magical strength out of five. All lots sold as is. The winning bidders will coordinate with Gains at the end to arrange payment. Let's start off the evening right," Vein crowed. "With a Meers."

Two guards moved to pull Sammy to the center, where the platform would raise him up. A trapdoor opened in the ceiling.

Briony's heart leapt. The auction was beginning.

Larissa was unfazed. "So, Parsons," she said. "You're not bidding? Stuck down here with us instead?" She hummed. "That doesn't seem right."

Sammy's hands were fixed together behind his back, and he had a black eye and a limp. He was shoved to the circle in the center, and the stage rose with him on it.

"Did they give you payment for your service to Mistress Mallow at the very least?" Larissa asked.

"Stop talking," Parsons snapped at her. He turned to face them. "Or I'll have to silence you."

Briony looked between them as Larissa grinned.

"I just think it's a shame. That's all," Larissa said.

Above, Vein read Sammy's catalog. "Thirty-one years old. Son of General Meers of Evermore."

The crowd hissed.

Parsons's eyes flicked to Briony, his lips tight with a decision he seemed to be making. Briony's pulse raced with the way he looked at her. Like she was a diamond in a glass case.

"Specialized in combat and strategy at school, so this heartspring would be perfect for someone in Bomard's army. The strength of his magic was measured at a four out of five. Most impressive."

Parsons glanced at the positions of the other guards. Almost all of them were staring upward, listening to the auction. He moved quickly.

"Let's start the bidding at two thousand gold pieces."

With a twitch of Parsons's fingers, Briony's hands were released from their position on the back of the wooden chair. Before she could fight him, his hand was on her arm, hauling her up.

Larissa tilted forward on her feet, the wooden chair lifted into the air behind her, and with a snarl she threw her body against Parsons. The three of them fell to the ground, the chair splintering around them. Briony's head smacked against the ground.

Parsons yelled out.

Her skull ached as she opened her eyes. Larissa's hands were raised with the shards of the broken wooden chair still stuck to them. She screamed, bringing them down like stakes into Parson's neck and chest.

Briony stared in horror as Parsons choked and the blood bubbled. Larissa bared her teeth at her. "Go, you idiot!"

Scrambling to her feet, Briony ran.

There was splintering all around the room. Grunting and yelling.

The guards cursed and scattered as they realized what had happened.

Briony ran the outer edge of the circle, her head spinning from where it had hit the ground. She searched for an exit as every chair she passed cracked and splintered against the ground.

Seventy-four prisoners following Larissa Gains's lead, and only a handful of guards to stop them.

As she ran by Cordelia, she saw pieces of wood firm in her fists, beating against one of the guards. Jellica Reeve had most of her chair still put together and swung it at the head of a running guard, knocking him back and climbing on top of him, slamming the wood against him. The rest of the guards moved quickly to restrain the men first.

Vein's voice floated down from above. "Some kind of . . . commotion. Nothing to worry about—"

Spells started flying. One slammed into Briony, and she flew against the outer wall, her shoulder popping, sickeningly. She yelped with no sound.

Someone hauled her up by her dislocated arm, and she tugged out of their grip. Blood dripped into her eyes from a cut on her head, and the pain in her shoulder blinded her.

"Briony!" It was Didion. He pulled her in a direction she hoped was an exit.

Running footsteps thundered from the stage above, and then the Bomardi were there, casting spells and kicking prisoners aside to beat through the crowd. She recognized Reighven's angry growl.

The smell of magic was thick in the air. The sizzle of it burned her nostrils. They'd only taken a handful of steps before Didion screamed, dropping to his knees at her side. Someone knocked into her, and they were separated.

Cohle screamed orders and Gains organized the restrained bodies, yelling for them to get to Briony.

A pair of arms wrapped around her waist from behind, tugging her back. She kicked, and he dropped her, her elbow slamming into the ground. Arms around her again, and she wasn't sure if they were the same.

She was pulled up, held against a man's chest with one arm wrapped around her shoulders and the other wound over her hips. She screamed silently, kicking the air. He moved with her, dragging her away.

Was he stealing her or bringing her back?

The air smelled of blood and pine, and her head was pounding.

She was being dragged away, toward the door.

She heard Gains's voice close by, and the man who held her turned.

"Good work, Hearst."

She had just enough time to wonder if it was Toven's or Orion's arms around her before Gains knocked her out.

* * *

Her head burst apart, and she gasped noiselessly against the pain.

Thunder rolled through, rattling her skull. She blinked her eyes open and found herself in a dark circular room. A gavel banged, and she knew where she was.

There were two guards on either side of Briony, hauling her up until she stood on her own. She'd been brought back to consciousness by one of them. She turned to look at everyone else in the holding area, but all she found were broken chair legs and drying blood.

Twisting to look around pulled at her shoulder, recently reset. She found a backstage mirror, cracked down the middle, and saw that they had banished the blood from her face. She couldn't tell if the concussion had been healed. She was nauseous and spinning, but they might have been the symptoms of a handful of other things.

She tilted her head back and looked up at the place where the stage lay on the other side of the ceiling. There was raucous yelling from above.

"Locklin, we all know you don't have that kind of gold!" Vein's voice cut through the pounding in her ears. The audience laughed. "Only serious bids here for Miss Hardstark, ladies and gentlemen!"

Briony's knees gave out, but the guards propped her up. She was going to be sick.

Cordelia was being auctioned. Then her.

She'd missed it. She'd missed the entire auction. She would never know where everyone ended up. Where Phoebe was sent, or Katrina or Didion or Sammy. She'd have to gather the information as best she could and hope to see them again in this lifetime.

She looked up to the ceiling as the gavel banged.

"Sold!" The audience erupted. "Cordelia Hardstark, love of the late Rory Rosewood, sold to Riann Cohle for twenty-eight thousand, five hundred gold!"

Her stomach heaved.

Such a lot of money. An insane amount. Would she really fetch her appraised price—over thirty thousand gold?

The noise from the crowd deafened her momentarily, and then she knew her concussion wasn't healed.

A circle opened in the ceiling, and there was Cordelia, lowering back down. Her white dress was spattered with red, and her spotlit face was impassive.

Through the hole in the ceiling, Briony saw Cohle come forward, his thin lips smirking at the crowd. Vein produced a scroll, and the yelling intensified as Cohle took the offered quill.

Cordelia jerked her arm as the platform brought her down, wincing as Cohle signed his name on the scroll. The brand on their forearms must change to reflect ownership. Where Cordelia's arm had once displayed Reighven's signature, now it must bear Cohle's name.

Briony's head pounded as Cordelia grew closer and closer to her. She wondered if there was something she'd missed. If there was something she could have done differently.

Maybe they should have hidden when Anna told them to. Maybe she should have let Katrina die in the dungeon.

Maybe she shouldn't have rallied everyone's faith around Rory. Maybe she shouldn't have let him go into battle at all.

Maybe she should have been by his side.

Cordelia's bottom lip trembled beneath somebody's dried blood as she saw Briony standing there, waiting, and Briony decided her only true mistake had been not killing Reighven in the dungeon corridors.

She should have killed Reighven, and then Gains, and then taken whoever was still alive and escaped. She should have let Katrina die. It probably would have been for the best.

Cordelia ran into Briony's arms, dodging the guards. "I will find you, Briony. It's not over."

The guards tugged Cordelia back, and Briony looked at Cordelia's face for the last time.

Briony voicelessly responded, *Not alone.*

The guards took Cordelia's arms, and she disappeared through the backstage door.

"And now . . . our grand finale."

She blinked, trying to focus. She needed to be present. Maybe once this day was over, she would fall asleep from her concussion and never wake up.

The guards pushed her onto the platform. The stage began to rise, and the roar of the crowd felt like a living thing. Vein was yelling, inciting them, but she could only squint against the lights as they hit her.

She looked down at her feet as the stage completed its ascension. Her gold dress shimmered.

The circus was full. Balcony after balcony. She turned to see the full circle of the audience. It must have been over ten thousand people, and Briony despaired at the thought that Mallow had this many eager followers already. How many of these people had been lying in wait, biding their time until the end of the war? And now here they were.

The noise continued for ages. Her eyes landed on the Bomardi on the ground level, filling up the majority of the front rows. Some of them on their feet, hollering. Some of them seated, whispering to one another and pointing to the stage.

She scanned the crowd. Mallow sat in the box reserved for the Seat of Bomard. She gazed at Briony as if she were no more than an elephant, about to balance on a ball. Gains was in the front, Reighven by his side. Cohle and Quill. She couldn't find the gray locks of Orion Hearst.

"All right! All right!" Vein laughed, sounding like his old self again—performing. "I know we're excited. Some of us have a new source of power to test out."

Briony slid her eyes to Vein as the Bomardi cackled. He'd been seduced by it all. Infected. He met her eyes and quickly looked away.

"Our final lot of the evening," he announced theatrically. He read off her appraisal notes. "Briony Rosewood." Hissing. "Eversun born." Booing. "Gold-blooded Princess of Evermore." Jeering. "Sister of Rory the Slain and enemy of Mistress Mallow."

They were on their feet again, yelling in the name of their Seat of Bomard.

She let it wash over her, like a cool bath.

Only one person sat perfectly still throughout. Four rows back on the left aisle. The stage lights blinded her from seeing his face.

"Ladies, gentlemen," Vein crooned. He raised his hands to call for peace. "I've not yet begun the bidding."

The lights were hot.

She focused on the lone person, still not socializing. Maybe he'd already bid on his lot and now was just enjoying a night at the circus.

Vein read out her grading. "As you know, much like Miss Phoebe Rosewood, this heartspring runs with golden blood. The Rosewood bloodline has an affinity for shield magic and protection spells. I do think I can theorize that whoever bonds to this golden heartspring will become flooded with more shield magic than anyone in Bomard knows what to do with."

Briony glanced at him. She didn't know if that was true or if it was part of the show he was putting on. Would the Bomardi who purchased her also receive her magical strengths?

Vein's voice was low as he continued. "Miss Rosewood appraised as close to a five as anyone did in our scale of measured magical power."

An intrigued murmur passed through the room. Mallow tilted her head.

"And in case you were curious . . ." His voice dropped low. "It will be an extra five thousand for this one."

The acoustics shivered with the hum of whispered interest. The lonely Bomardi did nothing but cross one leg over the other.

"Mistress Mallow," Vein said over the crowd. "Do we have your permission to begin the bidding at fifteen thousand gold?"

Mallow's gaze never left Briony as she waved her hand magnanimously.

Fifty hands shot into the air, orange flames popping from fingertips, calling Vein's attention.

Briony swallowed and looked down to find Reighven raising a lazy hand.

Hands were only raised on the ground floor, she realized. Perhaps they'd sold spectator tickets for the balconies.

"Let's weed you out a bit, shall we?" Vein quipped. "Sixteen thousand."

Only about five hands dropped.

"Sixteen five. Jumping up to sixteen five, ladies and gentlemen," Vein began.

She watched as hands slowly descended, Reighven and Cohle keeping up with each other, laughing at their little game.

Her knees felt shaky, and she wondered if she would be seeing food again anytime soon.

"Eighteen thousand gold. Do I hear—Yes, sir, eighteen thousand. What about eighteen five?" He pointed to Reighven. "Eighteen five to Reighven. Several others still in. Nineteen?"

She let her eyes glaze over, watching the unmoving Bomardi. He sat still, one hand on his thigh, head supported by the other. He looked young. Wide shoulders. Tall. Briony shivered with the recognition. With the intimate knowledge of his lazy posture and his long fingers.

"Nineteen five? Yes, nineteen five to Quill. Do we have—?"

"Twenty-five thousand," said a tense voice. Briony blinked as every person in the first three rows turned to look at that one solitary man. He'd raised his hand and produced a flare from his fingertips. Had she summoned his voice by staring at him?

Whispers and shuffling. She knew that Cordelia had just sold for a bit more than that.

"Er, yes. Twenty-five thousand to . . ."

"Twenty-six," Reighven snarled, sending a glare back at the younger man.

"Twenty-six five," from the fourth row.

"Twenty-seven."

"Twenty-seven five."

"Twenty-eight!" Reighven yelled, irritated with the man in the fourth row.

The man whose voice drawled out, "Twenty-eight five," as if money was no object to him. The man whose eyes she knew to be speckled with blue in certain light. Whose long fingers twirled his pen in class much as he was now, gathering the air and sparking it to produce flames.

Reighven hesitated, looking up to Vein. "Twenty-nine."

"Twenty-nine five."

And the thought floated through her addled consciousness that there was an auction, and she would belong to someone in a few short minutes.

And Toven Hearst was bidding.

The theater was buzzing. Most of the crowd had figured out that the Hearst boy was throwing his money against Lag Reighven.

"Thirty," Reighven stated firmly, like he'd ended a game of cards.

"Thirty thousand, five hundred," Toven hummed.

A crashing wave of whispers. Briony looked down at her feet, finding specks of blood on her shoes that they'd forgotten to clean.

"Do I hear thirty-one thousand?" Vein asked, speaking up again.

Reighven's hand shot in the air. Toven's followed.

Reighven had been so arrogant, so firm in his belief that he could afford her. But he didn't have the gold to back this up. Did he?

Her blood ran cold.

Cordelia. Cordelia's twenty-eight thousand gold now belonged to Reighven.

And Katrina. And the other women he'd caught.

Since he'd had several virgins, he now had a lot of money to spend.

"Thirty-two thousand," one of them yelled, but Briony was concentrating on her head pounding, her shoulder aching.

As the bids rose higher, she thought about Toven Hearst. How the last time she'd seen him, he'd proven himself a dangerous man.

"Thirty-three thousand," Toven said.

He'd chased her through a forest, toying with her, herding her like an animal.

"Thirty-three five," Reighven hissed.

"Thirty-four."

"Thirty-four five."

There was a saying in Evermore: *The demon who has shaken your hand is better than the one who hasn't.* She didn't know which demon would be better. Reighven was interested in possessing her body as well as her magic, but Toven . . . What had he said all those years ago when he'd asked her to dance?

I am accustomed to having the finest thing in the room, after all.

Could she hope that's all this was?

"Thirty-five thousand," Toven said, crossing his legs again.

"Getting a bit steep for you, whelp?" Reighven stood and faced the fourth row. "Hesitating?"

"Steep for me?" Toven laughed. "I'm surprised you can count this high."

Reighven turned to the stage again. "Forty-five thousand gold."

Briony swallowed as she listened to the hissing. She looked to Toven, still and silent.

"How much of that inheritance did Daddy give you to play with, boy?" Reighven smirked back at him.

And Briony wondered the same. Orion Hearst was the richest man in Bomard, and inheritance laws would dictate that Toven would have access to some of it . . . but was it anywhere near this amount?

Mallow shifted, catching Briony's attention. Her dark eyes were on Toven, assessing him.

Vein cleared his throat and said, "I hear forty-five thousand. Do I hear forty-six?"

Toven's hand lifted. Orange sparks.

"I can go all night, Hearst," Reighven said, throwing his arms out wide. "I've been making my fortune for a while now, and I just made fifty-two thousand off my lots for this evening."

"Fifty-three thousand," Toven intoned.

Reighven laughed and turned back to Vein. "Fifty-five."

"Sixty." Toven's voice cracked.

"Sixty-one." Reighven grinned, yellow crooked teeth shining at her.

She wasn't sure if it was the concussion, or the stage lights, or the future bearing down on her, but her lungs were begging for air.

She'd known that this would happen. That she'd be leaving with Reighven. She'd been mentally preparing for a week.

She didn't know if she would truly be better off with Toven Hearst, but now, as he hesitated before stating, "Sixty-two," she wished he'd never jumped in at all. Now she would always wonder.

"Sixty-five thousand," said Reighven, chuckling.

Vein was white next to her as he waited. "I hear sixty-five thousand," he said at last. The crowd started twisting, buzzing with whispers. "Do I hear sixty-six?"

She didn't dare look at him. Couldn't bear the idea that if she looked, she might see indecision in the way he held his shoulders. Maybe she could guess his thoughts as she had in school, when he'd roll his shoulders back and reset his posture before diving back into a problem.

"Sixty-five thousand going once."

Or the way he'd stare at the chalkboard in elixirs class, tilting his head to the side until suddenly grabbing for his pen, jotting his thoughts as if they'd disappear if he wasn't quick.

"Sixty-five thousand going twice."

Or in year three, when suddenly he stopped paying her any attention, not even to aggravate her. When he'd simply shut off, and only the strangest of circumstances would get him to fight with her or even just make eye contact with her.

A gavel banged.

The world cracked open, and a violent sound poured into her ears like lava.

Her eyes were on her feet as Reighven jogged up onstage and met Vein in the middle. The scroll. A burning on her left arm. And then a fist in her hair, dragging her head back. Reighven was there, grinning down at her.

She shoved at him, and the crowd loved that.

Mallow stood, applauding with the rest of them, as if asking for an encore.

Gains was smiling in the front row, like the cat who got the cream.

Briony couldn't make out sounds anymore. Too much in her ears.

As the platform lowered, taking her down to the backstage area, she chanced one last look to see the crowd on its feet, one seat in the fourth row empty.

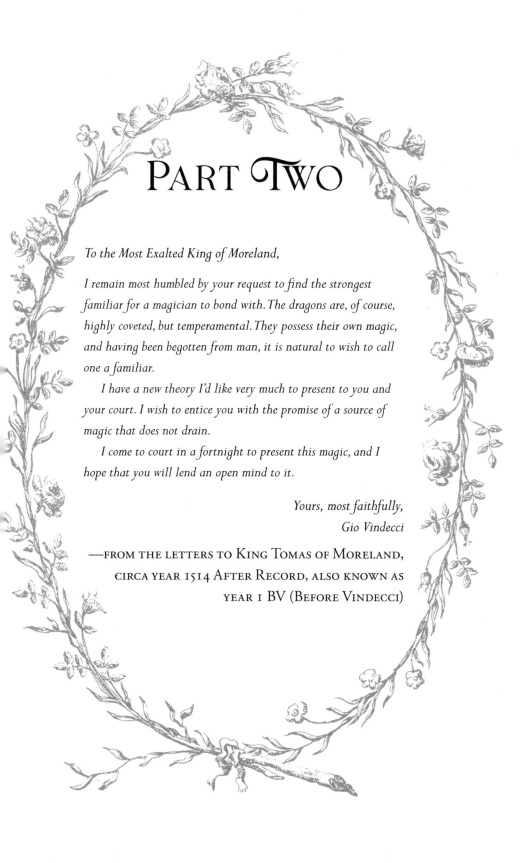

PART TWO

To the Most Exalted King of Moreland,

I remain most humbled by your request to find the strongest familiar for a magician to bond with. The dragons are, of course, highly coveted, but temperamental. They possess their own magic, and having been begotten from man, it is natural to wish to call one a familiar.

I have a new theory I'd like very much to present to you and your court. I wish to entice you with the promise of a source of magic that does not drain.

I come to court in a fortnight to present this magic, and I hope that you will lend an open mind to it.

Yours, most faithfully,
Gio Vindecci

—from the letters to King Tomas of Moreland, circa year 1514 After Record, also known as year 1 BV (Before Vindecci)

CHAPTER 12

Seven Years Ago

Y EAR TWO AT SCHOOL WAS VERY DIFFERENT, now that Rory and Cordelia were exchanging shy glances. And more.

It seemed everywhere Briony looked, they were holding hands or sitting with each other in the sun or even kissing ravenously in the suite Briony shared with her brother, at which point Briony loudly reminded them that the sitting area was a *shared* space.

Briony was alone more and more, except for when Didion asked to walk her back to her rooms upstairs. She'd let him kiss her after classes one day, and it was fine. When Didion kissed her again the following day, she had Toven's words in her head—*Do you really think anyone keeps their hands to themselves in year two?*—as his hands moved delicately over her waist, drifting upward.

He had a sheepish smile on his face when she pulled away, and Briony supposed that it had been nice. But the next day she made an excuse about needing to get back to her room quickly, and she spent quite a bit more time there.

At the Eversun school, the chill of the Bomardi mountains was a distant memory. The school was set on a lake and made of limestone, just like the neighboring Claremore Castle. The property sprawled outward instead of upward, like the Bomardi school. Briony's room had the perfect view of the lake, and it brought her so much peace of mind to look out the window and see the water.

That is, until summer came with its unbearable heat. And the Bomardi boys began using the dock below her window to strip down to their underwear and jump into the water.

Briony was concentrating on her maths one afternoon when she heard a familiar deep baritone voice drifting up to her window, joined by several others. She took a deep breath and tried to ignore them, just like she had every afternoon this week.

But then Toven Hearst's hearty laugh bellowed up to her, and she slammed her book closed and went to her window, careful to stand to the side so she wouldn't be seen.

Finn Raquin and Collin Twindle were already in the water, splashing and floating. Liam Quill was struggling with his boots. And Toven was just peeling his shirt off his shoulders, his back rippling with the action.

Briony sighed in exasperation. She couldn't say anything about it, because if they knew this was *her* window, they would probably find even more inventive ways to distract and annoy her.

As Liam shucked his trousers and jumped in inelegantly, Toven's hands went to his belt, taking his time. When he did slip his trousers off, he folded them neatly on the dock before diving into the water like a practiced swimmer.

His hair was darker when it was wet.

Briony watched the sunlight glisten off the water drops on his shoulders for longer than she cared to admit.

When she finally pulled herself from the window, she cast a deafening spell to block outside sound from her room.

The following week she took her schoolwork outside after classes, trailing the densely packed tree line around the lake toward her favorite tree. There was one solitary willow on the west side of the lake, with branches that dropped reedy vines all around, almost fully enclosing the tree. She loved to read there when it was balmy outside.

Only now, as she approached, she saw a person sitting at the base of her tree, with his own book.

Briony ducked behind a thick oak trunk and peered between the drooping branches.

Toven Hearst. Of course.

He was reclining against the trunk of the willow, a book in his lap and his collar undone. His shoes were off, and his socks were different colors.

For some reason it was the socks that kept Briony up at night after she'd walked all the way back to the castle and resigned herself to reading in her room instead. Was he blind to colors and patterns? Was he simply lazy about his undergarments? Briony couldn't figure it out, and she tossed and turned all night.

A week later came the hottest day of the summer. Briony loved the heat, but this was excessive. She was dripping and panting by the time she reached her tree, only to find bare feet this time.

Briony growled and pushed through the fronds.

Toven Hearst lay on his back, his book over his face as he snoozed. His feet weren't the only things that were bare.

His shirt hung from a knot in the trunk, and the expanse of his stomach and chest was there for Briony's inspection.

"No," she said. "Leave."

His hand reached up and removed the book from his face. "Excuse me."

"This is my tree," she said, still catching her breath. "Go away."

He lifted a pale eyebrow at her. "Your tree? Did you carve your name into it, Rosewood?" His eyes widened, mockingly. "Oh, that's right. It was your *brother* who showed skill in carving his name into trees, wasn't it?"

Briony flushed at the reminder that Toven knew her secret.

"Do you plan on telling anyone that I boost my brother, or are you just going to mock me with it for the rest of school?"

"Perhaps I'm waiting for the perfect opportunity to blackmail you." He placed the book back over his eyes, resting back on his arms.

She huffed. "I found the tree in the first week. It's mine. You have to leave." She knew she sounded abysmally petulant, but she couldn't help it.

"I'm not going anywhere. I was here first," he said, voice muffled behind the book.

And as he lay there, bare-chested and relaxed, she realized that he didn't think of her as a threat at all. She itched to change his mind about that, but knew what her father would say.

She tapped her foot against the damp shore, glancing around for some way to make him go and finding nothing. And then her gaze fixed on two mismatched socks at the base of the tree. She narrowed her eyes at them, wondering how someone who peacocked about school, caught his reflection in every mirror, and folded his trousers before jumping into the lake could possibly fail to match his socks.

"Are you still here, Rosewood?" he asked lazily.

She stamped her foot and marched away, determined to beat him to the tree the next day.

Which she did. When she saw him walking up to the willow, she cast a barrier charm on the curtain of fronds.

"I was here first. You'll have to leave this time, Hearst."

He glared at her and tried to push through the fronds. She *adored* the look on his face when he realized she'd barred him.

The next day, he was there first.

Briony raced from lunch the following day, grabbing an apple and nothing else. Didion tried to stop her, but she pushed past him apologetically.

She moved quickly to the lake, cutting a path along the shore to get to the tree first.

She heard footsteps in the tree line next to her.

Briony doubled her pace, her dress catching on tree roots and tearing as she barreled through the brush around the lake.

Toven came to keep pace with her. "Is this tree really worth so much to you?"

"Beating you is worth this much to me," she said, annoyed that his breath didn't seem to be affected while hers was straining.

Toven puffed what could have been a laugh, but then broke out in front of her with his long legs and then abruptly turned around to run backward, still faster than she could run forward.

"I'll tell you what, Rosewood," he said. "I'll leave the tree alone if you give me the top spot in elixirs."

Her feet stumbled. "I don't have the top—"

She stopped herself as he smirked knowingly at her. *Rory* had the top spot in elixirs.

"But of course, if you prefer to race me every day," he said, glancing down her body with a smirk. "I don't mind the view—"

With a sharp gasp, Toven was suddenly on his back, having stumbled on a root.

Briony burst out laughing, curling over to brace on her knees. The race was forgotten as she crowed at Toven's scrunched face, the wind knocked out of him.

He sat up, taking deep breaths and glaring at the root that had taken him down.

"Oh, that was priceless," Briony said, wiping her eyes. "Thank you for that."

"Stones, that was . . ." Toven reached behind his head and touched it gently. His fingertips came back red.

Briony blanched. "Oh! Are you all right?"

She dropped to her knees at his side.

"It's fine." He tried to shrug her off as he brought more blood away on his hand.

"Let me see—"

"No need."

"Really, Toven, I could fix it quick." She reached for his shoulder.

"Rosewood, get off me," he said without malice. "Like I'd trust an Eversun to heal."

Briony glared at him. "Mind magic works just as well for healing. I can handle a scrape fine." Her eyes widened innocently, playacting. "Unless you think I should call for a medical team? Are you so terribly injured that we should call all the tutors out to the lake—"

He sighed. "Just—hurry. And don't leave a scar."

Briony snorted and crawled around behind him, muddying the knees of her dress.

His silver-gray hair was matted with red. She winced, and quickly banished the blood with a pushing motion. There was a cut at the base of his skull, right at the hairline. She braced her thumbs and forefingers around the cut and focused on slowing his blood flow, encouraging coagulation.

There was a slight breeze, and his scent hit her. Peppermint maybe.

She passed her fingers over the wound, pulling the skin back together. Gooseflesh broke across his neck.

"Don't scar me," he repeated.

"Don't be a baby."

She worked the sides of the cut closed with small push-and-pull movements of her fingers against the air. Her face was close to his neck, and she could see her breath stir the fine hair above his collar.

And it hit her rather suddenly that they were alone in a dense tree line. Unchaperoned.

Briony's heart thumped with the intimacy of their position—her on her knees behind him, her hips and stomach almost touching his back.

His voice floated back to her from the winter solstice—*Do you really think anyone keeps their hands to themselves in year two?*

She swallowed and pulled her fingers away.

"You'll have to get the medics to finish," she said, knowing full well that she could have completed the stitching and left no scar. She pulled up from her knees to standing and grabbed her book and her apple. "I'm taking the tree today. You should go get that seen to."

He had just started to turn over his shoulder to look at her when she began walking away, her skin flushed and her ribs tight with something.

The next day, Didion found her sitting under the willow tree, and Briony pushed back the disappointment that he wasn't someone else. When Didion distracted her from her reading with a soft kiss, Briony let him. She let him curl over her as she reclined under the trunk, and with her eyes squeezed so tight that she could imagine his dark hair was a paler color, she brought his hands to her breasts. He couldn't untie her laces there, and he complained of a cramp the entire time, but she was desperate to relieve the burning inside of her, encouraging him to continue, to press harder, to rock against her.

No one keeps their hands to themselves in year two, anyway.

CHAPTER 13

S HE WAS SHOVED INTO A DARK CLOSET at the circus and locked in. It took time for her eyes to adjust, but she found a broom to snap in half, making a weapon. It felt like hours that she waited. Briony thought she'd be given to Reighven immediately, but maybe the payment process was more complex than she assumed.

When the door finally burst open and the light hit her eyes, she had lost all her adrenaline. Her heart kick-started into gear.

But it wasn't Reighven. Gains glared down at her as if she hadn't just made him a very rich man.

"Up."

Briony stood, not even bothering to hide the sharp stick from the broom handle. With a flick of his fingers, Gains tossed the stick aside.

"Come with me."

Slowly, she followed him out of the closet. He led her down a staircase and twisted her through the backstage of the circus. She didn't hear a sound behind any of the closed doors, and she wondered if every one of her friends was already gone.

When Gains stopped at a closed door that said *Acrobats*, he pushed the handle and stepped aside for her to enter. She expected to find Reighven. Maybe a cot or a chair where he'd force her down and push up her dress.

She didn't expect to find Larissa Gains. She hadn't expected to find her ever again.

Larissa seemed to feel the same as she sat up tall from the counter she'd been leaning on, eyes wide and hungry. They were in a dressing room with mirrors on the walls and large candles flickering.

Gains shut the door without looking at his daughter once, locking them in.

Before Larissa could say a word to her, there was a sharp burning on Briony's left arm. Her mouth opened in a silent hiss of pain. She looked down to where *Lag Reighven* had been inked into her skin. The letters sizzled. She squeezed her fist and watched as the ink lifted, rearranging until a different signature formed on her skin.

Toven Hearst.

She blinked down at the letters, her vision swimming. It couldn't be . . .

Larissa was at her side, grabbing her arm.

"Ha!"

The sound jarred her.

Larissa turned away, running her nails through her hair. The mirrors allowed Briony to see that she'd pressed her eyes closed, squeezing her lips together.

"Incredible." She spun around to face her. "How much?"

Briony shook her head, deciding that Larissa didn't need to know.

"Thirty thousand?" Larissa guessed, gazing at her assessingly. "Thirty-five thousand?" she said when Briony didn't answer. "Come on, now. I'm curious. Forty?"

Briony turned away but was unable to find a wall in which Larissa's face did not reflect back at her. Her own face was almost unrecognizable, with deep circles under her eyes and dry skin. Her jawline stuck out unpleasantly.

"Tell me," Larissa hissed over her shoulder. Briony met her eyes. Something stormed inside Larissa's expression, like the moment before thunder cracks. As Briony watched, Larissa's blue gaze flooded and she took a slow breath before asking, "More than forty thousand?"

Briony looked away, shivering. She caught sight of the ink on Larissa's arm—a matching *Toven Hearst.*

Before Briony could fully piece it all together, a furious gust of wind swept through the dressing room. She raised her hands to shield her face, and Larissa did the same. When she peeked, a wide gaping hole was in the room. A black entrance to a portal.

Larissa and Briony looked at each other. Briony didn't know what kind of choice they had. Someone would come to force them through, she was sure.

Larissa tried the door one last time to no success, and then she grabbed Briony's hand and tugged her through.

The pressure gripped her chest, and when they popped out the other side, Briony's face was battered with thick raindrops. She gasped soundlessly as lightning flashed the sky, illuminating a sprawling dark castle before them. The wrought-iron gates were closed.

Briony had read about Hearst Hall but had never seen it in person. It was built at the base of the Armitage Mountains, in one of the few plateaus of flat land in Bomard. Hearst Hall was only one of the Hearst properties, but it was their most prized and therefore their most frequently inhabited.

Larissa gazed up at it through the rain with apprehension, as if she didn't know if even she would be safe there.

Briony turned in a circle, finding the edge of a wood behind her in the lightning strikes, dark and impenetrable. They could make a run for it now. She could take Larissa's hand and flee into the forest, letting the Gowarnus elixir work its way out of their systems until they could properly portal away.

She had decided to do so when suddenly there was movement in the trees. Briony stepped back, and Larissa turned to see what got her attention.

A large fox had slunk around the trunk of a tree, watching them. Maybe it was a small wolf.

A clanking behind them made the women spin back to see the black metal gates swinging open. At the end of a long park, the door to Hearst Hall was open.

Briony turned in every direction. Was there a way out that wasn't toward the creature in the forest or toward the dark castle?

She grabbed Larissa's arm, pointing toward the left where a pathway split around the corner of the outer wall. Larissa shook her head mutely, her eyes flicking between the creature in the forest and the open door of the house. A ball of light was moving slowly down the long drive toward them.

Briony dropped Larissa's arm and made for the pathway. She could do it alone.

There came a snarling snapping of jaws, and Briony jumped back, finding the animal in her path. It was a fox, she could see, but with a deeper growl.

She stumbled and slipped in the wet grass, tumbling onto her backside. Larissa helped her up as the ball of light zoomed forward, stopping at the gates. It hovered, and Briony realized it was similar to the navigator flame that sailors used to guide them in the dark of the ocean.

Briony looked at the fox, who was licking its chops, and started forward to follow the light, dragging Larissa with her.

The fox lunged, and in a panic, Briony and Larissa separated. Briony fell forward past the gates, and Larissa scattered to the outside. A sharp pain sparked in Briony's left arm, and before she could get to her feet, the black gates were swinging closed, locking her in.

Briony ran for the gates, grabbing the metal and tugging while Larissa did the same from the outside. Lightning split the sky, and a crack of thunder followed no more than a second later. Larissa's wide eyes were on the fox as Briony tugged with all her might, her fingers slipping under the rainwater, and her relocated shoulder burning.

The fox turned with a final glance and headed back toward the trees. And a second later, a deep-black portal opened on the edge of the forest. A hooded man stepped out, and Larissa lunged for the gates with a cry, begging them to open for her.

The man held out his hand and screamed, "Don't!" He pushed off his hood, and Finn Raquin's anxious eyes were on them. "Don't cross the barrier, Larissa."

Larissa choked on a sob and ran into his arms.

Briony watched in silence as Larissa buried her face in her friend's chest. And she wondered what was happening to Cordelia at this moment. To Didion.

Without a glance to Briony at the gate, Finn grabbed Larissa's arm and pulled a vial from his pocket. He pulled the cork out with his teeth and said, "This is going to hurt."

Larissa's eyes went wide as he poured the elixir over her arm—over the tattoo with Toven's name. Briony watched in horror as Larissa's skin burned away. The blond woman screamed and tried to pull back, but Finn held her firmly. When the vial was empty, Finn tossed it on the ground and quickly started casting a spell over Larissa's arm. Lightning lit the sky, but not even the boom of the thunder could drown out Larissa's wailing cry as Finn pulled black smoke from her skin, inky and wet. Larissa drooped and passed out, but Finn held her tightly to his chest as he tugged and tugged until the smoke turned to blood.

He summoned a leaf patch to place over her burned skin, then tucked her up against his chest, carrying her back to the portal without a glance at Briony.

Briony's heart galloped. She banged on the bars, desperate to make him hear her. When he turned, she extended her arm as far as it would go, begging him with her eyes.

Me next.

Finn stared at her and took a deep breath.

"This is the safest place for you, Briony."

Her eyes widened in horror as she watched him glance at Hearst Hall and then turn to slip into the portal, Larissa dangling from his arms.

The portal closed with a *zip*, and then Briony was alone in the rain on the wrong side of the gates of Hearst Hall.

CHAPTER 14

RIONY PRESSED HER BACK against the wrought iron and stared up at the castle. It must have comprised three sprawling stories of stone, with a large dome in the center.

Was this to be her prison? She looked at her arm again. *Toven Hearst.* What had he given up to obtain her? She couldn't imagine that Reighven would have parted with her for anything less than an astronomical sum.

The Hearsts were rich; that much had been clear even without the evidence of it staring down at her. But why spend so much on her?

Toven had once killed four people just to get to her, so she supposed spending tens of thousands to have her now wasn't so much a surprise. A chill shivered through her as she remembered the way he'd chased her, running alongside her as if taunting her with how easily he could catch her.

The only reason he'd failed to capture her that night a year ago was that he'd been greedy with his magic. He'd misjudged what killing four people at once would do to his heart. It had been the first time she'd seen anyone take more than one life with a single Heartstop—an unheard-of skill. The Eversuns had known *Orion* was capable of it. Reports had come that he could kill two people with one casting of Heartstop. Even the most talented of heart magicians could use Heartstop only once at a time. Orion Hearst had been the dangerous exception, and Toven Hearst had had the potential to break every rule that came before him.

That night, Briony had moved through a dark forest, stumbling across corpse after corpse, four in all, until finally finding Toven Hearst incapacitated with the agony of ripping his heart four times in a single moment.

She'd wondered then, as she stared at the carnage that was normally impossible for a single magician, if she should kill him where he lay and save Evermore the problem of Toven Hearst down the line.

But she couldn't. Not then.

Lightning again broke across the sky, shocking her from her memories.

The navigator flame seemed to bob, as if it were saying, *Come along now.* It began floating to the house again, leading her inside.

Absolutely not, Briony thought. She glanced at the gates, her eyes following the long stretch of the wrought-iron fence into the inky night. Briony took off to the right, following the fence and hoping for an opening.

She looked at the castle again, half expecting someone to be watching her from the doorway or from behind an upstairs window. It remained dark.

The rain pelted her face and further soaked her dress. Her slippers were not meant for rain or even outdoors, much less the muddy grass along the fence. By the time it gave way to a stone wall, she'd lost one of her slippers in the mud.

Briony looked up the wall as lightning cracked the sky. It was ten feet high, at least, and with no footholds for climbing. She kept moving, circling the castle with one eye on the door where the navigator flame waited for someone to navigate.

As she rounded the southeastern side, her shoulder burned and her head pounded. Each breath felt like a stab in the ribs. She reached for her magic, either mind magic or heart magic, but wasn't surprised to find nothing responding to her.

Briony thought of Larissa. Did Toven know that Finn had taken her? Surely he had to. As she shivered against the wind in her thin dress, she found herself almost mourning the loss of Larissa. When there had been two of them, Briony had felt safer somehow. The idea of being alone, under Toven Hearst's roof, powerless in so many ways . . .

She'd never needed to know hand-to-hand defense. She'd always had Anna by her side. Briony had learned plenty of magic that would fend off attackers of all kinds, but she'd never needed to learn how to fight off a man when she was without magic.

As she curved around the back of Hearst Hall, Briony stopped at the sight of a large pond on the property. Maybe a small lake. The moon reflected off its surface, and the rain rippled the waters. Aside from the rivers that trailed down from the mountains, Bomard lacked bodies of water. Where Eversuns prayed to the waters that were so plentiful along the coasts and in their large inland lakes, Bomardi called upon the stones.

She refocused, finding the end of the stone wall just ahead of her. She rounded the wall and found she was at the top of a small hill that opened to a field. She could just see the base of the mountains in the distance. Her mind ran with the possibility of hiding out there. She didn't know what she'd find in the mountains, but all she needed to do was outlive the Gowarnus herb elixir as it drained from her system.

She just needed to run down this hill and toward the mountains.

It was worth a chance.

"I'd stop there, Rosewood."

She spun. Toven Hearst stood ten feet behind her, staring at her with guarded eyes.

Thunder rattled the sky, and she shook with the strength of it. Her heart pounded with the adrenaline of her near escape and her fear of him, this unknown Toven Hearst.

He wore the same clothes from the auction, but up close now, she could see that his vest was embroidered in silver. The rain made his hair darker, and she thought of the boys jumping off the dock at the Eversun school.

She blinked against the rain. He stepped forward, and it took everything in her power to keep from retreating from him.

"Would you consider continuing this tour of the grounds when it isn't raining?" he said, his wit as acerbic as ever.

Briony glanced over his shoulder at Hearst Hall, looking monstrous in the storm, then behind her to the mountains. To freedom.

Could she outrun him?

"Before you dash into the mountains to die of either cold or creatures, know that the grounds stop here for the purposes of that ink on your arm. If you cross the line, you will be harmed."

Briony looked down at the tattoo on her arm, the black and gold that glistened his name. Was that true? Or was it meant to scare her?

He was narrowing his eyes at her. She wondered if her non-responses unnerved him. Even if she'd had her voice, she wasn't sure she'd have the courage to give him hell like she used to. She used to fight back before she found out he was a murderer.

"Come now," he said, taking another step closer to her. "You're being stubborn—don't make me drag you."

She'd woken up in her first cell, been dragged on her back to her second, and been strong-armed into the dark closet of her third. And now she was being asked to walk to her final one.

The rain was slowing.

A breeze rustled the tree branches above them, and the moon reflected in his eyes.

It was worth a try.

If she was wrong, she'd end up in the cell like he'd planned anyway.

With an agility she didn't know she still had, Briony spun on her heel and leapt across the invisible barrier, into the field.

A spark of fire burst through her arm, burning, crackling, sizzling up her nerve endings. There was the squelch of wet grass under her and rapid movement as momentum rolled her over and over. Fire spread through her entire body, frying her from the inside. A yell echoed behind her as the pain surrounded her mind and plunged her into a spinning darkness.

*   *   *

Rocking. Swaying.

Briony was floating in the lake at school. The water was warm against her chilled body, and the gentle waves rocked her.

Her mind floated up, thoughts attaching to memories.

She'd been outside in the rain. She'd wanted to roll down a hill.

Toven Hearst had stopped her.

Her eyes fluttered, and she remembered the pain. Her body quaked, and arms pulled her closer.

Someone held her to their chest, warm, solid, a steady heartbeat, walking, swaying, rocking her back to sleep.

Her skin hurt. She could hear the rain but couldn't feel it.

Warm fingers pushed her wet hair off her forehead, and arms squeezed her tighter.

She fell back into the blackness, like blinking.

*   *   *

"What happened?" A voice burst into her mind, waking her. A woman's voice.

Her eyelids fought against the paste that closed them together.

"She jumped across the property line," rumbled a voice from the furnace against her ear. "This damned tattoo electrocuted her."

"Is she alive?" the woman said. It was the concern of a mother. But her mother was dead. "Toven, is she alive?"

The breath caught next to her ear. "I—I don't . . . She didn't scream."

The low vibration of his voice lulled her. She drifted out to sea again.

*   *   *

The first thing Briony became conscious of was the bed. Her eyes snapped open, and she stared at the low ceiling above her. Every limb sparked to life, but they only twitched when she tried to move them.

Tears pricked her eyes. She called out for her father, but no sound came.

She couldn't move her head. Her muscles were weighed down; even her eyelids worked too hard.

Then the pain came. She screamed and screamed into the silence of an empty room until her mind shut her body down and she slept again.

*   *   *

A cold compress touched her forehead, and her eyes blinked blearily at the movement in the room. A hum of voices, but she couldn't pick up the words.

She called for Rory. He could heal her. She'd healed him so many times—all he had to do was push magic down that vein in his chest to hers. Rory could fix it.

She remembered then. How he'd tried to say goodbye to her, and she hadn't let him. How he'd asked her, *Do you believe the prophecy is about me? Really? In your heart, Briony?* And how she'd let him ride to his death.

Tears tracked down her face as she sobbed. She tried to lift her hand to wipe them away, but her muscles didn't work anymore.

"She's crying," a deep voice said. "She needs something for the pain."

"I've already given her—"

"Then she needs more!"

Briony wept, unable to open her eyes. Unable to face a world where Rory was dead. She'd woken up in that world once before and they'd sold her, like she was a piece of land to harvest. Cordelia and Didion, too.

A terrible thought slithered down her spine. *That's how I truly know he's dead*, she thought into the darkness. *He didn't try to stop the auction.*

Even without a plan and without an army, Rory would have been there.

The pain of it dragged keening agony out of her.

*   *   *

The next time she woke, she could tell it was daylight. She turned her head toward the sun, peeking underneath heavy curtains and pouring out the side of closed drapes.

Briony's body still ached, but she could move slowly. She swiveled her neck to survey the room she was in, and her body jerked when she saw she was not alone.

Serena Hearst was stirring a teacup set on the bedside table. Briony watched the tall woman standing over her, her long limbs graceful in the dark.

"Hello, Miss Rosewood," she said, her voice unreadable.

Briony met her eyes. They shimmered a cold blue.

"How is the pain?" Mrs. Hearst asked. When Briony didn't respond, she continued. "Do you remember what happened?"

Briony remembered the rain. Toven's gaze as he told her to come inside. The sharp burst of electricity as she jumped into the field. *This damned tattoo electrocuted her.*

She nodded.

Briony glanced around the rest of the room. It was bare. No fireplace, no art. Only the bedding, the curtains, and the bedside table.

Toven's mother watched her guardedly. Briony tried to calm her heart as it whispered that she was in this woman's house. This woman whose son had just bought her like a prized horse. This woman who had married the most lethal man in Bomard.

"You had a concussion and a poorly reset dislocated shoulder. We staved off the hypothermia from the rain, but as you know, you were electrocuted quite severely. It may be another few days until your muscles are ready."

Another few days. That made it sound like days had already passed. She wanted to ask but let her mouth fall shut when she remembered her voice was gone.

Mrs. Hearst tilted her head at her. "Is there anything else wrong with you physically, Miss Rosewood? Are you in other pain?"

Briony shook her head. When Toven's mother continued to look her over, Briony slowly brought her hand up to her throat, each movement sending tremors through her muscles. Briony tapped her throat, her fingers brushing past the metal collar still on her, and she carefully shook her head.

Mrs. Hearst blinked at her, realization dawning. She lifted her hand and twitched her fingers. Heat flared in Briony's throat, and she tested her voice.

"Thank you," Briony said. Her vocal cords were gravelly with neglect.

Serena Hearst stared at her a moment longer, and Briony felt as if she were memorizing and cataloging her features. Then abruptly, she took the teacup from the bedside table, turning toward the door.

"Rest." A command not a suggestion.

Mrs. Hearst left. Briony tried to glance past her through the doorway, wondering what part of Hearst Hall she was in, but the effort to crane her neck was too much.

She heard soft voices outside the door, and as she tried to make out the words, her tired body fell into repose again.

* * *

Rory was screaming.

Briony ran through a maze of tall hedges, searching for him desperately. He called her name, begging her to find him. Every turn took her deeper and deeper into the maze. The sky was getting darker, and she could hear something chasing her. Hunting her.

When she looked up at the sky, the moon was beginning to blot out the sun.

"Briony!" Rory screamed.

She tripped, falling toward the earth. Falling, falling.

* * *

Briony jerked awake, tears wet on her face. The memory of her brother screaming rang in her head like a bell. Her chest heaved. She lifted her hand to wipe her face, and her muscles protested, but they did at least move this time.

As she shifted in the sheets, she realized she wasn't alone.

Toven Hearst stared out of the curtained window, facing away from her. The dusk sky backlit him, coloring his pale hair purple and orange.

She glanced at the closed door, the empty room. It was just the two of them, and she had no idea what he wanted with her.

CHAPTER 15

BRIONY COULDN'T BE SURE if he knew she was awake, but she supposed it didn't matter. She couldn't move her muscles fast enough to run. Her heart pounded with the unknown.

"My mother says your voice was taken," he said, breaking the silence. "Which doesn't explain why your *hearing* failed you when I said you'd be harmed if you crossed the boundary line."

She glared at his back. "Yes," she whispered fiercely, voice throaty with misuse. "Because I had every reason to trust you."

From this angle, she could just barely see his jaw clench.

Briony realized she'd been changed out of the dress from the auction and was now in a soft white nightgown. She hoped it had been a servant who'd done that.

She hissed through her teeth as she shifted to sit up, hating the way she lay supine before him like a rag doll. "Why is this such a hard recovery?"

His eyes were still on the view beyond the window. "Crossing the barrier should shock the tattooed individual and give them a chance to withdraw themselves from the perimeter. *You* jumped *through* the barrier, your entire body beyond it. Then you managed to roll down a hill. You were outside the boundary for almost a full minute."

She wondered if he would keep his back to her for the entirety of her imprisonment.

"Certainly took you long enough," she said.

That did it. Toven blinked slowly and turned to face her with furious eyes.

Why did all self-preservation leave her when this man was involved? She was wearing nothing but a slip, in a bed, in his home. With no one to come running if she screamed. Why did poking at him come so naturally to her?

She swallowed and looked away. A full minute of being electrocuted. Her muscles twitched at the reminder.

"And you brought me where?" She nodded to the small undecorated room. "Is this my cell?"

"The closest location for your recovery was the groundskeeper's cottage," he said. "It's temporary."

She glanced over the cobwebs in the corners. "And where is the groundskeeper?"

"We don't have one. Hearst Hall doesn't require any servants."

Briony blinked at him. A house that grand with no staff? Briony had heard of households cutting back on staff when gossip began creeping through the walls. Was it out of caution, then? The Hearsts were known to be secretive, but this was extreme.

She wanted to ask more questions, but Toven faced her fully and clasped his hands behind his back, a sour expression on his face.

"Mistress Mallow wishes to see you."

Briony's air caught in her chest. Her eyes flicked to the door, her muscles locked as she waited for it to open.

"We are to pay her a call as soon as possible," he clarified.

Briony glanced at him in shock. "Now? I can barely move."

"You'll have to manage," he said. "She has been kept waiting for three days."

Her eyes widened. "I've been in bed three days?"

"Six, actually."

Her mouth opened then closed, unsure how to respond. He stared at her, waiting. Would he drag her from the bed?

Briony shifted her legs, stretching them as she threw back the sheets. Her legs were bare, the nightdress twisted under her thighs.

Toven faced the window again, and she guessed that was all the privacy she would be afforded. With shaking movements, she pulled herself from the mattress, bracing on the wall to help her stand. There was a pair of hard-soled slippers on the floor, so she slid them on. With the bed between them, he turned to her as she tugged her nightdress to fall to her ankles. It was the only thing on her. She had no undergarments.

His unreadable eyes passed over her once before he brought his left forefinger to his right hand and magically sliced the pad of his thumb. She recognized the cast for a portal. On private property, an inhabitant's blood was needed to create portals in and out. Without, visitors had to portal from outside the front gates.

The portal's chasm grew wide in the empty room, and Toven gestured for her to come to him.

Briony moved on twitching legs, aware that she was about to arrive the waters knew where in nothing but her nightclothes.

"Your left arm," Toven said.

Briony looked down at it. The ink on the inside of her elbow glistened. *Toven Hearst.*

Toven wrapped his hand around the ink. The cool press of his hand on her hot skin had her wondering if she had a fever. Before she could wish for that sensation everywhere, he tugged her into the portal, and a flash of heat burned over the ink on her arm. When the void finished pressing down on her, she gasped.

She stood on the ledge of a great mountain, overlooking vast peaks and valleys. Briony's head swam with vertigo as she scrambled back from the edge. When she turned, there was a gothic castle carved into the side of the mountain.

"Come." Toven started up steep stairs in the twilight.

Briony watched him climb, her body groaning in protest already. She braced herself on the rock to her left and slowly followed him, taking the steps one at a time.

He waited for her at the next level, about fifty steps above her. When she was halfway up, she had to pause, panting. He made no effort to help her, but she eventually made it to the landing.

Before continuing he turned to her. "Mistress Mallow is now the supreme ruler of all Moreland. You will treat her with the deference she deserves."

Briony tried to catch her breath. "Or what? You'll electrocute me?"

Toven lifted a pale brow at her. "I know you've been *asleep* for six days, Rosewood, so you may not have grasped this," he said silkily, "but heartsprings don't need tongues. They don't need fingers. They don't need legs, even. Disobedience can be punished in whatever way Mallow sees fit, as long as your heart still beats."

Briony shivered, and it had nothing to do with the wind on the mountain.

He turned and continued up the next steps as she pieced things together.

It had been six days since the auction, and she was Toven Hearst's heartspring now. That was her only purpose in this world—to make Toven Hearst's magic stronger.

She slowly followed him up the mountainside.

Between burning torches on the next landing, there were two large stone doors adorned with an ancient Bomardi seal from the first civil war, and Briony realized where she was. Mallow had moved into the original home of the first Seat of Bomard, the Dragon Lord. He had been the first magician to ever take a dragon as his familiar—the same dragon that had bonded to Mallow.

As the stone doors opened, the firelight showed the entry guarded on either side by men in blue cloaks. One of them nodded to Toven as he approached and stepped aside, but the other's eyes fell over her body. She turned her gaze down.

A second set of doors opened deeper inside the cave-like castle, and Toven led her inside.

It was a grand hall with stone floors and an open ceiling, big enough for a dragon to land inside. One long wall was made of enormous arched windows, looking directly over the mountain range, vanishing into a large drop beneath them.

Veronika Mallow stood at the far end of the hall, staring off out across the peaks. There was no throne, no "seat," as was the custom in Bomard for audiences with the leader of the realm. Mallow simply stood in an empty room, wearing tight-fitted breeches, boots strapped up her calves, and a sheer top.

The whistle of the wind through the archways muffled the sound of their footsteps. Briony felt lightheaded.

Toven walked her to a spot on the stone floor, dark with dried blood, and dropped to his knee, dragging her down with him. He bowed his head, but Briony stared at Mallow's back, watching her turn slowly toward them.

Mallow's pale skin glowed in the rising moonlight, and Briony couldn't help but wonder again how old she was. Her eyes were as black as her hair as they landed on Briony, piercing through her.

"Briony Rosewood." The sound of her name sliding over Mallow's tongue made her skin crawl. "Welcome to my palace."

Briony breathed deep, the air thick in her throat. When she gave no greeting, Mallow continued.

"You went for quite a sum at the auction." Mallow's eyes glittered as her brows lifted, as if she and Briony had a little secret to themselves. "All those Bomardi men jockeying for you. I'm sure you were quite content."

Briony pressed her lips together, but then a deep rumble of chuckling chorused through the room. She looked to the archways and realized they were not alone. There were Bomardi guards hidden in the shadows.

"Stand," Mallow commanded, and then Toven was dragging her to her feet. "Toven."

"Mistress."

"You lost the auction, but then settled accounts with Reighven after," Mallow said.

"Yes, Mistress."

"Why?"

Briony waited, wondering why as well.

"I'm always drawn to the most valuable possessions," said Toven.

Mallow grinned and began to pace the room, continuing conversationally. "And is she everything you paid for and more? Have you completed the heartspring bond?"

"Not yet, Mistress."

The Bomardi guards shifted, whispering. She felt a dozen eyes turn on her as she wondered what the bonding process entailed.

Mallow's brow lifted.

Toven answered her unasked question. "She injured herself in an escape attempt, as you know. She's learned her lesson now, but she's been weakened."

"Do it soon," Mallow said swiftly. "What's the point in having a golden heartspring if you can't mine that gold?" She smiled. "Your father has resolved the issue with her collar, yes?"

"Yes, Mistress," Toven said. "All that's left is the bond."

Briony's mind was racing. The golden heartspring. That's what Vein had called her during the auction. She assumed it was just a reference to the legend that the Rosewoods had gold blood. Was there more to it?

And had Orion fixed the issue with her collar while she slept? Was it now properly suppressing any heart magic as well as her mind magic? Briony's body had been too weak to try earlier, but she reached for the pulsing vein in her chest, searching for heart magic. Then the humming thread between her eyes, her mind magic. Nothing responded.

A horrible thought materialized: Was this collar permanent? Would she never be able to take it off?

"Briony." Mallow's crooning voice interrupted her thoughts. Mallow faced her and clasped her hands behind her back. "Where is your cousin, Finola?"

She blinked. She couldn't hold back her surprise before Mallow saw it. "What?"

Toven's head snapped to her. "You will address her as Mistress," he hissed, eyes burning into her.

Briony almost glared at him. He'd warned her to be obedient.

"Finola Rosewood," Mallow continued, stepping forward. "Her safe houses. Her distant family on her mother's side—the Nottingdales, if I'm not mistaken?"

As Mallow inched closer, the air thinned in Briony's lungs. Her heart thrummed as she stared into the glinting eyes searching her.

Briony tried to remember the question as Mallow tilted her head like a tiger.

Finola. Finola was Phoebe's older sister. Finola was the person who'd taught Briony advanced mind magic after the war started—cloaking, blending, advanced subterfuge. Anytime she was home from a mission, she focused all her attention on lessons for Briony. She worked as a top adviser to the Eversun militia and had coordinated many of the strategic attacks on Bomard in the four years since Briony's father's death.

Finola was the first person who showed Briony that she didn't have to just be a pretty face for a political marriage. She could be useful to the militia, to the king's cabinet—even to a *Bomardi* cabinet had the war not broken out.

Briony's throat felt stuck on Mallow's questions, but something was becoming clear.

This was the reason why she hadn't seen Finola in the Trow dungeon. She'd never been captured.

And for some reason, Mallow was threatened by that.

A fire burned in her gut, something that she thought had been extinguished the moment she felt Rory's barrier fall.

"Finola was the Eversun army's head strategist and lead instructor in cloaking," she said. "Even if I had an idea of where she'd go, I'd be wrong." A slow smile spread up her lips. "I'm quite pleased to inform you that if Finola is out there, you won't find her until she wants you to."

Mallow's black eyes narrowed at her, and a moment too late, Briony remembered Mallow could take her tongue for that comment. Mallow's fingers traced a gesture, and Briony braced herself for painful magic, a punishment—

Something slammed into her face, stinging her cheek and snapping her neck to the side. She stumbled, regaining balance and pressing her hand to her face. Her eyes rocked in their sockets.

She searched for the weapon, preparing for another strike. Her gaze refocused as Toven lowered his hand, a sharp stone ring on his middle finger glinting at her. Her lip was wet with blood.

He'd backhanded her. He'd hit her, and she was bleeding.

"Watch your mouth. You are addressing the Mistress of the Realm."

She shivered at his voice and looked away from his icy eyes.

Though her head rang, it was the least of what could have been sent her way tonight.

Mallow seemed pleased with Toven's response. "She still has quite a bit of fire left in her, Toven. I look forward to watching it doused." She turned her gaze back on Briony and continued her questioning. "We know Finola Rosewood spent time on the outskirts of Kilwoven, on the coast. Where else?"

Briony stared at her, licking the blood off her lip. She had no idea what kind of answer would best protect Finola.

Mallow tilted her head. "I'll just take a look for myself."

She slithered forward as Briony realized what she meant to do. Briony tried to step back, but her muscles were locked. Her throat closed in terror as Mallow circled her, coming around to her front again and leaning in to her face. Briony looked into the black tunnels of Mallow's gaze, pulled to them inexorably.

And then there were daggers in her brain, sinking into her eyes and twisting deep. She couldn't breathe as memories floated through her head, yanked forward and pushed back.

She saw Finola with a sharp stinging pain, a teenager with wide teeth and braided honey-blond hair. She sat in the grass with six-year-old Briony, blowing dandelion tufts out into the field behind Claremore Castle. Her cheeks puffed wide, and Briony giggled.

Briony's mind was on fire as Mallow clawed through her thoughts, her memories—using magic only advanced mind magicians knew. Briony had heard of Mallow's power with mind reading—the benefit of the dragon bond—but this was so much like poorly done mind magic. Briony supposed there was no reason for Mallow to refine the technique into something less obtrusive and painless, as mind magicians studied to do. Mallow's magic felt like claws ripping at her cranium, prying open the plates.

Like a rubber band snapping inside her, Finola was now a young woman, standing next to Phoebe at King Jacquel's funeral.

Briony was a passenger in her own mind, aware of her own presence and Mallow's presence in every moment.

A ricochet to Biltmore Palace, and Finola was teaching Rory how to call upon their father's army—Rory's army now—as Briony took notes.

"Vindecci developed this himself," came Finola's melodic voice. She unrolled a large map across the dining room table. "You simply hover your palm over the castle that you wish to call upon."

She demonstrated by opening her hand over the picture labeled *Biltmore*. Twenty-one-year-old Briony gasped as the candles blazed hot, flames jumping to the ceiling, then dimmed as Finola took her hand away.

Finola turned to Rory. "The strategic advisers reside at Kilwoven." She tapped the map. "I'll take you there tomorrow—"

And like a whip cracking across her mind, she jerked to see Finola seated on Briony's bed at Biltmore Palace, with her arm wrapped around eighteen-year-old Briony's shoulders.

"No, it's not mutual." The younger Briony laughed through her tears. "I'm just an idiot."

Briony felt her heart hammering in her chest even as the pain of Mallow's mind cut through her thoughts, sizzling her nerve endings. Her pulse spiked, and her body tensed further.

No, no, no. Mallow couldn't see this . . .

There was a moment of stillness as Mallow seemed to hover, clueing in on Briony's reluctance to show this memory. Mallow's consciousness slithered through the scene, twisting around the two women on the bed and examining them.

"You're not an idiot," Finola said, pushing hair over Briony's ear. "I had a crush on a Bomardi boy when I was your age."

Briony looked up at her with surprised eyes. "What happened?"

"He married the day after school ended, and I begged your father to use me in any way but for a political betrothal with Bomard. He let me join the strategists' council instead."

Briony snorted. "*My* father? That would never be an option for me."

"You'll see. Come with me to Southern Camly this solstice. I have friends there who can teach . . . you . . . cloaking . . ."

Finola slowed, though she hadn't seven years ago. Mallow was pulling them backward, replaying the scene.

". . . Southern . . . Camly . . ."

Through the pain in her mind, Briony felt like screaming for other reasons. She'd just given Mallow a place to start looking for Finola. The country of Southern Camly, across the sea.

She waited for Mallow to release her mind, to be alone in her own head again and deal with the pain from there.

But Mallow was still staring at the two women on the bed with curiosity on her face. She pulled them backward again.

"I had a crush on a Bomardi boy when I was your age," Finola repeated.

Briony felt her real body twitch with terror, hovering in the receiving room of Mallow's castle. Her mind screamed at her to close off, like locking doors and shutting windows against a storm.

Suddenly, they were sliding through waves of memories and images. Briony's mind was forced to slither backward. She tried to fight, to pull any other moment forward, but Mallow's curiosity could not be quenched.

Briony was standing behind an oak tree, watching a boy with mismatched socks sit in her favorite spot under the willow on the lake.

Then she was in elixirs class, mixing together ingredients while the same boy read instructions to her.

"The dragonflies need to be more finely chopped—"

"Not for this one," Briony said. "The more uneven, the better."

"What are you talking about?" Toven said. He reached for her hand where it grasped the knife. "The bodies, yes, but not the wings."

Briony's gaze slid up to him as he showed her how he would cut the dragonfly wings. Her eyes ran over his jaw, his mouth, the way his cheekbones seemed to cut the air.

Briony watched her younger self stare at Toven, everything written on her face.

Mallow's consciousness hovered next to hers. Briony could feel Mallow inside her head, looking not at the younger her but at the one viewing her own memories. Briony turned inside her mind and met Mallow's shrewd, smirking face.

In the memory, Toven turned to look down at her, her body jerked away, and the knife fell to the floor.

Like a hook around her waist, Briony was tugged backward in time.

She was at the Bomardi Circus at seven years old, her first time in Bomard. She and Rory were in matching Eversun-green tunics. Her father was shaking hands with Orion, and Serena Hearst stood behind a cool-eyed seven-year-old with gray hair.

"They'll enter school together, I believe," her father said conversationally.

The gray-haired boy rolled his eyes.

She zoomed forward, lights bursting behind her eyes. Toven Hearst twirled his fingers and sent a cool breeze her way. She shivered and glared at him.

Mallow shoved them forward. Briony was in an itchy dress and Toven's hand was pressed to her back as he twirled them around the Biltmore dance floor.

"No?" Toven said to her, lowering his eyes to hers, bringing their faces together. "You don't know what I'm thinking now?"

Briony felt Mallow behind her, watching over her shoulder. Dancing with them.

Toven's eyes glittered, and her breath caught. "I never know what you're thinking."

Mallow could hear her heartbeat, feel the shiver across her skin.

She ricocheted forward. Her back slammed against a stone wall in a dark abandoned hallway, and Toven's hand was on her jaw, glaring down at her.

"Don't speak on things you don't understand," he hissed.

"I know *exactly* what I'm talking about."

"Your brother will be a head on a spike one day, and your body will be dragged through the street once Mallow has her way." His eyes glanced down. "And such a shame for such a fine body."

She spat on his face. He glared at her in shock. And then a smile crept across his features, curving and unfurling. Briony's breath was hot on his face, but his hand was cool against her cheek.

His body pressed up against her, pinning her in place. Her eyes widened to feel the long lines of him as he towered over her.

"If you insist on forgetting your manners, Rosewood, then maybe I'll be tempted to forget mine," he whispered against her mouth.

And with an abruptness that echoed of breathing air after drowning, she was alone in her mind. And Mallow was there with her in the grand hall, standing before her body as it hung limply in midair. She examined Briony through narrowed eyes, as if she'd presented an unexpected problem.

Briony's head felt the absence of Mallow's mind like a brain freeze, something chilling filling the plates of her skull.

Mallow released her magical hold on Briony's body, and it crumpled to the ground, legs bending in odd directions. It hurt to keep her eyes open, but Briony stared up at Mallow, seeing a slow idea forming in her eyes, a realization.

She knew that Briony once had feelings for Toven Hearst.

"Oh dear." Mallow tsked condescendingly. She smiled down at Briony, as if something grand had been given to her. But just as suddenly, her face fell, and she turned to Toven. Her hand shot out.

Briony heard Toven gasp, and his body lurched forward like a puppet on a string. His jaw stretched into Mallow's waiting hand. His legs struggled to find footing.

Mallow turned her black eyes on Toven's, and suddenly it was very quiet while Mallow searched Toven's memories and thoughts in a similar way.

Searched his thoughts for *her*. Briony was sure of it.

A drop of sweat rolled down Toven's temple as Mallow performed a thorough examination.

Briony didn't know how long she had been examined, but this felt longer.

Toven grunted, breath shallow.

And then after what must have been ten minutes, Mallow released him, dropping him to the floor next to Briony. Toven caught himself on his knees and stared up at Mallow.

Mallow smiled. Pleased.

She turned her gaze back onto Briony's weak body. And she chuckled. Briony flinched as the sound of it bounced around the hall.

Briony had—at one time—*yearned* for the man who would hold her captive and drain her of her magic every day for the rest of her life. A familiar boiling in her gut rose up and choked her—the same feeling she used to have in school whenever she'd have to tear her eyes off him. It was disgusting really. To want someone who thought so little of you.

A thought drifted through Briony's consciousness as it barely held together: If she had any doubts about how Toven felt about her, at least Mallow had given her reason to squash them. He didn't feel anything for her. If he had, Mallow surely would have found it.

Briony squeezed her eyes closed.

"Have fun with her, Toven," Mallow said. Briony could hear the smile in her voice. "I look forward to how powerful you'll become once bonded to her."

A shaking voice to her left whispered, "As do I, Mistress."

"Southern Camly," Mallow said triumphantly, reminding Briony that she'd given up more than just her own secrets that night. "Thank you, Briony. That will be all."

Toven bowed to Mallow and yanked Briony up by her elbow, dragging her along behind him.

After they passed the guards at the doors, they cleared the stairs built into the side of the mountain. A sharp tug through a portal sent them back to the grass inside the gates of Hearst Hall.

With Toven's hand over the tattoo, she felt the thrum of warmth as she was presumably locked in again. She kept her eyes on the ground as if Mallow were still there, bearing down on her. And maybe she was—inside her mind. Crawling and feeding on her. Perhaps she'd never leave.

Toven's hand didn't release her arm. His gray eyes searched hers, frantic movements across her face. "What did she find?"

She shook her head. "Nothing of consequence."

"Whatever it is, she thinks I'm complicit," he said.

The wind wove through them, casting his cloak in twisting patterns and dancing along her bare shoulders.

Maybe she could tell him. It was nothing really. *I had feelings for you.* It would be simple, and there would be no weight to it any longer. She could shrug and laugh.

But she was standing in nothing but a nightgown in front of a man whose power over her would go unchecked.

Briony shivered against the wind. She tugged her arm away from him.

"She looked into your head and found you innocent, Toven. So there's nothing to tell." She turned hard eyes on the silhouette of Hearst Hall down the long drive. "I'm cold, and I'm tired. My body aches and now my head is on fire. And my cheek hurts for some *unknown* reason—"

"I warned you not to speak to her—"

"And I'm starving—"

"Once a spoiled brat, always a spoiled—"

"Just let me go to bed," she begged.

Briony had no idea where the groundskeeper's cottage was, but she marched through the grass to the right. He'd said it was close to where she had injured herself.

"Rosewood. This way."

She looked back and found him standing on the pathway leading to the grand castle.

"It's time you were shown to where you'll be staying."

He gestured for her to follow him down the drive to Hearst Hall.

CHAPTER 16

THE FRONT DOORS GREW LARGER and larger as Briony trailed Toven down the path. He didn't glance back to make sure she was following.

He climbed the set of stone steps ahead of her and almost held the door open for her out of habit before he caught himself and went through first.

The entry hall was made of rich marble-and-gold walls stretching at least one hundred feet high. The candles were lit low, and the stairs turned around the entire hall, up to a second floor, then to a third. Above them was the domed ceiling, the most noticeable architecture. Grand paintings of Vindecci's era adorned the high walls in gilded frames.

Briony stared left, right, and center as she met three carved marble archways leading to dark wings. She'd never seen this much marble in her life. It wasn't native to the Moreland continent, so anyone who acquired it did so at a cost.

And he'd called *her* spoiled. Briony took in Hearst Hall, completely overwhelmed with the *wealth*. The marble floor was warm. She could feel it through her slippers. The chandeliers had no spiderwebs; the windows had no dust. It was marvelously taken care of, but by whom?

Toven flicked his fingers to close the front doors, and she ached to use that kind of simple magic again. He moved past her, and her stomach dropped when he started up the stairs.

She'd imagined a cell in the basement, or a nook near the kitchen. As she watched him ascend, she wondered if there were servants' quarters on the third floor. Perhaps she'd have an unfurnished room like the one she'd been in at the groundskeeper's cottage.

But when she followed him up the stairs, he turned off on the second floor. The family bedrooms, traditionally.

Briony gripped the marble banister and stopped on the landing. She braced herself there as remembered conversations flew through her head.

The Bomardi boys talking about what they'd do with their heartsprings once they got them.

The five thousand gold that she was worth because she'd been untouched.

Sacral Magic, which was foreign to her, but she at least understood that there was power to be gained by having sex in a heartspring bond.

"Where are you leading me?" she asked in a voice stronger than she felt.

He turned, several steps down a dark corridor. "To where you'll be staying."

"Which is where?"

"A bedroom," he said simply, seemingly frustrated with her.

She swallowed. "Whose bedroom?"

Toven Hearst stared at her, and she tried to hold on to the times he'd been decent. The way he hated when the other boys were crass. The way he flirted, rather than intimidated.

He blinked once. And his lips tightened.

"Yours," he said, voice soft.

When he turned and continued down the corridor, her breath was still tight in her chest, but loosening. She followed him, letting her eyes drift over the tapestries and wall sconces.

He stopped at a door on the right near the end of the hall, turned the knob, and stepped aside to allow her in first. When she approached, he gave her plenty of space.

It was a comfortable room, twice as large as the groundskeeper's bedroom. On the opposite wall were windows covered with thin curtains and a simple armchair. To the right lay a canopy bed and a wardrobe. The bedside table on the right had a candlestick and a decorative box meant for jewelry. To the left of the bed was a door that Briony could see would lead to a private bathroom.

She stepped farther inside and found that the wall to the right of the door had a bookshelf, though only three books were on it.

It was plain yet pleasant. It was the best she could hope for, really.

She turned to Toven, who was watching her closely from the other side of the door. For lack of anything better to say, she said, "It's nice."

He narrowed his eyes and puffed a scoff. "You'd prefer a cot in a closet?"

She shrugged. "I don't know why it matters. I thought heartsprings didn't need their tongues, much less a comfortable place to sleep."

She watched him take that in. "The healthier the heartspring, the healthier the magic."

"Ah, that's good. For you." She glared at him, and he matched it. "What does the heartspring bonding entail?"

"You won't need to concern yourself with that," he said, turning to the door.

She scowled. Oh, of course she needn't worry about it. It was just her magic.

"If you need anything within reason, you can ask the house for it," he said. "Meals, blankets, pain elixirs. It will provide."

He reached for the door handle, and Briony felt a spark of fear that she was about to be locked inside with no access to anything or anyone for the rest of her life.

"I'd like to know where everyone ended up," she said, the words rushing out. "The Eversuns."

He paused, then turned to lean on the doorjamb. "I thought you were tired and cold and hungry and your head hurt and your body hurt—"

She rolled her eyes, sighing at his petulance. "Bless the waters . . ."

"But if you'd like to chat more, perhaps you'll tell me what Mallow found in your head."

"I'm asking about people's *lives*, Toven—their safety."

"As am I," he said. "My family's safety."

He was deadly serious about this, and she didn't know why. Her gaze narrowed on him, and she crossed her arms.

"What are you *afraid* she found in my head?" Briony asked.

He stood from the doorway. "I'm not playing twenty guesses with you. Sleep well, your grace."

He pulled the door shut. Briony heard a lock click, and it echoed in her mind with finality. The walls felt too tight suddenly. She was locked in for who knew how long. Her breath caught, and she moved to the window to look at something that wasn't four walls.

The curtain would hardly keep out light, but she supposed she wasn't going to be worrying about getting beauty rest. She pushed it aside and squinted against the darkness. The room faced the front of the property, but she couldn't make out the gates.

She turned in a circle to examine her surroundings. Moving to the bookshelf, she looked at the three discarded books. They were non-fiction, one a medicinal textbook. The jewelry box on the bedside table held nothing. She tried the doorknob just to be sure she'd heard it lock. She had.

Briony peeked into the bathroom. It was sparsely decorated with marble and brass and a claw-foot bathtub in the middle of the room. She jumped at the sight of her own reflection. She was pale and thin, and her hair was brittle and unwashed. The nightgown hung off her bony shoulders.

Had she eaten since arriving six days ago?

She looked over the gold collar in the mirror, checking for anything she'd missed, but there was no way to open it.

Briony turned to the bedroom, about to ask for dinner. Before she could embarrass herself by requesting food from the walls, she spotted a side table that hadn't been there before next to the armchair by the window. A steaming plate of meat and vegetables greeted her. Her stomach groaned.

The potatoes were scalloped much the way Eversuns ate their potatoes, and her nose recognized a spice from home on the meat.

Briony considered what Toven had said about keeping the heartsprings healthy. There wouldn't be poison in this food, but it still felt wrong to eat it.

What was Cordelia eating? Did Didion get a bed and a bathtub?

Rory's face flashed in her mind, and tears pricked her eyes.

Briony dropped into the armchair, grabbing only the roll of bread and picking at it slowly.

What would they do now without Rory? Was there anything to hope for? She chewed the warm bread and thought of Finola. If she was on the run and able to make contact with others, was that enough? Would Southern Camly or any of the other countries across the sea have anything to say about Mallow's actions here? She'd ended the Rosewood line.

Briony's heart ached. She tried to tap into the vein that connected to Rory, but there was nothing there.

Why hadn't she hugged him goodbye?

Tears fell down her cheeks, and she tossed the bread back on the plate. There was an emptiness inside of her that had gnawed wider and wider since her father's death. Helping Rory and setting him up for success had been her only goal for the past four years, and now he was gone.

Where was his body? Had Mallow truly burned it?

Briony's eyes scrunched in pain: There was nowhere even to mourn him. He wouldn't be placed in the Rosewood mausoleum with their father and mother.

A shaking breath broke her chest, and she wept until the food next to her was cold.

When she finally wiped her eyes and sniffed back her tears, she turned to give in to the dinner plate, but it was gone.

In its place was a piece of paper, words appearing slowly as ink seemed to pull from below. She glanced over the first few lines as they were written.

Riann Cohle—Cordelia Hardstark

Del Burkin—Didion Winchester, Velicity Punt

Aron Carvin—Phoebe Rosewood

Briony gasped, snatching it up before it could disappear as quickly as it arrived. She devoured the information, separating her emotions from the facts.

Was this what Toven meant when he'd said, "If you need anything within reason, you can ask the house for it"? Had the house listened to her request? She watched the words fill out, all her questions being answered.

Liam Quill and his father had acquired Katrina and Simon, a young Eversun man they'd all gone to school with. She felt sick as she read that Canning Trow had bought Jellica Reeve, the woman he'd taken from the cell to test his elixir on.

The list didn't include Larissa anywhere, but of course Larissa was now with Finn Raquin.

Her eyes skipped over the page; there was something missing. Neither Sammy Meers nor his father the general was on this list. But Sammy had been auctioned. He had been the first Eversun called onto the stage. Briony's heart sank. If the Meerses weren't on this list, were they even still alive?

Briony memorized the list of names until her eyes couldn't stay open any longer. She didn't know what she could do with the information, but having a sense of where her friends had scattered to the winds was good.

She crawled into bed with the piece of paper crunched between her fingertips and slept a deep, dreamless sleep.

* * *

In the morning, she woke to the smell of breakfast on her side table. Hot honeyed pastries, spiced sausage, and more fruit than she could eat in a week. Briony picked at the tray and took a bath.

In the wardrobe, she found more empty hangers than occupied ones. There were two plain wool dresses in the Bomardi style, built for the cold, and two clean nightdresses like the one she'd been in since yesterday. There was a dressing gown, pairs of stockings, plain undergarments in pale shades, and shoes for all weather.

She plucked up the underwear quickly as if it would bite her and tugged a pale dress off a hanger. She slipped into the clothes, wondering if they were magicked to fit the wearer perfectly. Magical fabric was a very expensive luxury—but maybe the Hearsts' wealth meant they didn't even consider non-magical alternatives.

The sun had been bright through the thin curtains since she woke, but now she finally pulled them back. When the light greeted her skin, she realized she had not seen the sun since the day Rory died.

Hearst Hall was extraordinarily gorgeous. Where there had been gray shadows at night, this morning there were bright greens. She had a view of the front gates; the forest from which the fox had slunk was to the left. Her room was almost at the end of the wing. She pressed her face against the cold glass and could just see the end of the building to the left, perhaps only one more room at the corner. Briony turned and faced her room, letting the sun warm the back of her neck.

Was this her life now? She would eat, bathe, and sleep all in the same room, Toven Hearst would drain her from afar, and every now and then Mallow would slice through her mind for information.

She tried to think like Finola for a moment. Finola would be searching for an exit, but Briony already knew where the boundary line was.

Briony glanced down at her tattoo. Toven had placed his hand over it to transport her off the property. She could only leave with Toven Hearst.

The idea of using her womanly wiles to get off the property again made her laugh. Briony dropped her head into her hands and rubbed her face. Perhaps she should have spent more time learning a thing or two from Larissa Gains.

Her fingers trailed down her cheeks to her neck, stopping at the metal there. The collar took her magic, and the tattoo kept her on the property. She didn't know anything about either of these magics.

Her limited knowledge of heartspring magic came only from school rumors. Heartsprings hadn't been common practice in Evermore, because mind magicians didn't need them to fuel their power—and even their usage in Bomard had not been much spoken about until Mallow's ascent to power. As Katrina had told her years ago, heartsprings were actually a love-based magic originally meant for marriage. The two-way sharing of magic made each partner stronger. What Bomard had been doing was polluting the purpose, creating a one-way *taking* of magic. She had surmised that the collar took her magic and would soon funnel it into Toven once he completed the bond, leaving her with no access to her own power. And Sacral Magic was another thing altogether—an added push of magic for two heartsprings who were bonded and wanted to share their bodies with each other, sexually. *Canning* had found a way to pollute that as well with his elixir.

As for the tattoos, Briony had no idea where to start. If she had the Eversun libraries at her disposal, she would work day in and day out to find the magic they'd used for the tattoos.

Suddenly she remembered someone who'd gotten around the tattoo.

Larissa.

Finn Raquin had removed her tattoo at the gate, but Toven must have known Finn's plan.

Briony wondered if she could get that answer out of Toven.

Sighing, Briony went to the bookshelf across the room, grabbed a text on medicinal herbs and poultices, the least dry of her paltry options, and settled into her armchair for the rest of the day.

She dreamed about Rory that night. He was in formal black and white, with a rose in his lapel. She watched through a fog as Cordelia met him on the beach in a flowing Eversun gown, and they took each other in heart and mind under the sunset, marrying.

Briony woke up sobbing, unable to catch her breath. She turned into her pillow and screamed.

The next day she did it all over again, reading the second book on the shelf, a history of the Ash Wood in Bomard, meant for children.

And the third book on the next day: a biography of Vindecci's biggest opponent, whom Evermore barely bothered to mention in their history texts.

On the fourth day, she started the medicinal herbs book again.

Every morning, she tried the door handle. Every evening, she stared at the list of names the house had given her. Every night she dreamed of Rory, of Didion, of Cordelia. She woke sobbing. And then she tried the door handle again.

She lost the desire to bathe or change out of her nightclothes, so she simply stopped. When the food appeared, she glanced at it and went back to staring at a page or out the window.

Sometimes she pounded at the door, screaming to be let out, but no one answered her. She threw the candlestick and the incongruous jewelry box at the wall, and either she was incredibly weakened or the brass-lined box could not be broken. She received no attention. She tried to heave her armchair at the window, but the glass didn't crack.

Toven didn't disturb her again.

Was she just to exist like this?

She had no idea what the heartspring bonding entailed, so it was highly possible he'd already done it after Mallow's command. The collar was already on her. She knew heartspring magic was different than boosting. Boosting was a quick pulse of power, but heartspring magic was sustained over time and distance—a long-term supply of energy, unless one became overzealous. Either way, Briony felt no change to her lack of magic. She still couldn't access anything in her mind or her heart.

On the sixth day, Briony stayed in bed. She stared out the window with her head on the pillow, her tears leaving trails over her nose and onto the sheets. She wished to waste away. She could see Rory again, perhaps.

Her eyes were drooping closed against the sunlight when a harsh knock sounded on her door.

Briony jerked up, alert. She wiped her face and hurried out of bed. Before she could invite the visitor in, the door opened.

Serena Hearst entered, a displeased expression on her face. She wore a fitted blue dress, severely tailored in the Bomardi style of long sleeves and a tight bodice, and looked every inch the lady of the manor.

Briony was suddenly very aware of her unwashed body.

"You're not eating," Mrs. Hearst said plainly. "And apparently not bathing."

Briony swallowed, embarrassment rising.

"You must eat," Mrs. Hearst said. "You are not allowed to waste away. Your magic must strengthen Toven's. The healthier the heartspring, the healthier the magic."

Briony frowned, but before she could object, Mrs. Hearst flicked her fingers, and the wardrobe opened. The dressing gown flew out and landed on her bed along with a pair of shoes.

"Come," she said.

Briony slipped into the dressing gown and tied it around her waist. "Where?"

"You'll eat and get exercise. I'll walk you like a dog if I must."

Serena Hearst exited, leaving the door open.

Briony's heart skipped as she tugged on the shoes. She was being let out.

CHAPTER 17

BRIONY MOVED QUICKLY, eager to be away from those four walls, even if it meant spending time with Serena Hearst.

The blond woman said nothing as Briony joined her in the hallway. She only turned on her heel and walked slowly toward the stairs. Briony followed, glancing over the paintings and the tapestries she'd glimpsed in the darkness on her way in. Mrs. Hearst kept a slow pace, and Briony was grateful. Six days locked in Hearst Hall after six days recovering from electrocution after a week in the Trow dungeon . . . She wasn't quite herself, physically.

Mrs. Hearst swept down the staircase as Briony leaned on the railing. Her breath was thin, and she became aware of her hunger finally.

They passed a large window overlooking the back of the estate, and Briony's gaze caught on the large pond she'd seen on her first night. She wanted to ask Mrs. Hearst if it was magic-made or natural but refrained as the woman glanced back at Briony in frustration.

"Come," Mrs. Hearst said.

They twisted into the wing opposite where Briony's room was, and Briony had a host of new doorways to examine, some cracked open, some locked tight. She spied a formal dining room, an informal dining room, a study, and a sitting room—and those were just the *open* doors.

Finally, they arrived at the kitchen, and Briony almost laughed at the emptiness of such a grand room. There was so much food, but no servants, and only three in the house to feed. Four now, she supposed. Mrs. Hearst swept her hand over the counters, gesturing to the fruit and cheese, honeyed pastries, spiced meats, and boiled vegetables.

"Eat," she commanded. Her face was set in boredom, like she was beginning a long list of chores for the day.

A teacup steamed on the counter, and Briony sipped from it, beginning slowly. Her stomach growled as she approached the fruit and cheese. Mrs. Hearst stood in the corner of the room, her hands folded in front of her, waiting for Briony to obey. She nibbled on cheese and apples, but the fruit basket made Briony think too much of the Trow dungeon and the women who were so far from her now. She moved to the vegetables and meat.

"Toven says there are no servants in Hearst Hall," Briony said softly, testing the waters.

"No, there's no need," Mrs. Hearst said simply. Briony thought that may be all she would say, but she continued. "The hall was built from the Starksen stones, before they were declared magically protected."

Briony turned to look at her with wide eyes, her fingers in the middle of reaching for the serving spoon. The stones from the country of Starksen were from the early magic, predating even the system of magical gestures that magicians learned in school. The stones' very existence perplexed scholars and were at the root of phrases like *by the stones* or *stones' blessing on you*. The Starksen stones were very rare over in Moreland and usually appeared as honored marble statues or powerfully protected gatehouses.

"The entire hall is made from the Starksen stones?" Briony repeated.

Mrs. Hearst's cool gaze flicked over her. "Eat, Miss Rosewood."

Briony turned back to the food, ready to ruminate on that later. As she reached for the carved meat, her eyes lifted to the kitchen wall she faced.

On the wall hung a page from the *Journal*, the news source for the continent. Most households in Evermore and Bomard had at least one *Journal* page that updated daily. Her own household staff had one hung in the kitchen as well, but Briony was shocked by what was on today's page.

Sammy Meers's face stared back at her, and Briony's heart lurched.

It was a crude rendering, with sunken evil eyes and hollowed cheeks, but it was him. She'd know those curls and the shape of that jaw anywhere. The headline read: *Meers Most Wanted, Dangerous.*

Her mind whirled. Sammy wasn't dead. He was on the run and causing havoc, apparently.

That same spark she'd felt in her chest when she heard that Finola was still alive flickered again. How many more secrets could she learn from the *Journal*?

She glanced at Mrs. Hearst, finding the woman staring out the window without interest. Briony hovered at the spiced sausages, willing to eat twenty of them if she could just stand here and read the news.

Above the drawing of Sammy was today's date, and below the headline was a jumble of words Briony hurried to devour.

In the latest of killing sprees, a village on the northwest side of the Armitage mountain range was brutally attacked last night by Sammy Meers and his gang of insurgents.

"Are you finished?"

Briony jumped. Mrs. Hearst tilted her head at her. Briony didn't know how to delay this visit long enough to read more of the journal pages.

"Yes," Briony said, grabbing one more bite and glancing through the words again for any other familiar names or locations. She saw descriptions of people, but nothing stuck to her.

Mrs. Hearst gestured for Briony to follow her out of the kitchen. She hadn't noticed Briony's attention on the *Journal* page. Briony let her gaze rest on Sammy's face one last time, determined to find a way back to the kitchen and the source of information.

Briony was still considering how likely the chances were of Mrs. Hearst bringing her to the kitchens again if she staged a hunger strike when she realized they were walking in a different direction than before.

Her eyes took in more of Hearst Hall, trying to track which side of the castle they were on now.

"Where are we headed?" she asked finally when Mrs. Hearst led her past a sitting room before turning around the way they came.

"I'm walking you," Mrs. Hearst answered stiffly. "Seeing as you can't be bothered to do so yourself."

Briony pressed her lips together at the presumption that she *could* take herself for a walk, then followed the blond woman past a door ajar. Mrs. Hearst flicked her wrist, and the door closed with a click. Briony's pace stuttered before continuing. No other door had drawn Mrs. Hearst's attention like that. Letting her gaze take in as much of the corridor as possible, Briony memorized where they were—near the kitchens in the northwest wing, facing the back of the house next to a tapestry of the Ash Wood forest.

Briony stayed three paces behind Mrs. Hearst as they continued, finally pouring out into the entry hall with the staircase again. She glanced up at the sun cascading brightly through the domed ceiling, feeling the warmth of it on her skin and below her feet on the marble.

But instead of taking her up the stairs again, Mrs. Hearst walked her through to the other wing. Her mind spun with all the new paintings and tapestries and doorways to memorize. They were in the same wing as Briony's bedroom, but the floor beneath. A large set of double doors to the left were open and inviting, and Briony gasped as Mrs. Hearst led her past them.

A library.

It was the size of a small bookshop. Perhaps a large bookshop, as Briony couldn't see to the back wall. Tall as a grand ballroom with stacks reaching high to the ceiling, there was a half staircase up to a landing that housed even more shelves.

"Come."

Briony jerked her gaze to Mrs. Hearst and realized she had stopped to stare. Mrs. Hearst's expression was neutral but impatient. Briony gave the grand room one last glance before following Mrs. Hearst down a hall and up a simple staircase to the second floor. They twisted back to Briony's bedroom door, and Briony's breathing was labored by the time Mrs. Hearst led her inside.

"Please wash today, Miss Rosewood," she said in a voice that brooked no argument.

Briony nodded, embarrassment flooding her at Mrs. Hearst's gaze over her hair and oily skin. Mrs. Hearst stood in the doorway, and Briony wondered if she would wait for Briony to start the water.

"You must accustom yourself to this place," Mrs. Hearst said suddenly. "It may feel like a prison, but it really is not so bad. It is an elegant cell, is it not?"

Briony felt a hollow wind inside of her, settling around her ribs. She nodded in agreement for lack of anything else to say. Her mind was far away, on that *Journal* page in the kitchen, wondering how she could get walked around again.

Mrs. Hearst sighed, standing tall. "I'm sorry for all that you've lost, but I cannot offer you more than the assurance that Hearst Hall is the safest place for you."

It was the second time Briony had heard those words, and she understood them no better. Mrs. Hearst's gaze was even, and though she offered some comfort in her words, her tone did not show it.

Briony needed to gain this woman's trust somehow. Perhaps the "grateful prisoner" act was best.

"Thank you for lunch, Mrs. Hearst," Briony said softly. "The walk and the conversation did me some good, I think."

She was just about to smile and promise to bathe when Mrs. Hearst spoke.

"You may call me Serena."

Briony's eyebrows lifted in sudden surprise. For the first time on the woman's face, there seemed to be a hint of a smile there.

Mrs. Hearst—Serena—left the room, closing the door with a soft click. Briony stared at the spot she'd stood, waiting for the moment to make sense. She sat in the armchair, thinking of how best to force Serena's hand to "walk" her again, when she realized—

Briony hadn't heard the lock turn.

Jumping to her feet, she moved to the door, and with a shaking hand she pressed the handle.

It turned. It opened.

Briony's heart was pounding as she cracked the door open and peeked out.

She heard footsteps on marble down the hall, and she quickly closed it again. After five minutes of tense silence, she tried the handle just to be sure. It turned.

Had Serena been so distracted by her words of comfort that she had forgotten? Would she remember later?

Briony moved to the bathroom and filled the tub in a daze. She would try in the evening, when the house was asleep.

She would spend all night with the *Journal* page, draining it dry of information. Her chest burned with the possibilities.

* * *

At midnight, Briony stood barefoot in a clean dress, twisting her fingers and watching the clock move too slowly.

She waited a handful of minutes before opening the door and slipping out. Following the same path Serena had walked back with her, Briony took the small staircase instead of the grand one in the entry hall. She passed the library and paused only a moment before deciding her first priority was learning what was happening outside these walls.

The shadows of Hearst Hall taunted her every step, and the dim sconces seemed to flicker once she'd gotten close to them. She paused at the entry hall that she'd need to pass through to get to the other wing. The glass dome in the ceiling cast moonlight in odd angles over the walls and statues.

On quick feet, she silently skittered over the marble. It was easy to find the kitchen again. She made sure she was alone before grabbing a forgotten candlestick on a shelf and tilting the candle's wick to one of the barely lit sconces.

Briony hurried to the page on the wall, finding that day's news still up with Sammy's pictures. Vindecci himself had created the *Journal* nearly six hundred years ago to connect people all over the continent by sending news and information directly onto each household's page.

Touching her fingertip to the page, she whispered to the thick parchment, asking it to show her the news on the date of the eclipse—the day Rory had died. The ink drained and re-formed.

She read page after page of Bomardi propaganda, trying to find the cracks in the celebrations and successes. She skimmed the passages about the burning of Rory's body, unable to read the details, and focused instead on looking for three names: Sammy Meers, General Billium Meers, and Finola Rosewood. The day of the auction was reported on with information matching the list the house had given her. She noticed that Sammy Meers's fate was not mentioned in the *Journal*, either, despite him being the first to be auctioned.

Briony's skin tightened with a realization. Sammy had been on the stage when Larissa had attacked that guard and started the scuffle backstage. He must have escaped in the chaos. She breathed deeply, thanking the waters that something good had come out of that failed attempt.

The first mention of Sammy Meers came eight days after the auction. Briony counted the dates in her head, remembering that she had just come from visiting Mallow with Toven two nights before.

BREAK-IN AT BURKIN ESTATE

Del Burkin is dead this morning after a horrible tragedy at his estate last night. This coordinated and ruthless slaughter took place in the middle of the night and resulted in the kidnapping of Burkin's heartsprings.

Sammy Meers, escaped Eversun prisoner and known rabble-rouser, along with an unknown assailant skilled in "cloaking," or mind-control magic, killed Del Burkin in his bed and absconded with his two heartsprings.

Briony's fingers curled around the edge of the counter in desperation. Her eyes flew over the words again and again. Del Burkin was somewhere on the line, wasn't he? Someone's successor, she thought. The unknown assailant had to be Finola. Briony knew no one else on the run who was skilled enough in cloaking to be of note. But one other thought swirled in her mind: Burkin had bought Didion and Velocity Punt at the auction.

Sammy, Finola, Didion, and Velocity . . . Her throat clicked on hope as she swallowed it down. With Sammy's wily scheming, Finola's connections and skills, Didion's loyal bravery, and Velocity's tenacious fight, Briony would put money on that team in a heartbeat.

Her fingers were shaking as possibility bloomed in her chest. The rebellion was building.

She skipped ahead in the dates, finding another mention of Sammy and a description of Velocity: *dark-brown skin, missing left forearm.*

She pressed her eyes closed, sucking in a short breath. The tattoo. If Briony cut off her arm, she could get around the tattoo.

Briony tried to imagine it. Tried to think of Velocity at the boundary line of some gothic structure, staring at Sammy until she gave him the go-ahead to mutilate her. Sammy and Finola would have killed Burkin first, thinking that would do it—that the heartspring would be free if her master was dead. Another piece of information to file away: The death of the master didn't free the prisoner.

Had Didion cut off his arm as well? Her eyes welled with tears.

And did they have their magic back after Burkin died? Briony searched for mentions of a collar on Sammy or Velocity in their descriptions but found nothing.

Briony considered her own options. She could steal a kitchen knife right now and hack her way through her own flesh and bone.

Where would she go—armless and bleeding without magic? How would she find Sammy and Finola? Surely there had to be another way around the tattoo that didn't involve putting herself in such a vulnerable position.

Briony took a deep breath and whispered, "Next page, please," to the *Journal.*

The sconces flared to life in the kitchen.

She whipped around and found Orion Hearst leaning in the doorway, his shrewd eyes on her.

"Ah," he said. "It's always so disappointing to find vermin in the kitchen."

CHAPTER 18

RIONY'S PULSE WAS FLUTTERING, her muscles begging her to run. Orion stepped into the kitchen, stalking toward her with his arms crossed. She stepped backward, curling herself into the corner. He looked her up and down, then leaned in to view the *Journal* page. Every movement seemed exaggerated, as if he was playing with her.

"Ah, yes. Sammy Meers," he said, tapping the page. "I've been looking for him. Any idea where he might be, Miss Rosewood?"

He tilted his head at her, and Briony pressed back, hoping to become as small as possible.

"No," she said softly, when she finally realized he was waiting for an answer.

Orion turned and strolled around the counter, dragging his fingers over the knife block. A ring with a dark gemstone caught the light.

"And what might you be doing out of your room at this hour?" he asked.

"Couldn't sleep," she lied.

"And you found some reading," he said, lifting his eyes to her. He faced her. "I've been away on a mission for several days now, Miss Rosewood, so imagine my surprise to see how your circumstances have changed in that time."

Briony wondered what mission it had been, but before she could think long on it, he continued.

"Was it my son or my wife that let you wander about my house unchecked?"

Her knees were weak under his gaze.

"Neither. An unlocked door presented itself."

His lips curled in a condescending grin. "What luck for you." He rolled his shoulders. "Back to your room, Miss Rosewood. We wouldn't want you wandering through the estate boundary again without Toven there to *rescue* you."

He stepped aside and gestured for her to lead the way.

Briony squeezed past him and rushed into the corridor, through the entry hall, and up the stairs. She glanced down from the landing to see Orion Hearst following her slowly, like a predator ready to put on speed at the end. She barricaded herself in her room, with panting breaths, putting the armchair between herself and the door.

The lock clicked.

Briony pressed her eyes shut, trying to calm herself. Her chest pounded while her mind buzzed with everything she'd just learned. Her gaze slid to the windows.

There were Eversun rebels out there. Even now they may be on their way for her. The *Journal* page she'd read earlier today said that Sammy was "attacking" a village on the northwest side of the Armitage Mountains. That was the mountain range hugging Hearst Hall.

Briony moved to her window, staring out. There was a spark in her heart, catching fire. She reached for her magic, and she wasn't surprised when it didn't respond. Touching the collar around her neck, Briony knew she needed to get into the Hearst library. The tattoo or the collar—either or both could be solved with the right book, she knew it.

She just needed one of the Hearsts to let her out again.

*　*　*

Briony stopped eating again. Only this time, she was hungry.

Every morning she salivated over the breakfast tray, every afternoon she hid in the bathroom from the lunch tray, and every evening she stared at the dinner tray until she was faint.

It only took three days this time before there was a knock on her door, but now it was Toven.

He opened the door as she stiffly got out of bed, glad she'd at least been bathing and changing out of her nightgown this time around. His eyes raked over her and then cast to the lunch tray that had been calling her name for an hour. He wore a navy shirt with a light-blue waistcoat, and the combination made her stomach tumble, causing her to wonder what kind of hunger she truly felt.

When he glared at her and slipped his hands into his trouser pockets, she leaned on the bedpost and matched his expression.

"Do you plan to wither away in here?" he asked.

"Well, there's nothing else to do."

Something sparked behind his eyes. He looked away from her and strolled farther into the bedroom, heading for the lunch tray near the window.

"You need to eat. You need to remain healthy as my heartspring."

She narrowed her eyes at him. "I have to say, that's not the most compelling argument for me. Does my magic have a different *flavor* when I'm weak, Toven? Does it not *taste* the same? Is that golden heartspring magic not as succulent?"

"Sounds like someone's hungry," he muttered, picking up a tart and popping it between his lips.

She watched his mouth move, his jaw chewing, his tongue swiping out for the sugar on his lips. She glanced away.

"So, what's the plan, Rosewood?" he asked, plucking up a honeyed pastry next—her favorite, the sticky buns with sugar crystals on top. He bit into it and stared at her. "Are you waiting for someone to take you to the kitchen again so you can read the *Journal* page?"

Her eyes lifted from the pastry. She didn't bother looking innocent.

He sauntered toward her with all the swagger she remembered from school before he'd become cold and unreadable. Her gaze moved between his chewing jaw and the second half of the pastry in his hand.

"Are you waiting for someone to forget to lock the door again?" he asked slowly, coming to stand in front of her. She had to tilt her head back to meet his eye.

"Well, if you're offering," she said.

His lips twitched. He brought the bun up between them, and she prepared to watch him finish it, to bite back a pained groan over how hungry she was. But then the sweet pastry was extended to her lips.

And her mouth opened before she could stop herself.

Briony's eyes fluttered shut as Toven softly pushed the bun into her mouth, his thumb tugging on her bottom lip as he pulled away. The sugar burst on her tongue, and her stomach was tight and loose all at the same time. When her eyes opened, she realized she'd just let Toven Hearst feed her. During her hunger strike.

He stared down at her triumphantly, sucking the sticky honey off his thumb before stepping back. She swallowed thickly.

"Do you need me to hand-feed you at every meal? Or do you think you can manage now?"

Her cheeks burned and she straightened.

"If you want your heartspring healthy and happy, then I need more to do, Toven. More to read." She breathed deep and said boldly, "I'd like access to the library."

He laughed. And he was so handsome, it pained her.

"The library," he repeated.

She stared at him, waiting for him to concede, knowing he wouldn't.

"You can tell me what you're eager to read, and I'll bring it to you," he said.

"No."

He scoffed. "No? You don't want me knowing what books you're reading, Rosewood?"

"No. I first plan on looking up 'How to maim and torture Toven Hearst,' and I'd hate to tip you off to my methods."

He sauntered forward. "You—a prisoner—wish to have unlimited access to one of the world's most expansive libraries," he said. She swallowed and kept his gaze. "And what do I get out of this bargain, Rosewood? You do plan to barter something, yes?"

Briony's skin chilled, and her heart beat faster. There was nothing in his expression that led her to believe he was threatening her. Her pause, though, seemed to make him reevaluate his words. His playful expression dripped off his face.

"What do you want?" she asked quietly.

Toven blinked. Then he sneered at her with a laugh, stepping back and turning to the windows.

"My, my. What would the royal family say. Bargaining with your body so soon into our arrangement. And all it took was a honey bun—"

"I wasn't offering my body," she said quickly. She lifted her chin. "I just meant, what do you want? To know what Mallow found in my head? To know where Sammy Meers might be?"

Toven's eyes flickered over her. He pursed his lips and looked down.

"Don't show your hand when you're bartering with information, Rosewood," he said wryly. "What's in your mind can be taken from you."

Her brows drew together. By Mallow? Was that what he meant? Before she could ask, he sighed and nodded at her tray.

"Eat, then I'll give you five minutes in the library," he said.

Her breath caught. "Fifteen minutes."

"Ten."

"Deal."

She moved to the lunch tray on shaking legs, hoping she wouldn't faint in the handful of steps she took to the side table. Briony devoured half a sandwich and a few vegetables before grabbing another honey bun and patting her mouth with the cloth napkin. She took a sip of tea to wash it down.

"Ready," she said, biting into the bun.

He tore his gaze from her mouth and walked out the door.

She followed him down the corridor and down the stairs, chewing thoughtfully. She had no idea what kind of books to look for. Magical brands, perhaps? Cross-reference tattoos and boundary lines?

Toven pushed open the double doors, and Briony stumbled at the sight again. She thought she'd imagined how large the library had been, but she hadn't.

As she stepped inside, the smell of old books filled her senses. She wanted to zoom through the stacks and bleed the Hearst library dry of information. There was a long table for spreading out research on the right, and comfortable couches and chairs in the middle.

Toven moved to an oversize book in the left corner. "This is the cata-log. You can ask for a subject or a specific title and the books will organize themselves, either by guiding you with a navigator light or bringing the books directly to you."

Briony nodded but steered clear of it, not wanting any traces left of what she was researching. She climbed the six stairs to the upper landing and turned around a stack to find rows and rows of books. She gasped, loud in the quiet hum.

"Ten minutes," Toven reminded her from near the door.

Briony moved to a section on magical protection, cracking open spines on boundary lines and estate magic. She was searching her fifth table of contents when a terrifying thought crossed her mind.

Her *mind*.

The images she saw . . . the things she read . . .

Mallow could see them all if she looked into Briony's mind again.

And hadn't Toven just said: "What's in your mind can be taken from you."

It wasn't just her important memories that Mallow would have access to. She could see anything Briony did, no matter how mundane. Pages and words and information. Her favorite things.

Briony put back the book with shaking fingers, knowing that research-ing the tattoos was enough to incriminate her. She'd never been afraid of her own mind before.

Staring at the shelves of a library so dark and powerful that it could defeat Mallow and all Bomard with only its pages wielded by the right per-son, Briony realized she couldn't use any of it.

She stepped back, breathing hard. There was nothing she could research. Nothing was safe. She blinked quickly at the stacks, focusing on her breath, feeling a sharp pain in her ribs.

Her mind wasn't her own. She felt Mallow's presence inside still, slick like oil. Perhaps she wouldn't ravage Briony's consciousness again, but could she count on it?

She leaned back on the shelves, closing her eyes. "How do I keep her from reading my mind?" she whispered to herself, scarcely more than air.

The sound of shuffling to her left snapped her eyes open. A book slithered from a shelf down an aisle and floated, as if it had been called. Blinking, she peered between the shelves to see if Toven was calling books from the catalog at the front.

He sat in the armchair with one leg crossed over the other. It wasn't him.

But still the book hovered. Briony moved down the aisle, walking carefully toward the text. Close enough to grasp it, she read the spine.

Mind Barriers for Beginners

Her heart stuttered in her chest as she reached for the thin book. It fell into her hands like an apple from a tree. She stared at the cover blankly for a minute before she flipped to the table of contents, fingers trembling.

It was a book on shielding one's thoughts. Briony frowned. Had the library heard her? Did the catalog provide help without prompting? Perhaps this was more of the magic of the stones in Hearst Hall.

Mind barricades would be the best protection from Mallow's probing, but it was a magical ability. And she didn't have magic.

She read the chapter titles:

Meditation

Clearing Your Mind

Walls and Doorways

From the little she knew of mind barricades from her own reading, they required a focused mind. It was extremely advanced stuff. Year fives barely touched on it before leaving school, but these first chapters sounded simple enough, possibly non-magical.

Briony slid the thin book into the slipcase of a large text on agriculture and quickly glanced through the fiction shelves, grabbing two of her favorite books as decoys.

When she descended the stairs, Toven checked his timepiece in surprise. "Would you like the last twelve seconds or are you done?"

She swallowed thickly and smiled. "I'm done."

Briony felt like a child that had stolen from the marketplace, waiting to see if she'd be caught by the vendor. Toven looked at the spines in her arms, seeing only the agriculture slipcase and two novels.

He led her out of the library, and Briony sent one last loving glance over her shoulder. They walked upstairs in silence, and he opened her door for her. She held the books to her chest like a shield.

"You'll be eating from now on then?" Toven said, one hand on the doorknob.

"Until I run out of things to read," she said lightly.

He frowned at her and shut the door. The lock turned.

Briony dashed to her bed, dropping the books and flipping open *Mind Barriers for Beginners*.

She still didn't know how far she could get without magic. When Finola had taught her cloaking, there were *weeks* of only meditation. Finola had an entire room dedicated to meditation. Briony had been inside it once, but it was so blank that it had dizzied her. No windows, white walls, and the door disappeared once it was closed. She'd gotten claustrophobic and needed to leave.

Briony looked around her bedroom, grateful for the first time that there was no distracting decor or large pieces of furniture. She could perhaps create her own meditation space.

She read all night, devouring the techniques in the book. The next day, she put them into practice, finding familiarity in the same meditations from her cloaking studies. So much of it reminded her of Finola that she burst into tears after an aggressive hour of concentration, feeling completely worn out.

Briony slipped into bed early and tried to focus on emptying her mind before sleeping, but dreams spun into her head like spiderwebs.

*   *   *

Her consciousness lifted from her dreams in slow waves, a weightless floating back to the surface. Every time she dipped back into dreaming, Rory was there. She wanted to stay there, in a place where her twin was still alive, but something tugged her relentlessly toward the surface.

Untwining her wishes and memories, Briony felt a pricking across her skin, her body dragging her back into her bed at Hearst Hall, where Rory was dead. Her arms prickled with goose bumps, and that familiar sensation of watchful eyes washed over her.

There was a soft tug at her hair, tickling at her neck.

Her lashes fluttered, and she opened her eyes to her dark bedroom. She tilted her head to the door, certain for a moment that she hadn't been alone. That a hand had passed through her hair, a gaze steadily watching over her.

That maybe someone had come to check on her.

She blinked away her silly thoughts, twisting her legs in the sheets, and turning over to her other side to snuggle in.

A shadow in the darkness moved.

And a low growl breathed hot air across her face.

Briony screamed as the gray fox from the forest pushed a paw into her chest, holding her down. It stood for a moment above her, canines bared, hot meaty breath gusting over her frozen skin. Then it snapped its jaws, and its teeth sank deep into her neck.

CHAPTER 19

I T WAS HEAT AND PAIN and a white-hot agony, and her scream broke off in a gasping cry. Briony kicked her feet and tried to push the fox off, but her muscles were still too weak from starving herself.

The fox unlatched its teeth and snarled at her again, its jaw glistening red in the moonlight. It reared back to attack again, and Briony cast up her arms, protecting her face.

Teeth slashed at her forearm.

"Vesper."

The room shook with the word that sounded like a command, and Briony peeked through her arms to see Toven in the center of the room in only his pajama bottoms. His eyes were wild but concentrated on the fox that had turned over its shoulder to growl at him.

"Vesper," he repeated. "No."

Briony momentarily forgot the gashes to her neck and the hot sensation of life leaving her. She could only watch as Toven stood perfectly still, commanding the animal as if he was its master.

Was he its master?

The gray fox huffed, and Briony saw her blood fly from its jaw, speckling her sheets. It turned its head back to her, baring its teeth. And then it lifted its paw from her chest, and Briony rolled to the side as quickly as she could. The room spun as she tumbled off the bed and pushed herself flat against the wall, watching in anticipation as the gray fox turned to face Toven again.

His hands were at his side, as if he wasn't afraid for his own safety at all.

They stared each other down, Toven standing half-naked in the moonlight, and the bloody fox on the bed.

And without knowing what passed between them, Briony watched the fox hop from the bed and trot out the door.

Adrenaline drained from her body, and her vision spotted black. She tried to put pressure on the bite, but the collar was in the way. She felt the wall behind her moving sideways. She braced for hitting the ground, but it never came.

"Rosewood."

She opened her eyes, finding herself horizontal and staring up into Toven Hearst's gaze.

Her consciousness dripped in and out of the present. There was a burning in her neck. Maybe less a burning than a humming.

She faded into the blackness again, and when she came out of it, Toven's mouth was pressed into a tense line. She stared up at his lips, pondering the poison that could drip from them. She felt her neck stitch back together as his fingers twisted through difficult patterns, skimming gently over her skin, pulling the edges of her wound together.

It had been so long since she'd been touched in anything other than force or imprisonment, and she tried to stop her whole body shuddering with pleasure. A sugary thumb brushing over her lip burst across her memory, but she was too weak to place it.

Her body was draped over his lap, her limbs twisted at odd angles and her head against his thigh. His torso gleamed in the moonlight. She ached to trace her fingers over his chest, to feel the softness of his skin against the firm muscle. She imagined her hand floating up, her fingertips slowly placed over his heart, and the shivers that would follow her movements— the gooseflesh she could incite in him. As in their race to the willow tree.

One of his hands moved to cradle her skull, and the firm pressure of his fingers sent a soft sigh cascading from her lips. His other hand reached for hers where it was trailing over his ribs, and he turned her forearm to work on the bites dripping blood down her elbow.

Her neck was sticky with dried blood, but she could feel herself getting stronger.

She tried memorizing his face, his tight jaw, the pale skin of his collarbones that was brushed with color. She lifted her eyes and found him looking down on her.

Briony was vulnerable in only a nightgown. He made no motion to move her, so she still lay across his thighs, with one arm supporting her and the other resting softly over her heart.

His gaze traveled over her throat and chest, and she wondered how soaked with blood the cotton was.

See? My blood isn't gold, she wanted to say.

The cool air over her skin and his attention made her nipples pebble, but she didn't have the energy to cover herself. She could tell the moment he saw the peaks of her breasts calling for attention under her nightgown.

"The bleeding stopped," he said perfunctorily, gaze coming back to her face. "We'll get you some elixirs for the blood loss. You should bathe and rest."

He didn't move. She felt the warmth of his fingertips on her collarbones, his heavy palm over her sternum, as if he was counting her heartbeats.

"Sleep here?" she croaked. "After this?"

"She won't be back," he said.

She watched his face, waiting for an explanation, and finally her addled mind found one.

"She's your familiar," Briony whispered.

Toven seemed to glare at the doorway. "We're still . . . working it out."

A hollow laugh burst out of her chest. It was such a casual sentence. Something couples would say. He turned his glare down to her.

"Shouldn't familiars do the magician's bidding?"

He pursed his lips. "I suppose I've never sought anyone who obeys easily."

His eyes turned to her, as if he just realized what he'd said. Briony felt another shiver crest over her skin. And his eyes dropped to her breasts again.

"Why did she want to kill me?" she asked. "Doesn't she know I'm here by your wishes?"

"She's . . . a jealous creature. We both can be."

Briony watched his throat bob as he swallowed. She didn't want to move, didn't want to call his attention away from her body. She'd felt his gaze on her body before, but never when she was so exposed, so undressed.

The way Toven's arms held her, the way his palm was inches from the swell of her breast, the way his eyes lingered in all the places she'd dreamed of his mouth kissing . . .

Did he want to touch her? Would he touch her? All he had to do was shift his hand and he'd be cupping her breast. Did he know she was aching for it?

His eyes were so soft and his arms warm, and she didn't know how to reconcile the man who had hunted her with the man who now held her so tenderly.

"Jealous of what?" she whispered.

His eyes slid up to hers again. "She understands that you are the new magic source."

Her mind was foggy with blood loss and the torture of his touch, but she tried to make sense of his words. "But heart magicians can have a familiar and a heartspring, can't they? Multiple sources?"

Toven nodded. "They can, but because of your power, your Rosewood blood, I wouldn't have need for more." He swallowed, his eyes flicking over her clavicles and lower. "She would become obsolete if I were to use you as a heartspring."

If I were . . .

Her eyes drifted across his face, wondering if he was aware of his admission.

He hadn't bonded to her yet. She assumed something had been done already without her knowledge, but Katrina *had* said it was a ceremony of sorts. Whatever that bonding ceremony entailed, they hadn't completed it, and Mallow had requested it over a week ago.

"Very jealous, then," Briony said, trying to think of anything else to keep him, but she was too slow.

His muscles moved under her, his hand lifted off her sternum, and before she could help by sitting up herself, he had unfolded himself to standing, with her in his arms.

She instinctively draped an arm around his neck, and he moved with her to her bathroom. He flicked his fingers and turned on the hot water in the tub.

When he set her on her feet, she looked up at his mouth, his eyes—but his expression was firm and cold again. The open gaze over her body had disappeared. Her arms unwound from him, and her fingers trailed over his stomach one last time as he stood from bending.

"Clean yourself up. Get some rest," he said.

He didn't look at her again as he left.

Briony watched the tub fill, wondering at how he'd come so quickly when she screamed.

And wondering at the heat she felt behind his eyes as she lay in his lap in thin, blood-wetted cotton.

* * *

Briony woke the next morning feeling completely wrung out. She stared off for hours, reliving the fox's breath on her face, the sound of her skin tearing. And then piecing together what she remembered of Toven. Seemingly appearing from nowhere, still as stone as his familiar left the room, and then suddenly holding her, healing her.

And the most perplexing thing of all: Toven Hearst was not using her as a heartspring. Her mind drifted through all the possible reasons why not, but she couldn't come to a clear conclusion.

Elixirs appeared with her breakfast, and she didn't hesitate to take them. The pain in her neck and forearm was unbearable.

She slept on and off throughout the day, letting her dreams alternate between snapping, blood-wet jaws and bare skin and hungry eyes.

* * *

Toven did not come back to check on her. Briony was too exhausted with her injuries to try another hunger strike, but even with the door locked again, she had *Mind Barriers for Beginners* to read.

Three days after the attack, Briony was on her sixth reread and finding it very difficult to memorize theories and techniques without the practical application. There were certain meditation techniques that could be practiced without magic, however, that were interesting enough.

Meditate on a cool blue lake with still waters, stretching out past the horizon. There are depths below, but a still and tranquil surface.

Briony imagined the lake at the Eversun school and her favorite willow tree kissing the water.

Or sometimes the task was to focus on a moving target, blurring the edges of everything else. For this, she'd found a large seabird that flew in lazy circles around Hearst Hall, but even as she tried to focus on the albatross and blur the rest, her mind wandered, trying to guess why a seabird would be found in the mountains. One day a large hawk joined the white bird, dancing and diving. She'd meditated on the two of them for hours before realizing she recognized the large hawk. It was Orion Hearst's familiar. Her chest had squeezed tight in anxiety with the knowledge that the man himself was at home at that very second. She stuck to the image of a lake with still waters after that.

The beginning theories were familiar due to her studies in cloaking and blending, the abilities to change form or become unseen, but without a thread of magic behind her eyes to tug on, Briony didn't know what to do with the meditations. Her hand reached up for her neck, fingers running over the healing fox bite as she tapped the cold metal. She needed to get back to the library and research a way around these collars, but what if Mallow was going to read her mind again? Mallow would see her research if Briony couldn't shield it from her.

Briony was sitting in her armchair, staring out the window at the grounds and imagining the Eversun lake in the place of the front gates, when a knock came. She blinked. The intrusion brought her mind back to the present.

She stood, and when no one pushed their way in, she said, "Come in."

Toven opened the door, and her breath caught in her throat. She flushed at the memory of the last time she'd seen him, when he had been wearing hardly anything.

He stood in the doorway as if there was a spell keeping him out. She watched his eyes drift down to her throat. "You're healing well?"

She nodded. "Yes, thank you."

He said nothing else, just stepped into the room and looked over the furnishings. She eyed him, waiting for the purpose of his visit to become clear.

He stared at her bookshelves, his fingers playing with the ring on his right hand. It looked like it could be onyx, but there was also a green tint in certain lights.

Orion had a similar one.

"Is that a Hearst family ring?" she asked, taking advantage of the unrushed nature of the conversation.

He looked down, splaying his hand. "No. It's a symbol of the line."

Briony hummed, a thought coming to her. "Del Burkin is dead. How will that affect the line?"

He quirked his brow. "I see the *Journal* page has been informative," he said. "Burkin was Cohle's successor. Cohle will need to choose a new one now."

Riann Cohle was first in line to the Seat, should anything happen to Mallow. Briony crossed her arms.

"That's what I never understood. Burkin is not a blood relative of Cohle's, but he was chosen to succeed him?"

"Yes. Not everyone on the line chooses their firstborn to be their successor. Some align themselves with other influential families by giving them a place." He gave her a pointed look. "*Blood* doesn't matter to us in Bomard."

She scoffed. "Says the man who will *inherit* his father's place in line—"

"My father and all Hearsts before him have chosen to pass the position to the firstborn," he interrupted. "It is predetermined, yes, but it *is* a choice. The hall and the Hearst wealth follow similar inheritance laws."

"Isn't that odd then?" she asked. "When Cohle does name his successor, that completely random person could now supersede your father in the line should anything happen to Cohle?"

His lips curved. "Yes. But the politics of the line only matter to the line at the moment. Mistress Mallow will live for a very, very long time with the bond from her dragon, and there will be no need to plan for succession. The line is nothing but a symbol now."

Briony's brow furrowed as she tried to pivot the conversation somewhere useful. When he gave no further clue as to the purpose of his visit, she decided to be direct.

"I was wondering when I might have another visit to the library," she said.

He pressed his lips together, irritation clear on his face. "Were you?"

Glancing down innocently, she said, "I find that I need to keep my mind occupied, after being viciously attacked in my bedroom."

He sighed, and she looked up at him as he ran a hand over his face.

"And what of your other books?" he asked.

"I've finished them."

He leveled his gaze on her and hummed. "And you think you've learned all you can . . . about agriculture?"

Briony's skin tightened, and her stomach flipped over.

He glanced down to the mind barriers book on the side table near her hip. The one covered in a slipcase for a book about agriculture.

She was caught. Would he punish her for hiding the book from him? Her heart was in her throat when his eyes returned to her, but there was an intensity in them that stopped her. As if he was asking her an entirely different question.

But he had to know, surely, that there was little she could accomplish without access to her mind magic.

"I've learned quite a bit about agriculture," she said softly, testing. "But I find I lack the tools for a practical application."

They stared at each other, unblinking. Finally, Toven slipped his hands into his pockets.

"You think you are ready for a practical application?"

The room grew hotter, and the walls felt closer. They were dancing on the edge of a knife.

"Yes. I learned the basics years ago," she said, and then as an after-thought: "Of agriculture." Her lips twitched.

Toven nodded slowly. Then he spun on his heel and said, "Come with me."

Briony stood frozen before jerking forward to follow. Her pulse raced as quickly as her thoughts. She'd all but asked for her magic back, and this was his response?

He led her down the stairs, and instead of turning toward the library, they crossed the entry hall to the other wing. Was he taking her to the kitchen? For the *Journal*? She almost asked, but then he stopped in front of a familiar door next to the tapestry of the Ash Wood forest.

Toven's face was guarded as he reached for the handle, and Briony

realized it was the door Serena had carefully closed on their walk. He let
her in, and her gasp echoed off the bare walls inside.

The room was small and completely empty but for a plain white chair.
There were no windows and no other doors. The walls were pearly white,
and an eerie glow seemed to emanate from the room itself. There were no
lamps or candles.

It was a meditation chamber. It had to be.

Briony stepped backward in dread, and her back met Toven's chest in
the doorway.

"No—"

"You said you lacked the proper tools," he said. His hands took her
shoulders and moved her forward.

She spun, eyes wide. "I don't want to use it."

His face was a mask, but his eyebrow lifted in derision. "You *do* know
what this is?"

"Yes, but—I—"

He scoffed. "What did you expect, Rosewood? You bat your lashes at
me, and I give you back your magic?"

He stood on the threshold, blocking her exit. Briony turned back to the
white room, looking it over and wondering if it could truly help her with
mind barriers.

She stepped forward slowly. The door shut behind her, and the wall
swallowed it up. There was no doorknob, just a blank wall. She was alone
in the chamber. The only sound was her heartbeat hammering in her ears.

She sat in the chair, trying to conjure Finola's instructions while staring
at the vast emptiness of the blank walls.

*The white walls help you empty your mind. The world outside falls away. Your
body falls away. It is just your mind.*

Briony swallowed, feeling the same tightness in her chest from years
ago. The room was simultaneously too small and too wide. She stood from
the chair, her legs shaking, and turned in a circle to find the door.

White in every direction.

Her heart raced as she pressed her hands along the wall, desperate to
find the way out. Tears pricked her eyes as her breath shivered in her lungs.

"Please," she whimpered, fingernails scrabbling for any seam she could find. "Please!"

He'd left her in here. She'd never get out. He was punishing her for taking the mind barriers book.

"Toven! Please!"

The doorknob appeared at her request. Briony tumbled out into warm arms. Dragging in deep breaths, she pressed her forehead against Toven's chest and stifled her sobs.

"Don't lock me in, please," she begged, clutching him.

She had only a moment to feel his arms around her before he pushed her to step back. She took a shuddering inhale and prepared an apology for wanting to learn mind barriers—for presuming he would return her magic to do so.

His voice rumbled first. "There are other techniques. Meditation chambers are not for everyone."

He dropped his hands from where he'd curled them around her upper arms. She stood so close to him she could feel his breath on her forehead.

The air between them pulled tight, vibrating like a string.

Toven turned and led her back the way they'd come, taking her to her room. Briony relaxed the farther she walked from the chamber. Her mind whirred with ideas that the panic hadn't let her consider before.

Someone at Hearst Hall used a meditation chamber. Someone at Hearst Hall practiced mind magic, though it had been outlawed in Bomard for five years.

The advanced mind magic skills—cloaking, blending, and mind reading—all began with meditation and a clear mind. Toven had shown an interest in mind magic in school. She'd caught him using it a few times. But Orion would also see benefits in mind reading as Mallow's favored soldier. And what had Toven said?

Don't show your hand when you're bartering with information, Rosewood. What's in your mind can be taken from you.

When they arrived at her bedroom, Briony had more questions than when she'd left it.

She moved through the door and turned to ask some of them directly.

Just then, every candle in the room flamed to twice its size. Briony jumped as the corridor behind Toven seemed to ignite. And just as soon as it began, it was over.

Briony knew this system, as her father had used a similar one. The leader of the realm was demanding the immediate presence of the inhabitants of Hearst Hall.

Toven stood still for a moment, staring at the candles. "I have to go."

Briony's pulse accelerated as she was abruptly reminded that Toven was one of Mallow's skilled soldiers. Underneath his warm hands and his mercurial eyes, he could be as ruthless as his father in battle. He was a killer. She'd seen that firsthand.

"All right," she said.

He glanced at her one last time, as if he wished to say something, but then spun to leave. The door locked behind him.

Briony dropped into her chair, staring at the mind barriers book and pondering the last ten minutes with a racing heart.

* * *

She woke late the next morning. It was past nine when her stomach rumbled, used to a prompt breakfast tray delivery.

It seemed the house was behind schedule.

Briony bathed and dressed, but there was still no breakfast tray on her side table. Instead, there was a note.

Miss Rosewood,

> *I have gone on an emergency. Toven is injured. I don't know when we'll be back.*
> *The house may have trouble, but just ask for what you need.*
>
> *Serena*

Briony's fingers trembled around the paper.

Toven was injured. And it was serious enough that Serena had left to be with him.

She wondered at the small kindness of leaving a note for her. Serena could have left her completely in the dark, but she hadn't.

Briony stared at her bedroom door, wondering what would happen to her if Toven died. Would the tattoo alert her somehow?

A sudden, inexplicable terror seized her ribs, the pressure so overwhelming she found herself gasping for air. She screwed her eyes shut and drew on the meditation she'd been practicing until it passed.

If Toven died, would she go back to Reighven?

She forced herself to breathe.

Briony ran for the door, hoping against all odds—

The handle turned under her fingers. She cried out in relief, hurrying out of the room that had started to press in on her.

She stood in the middle of the corridor, her fingers over her mouth and Serena's note in the other hand.

"Hello?" she called out like a child. She had to be sure she was alone.

There was no response.

Briony moved slowly toward the stairs, piecing together what she knew. Mallow had called for Toven yesterday, and now he was injured. Did that mean there was a confrontation? Had Sammy or Finola or Velicity or Didion done something to Toven?

She tried, but failed, to find a scrap of joy that maybe there had been a victory against Mallow.

Gasping, she remembered the *Journal* page in the kitchen. She raced down the stairs and flew down the corridor. She ran into the kitchen and skidded to a stop, the headline numbing everything inside of her.

REBELLION SQUASHED AT CASTLE JAVIS: ANOTHER ROSEWOOD SLAIN

There was ice in her veins and a cold wind between her ears.

Finola was dead.

CHAPTER 20

MISTRESS MALLOW IS VICTORIOUS AGAIN!

A small rebellion broke out at Castle Javis last night, led by insurgents and Evermore sympathizers. The rocky beach at Javis provided minor cover for the rebels as Mallow's forces gathered and vanquished their foes.

There were limited casualties for the Bomardi at the skirmish, but considerable losses for the rebels who scrambled back to their hole in the ground, their tails between their legs.

In the wake of the new International Portal Prohibition, the rebels attempted to cross the portal barrier by boat, bypassing the line by non-magical means. Orion Hearst was first on the scene, ruthlessly cutting off the boat supply and taking out several essential faces of the rebellion in the process, including cousin to Rory the Slain, Finola Rosewood.

BRIONY SQUEEZED HER EYES SHUT, struggling to take in air.
Finola was dead.
Orion had killed her.
It felt like her chest had been cracked open. Briony's breath trembled.

Who else had died that day? Sammy? Didion? Would they have been mentioned?

She pressed a hand to her stomach and focused on breathing, swiping away the tears pouring down her face. She called back on her meditations.

Think of a lake with still waters.

After several minutes of deep breathing, her eyes dry once more, Briony was able to close off her emotional reaction and focus on the things she needed to cogitate.

There were portal boundaries, limiting travel to inside Moreland only. Although it was rare to portal across countries and large bodies of water, it wasn't unheard of. People with exceptionally powerful magic could manage it. But if Mallow had tightened the borders, if there were now actual magical limitations, that would make it incredibly difficult for people to get out of Bomard.

Was escape truly the plan for the remaining Eversuns? Not fighting?

The lake inside her mind rippled.

Orion Hearst killed Finola.

She braced herself on the wall, feeling breath pull sharply at her lungs.

How many others had died? The article only mentioned Finola.

The words "limited casualties for the Bomardi" ran across her eyes over and over. Was Toven one of the "limited casualties"?

She knew that the *Journal* was probably filled with propaganda these days, but would it actually gloss over the death of one of the Ten's successors?

She took a ragged breath and pressed her face into her hands, trying to find that lake with still waters in her mind. When she opened her eyes a few moments later, a determined fire filled her chest.

Briony marched to the library. It didn't matter if Mallow could see into her mind; she could no longer sit and wait.

The double doors swung open easily for her. She moved to the catalog and called up all books on magical brands. The shelves shook, and books of all sizes slithered out to hover in the aisles. Briony collected each of them and laid them out on the long research table.

She sat herself down and dove in.

*   *   *

The house began to respond to her requests gradually. It was almost as if the walls were in mourning—slow to respond, distracted in granting requests. She asked for breakfast the next morning and received roast duck. It was delicious, but it wasn't breakfast.

Briony checked the *Journal* page first thing in the morning, researched in the library after breakfast, and explored Hearst Hall when she began to go cross-eyed in the afternoon. Pacing and meditation failed to banish the horrified dread in her stomach, so she went out to the grounds and found the boundary again, reaching her arm out to test the tattoo. It shocked her—unpleasant but not truly painful. Walking the perimeter, she kept trying her arm on different spots until her fingers went numb and all her racing thoughts were forgotten. She looked for Vesper in the forest, until she realized the fox must be with Toven as he recovered.

On the third day of her solitude, Briony was leaving the kitchen after a quick lunch when she passed the tapestry of the Ash Wood and the door to the meditation chamber. She pondered, again, who it was that used it at Hearst Hall.

Since Toven was the one to bring her to the chamber, did that mean he was the one who used it? And why had he shown her where it was? Surely it was dangerous for Briony to know about such a room when it implied that the Hearsts used illegal mind magic in some way. Especially if Mallow were to look inside her mind again.

Briony tilted her head at the door, thinking. She reached out to open it but didn't step inside. The white walls stared back at her.

What an incredible risk he'd taken in showing her the meditation chamber . . . unless she was supposed to learn how to conceal its existence in her mind.

Briony thought of the moment the mind barriers book had slid from the bookshelf. The way it had come as if called. And Toven Hearst sitting innocently near the catalog.

If Toven had given her a book on mind barriers and then shown her the meditation chamber . . .

Toven Hearst *wanted* her to learn mind barriers. *Why?* Because he wasn't using her as a heartspring? Or were there more secrets in Hearst Hall than she could possibly imagine?

She gazed into the white room as if it held answers for her.

A chill passed over her as she remembered being locked inside—the way she'd scratched at the wall until the room released her.

Briony's lips parted in thought. She'd believed Toven was punishing her for taking a book on mind barriers by locking her in the room, but he'd been just outside the door, waiting for her. Hadn't he?

It reminded her suddenly of the night Vesper had attacked her. He'd appeared in the center of her room within seconds. She'd never considered where Toven's bedroom was, but if he'd been ready for bed when he heard her scream, certainly his room was nearby.

Briony headed up to the second floor. She checked over every room on the floor, finding nothing. Frowning at her own door several paces away, she considered if Toven had just been passing through that night. If perhaps he'd come to check on her.

Sighing and resigning herself to searching the other wings of the hall in the morning, she turned to go to bed. Something flashed, catching the light, and she stumbled to a halt, turning to see the figure of a fox with an onyx eye winking at her from an ornate carved wooden door.

She blinked back at it. That door hadn't been there a minute ago. It was charmed to blend in.

Her fingers touched the cool brass doorknob, turning it. The carved fox stared at her as she pushed the door open and stepped inside.

This was undoubtedly Toven Hearst's bedroom. Grays and silvers. A Bomardi crest on the wall across from her. A dark-wooded bed. Bookshelves filled to bursting.

She moved inside, her nose picking up his familiar scent. She wondered again if he would ever return. Her chest tightened, and she swallowed.

The bedroom was on the corner of the house, with windows facing north and east. It was almost twice as large as her room, but there were similarities in the design. As she looked it over, Briony realized that Toven

Hearst had set her up in a suite as close as physically possible to him, and yet had not used her as his heartspring.

Why?

Briony wondered if the meditation chamber downstairs only scratched the surface of the ways the Hearsts rebelled against the Bomardi laws and customs. Was it possible that they did not support Mallow as fully as Briony had thought?

She turned her attention to the shelves, to the trinkets, searching for answers.

There was a carved statue of a fox next to a framed sketch of Toven with Finn and Liam. Neither item gave her any information.

Sliding closer to the bed, she gave in to the urge to drag her fingers across the fabric. His sheets reminded her of her life before, when the thread counts were high, and gold and silver wound through every brocade. The bed was made, and when she remembered the way he'd folded his trousers on the dock, she thought maybe it wasn't the magic of the hall that took care of the tidiness. She pulled open the drawers in his bedside table, finding nothing but trinkets. The bookshelf near his bed was filled with familiar titles, and she let her hands drift along the books he kept close to him.

The bathroom had a similar tub to her own, tidy counters, and a mirror she could imagine him in, sweeping his hair back or deciding to let it loose. She examined his products, some with expensive-sounding names. She could imagine him here, stepping out of the tub, wrapped up in luscious towels, taking care of his fair skin with the creams and products in the drawers. Her smile faded in the mirror as she wondered if he would ever complete those rituals again.

She pulled open the closet doors, finding a vast space for all of Toven Hearst's grays and cobalts. She checked the pockets for anything interesting, some clue as to who he really was, and found nothing.

Although rifling through his drawers was a clear breach of privacy, she had bigger issues to worry about. She shoved aside her guilt and pulled open the next drawer.

Laid on top of other grays and blacks was a soft blue sweater that she wasn't sure she'd seen him wear. It reminded her of the rich fabrics she used to wear as the Princess of Evermore. She had to resist the urge to bury her face in it.

She pulled open the drawers against the wall and blushed to find his trunks. Black. Of course. The next drawer was socks—none of them properly paired. She scowled down at the sock drawer, as if it was a problem to solve.

The bottom drawer had extra blankets and a black shoebox. She pried the top open and found nothing inside but a green lace ribbon.

Briony stared down at it for several moments, trying to place it, trying to account for its presence here, in Toven Hearst's closet.

Because the ribbon looked an awful lot like one to tie back hair. Girls' hair.

And as her mind cataloged it, bringing up thoughts and sending others back, she couldn't shake the feeling that she knew this ribbon.

She carefully placed the lid back on the shoebox, feeling like she'd been caught doing something terribly invasive. Leaving Toven's room, she returned to her own, letting her mind run as she leaned back on her closed door.

She blinked, rearranging the ideas in her mind, categorizing her findings.

There was a drawer in Toven Hearst's bedroom that contained a shoebox. Inside that shoebox was a hair ribbon.

And try as she may to rationalize it in any other way . . . that ribbon was hers.

CHAPTER 21

Six and a Half Years Ago

BRIONY NEVER HAD TROUBLE SLEEPING IN EVERMORE. The breezes seemed to sing to her on hot nights, and she never underestimated the benefits of a cool bath instead of a warm one.

But in Bomard, the chill at night turned to pins and needles in her legs. She thought perhaps she was having a growth spurt, like all the boys had, but the nurse had said that at eighteen, she should be done. She'd sent her off with an elixir for relaxing at night, but it was now the third time this week that Briony had rolled out of bed, tugged on a thick robe, and gone for a walk after midnight.

And it was the second time she'd run into Toven and Larissa fooling around in the hallways.

Briony stopped dead as she turned the corner, the itching sensation in her legs giving way to a weighted feeling, like prey ready to run.

When she'd found them three days ago in a similar state of passion, Toven had been crowding Larissa against the stone wall near the staircase, his long body pressed to hers and his thigh shifting forward to press between her knees, drawing moans from her throat. That time, Briony had quietly backed away and run back to her shared suite with Rory, throwing the covers over her blushing skin and just waiting for the pins in her legs to cease.

But now Larissa was seated on the ledge of the window, her legs twined around Toven's hips and her head tilted back, exposing her neck to his ravenous mouth. He had an arm snugly wrapped around her waist; otherwise, Briony thought, she might fall back and out the window. And his other hand had slipped below the fabric of her skirts.

Briony was frozen still as the muscles in Toven's back moved under his thin shirt, and for some reason, her first thought was—*why aren't they cold?*

Larissa's lips parted on a silent sigh.

They had obviously mended things after the state dinner where they'd been playing games, using her as a pawn. It was all but given that they would marry after school ended.

She should sneak away. She should ignore the couple and just go walk the twenty feet between her room and the opposite hall one hundred times until her legs stopped bothering her.

But this was *her* landing. Hers and Rory's. And yes, it was clearly a great place for groping someone because it was so isolated up here by the heir's private suites, but it was *her* floor.

Briony crossed her arms and cleared her throat.

Nothing happened. Toven's arm tightened around Larissa's waist, and she turned his face to kiss him. Briony watched the hungry way his mouth moved over hers, as if Larissa could barely keep up.

She rolled her eyes. "They say across the sea, when the lord and lady become intimate, the entire village is made aware of it. Is that what you're trying to accomplish here?"

Larissa seemed to slowly come back to the present, her mouth going slack and her eyes fluttering open to glare at Briony. Toven, on the other hand, moved his lips back to her neck, unaffected.

"See something interesting, Princess?" Larissa drawled, pushing Toven back slightly. He took a deep breath with his eyes closed, then twisted to land his gaze on Briony.

"Interesting? Not at all," Briony responded. "*Grossly brazen* is the phrase I would use."

Larissa opened her mouth to retort, but Toven beat her to it.

"It must be difficult," he said loftily, "being so wound up that you have to ruin everyone else's good time."

She narrowed her eyes at him. "I am not . . . wound up. I simply think you should fondle each other on your own floor."

His eyes sparkled. "Do you do your own fondling up here? Are you out for a clandestine meeting yourself? Or do you manage that part solo?"

Heat rose in her cheeks. Why were Bomardi so crass?

Before she could snap back, Larissa leaned in to his ear and whispered loudly, "Perhaps her brother *does* manage it for her."

"You spend an awful lot of time wondering what my brother and I are up to, Larissa," Briony said.

"And you seem to care a great deal about our intimacy—"

"I *don't* care!" she snapped. "I just wish I didn't have to see it."

"Perhaps you could learn a thing or two," Toven whispered.

His eyes glittered on her, black pools of desire that hadn't faded yet. She saw him shift his arm, and then Larissa gasped. Briony flushed with embarrassment. He was still . . . working her . . .

She spun on her heel and all but ran away. "Have a grand evening, you two," she called.

"Do come back anytime you need to stretch your legs, your grace." Toven's voice followed her down the hall.

It wasn't until she was in bed again, heart racing and fighting the memory of how their mouths came together, how his shoulders flexed, how his hand slid between her thighs—that she realized Toven Hearst knew about her pins and needles without her saying it.

Which would be preposterous.

Because only incredibly advanced mind magicians could read one's thoughts. Not even Briony had learned the skill yet.

And Toven Hearst was a *heart* magician.

CHAPTER 22

THE NEXT MORNING, TOVEN'S DOOR WAS LOCKED.

"Of course," she whispered to herself, glaring at the walls of the house.

After finding nothing new on the *Journal* page, Briony went to the library and looked up another book on mind barriers, though she knew it was foolish to think she could use the techniques inside one day. Her mind wandered to Mallow and to how one could possibly learn mind-reading skills without a formal education in mind magic. Was the dragon truly that powerful, to help her bypass years of study?

She began to research the dragon that afternoon. Legend had it that the first known dragons were magician-made. The most powerful mage of thousands of years ago, in what was currently known as Starksen, created a dragon and his mate out of the ether. The dragons pledged their allegiance to that mage and completed the familiar bond.

Briony read through sightings of Mallow's dragon over the past six hundred years, trying to learn as much as she could about where it had been and why it could have been called to return. Her research left her with plenty of notes without a central thesis.

When she'd had enough of the dragon, she spent hours reading and rereading the books on mind barriers. There were so many tricks to meditation, but the water imagery in particular was effective. It helped her to think of the lakes of Evermore.

Think of a lake with still waters.

Briony began to walk the grounds, spending a few hours a day near the pond, sitting on the grassy shore and meditating. On the far side, close to the forest, there was a tree on the water's edge, dangerously close to losing its balance into the pond. It reminded her of the willow tree at the Eversun school.

She plopped herself down in the grass near the tree, dropping several books next to her. Gazing at the water's surface, Briony blocked the sounds and smells around her, focusing on her sight only.

Think of a lake with still waters.

A breeze kissed the surface, rippling the water. Briony focused on the depths below, still not visible even after the water stilled again.

The sun dipped lower as she meditated, her hands clasped together, and her thoughts far away.

"You've mastered meditation, I see."

She blinked at the pond, the voice beckoning her mind forward. She turned, and Toven stood behind the tree. She stumbled to her feet, a book falling from her lap. There was a flurry of movement as she retrieved it and he stepped forward.

Standing tall again, the book held tightly in her hands, she met his eyes. "You're back."

"Yes, just twenty minutes ago."

Her eyes scanned him. He wore comfortable trousers and a buttoned shirt. Not a hair out of place. Not a scratch or tremor or bloody stain. But his left arm—he held it across his stomach as if it were in a sling.

"Your arm." She stepped toward him and stopped. She watched his throat bob. "What happened to it?"

"An injury," he said quickly. "It wasn't my intention to leave you alone—"

"What kind of injury?"

He looked down at his shoulder. "A Blood Boil that started toward my heart, and a Bone Dust spell that got my shoulder. I'm almost healed. I just shouldn't use my arm for a few more days."

Blood Boil and Bone Dust. Briony swallowed, visualizing how incredibly painful it must have been to feel his blood boiling and his bones shattering into pieces. Terrible heart magic.

And then she remembered Castle Javis. And the people his father had killed.

She closed down her concern and joy at seeing him alive. "Did it happen at Javis?"

His eyes snapped up from the path they were taking over her clavicles. He examined her, and then it seemed to dawn on him.

"So you've been reading the *Journal* page."

"Is it true that my cousin Finola is dead?" She could hear the blood rushing through her ears.

"She's dead." The answer was swift and merciless.

A heavy weight settled in her chest. "And your father killed her? *My* cousin is dead because of your father?"

"This is a war, Rosewood." He stepped closer to her, and she noticed that he wobbled on his left leg. "Or have you forgotten?"

"The war is won," she hissed. "You won. But of course, you won't stop until every last one of us is dead or in chains."

"How in the stones is this my fault? It was my father who killed her—"

"Just because a few people were trying to escape—"

"No, to kill the woman murdering his son."

Briony's lips opened. And closed.

Finola had been responsible for the Blood Boil and Bone Dust curses?

She swallowed, feeling her stomach churn and tumble as her fingers dug into the spine of her book. She felt a desperate need to turn the conversation away.

"Any other questions, Rosewood?" he said, but it was a whisper in the space between them.

Millions, actually.

"What would have happened to me if you'd died?" she whispered, watching his brows furrow and his eyes clear. "Would I have gone back to auction?"

His face twitched violently, as if he'd been slapped. He stepped back from her, eyes tracing her from top to bottom, and he exhaled sharply. Blinking, his mask fell back into place.

"My mother would have taken care of you—"

"Your *mother?*" Briony laughed, thinking of the woman whom she'd hardly interacted with. "Why would your grieving mother spare a thought for me?"

He swallowed. "She wouldn't have let you go back to auction." But he didn't sound convinced. He looked over her shoulder at the pond, and her confidence faltered.

"Would I have been returned to Reighven?"

His head snapped back to her, and his eyes turned hard as stone. "No. He has no claim on you any longer." She felt a chill across her shoulders, and a darkness rolled off him. "You don't need to worry about Reighven."

She looked up into his dark eyes, searching for the source of it all. "What did you give him in exchange for me?"

He swallowed, and she waited for him to tell her the truth or a lie.

"The one thing he wanted more than you," he said.

Her heart pounded and her breath left her as her mind worked through all the possibilities. "Which was?"

"It's a private agreement," he said softly. "I couldn't tell you even if I felt compelled to."

She glared at him. "Why even buy me if you aren't going to use me as a heartspring?"

He took a breath, and she prepared herself for the range of answers he could give. She thought of the ribbon in his drawer, her bedroom close to his, the way he held her while she bled. She thought of the esteem she brought the Hearst family, the way Mallow had smiled when Toven boasted about the money spent to obtain her.

But she thought about the answer she most hoped to hear, even for all her logic.

That she was more than a heartspring to him. That she was more than an Eversun princess.

His eyes turned to a spot over her shoulder, and his lips pressed tightly together.

"What kind of answer would you prefer, Rosewood?"

"I'd prefer the truth, but I don't assume I'll get that from you."

She grabbed her extra books from the grass and marched past him.

She was boiling. She'd made it ten steps beyond the tree before he spoke. "Rosewood, can't it just be the right thing?"

Spinning back to him, she laughed dryly. "The right thing? The right thing would have been stopping the auction altogether. The right thing would have been not going with your father the day the Bomardi school was attacked." Her voice cracked, and she swallowed.

She shouldn't have brought up that day.

He lifted a brow, and the haughty look he sent her sizzled her nerve endings, firing up her blood.

"But if I'd fallen on my sword, Rosewood," he said, "who would have set you up in a private suite?" He prowled forward, his injured arm hanging uselessly across his chest. Her skin was buzzing. "Who would allow you privacy and leave your magic untouched—"

"I didn't ask for any of this, Hearst—"

"—certainly not Reighven."

Her lips curled back as she bared her teeth at him. "Is it gratitude you're looking for? You want me to say *thank you*?"

"It'd be a fucking start."

His breath was hot on her face. He glared down at her, his eyes flashing. Her fingers itched to hit him, to push him back. She was shaking with it.

"I won't say thank you for something so selfishly motivated. Clearly, nothing you've done has been for the greater good if you need validation for it."

"'Selfishly motivated'?" His eyes dragged over her lips and shoulders, down to her chest. "You're the one who sought out *my* bedroom, Rosewood."

He smirked at her, and she saw red.

She vibrated with the need to hurt him. It shook her every muscle until her hands fisted with her determination not to raise a hand to her captor, and the energy punched its way down her legs. Ready to snap back at him, she stomped her foot on the ground, freeing the electricity—

Toven jerked back, flying through the air as if on a string, his lips parted in a silent gasp. His body slammed against the tree trunk with a crunch, and he crumpled to the ground.

Briony stood, mouth wide and eyes popping, looking for the source of the magic. Looking for the reason . . .

Her fingers shook, life sparking in them.

Her magic.

The collar wasn't working. When had that happened?

Her eyes snapped back to Toven, curled in on himself, wheezing.

Had he granted her request? Had he given her back her magic?

"Toven, I . . ." she stammered, "I didn't mean to—"

He gasped a rattle. His eyes were pale, and his skin was gray. His injured arm still held across his chest, leaning back against the trunk, but his entire left shoulder seemed disfigured.

His shoulder had been dust not long ago, and she'd just slammed him against a tree.

She was running to his side before she could command her feet. Dropping to her knees, her hands reached for him, stopping short when she didn't know where to touch him.

His head turned away from her, eyes squeezing shut. A tear dripping out of his closed eye. He wheezed.

"Toven, can you"—her voice shook and fingers trembled—"can you stand?"

He coughed, and blood sprayed from his lips onto her dress.

Her head whipped to Hearst Hall. "Help!"

But they were too far away, and his lungs sounded wet. She couldn't run and make it back in time.

She looked down at him. "Tell me what to do. Tell me how to fix it."

He wheezed, his eyes locked on her face. He seemed calm. Almost resigned.

She would not be.

Briony dropped his hand and rose to her feet. She turned to the forest.

"Vesper!" She scanned the forest, eyes darting for movement, heart pounding in fear. "Vesper! You must come!"

There was a crunch of leaves to her right, and the sly gray fox poked her head out from behind a bush. The fox let out a high keen and bounded toward them. A gust of relief whooshed from Briony as she dropped back to her knees beside the animal.

Vesper sniffed at Toven as he lay wheezing, and then she snapped her jaws at Briony.

"I know," she said, raising her hands. "Just fix it, and then you can bite me again."

The fox bit down on Toven's collar—and with a burst of wind, they were gone.

She gasped. She'd never seen a familiar's magic up close like that.

She was alone at the pond. She was alone, and she'd hurt him.

Gasping with sudden tears, she looked to his bedroom window—the corner bedroom on the second floor.

The candles were lit inside.

She grabbed up the books she'd dropped and ran. Her legs carried her through the gardens and up the stairs to the entrance. Then she was at the base of the marble stairs, her feet thumping as she ran up to their shared wing, barreling toward the door with the fox carving. The door handle didn't turn. She had to see him.

Suddenly the door flung open, and Serena Hearst's face was there, scowling at her.

"Miss Rosewood. You must let us fix this before you cause more damage."

Briony sobbed. "I didn't mean to harm him, please—"

Toven screamed beyond the cracked door, and she shuddered, craning her neck to see into the room. Serena closed the door on her and locked it before Briony could blink.

She stared at the carved fox, her hand covering her mouth. He'd been recovering for a week, and she'd undone it all.

Briony stumbled back, still confused where her magic had come from.

She felt someone in the hall before she heard them. Glancing up, Briony barely had a second to take in Orion Hearst's vicious expression before she was flung back against the wall, her body hanging by an invisible force, her throat closing with the magic he held her neck with.

Briony's eyes bulged in panic, and her feet kicked at the air. Her shock battled with her fury over seeing her cousin's killer in the flesh.

Orion Hearst snarled in her face, one hand held out as if he were choking her.

"Do you have *any* idea how difficult you make my life, Miss Rosewood?" he asked her, his voice deceptively calm.

She tried to speak, croaking, "It was an accident——"

"It would be so easy to just be rid of you," he said softly. His fingers twitched in the air, and fear choked her as she wondered if he would just snap her neck. Her legs scrambled against the wall. He leaned in to her and whispered, "You wanted your magic back to learn mind barriers? *Go learn mind barriers.*"

He released her, and she dropped to the floor in a heap of limbs. She gasped for air as he spun on his heel and disappeared into Toven's bedroom.

Toven's groaning filled the hallway, and Orion hissed, "The medics told you it was too soon, Toven."

The door slammed, and she listened to the echo of it bounce over the hall.

Briony's heart raced. Orion Hearst knew she had her magic, and he didn't plan on taking it from her.

Briony pulled her legs into herself, trying to catch her breath until her shoulders stopped shaking and the image behind her eyelids of Toven crumpled under that tree vanished.

She lifted her hand and slowly rotated her fingers . . .

The string behind her eyes that felt like home vibrated.

A soft wind filled the hallway, and Briony sighed in relief.

Tears fell down her cheeks with the onslaught of emotions. The simultaneous fear and fury that Orion Hearst arose in her, the hollow grief over losing Finola, and the guilt sitting heavy on her chest for the agony Toven was in. But as she plucked that string of magic again and felt her body sing, all of it washed away.

She kept vigil outside Toven's bedroom, with only one set of thoughts chasing each other around her mind. She had her magic. She'd asked for it, and Toven had given it to her.

The Hearsts must be desperate for her to learn mind barriers, and Briony couldn't imagine why.

CHAPTER 23

B RIONY STOOD AT HER DOOR, her ear pressed to the wood, listening to Serena's footsteps grow closer.

Every day, she left the door to her room cracked so she could listen for a scrap of conversation as Serena went in and out of Toven's room, and every day she heard nothing.

Waiting for Toven to recover from his injuries was somehow even more agonizing when they were only separated by a wall. She suspected his condition was serious, but not critical, as Orion had left Hearst Hall again the day after Briony had injured Toven.

Some days, after Serena had left Toven's room, Briony would creep to his door and try the handle. The carved fox's mocking black eye stared back at her, refusing to budge. She attempted to open it with magic on several occasions, but without success.

Now, a week later, as Serena grew closer, Briony held her breath, waiting for the sound of Toven's door opening.

The knock at her own door rattled her head, and she jumped back.

Serena stood on the other side with a strained smile and folded hands. "Hello, Miss Rosewood. I thought it was time we spoke."

"I'm so sorry, Serena," Briony said, words pouring out of her. "I swear I didn't mean to hurt him. I had—I had no idea that I had magic, and I was angry and—and it just happened. Believe me—I wish I could take it back."

Serena blinked down at her, lips twitching. "Thank you, but I think you are apologizing to the wrong person."

"He locked me out." She shut her mouth with a click, regretting speaking so quickly. "I mean to say, he . . . he obviously doesn't want to see me." Something sparked in Serena's eyes, and Briony felt her face heat. "Or he's resting, I'm sure."

"Resting, certainly. It's been a trying few weeks for him. For the whole family, really."

Briony nodded at her feet. "Is he healing all right?"

Serena paused. "May I come in?"

Briony nodded, waving Serena in and perching on the edge of the bed as the woman fluttered into the armchair.

Serena gave her a tense smile. "His shoulder and half his rib cage needed to be rebuilt, but aside from that, he's in good condition."

Briony felt her tongue stick to the roof of her mouth. Her vision blurred, and she blinked away the memory of his body on the grass, the way his torso had slammed against the tree trunk . . .

She'd done that. She'd broken countless bones in his body, puncturing his lungs. And then she'd fumbled over him for what felt like hours instead of calling for help immediately.

Briony's lip trembled. She glanced back at Serena to find the woman staring at her with an assessing gaze.

"Don't fret, dear. He's healing as we speak," she said. "And if I know my son, I know he probably deserved at least a slap across his mouth."

Briony forced her lips into a parody of a smile. She asked a few more questions, steering away from Toven's health or the battle at Javis that had injured him originally. Serena revealed nothing, except that they had stayed in a cottage on the outskirts of the remains of the castle while Toven recovered, and that Orion was currently gone on a mission for Mallow.

Briony had no desire to press her on either topic.

As Serena stood to leave, she said, "Do be advised, Vesper is in Toven's room while he heals; it speeds the process, as I'm sure you know."

Briony nodded, and irritation flashed in her briefly before she realized she was feeling jealous of a fox.

"Perhaps you can distract yourself with reading," Serena said, letting her gaze land on the collection of mind barrier books that Briony hadn't thought to hide.

Shock spiked through her. It was Toven, Orion, and now Serena who all were pushing her to learn mind barriers. Briony looked at Serena warily.

"Yes, I will." Her voice was careful.

Serena crossed to the door. "Good day, Miss Rosewood."

Briony stood. "You may call me Briony," she said.

Serena paused and gave her an inscrutable smile before closing the door.

Briony sat alone, thinking about the fact that Toven wasn't using her as a heartspring. Why wasn't he? And was that defiance punishable? Was that another thing Briony was supposed to hide in her own mind? Were the Hearsts worried Mallow would see that in her thoughts?

Her mind spiraled for the rest of the afternoon, thinking of hundreds of possibilities.

*   *   *

The next day, Briony tested out her newfound freedom a bit. She slipped down to the kitchen to check the *Journal* page for information. She met no inhabitants of Hearst Hall and no resistance. There were a few skirmishes reported in the page, but no sightings of Sammy, Didion, or Velicity.

The only thing that caught her eye was today's date. A weight dropped in her stomach as she realized Toven was mending broken bones on his birthday.

When she climbed the stairs, she passed her room and went straight to Toven's door. She'd forgotten to try it on her way down to the kitchen, even though it was a force of habit by now—

The handle turned. She pushed open the door and entered the room before it barred her.

Knocking hadn't even occurred to her. She shut the door swiftly once she was through. Vesper sat the foot of the bed, lifting her head to growl in warning, but Briony paid her no attention.

Toven lay against his pillows looking deathly pale. When he saw her, he began shifting, attempting to sit up, possibly saving his dignity.

"Don't," she cautioned, moving toward the bed. "Don't injure yourself further. I'll be quick." She wrung her hands. "I'm sorry. I'm very, very sorry, Toven."

His eyes grew wide, and the color returned to his cheeks as she came closer.

"I had no idea that I had my magic—which, actually, I'd like to ask about, but—no, another time."

She was stammering, and she felt a blush rise from her chest. He pushed his limp hair off his forehead, raking his fingers through it.

"I would never have—have injured you further on purpose. I promise that wasn't my—" She swallowed. "I mean to say, I was just very angry, and I felt out of control—"

"Rosewood—"

"Please let me finish." She stepped forward again, and for a wild moment she thought about taking his hand, sitting at the edge of his bed. "Hurting you was unintentional. I hate your father for what he did to my cousin, but I'm aware that things could be much worse for me here, and I know you're just doing your best—"

"Rosewood, we have company."

She froze, heart stopping. He didn't mean Vesper.

Spinning to the other side of the room, she saw Finn Raquin reclining comfortably in Toven's wingback chair, sipping merrily from a glass and smirking.

"Briony," he said. "So good of you to drop by."

Her lips parted uselessly, staring into Finn's dark eyes as he smacked his lips, drinking in the brandy and the show.

"Finn," she said, heart thrumming with panic. She'd just admitted that she had her magic. How could she have been so stupid? He might have freed Larissa, but he surely had no loyalty or care for her.

Of course he was here. It was Toven's birthday, wasn't it? She looked back to Toven, a strained expression on his pale features, and her cheeks flushed in mortification. The anticipation of seeing him again had been too great, and the need to apologize had overwhelmed her logic.

There was a noisy sip from the armchair, and Finn smiled at her over his glass as her attention returned to him.

"Rosewood, pull up a chair. Let's catch up." He crossed one leg over the other, eyes sparkling.

She gaped at him, blinking quickly before blanking her features.

As she worked to calm her racing mind, it dawned on her that, on balance, Finn Raquin might be the only Bomardi that Briony could make this kind of mistake in front of. He had never cared much for the politics of Bomard, as his mother was Eversun. He'd always remained quiet when the rest of them were boisterous about their plans for their heartsprings.

"I've just come to . . . to clear the air. About . . . something." She glanced to Toven quickly, where he sat up in bed as much as he could, leaning slightly to his right. "And—and I have . . . so . . . Enjoy your visit," she said, nodding to Finn.

She hurried to the door, pulling it open, and in a moment of sheer impulse before she could stop herself, tossed back over her shoulder, "Happy birthday, Toven," before sliding through and shutting the door behind her.

*　　*　　*

She was still blushing when she got out of the bath an hour later, having allowed her mind to concoct all the different ways Finn Raquin and Toven Hearst might have reacted to her flustered intrusion and intimate birthday sentiments. Sighing, she slipped on her bathrobe and tossed her wet hair up in a knot, exiting to her bedroom.

Finn Raquin sat in her armchair, flipping through one of her books—thankfully not one of the mind barrier books; she'd hidden those yesterday. He smiled at her from across the room, sipping on her afternoon tea.

"The water temperature is decadent, isn't it?"

Briony pulled tightly at her bathrobe, her heart pounding under her fingertips. She knew Finn a little, since their mothers had been close. After Briony's mother had died in childbirth, Ember Raquin had become almost an unofficial godmother, visiting Briony and Rory frequently as children with Finn in tow. As they grew older, the visits became less frequent, perhaps due to tensions between the two countries, but she had always offered a friendly word or smile when she'd seen Briony at official functions. From the little Briony had seen of him as a child and how unpolitical he'd been at school, she knew Finn wasn't as bad as the other Bomardi—but then she had no idea what this new world was like.

"What do you want?" Her voice was stronger than she felt.

He waved his hand. "The room was quite difficult to find, actually. Charms and the like." He crossed his legs and smirked. "But I knew it would be close."

She glared at him. "Well, thanks for dropping by, but—"

"This doesn't look like a sex dungeon at all, really." He stood, straightening his unwrinkled shirt and taking in the suite. "I'm quite disappointed."

She stared at him incredulously. "A sex dungeon," she snorted. "And where did you get that idea?"

He turned to look at her from where he'd just parted her curtains to examine the grounds. "Toven."

She blinked, mind twisting to work through it.

"He's very coy with the details of course," Finn blithely continued, "but he said that once he'd completed the bond with his heartspring, that Sacral Magic became undeniable. You two have been at it like rabbits, from what we can tell."

The mention of the heartspring bond—which Briony understood was *not* being used—and Sacral Magic . . . It was possible to have a heartspring bond without experiencing Sacral Magic, surely, but apparently Toven had been crafting quite a tale about what went on behind closed doors at Hearst Hall.

"My ropes and chains are in the closet," she deadpanned. "Who is 'we,' exactly?"

Finn wandered toward her bookshelves. "The boys." His fingers drifted over the handful of titles, then the bare shelves surrounding them. "At our gatherings." He eyed her, his features giving away nothing.

Briony considered her next move carefully.

"How is your mother in all of this?"

Finn blinked once, expressionless. "She's gone. A traitor to Mistress Mallow."

Briony's lips parted. Her chest tightened. "She's gone? What does that mean?"

Finn glanced out her windows. "She was at Castle Javis with the Eversuns. She's either dead or she's none of my concern any longer." He looked at her. "She's . . . gone."

What did he truly feel about it? He seemed so controlled in the way he gave information, in the same way that Toven could be emotionless. She tried one more question.

"Where is Larissa?"

His dark eyes danced over her face, pausing. "Dead."

Briony felt the wind knocked out of her. She resisted the need to lean on something. Her fingers tightened in her robe.

Her mind worked. The last time she'd seen Larissa, she'd been running into Finn's waiting arms . . . as he rescued her.

Her eyes dug into him. "Why?"

"For disloyalty to Mistress Mallow," he responded smoothly. Too smoothly.

"You're lying."

Finn paused. Then shrugged, and said, "Ask Toven." He sauntered into her sleeping area, drawing closer to the bed. He ran his fingers over the decorative jewelry box, almost dearly. "He'd be more than happy to give you more information."

"Wonderful. Anything else? Or can I get dressed now"—he opened his mouth—"in privacy."

He grinned. "I was just interested in seeing the sex dungeon, but . . ." He sighed dramatically. "I'm afraid you've let me down."

"Apologies." She moved to her wardrobe, dismissing him.

"It does tickle me to see how close you and Toven have gotten."

She froze in the middle of reaching for a clean dress. Finn leaned against her bedpost, watching her closely.

"We're not close."

"Yeah?" He lifted a brow at her. "When's my birthday, Rosewood?"

She pressed her lips together, fighting the blush creeping up her neck.

He smirked and sauntered out the door.

*   *   *

All further news of Toven was passed on from Serena. He finally left his room for the first time a day later. He walked by himself through the estate's gardens on the next, and finally on Friday, he left the property for the first time.

She looked for him in the mornings from her window, hoping to glimpse him walking through the grounds, testing his new ribs, but she never spotted him.

Briony had begun tugging at her magic again. It was slow to respond, like a muscle weak from lack of use, but she started small: turning the bath taps, calling books from her shelf, warming her cold teacup. She was eager to try the next steps of mind barriers.

On Tuesday, she moved her meditations to the library, choosing a book on different barrier techniques. One that had resonated with her was thinking of her mind as a bookcase or a series of shelves. Her introductory textbook had included a short summary of it, and she'd experimented with it before using pure intuition. But now she had pages of detail and theory at her fingertips.

She found ideas for bringing other memories forward—in her case, displaying a memory on an easily reachable shelf. Although the techniques were incredibly advanced, Briony couldn't help but soak in the information, always seduced by the most challenging ideas.

Hours later, Briony sat in one of the grand armchairs, facing a large window that overlooked the pond as she focused her mind on still waters and hidden shelves. She tried to bring forward only memories of her father, but it quickly became apparent there were too many other things at the forefront of her mind, making her shiver as they played again and again.

Toven's bare shoulders as he mended her neck back together.

The echo of Didion screaming that it would be all right off the stone walls of the prison.

A body flying backward, hitting the trunk of a tree.

Rory's easy smile on the day he rode off to his death.

The dried blood on Cordelia's temple as she turned to her, pale skin translucent in the spotlight.

Briony took each of them, holding them like books, and placed them on tall shelves, or shoved their thin spines inside larger ones and hid them on bottom shelves. It was like tidying away the things that cost her most— both in love and in pain.

She pulled forward the memory of her father taking them to the circus. Her father's aftershave. Rory's easy laugh at unfunny jokes. An entire shelf was open at eye level, now that she'd replaced the other thoughts. She filled it with happy memories of her family.

"Rosewood."

Her eyes blinked. She was staring at the pond from a deep armchair in the library.

The books inside her mind shivered, thrumming with the energy it took for her to contain them—to keep them in place. Only happy memories of her family available to prying eyes.

"Rosewood," someone said again.

She swam back to herself. There was someone next to her. But if she looked at him, the books would fall off their shelves and she'd be left only with bare shoulders and echoing screams and dried blood—

"You're feeling better?" she asked, drawing breath from her lungs and preparing to look away from the pond and the still waters. "How are your ribs?"

She focused her mind and called on her strength to keep her shields up. Her heart pounded with excitement to look up; to see him again. And she quieted that book, pushing it away.

"Better," his voice rumbled.

Breathing deep, she turned her eyes to him, taking in a tall body leaning slightly to the right, and curious eyes gazing down at her.

Only happy memories of her family.

Her gaze flitted away, her energy focused on the bookshelves in her mind.

"How was your birthday?" She knew her own lips had asked the question, but the voice was unfamiliar to her. "Were you able to enjoy it—?"

"Look at me."

She felt the request in her bones. Turning her head to him, finding his gray eyes, she saw him twitch at the sight of her. He looked down at the book in her lap, then back up at her.

Briony saw him through a haze, recognizing him, but also failing to place him. Her body filled with cotton, her head filled with dust.

She blinked, and it was as if he swam back into focus. Toven Hearst stood next to her, staring down with concern.

Her bookshelf cracked, and the texts fell open at her feet.

She sucked in a deep breath, and his bare chest, his broken ribs, his crumpled body, his cool eyes—all those carefully placed books fell off the shelf in her mind.

Her eyes stung, as if she'd looked directly into the sun. She pinched them closed and pressed her hand over her forehead, blocking out the light.

The advanced mind barrier book slithered away from her lap, lifted away from her.

"You're too expressive for this specific technique," he muttered. "It will be obvious that something is wrong with you." She listened to him turn the page and then close the book with a snap. "You skipped intermediate studies?"

"Of course," she said, her lips pulling in the ghost of a smirk. Her head spun. She felt like she'd been awake for days. "Did you expect anything less of me?"

Her eyes slipped open, staring at the pond through the window again. She tried to grasp onto the idea of still waters, calming her racing mind, but her energy was depleted.

"It can be exhausting," he said, barely a whisper.

She nodded, drowsiness in her veins. She wanted to close her eyes and sleep. But she had more pressing questions while she had him here.

"How is Larissa?"

She watched his eyes harden, like a swift close of a book. "She's dead."

Briony pressed her lips together. "How?"

"She was killed for her disloyalty to Mistress Mallow."

She frowned, watching him closely. "Those were Finn's exact words as well. Curious."

His eyes snapped to her. "When did you speak to Finn?" There was a bite in his words and ice in his eyes.

"He stopped by. Entered my room and drank my tea without a care in the world." She shifted in her seat, lifting a brow at Toven's dark expression. "He also mentioned some fascinating stories you've been spinning to 'the boys.'"

Toven's gaze flickered to her.

"Is your confidence so low that you must describe your conquests in such detail to your friends, Toven?" she asked.

He swallowed. "When the 'conquest' is the Princess of Evermore, yes."

She curled her lip. She decided to push her luck.

"What exactly goes into a heartspring bonding?" she asked.

He looked away from her. "It's an exchange of jewelry imbued with a drop of the wearer's blood. It's different from boosting because the jewelry ties two people together over distance. You have to be physically next to someone to boost, but heartsprings don't even need to be in the same country to share magic with each other." He shifted his weight, leaning away from his weaker side. "When the Bomardi adapted the heartspring bond for their own purposes—for the Eversun heartsprings—they developed the collar for a one-way taking of magic." He glanced at her neck. "The collar siphons all magic—heart, mind, and Sacral—into another piece of jewelry or into a location, like the Trow dungeon."

"But you never bonded to me, despite Mallow demanding it?" she said. "Does that mean you never took my magic?"

He swallowed and answered carefully. "Heartspring magic cannot be taken if it's already freely given."

She squinted up at him, trying to understand.

"*You* started giving away your heart magic to your brother years ago," he said. "Boosting him. My father doesn't quite understand it, but even in your brother's death, you give your magic to him. We think it has something to do with being twins. It created a heartspring bond without the ritual or the jewelry. That's why this collar doesn't work to take your heart magic."

He traced his finger over the gold around her neck. Briony thought that over.

"So my heart magic couldn't be taken because I was already unknowingly . . ." She choked. "Bonded to Rory. As his heartspring?"

He nodded. A surge of sadness crested over her, thinking of Rory and the bond to him that she'd never understood. It was a heartspring bond.

"We kept you on the Gowarnus elixir to keep all of your magic subdued. It was in your tea. Sometimes your food."

Irritation flickered in her as she remembered how Serena and Toven had been insistent that she eat. It was no wonder; they were dosing her.

"I requested that we stop the Gowarnus elixir, so you could access your mind magic for your practice in mind barriers," he said.

Her heart pounded. She wanted to ask why—why it was so important—but she needed to get all the facts straight first.

She pressed her eyes closed, the headache becoming worse. "So in the Trow dungeon, the collar took my mind magic but not my heart magic—because I was already giving it away. Then after I got here, I was being given the Gowarnus elixir." She stared up at him and reached for the band around her neck. "Does this collar even do anything?"

"Not yours. Not at this time. Without us bonding, it's just for show."

Her thoughts were becoming fuzzy. It was too much to work out for now.

She moved to stand, and blood rushed to her head. The mind barrier had drained her far more than she'd thought, and she stumbled back against the arm of the chair.

A hand on her elbow. Her head pounded as she squeezed her eyes shut, registering Toven's touch, the warmth of his fingers on her skin through the thin cotton of her sleeve. When she opened her eyes and righted herself, he said, "You should be careful next time. It can be very draining."

She blinked to find him staring down at her, body close and fingers still light on her arm. He wobbled on his feet, looking pale.

"You're still injured," she said. "You should be careful as well."

His eyes danced over her face, a hint of a smirk on his lips. "We're quite a pair, aren't we?"

She had an image of another life. Another reason for his hand to take her elbow. Another use for the closeness of his body.

Perhaps things could have been different. Perhaps the Hearsts would have been the top contenders for the Rosewood daughter's hand.

Toven's smile dripped off his face, but he held her eyes.

Perhaps she would have lived here after all—in some other life.

The library doors creaked open, and he stepped back from her, dropping her elbow.

"Toven," a sharp voice called from the door, and Briony turned with an aching head to see Serena, her mouth in a tense line. "You have guests."

Toven stepped in front of her as Briony focused her mind on what the words meant.

"Shall I send them to the drawing room?" Serena said firmly, but before Toven could respond, a raucous voice called from the hallway.

"A look at the old library wouldn't be bad, would it, Can?"

Liam Quill pushed through the door with Canning Trow and Finn Raquin behind him.

CHAPTER 24

W ELL, WELL, WELL!" CANNING SAID with a slimy grin. "If it isn't the Eversun princess."

Briony watched in tense anticipation as Finn, Canning, and Liam entered the library, spreading out like a blockade across the only exit.

"Gentlemen," Toven said coolly. "To what do we owe the pleasure."

"It is your birthday, isn't it?" Liam said, flipping through an open book on the research table.

"Last week, but I appreciate the care," Toven said.

Briony met Finn's eyes as he stood near Serena at the door. He looked nervous. And Briony immediately could tell that this wasn't his idea.

"Shall I take the girl back to her quarters?" Serena asked.

"Yes," Toven said, turning to look at Briony. "I was having her refile all the books based on how many times the word *the* appeared." He grinned at her coldly.

"Oh, have her stay," Canning said, throwing himself down on an armchair. "We haven't gotten a chance to play."

"You know I don't share," Toven said dryly. "Mother?" He nodded at her.

Serena moved toward them, ready to collect Briony.

"Have her stay," Canning said firmly, staring Toven down.

Serena paused.

The room watched closely as Toven and Canning studied each other.

Aside from the state dinner when they all stepped in front of one another to dance with her, Briony had never seen how the rank in the line worked in casual social situations.

If this could even be called casual; it felt very charged.

Toven nodded. "She'll stay, Mother."

Serena hesitated before smiling. "Of course. You boys behave yourselves."

"Wouldn't dream of it, Serena," Canning said, twisting his head on the arm of the chair to watch Toven's mother glide out of the room. Once the door was closed, he turned to Liam. "Has Serena Hearst always had that rack?"

Toven tilted his head at him coldly.

Liam snickered.

"Whiskey, anyone?" Toven said. "From Father's private collection." The house obeyed, and a tray with glasses and a crystal decanter of whiskey arrived on the table next to Finn.

Finn began pouring. "So, Toven," Finn said. "How are the ribs?"

"Ribs?" Liam asked. "I thought you shattered your shoulder."

"I did," Toven said, plucking a book from the shelf and handing it to her absently. Briony fumbled with it before deciding to reshelve it for him. "But then I went and played Dodge with Finn and he slammed into me."

Finn shrugged sheepishly. "What can I say? I have a competitive streak."

"Why don't you bring the slut over here."

The room paused and turned to Canning. He beckoned her with a finger.

Briony froze. She was in danger, but she didn't know what Toven could do for her.

Toven shifted to the side slowly, allowing her to move forward. Briony stepped into the center of the room on shaking legs, feeling unwanted eyes dripping over her. She stopped in front of Canning. He was draped lazily over the arms, staring at her body.

"She doesn't look like she has the pox to me."

Briony blinked. The pox was an infection primarily occurring in Evermore's humid climate, resulting in pustules and boils if not properly attended.

Toven's heavy footsteps came closer. "She's almost healed. It made taking her almost revolting some days, but that pulse of Sacral Magic is too good to pass up."

She recalled Finn's quip about a sex dungeon. Toven had implied to these men that he was having sex with her.

A warm hand dropped on her hip, and Briony tried not to jump. Toven's crisp scent fluttered around her.

"But you *have* taken her." Liam lifted a brow at Toven from the catalog. "Because there are rumors that you haven't."

"And who might be the root of these rumors, Liam?" Toven asked pointedly. "I might ask you the same question, but of course, you couldn't snag yourself a woman. Just a male Eversun for a heartspring."

Briony remembered the list. The Quills had ended up with Simon, a young man a few years older than her, and Katrina. Bile crept up her throat as she guessed that Katrina belonged to Liam's father. Were many Eversuns being abused in the name of Sacral Magic?

"Not all of us like to drop sixty-five thousand on our whores," Liam snipped.

"Yes, only those who like the best," Toven said.

Finn hovered tumblers of whiskey over to them.

"Well, cheers to your birthday, Tove," Canning said.

Toven lifted his glass, and the others followed. "To Mistress Mallow," Toven offered. "May she reign forevermore."

"Forevermore," they echoed, as if it was a common toast.

After finishing his entire glass and handing it back to Toven to fetch him another, Canning said, "So I suppose now that she's well, you'll be bringing her to the revels." He nodded at Briony.

There was a tense silence for only a moment before Toven broke it.

"I plan to, yes. As long as I'm not called into service." He walked the glass back over to the whiskey decanter, and Briony watched him meet Finn's eyes.

"Of course, you could always let a friend borrow her," Canning said, his tongue running across his teeth.

"Oh, haven't you heard?" Liam spoke from a shelf that he'd wandered to. "Toven Hearst doesn't share her."

Canning grinned. "Is that right."

"That's right," Toven said. "I paid too much to let anyone else take a dip." And then, changing the subject, "Liam, can I *help* you find the book you're looking for?"

Liam turned around and hid his blush behind his whiskey glass. He smacked his lips and said, "My father was hoping to borrow something."

"Strange," Toven said coolly. "I received no letter of interest."

Liam smiled thinly. "He sent me to ask."

"Then ask."

Briony tried to focus on the conversation as Canning suddenly stood and stepped toward her.

"It concerns the portal boundary line. And the incident in Ashmont last week," Liam was saying.

Briony's ears perked up even as she kept her eyes on Canning, trying as subtly as she could to step back. The last time she'd heard of the portal boundary line, it had to do with Castle Javis, where people were trying to get out.

"We're looking for texts on obscure wards, ones they're less likely to—"

"Have you sampled my elixir with her yet?" Canning interrupted, as if the conversation bored him. "Jellica practically vibrates when she's on it."

He lifted a hand and brushed his knuckle down the side of her jaw, drifting lower, lower. She stood her ground, unsure what she could do, but trembling in fear and fury as Canning's knuckles skimmed down her neck and over her clavicle, then caressed the side of her breast and under. Her throat was tight as she choked on bile.

"I can't say that I've had a need," Toven replied. His voice came from behind her, and then one hand was pressing Canning's glass into his trailing fingers and the other was pushing a glass into Briony's sternum. Her hands came up to grab it in surprise. "We've been having plenty fun as it is."

Toven wrapped his arm around her stomach, pulling her inches backward from Canning.

Canning sipped from his glass, watching the two of them as Toven settled his fingers just beneath her breast, tugging her ever closer to him.

She'd never been so aware of how special her circumstances were until that moment. It wasn't just that her friends were being drained of their magic—some of them being raped if Canning's elixir was being used—and all living in the waters only knew what kinds of conditions. Were some also being flaunted or shared? Possibly expected to entertain many?

She looked down into the glass Toven had given her as Liam continued his description of the book he needed and Canning glowered. She lifted it to her lips, and it jumped out of her hand, hitting her chest and spilling whiskey down the front of her dress. She gasped as Canning swiftly stepped back from the spray. She hadn't dropped it.

Toven tutted.

"Do you have any idea how much this whiskey costs?" he snapped. "Go upstairs and clean up."

Briony turned to look at him. It was him. He'd spilled it on her, to give her a chance to leave.

She looked to the ground and moved to the door.

"Come on, Toven," Canning said playfully, stepping into her path. "We can clean her up, can't we?" He leered, and then he swiped his finger over her clavicles, gathering drops of whiskey to bring to his mouth. "Get that dress off, though. So it doesn't stain," he said mockingly.

Liam laughed, and Briony saw Finn shift in the corner.

Toven stood very still while Briony's heart pounded.

"I don't share, Trow," Toven said.

"We can look but not touch," Canning said innocently. "Can't we, lads?"

"Absolutely, Toven," said Liam. "Unless you'd like to wait for Friday. When there's more of us."

Toven's unamused mask slipped into place, and then he looked down at her. "Off."

Briony gaped in disbelief; was she truly being forced to undress in front of Canning Trow and Liam Quill? Not to mention Toven and Finn. Hesitantly, eyes silently begging for intervention, she reached up for the sleeve at her right shoulder and pushed it down. Then the left. Her skin didn't feel her own, and her stomach turned over. Toven held her eyes while the fabric slipped down her arms, her breasts, her stomach. She pushed it off her hips, and then she was in only her bra and underwear.

She thought of Reighven watching her shower and closed her eyes to the mortification, the shame. At least it wasn't that.

One of the young men whistled.

"I always knew she had those tits," Canning said, sucking his teeth.

She felt eyes on every inch of her skin, and another set of eyes hard on her face.

Toven reached forward and curved his palm around the back of her head, threading his fingers through her hair and holding her firm. He pulled her forward slowly, and she was forced to step closer.

He held her eyes as he whispered, "Don't ever spill a glass I give you again."

She wondered how much he regretted trying the "whiskey spill" trick now.

"Do you understand?" he said softly.

"Yes."

"Yes, what."

"Yes, Master Toven."

In his other hand, he held a whiskey glass. "Open your mouth."

Briony could do nothing else but obey. She parted her lips, and Toven tugged her head back by the hair.

He poured the whiskey into her mouth, letting it splash over her lips and trail down her chin, dripping down her chest.

She squeezed her eyes closed, trying not to cough against the burn of it. She heard the whiskey glass shatter as it was tossed away, and then his hand was low on her hip, his fingers curving around to press against her backside as he coaxed her against him.

She grabbed for his shoulders as he tugged her head further back, exposing her chest and throat to him.

She could only see the upside-down ceiling, but she nearly jumped out of her skin at the electric burn of Toven's hot mouth on her chest. His tongue glided from the top of her bra up to the pulse in her neck. He was licking up the whiskey. A squeak popped from her throat, and her back ached at the position even as fire pooled under her skin.

She could feel his teeth at her throat, and then he was sucking kisses over her breasts, licking up any drops still left. Her chest heaved for air, and just before he pulled her up to stand tall, she felt his fingers release her backside before swiftly coming back to slap a cheek.

She grunted, and his tongue slipped over her throat as he raised her, up her chin, stopping before her mouth.

When she was upright, she couldn't meet his eyes.

"Go," he said, throatily. "Take your dress and wash it out."

Briony nodded, her heart thundering. She gathered her dress and ran to the door, not daring to look at any of the men in the room.

*   *   *

Briony turned the water to scalding for her bath. Her skin was electrified in every place Toven's mouth and tongue had been, and she was mortified that in any other situation, she would relish the memory of it. But now she wanted the water to burn the memory off her.

To be so reminded that she was *property* in the same breath as feeling Toven Hearst's mouth on her skin . . . a mess. And she cringed with the knowledge that this was surely just scratching the surface of what others were going through.

Once she'd scrubbed every single inch of her body, twice, she was better able to focus her mind, and after reheating the water, one thing came back to her.

Liam needed a text on boundary lines. Specifically his father did. And Liam had mentioned Ashmont, too, an abandoned village in the west on the other side of Bomard's dead tree forest. What could they be doing in the west? Was it another attempt at leaving Moreland?

Not for the first time did she wonder how the countries across the sea felt about Mallow's seizure of Evermore.

When Briony thought she had burned off the feeling of Toven's tongue and Canning's knuckles, she wrapped herself in her dressing gown and stood by the window.

There was a quiet knock on her door. And even though she knew exactly who it was, she told him to come in, even in just her robe with wildly drying hair.

The door opened quietly, and Briony continued to stare out the window. When he didn't say anything, she finally turned to face him.

Toven stood in the doorway, not daring to enter. He leaned against the frame, affecting casualness, but his fingers were twisting his Bomardi ring.

She didn't know what to say. So she skipped it.

"Why did I have the pox?" she said tiredly.

Toven pressed his lips together in a fine line. "There is a party every weekend. You've had pox for four weeks, too ill to attend. And now you are no longer ill. Clearly."

"What kind of party?" Her voice cracked. "Is it anything like that," she said, indicating what had happened downstairs.

He looked past her shoulder, out the window. "It's a chance for Bomard to mingle and gloat over their victories. Nothing like that happens in public, but behind locked doors . . . in many ways, it's worse."

Trying to keep her breath steady under the weight of her ribs, she realized something. "Are there other Eversuns there? The heartsprings?"

When he nodded, her heart skipped a beat, her mind running wild with the opportunities—

"Cordelia Hardstark is no longer in attendance," he said, clearly reading her. A heavy silence. "She doesn't tend to play nice with others."

She stared up at him, feeling a familiar irritation surge through her. "And will I be expected to 'play nice'?"

His eyes flashed at her, and he said, "You're too smart not to."

He was right. She'd been looking for a way out of Hearst Hall. And now that it was here, in front of her, she wouldn't spoil it.

"So we'll go this Friday," he said.

She turned back to the window. She felt him start to leave and said, "It was a good try. The whiskey." He paused, and she didn't look at him. "It's a shame Canning thinks he owns the line." Her mind twisted, and it felt like when she and Rory used to stay up all night, trying to plan for every eventuality on the battlefield. "You'll have to get one over on him somehow." Her voice was cold. "No one should order a Hearst around like that."

Toven didn't say anything in response. And a few moments later, the door clicked closed.

* * *

Friday evening arrived, and with it a new dress in her wardrobe. Briony stared at the green silk swinging innocently on the hanger—the finest fabric she'd been offered yet. It was draped like an Eversun dress, with thin straps and a drop back, but the silk would cling. She traced the long hem; it would trail past her ankles. A pair of black heels sat at the base of the wardrobe. There was no bra appropriate to wear with it; that was, of course, the point of it.

She was to be shown off. What had Toven said? A chance for Bomard to gloat over their victories? Was she one such victory?

At a quarter past ten, he knocked on her door. He glanced over her once, his eyes not resting anywhere too long, and stepped inside to begin a portal. He was in relaxed Bomardi clothes—trousers and waistcoat, with the sleeves of his black shirt loose.

The portal yawned in the center of her room, and he reached his hand out for her tattoo.

Briony paused, wanting to ask a million questions before stepping into the unknown. "Will Mallow be there?"

"No. My father is with her elsewhere."

Briony now had two million questions.

She stepped forward, feeling the silk move against her skin like water. Her back was completely bare, and she wanted to ask if she'd worn the dress right, but he still hadn't really looked at it. As much as she had been violated the other day, hadn't he been as well? Forced to do something he didn't want to?

"Will something similar happen tonight?" she asked, not elaborating. They both knew what she meant.

His eyes were cold and dead as he looked at her. "No. You will stay close to me, and we will let everyone see you so that we don't have to return for several weeks. That's all."

She swallowed, shivering.

"There will be minor contact," he said, clarifying her question. "Between us. No one else." His eyes were on the portal, and she wondered how much minor contact either of them could stand.

She was about to ask him which estate the party was at when he reached for her again, grabbed her arm, and tugged them both through the portal.

She wished she'd asked. She wished she'd prepared.

The wind whipped her dress and her hair, and she heard the crash of the ocean.

They were at Biltmore Palace. They were at her family home.

CHAPTER 25

Six Years Ago

RIONY'S SUMMER SOLSTICE WAS ALWAYS SPENT at Biltmore Palace, on the hill overlooking the main ports of Evermore. The solstice divided the school year in half, allowing a weeklong break from classes— and a break from the Bomardi students.

While Briony usually opted to invite Cordelia to spend the week with her at Biltmore, Briony's father had decided that Rory and Cordelia couldn't share a roof while they were courting.

So instead—

"Stones, is it always this hot on the solstice?" a loud voice said from next to Briony, where she lay on the grass in the garden.

Briony took a deep breath, channeling patience, before cracking her eyelids. Katrina sat fanning herself, looking not at all relaxed in the sunshine.

"Would you like to retire to the courtyard? There's more shade there," Briony said as politely as she could.

Katrina sipped her fairy wine and shook her head. "No. If this is what you do on the break, then I'll do it, too." She twisted up her straw-colored hair and lay back onto the grass. "You'd think that as a princess, you'd have someone fanning you with a large leaf at all times."

Briony's face scrunched at the insinuation that she had servants dedicated solely to her comfort. She bit back her comment just as the boom of a cannon shook the garden.

Katrina shrieked and Briony continued her sunbathing, unfazed.

"What the fuck was that?" Katrina scrambled up, clutching her chest.

"It's the Summer Cannon," Briony said lazily. "It happens every day at noon at Biltmore."

"*Why?*"

"To mark the time for the ships just off port," she said. "It's traditional."

Katrina slowly lowered herself back down on the grass, breathing deeply in a way that Briony found overdramtic. After a few blessed minutes of silence, Katrina spoke again.

"Did you hear that Toven Hearst and Larissa Gains will be formally betrothed when we return to school?"

Briony snapped her head to Katrina. "What?"

Katrina hummed, closing her eyes against the sun. "She's spending the solstice at Hearst Hall. The talk is that they'll be engaged by the end of the week."

There was a gnawing in Briony's chest. She didn't trust herself to speak.

It shouldn't have been surprising to her. She had run into Toven and Larissa in the dark corridors several more times during the spring, always clutching at each other. They'd been assumed to be courting for most of school, so this was just the next natural step.

But Briony couldn't help the way her ribs seemed to stick together at the thought of Toven engaged.

They'd been partnered in elixirs class all spring, and she'd had the agonizing pleasure of watching his hands work through the ingredients every day for two months. Slicing roots, plucking plant leaves, roughly chopping insect wings. She hadn't known where else to look but at the veins in his forearms as he worked.

And it wasn't just his appearance that was distracting. His crisp scent hung onto her clothing for the rest of each day. His voice teased her quietly, needling her about knowing all the right answers and refusing to share them with the tutor. His warm skin brushed against her fingers whenever they reached for the pestle at the same time.

Briony stared at the sky, letting the sun burn her eyes. She hadn't understood until that moment how inappropriate it all was. If Toven was courting Larissa with the intention to marry her, then the small attentions he gave Briony were childish games. Anger boiled in her suddenly, and every coy smile he'd given her, every whisper against her ear, every time he'd stolen her chopping knife at the end of class "by mistake" and made her chase him down in the hall to get it back from him—all of it felt tainted now.

"It's weird, right? I know people get engaged during school all the time, but I didn't expect it of anyone I *know*." Katrina rolled on her side to face Briony. "Will you and Didion be next?"

Briony squinted at Katrina. "What? Didion and me?"

She smiled. "Yeah. He's very handsome. And kind."

"Sounds like *you* should marry him," Briony said, turning back to the clouds.

Katrina snorted in response.

There was the sizzle of a portal opening in the far end of the garden, overlooking the sea. That was the only place you could portal into, if you had high enough status.

Briony sat up and found General Meers and her cousin Finola marching quickly to the palace, their pace determined. Finola didn't spare her a glance.

"You go find shade," Briony said to Katrina. "I'll be back."

She got to her feet and followed them inside the entry hall.

General Meers was barking orders as if he were the king himself, and Finola was speaking quickly to her father's equerry. Briony kept to the walls, stepping behind the pillars that held up the scalloped arches.

"I need the king *now*," General Meers demanded.

Rory and Didion popped out of the far hall, watching the commotion.

"He's in his study," the housekeeper said, gesturing for them to continue upstairs.

General Meers raced ahead, taking the stairs two at a time, with Finola close behind.

Briony darted for the stairs, just barely beating Rory to them, and both twins climbed quickly to the second floor, where they followed the general down the open arcade.

Their father's study overlooked a cloistered garden and was lined with lattice windows that let air in but kept prying eyes out.

General Meers was already talking by the time Rory and Briony reached the door.

"Seat Pulvey is dead."

Briony skidded to a halt in the doorway, watching as her father dropped his pen and steepled his fingers on the desk.

"Mallow?" he asked.

Briony remembered that name. The woman with the shrewd eyes and pin-straight hair, who'd talked of using children as collateral.

General Meers nodded. "Scouts say that Veronika Mallow now holds the Seat of Bomard."

Briony gasped, and the room looked at her and Rory in the arched doorway. Finola gave her a tight smile in hello.

"Children, you'll excuse us," General Meers said.

Briony glowered and Rory said, "I'm nineteen. I'd like to know the political happenings in my future realm."

King Jacquel nodded and gestured for Rory to sit in the chair in the corner. Rory waved his hand and conjured a second chair, twin to the first. He met his father's eyes as he pulled the chair for Briony.

"My king," the general began. "I really must object to so many ears in a confidential meeting—"

"You're a fool if you think Briony's ears to be the least useful of the five of us here," Rory said, and Briony's chest warmed at the unexpected praise. Rory met her eye with a supportive smile.

Her father cleared his throat. "Go on, General."

Briony and Rory sat in the corner as General Meers pursed his lips in displeasure.

Rory asked, "How did she supersede the line?"

"She ascended properly," Finola said. "At the time of Gin Pulvey's death, Veronika Mallow held the position of first in line."

"How?"

"Riann Cohle killed his father last night," Finola said. "He then ascended to first in line, named Mallow his successor, and immediately abdicated.

Before killing Gin Pulvey, she named Riann Cohle *her* successor. They ascended together upon the death of Pulvey—her to the Seat, him to first in line. So there will be no changes to the line below them. Riann Cohle only needs to choose a successor."

Briony's lips parted, shocked at the political maneuvering.

General Meers paced to the desk. "We think she seduced Riann Cohle—"

"There's no evidence of that," Finola objected.

General Meers rolled his eyes. "Regardless, she convinced Cohle of this plot, and now she sits on the Seat."

"Has she made any manifesto?" King Jacquel asked, staring out his lattice windows thoughtfully.

"Not yet, my king," General Meers said. "Bomard woke to the news, and my sources are keeping a lookout for any objections from the line."

"There won't be," her father said, rubbing his chin. "She's gotten to them all, I'm sure."

"There is one thing," Finola said hesitantly, and they all looked at her. "There is a rumor that Mallow will order the end of mind magic in Bomard."

Briony's face twisted. "How would she do that? We're halfway through a Bomardi school year. How will the Eversun students practice mind magic?"

Finola nodded at her, as if Briony had answered her own question.

The room was still for a moment. And then Rory said softly, "Well. I'll be interested to see how the Bomardi return to school after the solstice."

CHAPTER 26

BRIONY'S GAZE TRAVELED UP the tall cliffs on which Biltmore Palace was built. She knew those cliffs intimately. She'd scaled them as a child, hiding from guards and scurrying to catch up with Rory and Sammy.

At night, it was beautiful, lit from within like fireflies caught in a jar. Tonight was no different, even though the Eversun flag had been replaced with the Bomardi crest. She could imagine for a moment that she was with her father, arriving for a long week of hosting dignitaries and deciding important world matters.

Then Toven took her elbow and encouraged her forward, and the memory-film over reality broke away.

Biltmore Palace was monstrous.

She stumbled up the path next to him, staring up at the burning light coming from inside; it flickered up the walls as if a fire were devouring the hillside. Turning back over her shoulder, she looked down to the port—or what was left of the port.

Mallow had decimated the docks a year ago in an effort to cut off Rory and Evermore from the countries across the sea. Only one ship had made it out before the Bomardi militia started burning all of them down, and the Bomardi fleet hunted it down before it could travel across the sea for help.

Phoebe and Finola's father had been on that ship.

Now Mallow was rebuilding the docks, it seemed. Briony could see the flare of magic in the moonlight.

"Focus," Toven whispered under the wind.

She turned back to the long walk up to the gates. She looked to the top of the portcullis and gasped. A gray wolf and a black bear prowled over the archway, staring down at the two of them. Inside the gate, two men in Bomardi-blue cloaks were chatting casually. When the wolf snapped its jaws, the man on the left glanced out the gates at them.

They were their familiars.

The wolf's master stood up straight and said jovially, "Toven Hearst. What did you bring for us tonight?"

"Ah, you couldn't handle her, Roth," Toven said smoothly, and the men laughed.

Toven reached down for the ink on her arm, covered his hand with it, and tugged her forward through the gates. Briony felt a burning under her skin. It was a magical barrier, just as at Hearst Hall.

One of the men whistled at her as she passed, and Briony tried to keep her balance in her heels. The path was made of silt and dirt, eventually hardening into stone on top of the hill.

They twisted up the path, and once they were out of earshot, Briony asked, "Am I locked in now?"

"Do not speak unless you are spoken to." Toven's voice was harsh and deep. "Not until we are upstairs."

She glanced at him and found his expression impassive, but the skin above his right eye was twitching with tension.

The path opened into the gardens where she and Rory used to wait for her father to be done discussing matters with Sammy's father, anxious to get down to the docks and play with the sailors' children. A stone pathway wound through the grass, crossing over the water that trickled through the entire palace in tributaries.

There were a handful of people walking in the garden having private conversations, and Toven slowed once they were under a lamp. He turned to face her under the pretense of checking her over.

"Do not let your eyes linger too long on any one person. Do not try to interact with your friends." His fingers came up to the strap on her shoulder, and she felt the whisper of his touch across her collarbones. His gaze was following his fingertips. "Be smart. Be obedient. It will be over soon."

She had the distinct impression that he was saying the last bit to himself.

When he didn't say anything else, she became aware of eyes on them. The people in the garden had turned to look, speaking quickly to one another.

Before she could wonder if he was waiting for her to respond, he turned them toward the entrance and slipped her hand into his elbow. As if they were courting. She glanced up at him, finding his gray eyes forward, the lamps lighting his hair in yellows and oranges.

As they approached, the music grew louder. She wondered what kind of horrors she would find inside. Would her friends be in chains? Would she find them beaten and bloody?

The doors opened, and a young woman in a scarlet dress smiled coyly at the two of them from in front of a heavy curtain.

"Master Hearst. Welcome." Her voice was silky, and her eyes danced over Briony for a second too long. "Miss Rosewood. What a pleasure."

Briony blinked at her. She had luscious brown hair and olive skin, but Briony's gaze was concentrated on the collar around her neck that matched Briony's, only in silver.

"Ilana," Toven said in greeting. "Enchanting as ever."

Ilana pulled two champagne glasses from a side table, and Briony was shocked when one was handed to her. She held it close to her chest.

"Tonight, we have General Tremelo in attendance," Ilana said, handing Toven a piece of paper. Briony could just glimpse the sketch of a man and a few paragraphs. Toven glanced it over. "Have you been introduced?"

"Yes, my father has bartered with him before." Toven handed the page back to her. "Anyone else?"

"Just the usual riffraff," Ilana said playfully. Her eyes flicked to Briony faster than quicksilver. "Mistress Mallow does not plan to be by."

"Thank you, Ilana," Toven said. He ran a hand over his hair casually. "Can I ask if Lag Reighven has made an appearance yet?"

Briony felt her throat close.

"No, Master Reighven isn't on my list." She smiled and reached for the curtain.

The sound slammed into Briony like running into a wall.

Beyond the curtain in the large entry hall were at least one hundred people. Their conversation, their laughter, the sound of their glasses clinking together—all of it burst through the curtain at once.

Briony's eyes were drawn in every direction as Toven led her inside. The entry hall was packed with people whom she'd once welcomed in a receiving line, next to her father and Rory. To the right, she spied Caspar Quill talking animatedly with a group, champagne sloshing as he gesticulated. Katrina was draped on his arm, wearing a tight dress, a gold collar, and a vacant stare. Briony stepped toward her without thinking, but Toven steered her away.

She spied a woman she'd been to school with sipping from a glass and laughing heartily at everything her escort said. Briony did a double take when she saw dark hair and sun-kissed skin. Phoebe was less than ten feet from her for the first time since the Trow dungeon. Briony's eyes dug into her, begging her to look over, but Phoebe was smiling up at Aron Carvin, a short, red-faced man who was second in line for the Seat. Phoebe's gold collar sparkled in the candlelight, and her nails were bright red on her glass of champagne.

"Don't linger," Toven hissed.

Briony snapped her gaze forward just as two young men stepped into their path, one thin with golden-brown skin and the other heavyset and pink-cheeked. Lorne Vult and Collin Twindle, who had been a part of Toven's gang in school. Collin's mother was seventh in line, and Lorne's aunt was somewhere behind Finn Raquin's father, but Lorne had been dogged in his attempts to barter his way to a better position as a successor.

"Toven," Lorne said. "Cutting it close, aren't you? You're almost late."

"Almost, but not." Toven shook both of their hands.

Briony tore her eyes from them as they looked her over. Lorne Vult had been a close friend of Canning Trow's and had a reputation for making girls uncomfortable in the halls. Collin had been shy when he was younger but had become crass and status-obsessed over the school years. He'd been one of the first boys to join his father in hunting down the Eversun children on the day the Bomardi school was attacked—the day her father was murdered.

Collin's amber eyes dripped over her exposed skin. "So you've brought her," he said.

"I have." Toven sipped from his champagne. "Her pox finally cleared."

"Will you be sharing her?" Lorne asked, voice lilting.

Briony's eyes snapped to him, and he smiled at her.

"Unfortunately, no, gentlemen. If you wanted a golden heartspring, you should have bought one yourself."

"Not a heartspring I'd be using her for," Collin said, and Lorne laughed.

Briony glared at the larger man.

Toven checked his timepiece. "It's almost that time, gentlemen. Gather your heartsprings, and I'll see you in the suite."

Before either of them could say another word, Toven was guiding her to the left and away. Her mind stuck on the word "suite," and she wondered what was ahead of her.

Toven steered them in a wide circle around the room, and every time they neared a door, she thought he would take her through it. He shook hands but didn't stop. When they finally came back to where they'd started, Briony realized he was showing her off—making sure as many eyes were on her as possible.

Briony looked for people she knew, finding familiar faces from the Trow dungeon. She tried to keep track of the Bomardi elite she was recognizing, but there were too many. Katrina had disappeared, but she found the back of Phoebe's head twice. Either her cousin was making it a point not to look at her, or she was truly clueless to Briony's presence.

When Toven finally directed her toward the staircase that led to the second floor, she thought they'd be done with the whispers that followed them as they moved through the room.

At the base of the stairs, Hap Gains stood smoking a cigar and talking with the man from the sketch Ilana had showed them. Briony steeled herself to be in Gains's presence again, and she felt the smallest of pauses in Toven's gait before he ushered her forward.

"Hap, good to see you," Toven said, reaching for Gains's hand. "And General Tremelo, what an honor it is to host you tonight."

The general took Toven's hand with a grin. "Orion's boy. Your father owes me a game of cards!" His accent was crisp and tight.

Her mind twisted through what this could mean. Bomard was entertaining a general from across the sea? Was Mallow's reach spreading?

"Please accept my father's apologies that he couldn't be here to escort you himself," Toven said, with a glance at Gains. Gains narrowed his eyes at him. "I know how he appreciates Daward's business."

Daward was one of eight magical countries in the east. They also practiced heart magic, but it had been centuries since they had abused heartspring bonds in the same ways that Bomard currently did. Briony had no idea what kind of "business" Orion Hearst had with Daward and its general, but she could assume it would not be something her own father would have condoned.

"Please send my regards to your father." General Tremelo had a kind smile, but as he turned it on Briony, she braced herself for another lecherous gaze. "And who is this?"

"Briony Rosewood," Toven said with a hint of arrogance. His arm wrapped around her waist loosely, his hand landing over her hip. "My heartspring."

Tremelo's eyes blinked twice, very quickly.

"Ah. Jacquel's daughter."

What did that tone mean? Had he been friendly with her father? Was he perhaps upset to see King Jacquel's offspring being treated like property by Bomard? Briony couldn't decipher it.

"Young Hearst has been rather ungenerous with her," Gains said, his smirk returning as he sucked on his cigar. "This is Miss Rosewood's first visit to Biltmore."

Briony bit down on her tongue, resisting the urge to correct him.

"Far from her first visit," Tremelo said lightly. "This was her father's house not too long ago, was it not?"

His words seemed to steal the air from the room. Gains puffed on his cigar, and Toven's lips lifted in a tight smile. Briony stared at the general, trying to figure out his intention in bringing up the real facts of the matter.

"Very true," Gains said, covering. "I only meant that Toven has avoided bringing her to our weekly parties."

Toven's fingers tightened on her hip. "Well, after what happened with Cohle's heartspring last month, I wasn't in a hurry to bring her."

Toven looked to Gains as the man's eyes hardened.

Anxiety sparked in Briony's blood. Something had happened to Cordelia?

244 ~e~ JULIE SOTO

"But surely with a golden heartspring, there would be no danger in showing her off a bit," Gains said.

"Ah, yes. I've heard much about golden heartsprings," Tremelo said genially, "and yet I still have no idea what it is that makes them so special."

Briony's ears pricked.

Gains tapped the ashes off his cigar. "The Rosewood blood, said to be golden, creates a more powerful heartspring bond. Both golden heartsprings measured considerably high in magical ability on our scale." He nodded at Aron Carvin and Phoebe across the room and then grinned at Toven. "Which is why we're all so anxious to see Aron and Toven in the arena together."

Briony's head was spinning with all the new information. An arena?

Toven's expression remained placid. "I prefer to save my magic for whatever Mistress Mallow requests of me."

Tremelo laughed. "Good soldier. My, I bet you're up to your ears in power. It's good to see Miss Rosewood looking no worse for wear because of it."

There was something in the way Tremelo spoke—in the way Gains paused, in the way Toven's fingers tightened on her hip—that made Briony wonder what was behind his words.

Daward didn't practice mind magic, so she didn't find any resistance when she carefully extended her index finger in a penetrating gesture and grasped the thread between her eyes. Tremelo's mind was a maze of strategy and tactics, but at the forefront she saw herself as Tremelo saw her: healthy and unharmed.

Briony slithered out of his thoughts and wondered what Tremelo's true motiviation was here tonight. Who was he to report back to? And why was it important to him that the daughter of Mallow's enemy was safe, though captive?

If Bomard was extending its influence, was Daward worried about their own futures?

"Quite a bit of power," Toven said, agreeing. "I'll leave you two to your evening."

He shook both men's hands and steered her around them.

"No need to keep the woman wound so tightly, Toven," Gains said to their backs.

Bile curdled in Briony's stomach. That was one innuendo she didn't need unraveled.

She'd learned too many things in too short a time: Something had happened to Cordelia, there was an arena of some sort, and General Tremelo of Daward was not fully on board with Veronika Mallow's Bomard.

Toven led her to the stairs that ran with the sacred waters. Railings splashed with flumes of trickling streams. She wanted to ask him what was going to happen in the "suite," but before she could open her mouth, they'd arrived at the landing and were faced with a young guard in Bomardi blue.

"Toven." He nodded at them. "Everyone's inside."

"Wonderful," Toven said, raising his hand to present his black ring for inspection. "I love to make an entrance."

The guard unlocked the door behind him that led to her father's old open-air dining room.

When the door opened, raucous laughter beat against her eardrums, and Briony found a table set for eight. Seven young men were seated, drinking and smoking, and seven young women in collars lined the walls, eyes cast down.

The conversation came to an abrupt halt, and Briony finally focused her eyes on the men at the table as every gaze turned on their arrival.

Finn Raquin, Liam Quill, Lorne and Collin, two others she didn't recognize.

And Canning Trow, standing from the head of the table. His smirk was wide and his eyes were hungry as he lifted his glass.

"Miss Rosewood. It's our honor to host you tonight."

In a disturbing show of chivalry, the other six men came to their feet, and Briony was abruptly reminded that she had no idea what the rules were in this new world.

Canning Trow grinned at her, his eyes sliding down her body. "Gentlemen, the golden heartspring is here."

CHAPTER 27

SORRY TO KEEP YOU ALL WAITING," Toven said, stepping forward and shaking hands with Canning. "General Tremelo took an interest in my heartspring."

Behind her, the door closed, and the guard locked it.

Briony's eyes moved quickly over every woman in the room, standing behind an occupied chair like a serving maid. Every gaze was cast down, but she recognized several of them.

Behind Canning's chair was Jellica Reeve, whom Canning had boasted only days ago about using his elixir on. A woman named Octavia who had always been quiet and kind in school stood next to Jellica, behind Lorne's chair. Where she had been full-figured in school, she was now skin and bones. Across the table from them, Cecily Weape, daughter of a high-ranking Eversun, stood behind Collin's chair. Something in Briony broke when she remembered that Collin used to send her love notes at school.

Other faces came and went in her memories, failing to attach to names.

On the table were several opened bottles of wine, herbed vegetables, and a full roast pig complete with an apple in its mouth.

She quickly adjusted to the idea of "dinner," and lifted her eyes to the men in the room.

"Well, the general has always been known for his exquisite taste," Canning said, eyeing her.

Toven quickly moved to the open chair, facing Canning at the other end of the table. Taking note that Toven was one of two top dogs in this room, Briony followed behind him and quickly took her place against the wall, behind his chair.

Toven picked up his empty wineglass and extended it out to his side, waiting. Briony stared at it.

"Do keep up, Rosewood," he said snidely.

The men chuckled, watching her.

Then a woman with strawberry-blond hair stepped forward from the wall behind Liam, reached for a wine bottle, and met Briony's eyes as she filled Liam's glass.

Briony jerked forward, following her lead and filling Toven's glass. The men's eyes glittered at her, while Toven simply stared forward, away from her.

Once his glass was full, she set down the bottle and stepped back, glancing at the blond woman in thanks. When the woman smiled back at her, Briony's mind rearranged like tumblers in a lock.

It was her maid from Claremore Castle. The one whom she had saved on the day of the attack—the day Rory died. The one who had led Cordelia and her down the stairs and who had run when Cordelia stayed behind to find her.

Briony swayed on her feet, her heels tilting under her ankles.

The strawberry-blond woman looked down at the floor again.

It was some comfort, Briony supposed, that there were no winners that day. If she'd hid like Anna wanted, she'd have been found. If she'd been a few steps faster down that passage and missed the cave-in, she'd still have been captured, like this young woman was.

Briony glanced her over, finding a silver collar around her neck, instead of gold. There was obviously a difference there—but what did it mean?

Toven lifted his glass. "To Mistress Mallow. May she reign forevermore."

The room chorused, "Forevermore."

"And may her enemies," Toven continued, and turned his head to give her his profile, "be *nevermore*."

The men laughed and sipped their russet-colored wine.

And all Briony heard was the echo of her country's name in both statements. There was a window ledge behind her, and she leaned back on it, letting the breeze move across her shoulders and taking the weight off her too-tall heels.

Conversation spun quickly after that.

"Your father back yet from across the sea?"

"Lorne, do you have that painting I was asking about?"

"—new batch of elixir soon?"

"She was *gagging* for it, I tell you—"

Briony tried to follow the speakers with her gaze, but the men kept glancing at her. Across the table, Jellica Reeve shifted on her feet, swaying forward as if her body were tied by a string to Canning's chair. Her eyes were dilated, gaze hot on the back of Canning's head.

Briony's brows drew together.

"Her pox has cleared beautifully, Toven." Lorne's voice rang out over the table, a sparkling smile on his face as he appraised Briony. "She hardly looks like she had it."

"Well, of course," Toven hummed. "I couldn't let my property look so tarnished, but I assure you, the boils and puss were disgusting." He glanced over his shoulder at her in distaste. "You tired? Can't stand straight?"

Every eye turned on her. She pushed up from the windowsill, realizing that none of the other women were leaning.

"No, sir. Just not used to my shoes, sir," she mumbled.

Toven's eyes flashed at her while the table erupted into laughter.

"Oh, Rosewood," Liam said with a grin. "You can have a break from your footwear. Come sit on my lap."

The men howled. Toven sipped his wine, set the glass down, and cleared his throat. "She will do no such thing."

The laughter dissipated at his tone.

Liam rolled his eyes. "Stones, why even bring her if we can't have a little fun?"

Toven drummed his fingers on the tablecloth. "*I'm* having fun, that's all that matters. Lorne? Will you do the honors?" He nodded to the pig in the middle of the table. "I'm starving."

Lorne stood with a smirk and produced a carving knife. Briony listened to the men chat while the women approached Lorne one at a time to take a plate to their escort. Cecily Weape retrieved Collin two servings, and he thanked her with a pinch to her backside. Jellica Reeve almost dropped Canning's plate, her hands were shaking so badly, but Briony noticed that it didn't seem to be fear driving her. When she set the plate of food down in front of Canning, she hovered, her fingers curling, almost reaching to him. He smirked up at her and said, "You may go." Jellica whimpered and stumbled back to her place behind his chair.

Briony moved around the table to Lorne's side when it was her turn. She could feel him watching her as the conversation continued, eyes raking her body.

"She looks pampered, Toven," Lorne said, twirling his knife. Briony's heartbeat quickened as he began spinning the blade on his thumb. "My heartspring gets so weak after I drain her; dry skin and tired eyes." Lorne's gaze dropped over Briony's neck and chest. "And no other kinds of marks, either. You must not be having *that* much fun."

The table laughed. Briony glanced to Octavia, standing ghostly behind Lorne's chair, peeling an orange for him with her eyes glued to his knife as it spun.

"You know how much I paid for her," Toven drawled. "Of course I bathe her in milk and lavender every night."

Canning laughed. But Lorne's eyes were darting across Briony's skin. She drew in a slow breath, wishing she could go back to Toven's side of the room.

Quick as lightning, there was a glint of metal, and then Lorne was a breath away, his knife between her skin and the green strap of her dress. He tugged on it.

"She's an Eversun, Toven. She only needs to lie on her back." His crisp white teeth flashed at her, his breath hot on her face. "Besides, I always heal them afterward."

She froze in horror as the knife cut through the strap, her heart fluttering wildly and her eyes wide—her dress slipping down her chest—

The knife zoomed away from her skin, spinning through the air to pierce the stone wall as Lorne jumped backward.

Her strap repaired itself, and she turned to see Toven's hand outstretched, hot rage simmering beneath his cool facade.

"I'm not sure how many more times I need to say it," he whispered, and the room was barely breathing. "That heartspring is mine. Her mouth is mine, her magic is mine, her skin is mine." His teeth bit through the words, and he met eyes with every person at the table before saying, "You will not touch her, under any circumstances. I purchased her. I do what I please with her."

Her skin tingled where she could still feel the ghost of Lorne's knife. Her breath was shallow as she watched Toven glare at them, still as a statue, until he was satisfied that he had been heard.

"Now bring me a plate. I said I was hungry."

Briony took the plate and hurried to the other side of the room. As she set it before Toven, she reached to refill his wineglass, too. An arm snaked out around her waist, and she was suddenly tugged into Toven's lap. She stifled a gasp and righted herself, sitting sideways across his thighs. His left arm slipped around her back, steadying her with his palm against her left hip.

Toven picked up his fork with his free hand and turned to the table. "Now, what were we talking about?"

Briony tried to concentrate on anything but the firmness of Toven's thighs beneath her. She'd never sat in a man's lap before. It wasn't proper for any unmarried young woman to do so in public, much less the daughter of the king. She'd been close to a man's body like this when she was unchaperoned with Didion, but this was far more intimate.

It wasn't just the feeling of Toven's thighs through the silk of her dress, but also his hand steadying her. The brush of air across her naked back.

Conversation slowly flowed again, tension high in the air after Toven's outburst. When Cecily refilled Collin's plate, he pulled her into his lap as well, nuzzling his face into her neck. When Briony next glanced up, Octavia was in Lorne's lap, his fingers twirling her hair absently while he talked to Canning about betting scores. Guilt boiled in Briony's gut at the thought that she and Toven had changed the tone of the evening.

Her gaze drifted to Jellica again. While Canning made no move to bring her into his lap, she stood barely a pace behind him, her body shifting and lip pulled between her teeth in what Briony would call desire. She reached for Canning's shoulder and then dropped her hand, as if remembering herself.

Finn was the first one to offer his heartspring a bite of cheese. Then suddenly the strawberry-blond woman had a glass of wine in her hand, laughing at everything Liam Quill said as she sat in his lap.

To Toven's right was a muscular Bomardi with rich bronze skin whom Briony thought was called Kleve. He'd been in final year at school when she and Rory started and had been kind as far as Briony could remember. He looked rather displeased about the entire evening, sipping quietly from his wineglass, while his heartspring, a dark-skinned woman Briony didn't recognize at all, stood still as stone, eyes a thousand miles away.

Then sat Collin, whom Briony could hardly look at without feeling ill as he forced Cecily to kiss him at the dinner table. Between Collin and Canning sat a man whom Briony thought was the successor to Gains's place in the Ten, though she didn't remember his name.

From her left, Finn reached forward for his glass of wine, and a black gemstone ring caught the light. And like a bolt of lightning hitting the sky, she suddenly realized why these men had dining privileges like this.

They weren't just old friends from school. They were the successors.

Cohle, Carvin, Trow, Gains, Locklin, Quill, Twindle, Hearst, Kleve, and Gidrey—those who stood in line to the Seat—passed their place in line to one person of their choosing on their death or abdication.

She glanced at their right hands. Dark gemstones gleamed back at her from their middle fingers, like Toven's. Even Finn, who had previously been successor to his father at fourteenth, was wearing a ring that symbolized the Ten. He must have moved up. Lorne's ring had no gemstone encased in it. She itched to ask Toven about that.

These eight men were all on the line, somehow. In fact, if she matched each known successor to a position on the line, she would probably find that the two other successors not here were women. She would have scoffed if she could, knowing how much Bomard looked down on

Evermore for relying on male-born primogeniture. Now look at them. Some of their mothers or aunts may be on the line, but the second generation was certainly a boys' club.

"Toven," Canning called across the table, his cheeks flushed from the wine. "Since we won't be getting a taste, tell us a bit about the princess in the bedroom?"

A guffaw burst from someone, and then the table went silent. Briony's face grew hot, and Toven's throat clicked as he swallowed.

"What do you want to know?" He lifted his wineglass, draining it. Her heartbeat drummed against her ribs.

Behind Canning, Jellica had tears rolling down her face that Briony couldn't understand. Jellica's hands were squeezed tightly into fists, and her chest and neck were flushed.

"I seem to remember she was aloof in public, but fiery in private." Canning smirked at Briony, and she remembered the way he'd stolen her for a dance at the state dinner. "Is she just as blazing in bed?"

Laughter clattered against the spoons, and she lifted her head to find every eye on her, hungry with lust or cruel amusement.

"In the beginning," Toven said finally, a low hum through her back. "Now she knows how to relax."

She felt a shiver at her shoulder blades, spreading outward and sinking into her skin.

"What's her cunt like?" Lorne asked, biting back a smile.

"Delicious."

There was stillness, and Briony thought perhaps Toven had said the wrong thing. Because it wouldn't be necessary to . . . it wouldn't be something that he'd . . . that they'd—

"You go down on her?" Collin asked, voicing her concerns with a grimace.

"Well, if she's misbehaving I don't bother," he said, as if he'd been asked about the weather.

"That's what the elixir is for, Toven," Canning said with a laugh.

Behind him, Jellica whined in her throat. Canning beckoned her forward and sat her across his lap. Briony's stomach churned as Jellica finally calmed once she was touching him. Canning shushed her and whispered, "Just a bit longer."

Briony hid her disgust as Jellica pressed her face into Canning's neck and began to kiss his skin desperately. Jellica was on the elixir at this very moment. This was what it did, Briony realized.

"We get on fine without the elixir," Toven said. "It's so much more satisfying to have them moaning and begging for it all by themselves, don't you think?" Toven's hand lifted off her hip and reached for a curl, twisting it lightly. "That rush of Sacral Magic is so much sweeter that way. No offense, Canning."

Canning's lips twitched without smiling. Jellica was writhing in his lap, pressing herself closer, kissing his skin, and trying to get her fingers under his collar. Almost lazily, Canning pulled her hands off his buttons and pushed them into her lap.

"But you have *used* the elixir?" Canning asked. There was a challenge in his expression.

Briony felt every eye on them, the men and the women. All but Jellica who sobbed against Canning's neck, as if she'd die if he didn't allow her to touch him.

"No. Rosewood doesn't need it," Toven said conversationally.

Liam picked up his glass and said grandly, "Oh, that we might all be blessed with Toven Hearst's sexual prowess." His eyes glinted.

Toven breathed deeply against Briony's ribs. "The stones bless us all with different skills," he said dryly. "I'm sure you and your heartspring will find your own rhythm, Liam."

The table chuckled lightly, and Liam glared at him. Liam's heartspring was a man. Briony had heard rumors in school that Liam preferred men, but he was always quick to deny it and quick to anger over it.

Toven sipped his wine as Liam opened his mouth to retort—

"We'd be honored to have Miss Rosewood partake next week," Canning said. The room went quiet. "Seeing as you won't be sharing her, we'd love to have a glimpse at what she's like." Canning ran his tongue over his teeth. "On the house, of course."

There was a tense pause. Every eye flickered between Toven and

Canning. Toven tilted his head, and she could feel the breath he drew before replying.

"That's kind, but quite a waste. Like I've said, we get on fine without."

Toven ran his hand up her hip, over her rib cage, and Briony's body froze at the sensation before she could mask it. She glanced up at Canning; a slow smirk was curling over his face.

"No need to be shy, Toven. You know what happens in this room, stays in this room. I want to see her gagging for it, like you've described in such detail to us," Canning said. It had an air of finality. He snapped suddenly, with an idea. "And it doesn't need to be a waste. You could sign up for the arena next week!"

Briony had no idea what that meant.

Toven set down his wineglass. "I assume that's why Miss Reeve is currently gnawing on your neck?"

With a laugh, Canning softly instructed Jellica to leave his lap and return to the wall behind him. She whined, pressing herself closer. He kissed her cheek and gave her a push.

"Yes, you'll see me in the arena tonight," Canning said. "Jellica will give me a bit more strength, won't you dear?" He blew her a kiss. Jellica shivered, her hand running over her skin.

The men started trading stories about the women in their laps or women in the past, as if they were all back in the boys' dormitories. The laughter started again. The man to Canning's left, Gains's successor, told a particularly nasty story, and he bounced the woman on his lap in a crude imitation of it, jostling her until she spilled her glass.

Briony tried to focus on the women, the exits, the sharp cutlery— anything but the vileness happening in her father's old dining room. Or the way Toven's hand stayed in her curls, threading and twisting softly.

One of the women passing out fruit and sweets smiled demurely every time a wandering hand squeezed her backside or drifted up the side of her thigh, and Cecily looked as if she might be sick as Collin turned her to straddle him in the chair.

Briony felt acid in her throat, burning away at her lungs. Toven had told her that behind locked doors, things were worse. She braced herself for the evening to spiral further. Not even the slow rub of Toven's thumb behind her ear could distract her from the tightness in her chest.

The men were talking over one another, louder and louder. She felt Toven laugh when Liam made a joke, bellow when Finn dared Canning to chug the rest of his bottle, chuckle when Kleve left to grab more wine from the attached serving room. As her eyes followed him out, they landed on Collin pushing on Cecily's shoulders, urging her down to her knees.

She gasped, choking on the air. No one batted an eye. One more glance showed Cecily's shaking fingers unbuckling Collin's trousers. Her face was pale but resigned, as if she saw no other option.

Briony couldn't breathe.

"Who's against you in the arena tonight, Canning? Not Carvin, I hope," Finn said.

"No, Carvin takes a break this week," Canning said.

"After what happened to Hardstark last month, I'd be hesitant to get anywhere near Carvin," said Liam.

Briony's ears pricked at the mention of Cordelia. She looked away as Cecily took Collin out of his trousers, bile rising in the back of her throat.

"Cohle was too ambitious," Canning said. "He should have known Hardstark would be husked."

Her eye twitched. Her shallow breath felt like ice in her chest.

Husked. Cordelia had been husked—all her magic taken, used up, with no promise it would ever return.

Briony squeezed her hands into fists.

A glass shattered—a spray of crystal shards across the dinner table, fruit and cheese exploding outward and bouncing away. The men scattered to their feet, and a pressure released in her chest as Toven stood with her, spinning her body away, his hand outstretched to cast protections.

Collin's fist was bloody where his glass had been just a second ago. Looking down at his hand in amazement, Collin flexed his fingers. Cecily crawled out from under the table.

Briony breathed deep.

Her magic.

She'd just let her magic loose in front of the successors to the line.

Chapter 28

TOVEN WAS QUICK TO BEGIN.

"Stones, Collin! Too excited?" He bellowed a laugh, tucking Briony behind himself subtly.

Slowly the others caught on. Collin had squeezed his glass too hard. That's all it was.

"You'd think he'd never been sucked off before!" Canning barked, and Lorne snickered. Collin smiled down at his hand in confusion.

The fear seeped out of her as those awful words came back to her.

Cordelia had been husked. Completely drained of her magic, her heart unable to produce more. She was alive, but barely.

Tears gathered in her eyes, and she turned her face away to let them fall. She couldn't mourn Cordelia here, now.

Kleve came back in from the other room, arms full of bottles, and took in the scene. "What's all this glass?"

"Excellent point, Kleve." Canning turned malicious eyes on the women. "Ladies, on all fours! I want every piece of glass collected and every boot kissed." He wove his fingers together behind his head and smiled at Toven specifically.

Toven's fingers twitched on Briony's waist as several women immediately dropped to their knees.

Briony was still trying to calm her heart and focus on tucking Cordelia away in a book on a low shelf in her mind's eye.

She began to go to the floor, but Toven's hand on her wrist stopped her.

"What's wrong, Tove?" Lorne said. "Do you think your heartspring is too good to do our cleaning?"

"I do, actually," he said. "I don't usually let sixty-five thousand gold drop on the floor."

Briony glanced between them. Every other woman had gone to her knees.

"It's strange to me how you let her act like a gold-blooded princess still," Liam said, examining his reflection in his spoon.

The room quieted, holding its breath. The only sound was the tinkle of glass as it was collected under the table.

Toven released her wrist with a look of disdain. She fell to her knees quickly and crawled under the table, feeling small pieces of glass dig into her palms and knees. She took a deep breath and centered herself, relishing the first moment without eyes on her.

When she looked up, several of the women were working fast to collect the fallen food and broken glass, but Cecily was frozen. She was curled over her knees, a palm to her mouth, and a silent screaming sob choking her. Briony watched as the woman between them—a dark-skinned woman in a silver collar—wrapped herself over Cecily and squeezed her body tight on every shuddered inhale.

Jellica Reeve was across from Briony, her gaze vacant and her mouth parted as she seemed to take in more air than she could possibly need on every breath. She had a palm full of glass.

The conversation hummed to life again, and Briony began reaching out with shaking hands to collect anything she saw on the floor.

Her eyes blurred as Cecily took a gasping breath.

She had a sudden memory of Cecily's laugh, breaking through the dining room at school. It had been wild and jarring from such a small body.

Briony reached out for a stray grape, brushing fingers with another person. Before she could retract her hand, pale freckled fingers grabbed hold of her tightly. When she looked up, the strawberry-blond maid was focused on her, squeezing her hand, grounding her.

Briony wanted to ask a thousand questions about this young woman's life before the Eversun palaces and where her brother was and if she'd *almost* gotten out.

Another hand took her other and squeezed. She looked to her right. The dark-skinned woman was still curled over Cecily as her breathing calmed, but she'd reached out, connecting herself to Briony.

As Briony looked around, she found every woman slowly squeezing another's shoulder, hand, wrist, support vining among them all. Octavia and Jellica and five other women she didn't know were holding tightly to one another, as if they could all infuse Cecily with what she needed to stand up and sit back down on Collin's lap. It almost felt like magic—this connection, this contact. Tears pooled in Briony's eyes at the thought.

And as quickly as it had begun, it was broken. Briony found her hands empty but for the glass and grapes, missing the vine already.

When she came to her feet, she discarded the rubbish and picked shards out of her palms with a hollow feeling in her chest.

Before she could decide if she was to sit in Toven's lap again or not, a soft bell rang in the courtyard below.

Canning clapped. "That's our cue."

Jellica stumbled forward, clutching onto him in relief.

All the men but Canning rose from their chairs, and Briony hoped it was almost over. Her eyes were tired with unshed tears, but she sniffed them back.

"Best of luck in the arena," Lorne said, taking Octavia by the waist. "Toven, you'll sit with us, of course."

Toven passed a hand through his hair and said, "I'm afraid not. My father is to be home this evening. I need to be there to greet him." His hand drifted to the small of her back, ready to guide her out.

"I knew he wouldn't," Lorne slurred to Liam.

"Come now, Toven!" Canning gestured dramatically. Jellica had fallen into his lap again, only this time she straddled him. "I've already won ten gold from Kleve. He bet you'd never bring her to dinner." Canning smiled and pointed his thumb to Lorne. "This one says we couldn't get her into the arena, but I know one day you'll jump in."

The way they grinned made Briony's stomach churn. Toven forced a smile and fiddled with the ring on his middle finger.

"Perhaps another time."

The men glanced among themselves. Canning smiled over Jellica's shoulder as she peppered kisses down his neck, panting with desire.

"What time is your father due home?" Liam said, his tone deceptively casual.

Toven paused, and Briony wondered if he was trying to figure out the time. "Half past twelve. So we——"

"Plenty of time!" Lorne clapped Toven on the shoulder, as if the deed were done. "You'll see Canning in the first round for certain!"

Toven's hand was tight on her back, sending tension up her spine. "I suppose we have twenty minutes."

"Ahem, speaking of . . ." Canning said, trailing off suggestively. Briony realized Jellica was unbuttoning Canning's trousers eagerly.

Briony swallowed back bile and looked away. He was going to have sex with her before he fought in the arena, because it would give him a boost of Sacral Magic. Briony had gathered that much.

Lorne knocked on the door, and the guard opened it from the outside. Briony took note of the extra precautions they had taken for their clandestine dinners.

They made their exit, the men laughing at Canning and Jellica, the women's eyes turned away. They wound back down the stairs and into the entry hall again. The crowd had thinned, but there were still enough eyes on all of them as they passed like a royal cavalcade. Several people were mingling in the garden, having hushed conversations over sloshing drinks.

As they walked through the garden that Briony used to read in on hot summer nights, she faintly heard the crowd over the sound of the water trickling through the fountains. They passed her father's old gallery, an ornate building perched at the top of the cliffs, hosting original paintings, sculptures, and weapon designs by Vindecci himself.

She summoned what was left of her control. *Think of a lake with still waters.*

They were headed to the amphitheater, where lectures and plays and great speeches had been made for centuries in Evermore. *It isn't an arena!* she wanted to scream. *It's a palace for art and philosophy and science.*

As they reached the arched stadium entrance, the woman from the beginning of the night—Ilana—stood with a tray of champagne and scotch.

"Gentlemen," she greeted with a wide smile. Her lips were still violently red, her hair still falling in perfect waves.

Lorne plucked a scotch from her tray. "Ilana, dear," he cooed. "You look ravishing. When are you finally going to come home with me?" He stroked her arm.

"Flattery will get you everywhere, Master Vult." Ilana winked at him and turned to offer the tray to Toven. "But you know the Barlowes wouldn't allow it."

Briony stared at her, filing that information away as Toven pressed another glass of champagne into her hand. Her eyes fell on Ilana's silver collar as the pretty woman batted her lashes at Toven, then Finn, and glided down the line with her tray.

Toven led her through the passageway under the tiers of seats and into the circular arena. Sand lined the floor where at least two hundred people stood drinking and socializing before finding their seats. Every step closer to the middle made Briony feel sicker.

Toven and the others moved to an area that was apparently being kept clear for them. There were rising benches to sit on, but the men remained standing and socializing. General Tremelo was sitting near the front with Gains and Canning's mother, Genevieve Trow. She cast her gaze around the amphitheater, finding Katrina on Caspar Quill's arm, expression empty. In the front, across from Briony and Toven, Phoebe teetered on tall heels next to Carvin. She looked exhausted, but Briony felt cold dread inside of her as Phoebe laughed at something Carvin said.

Carvin smiled down at her and pressed a kiss to her lips that Phoebe returned.

Briony's ribs felt stuck. Was Phoebe on Canning's elixir? Her behavior was nothing like Jellica Reeve's, but how was it that Phoebe looked almost natural on Carvin's arm?

Briony stared across the arena, begging Phoebe to look at her, to prove that she was still behind the shy smile and fluttering lashes.

She never glanced her way.

After about ten more minutes, Mr. Vein, the same man who'd hosted the auction, entered the arena to thunderous applause.

"Ladies and gentlemen of Bomard," he greeted, his voice amplified. "As you remember from last week, Mr. Carvin is our reigning champion."

The crowd hollered, and Carvin waved, wrapping his arm around Phoebe's waist. She sipped from her champagne glass and smiled at the crowd.

"He and his golden heartspring will take this week off, as you know—but! Who will he face next week?"

Briony's head pounded with the screaming. She felt like she was back at the auction, with Mr. Vein's gleeful voice riling up the crowd.

Canning Trow entered the circle with Jellica trailing behind him. The crowd whooped, and Genevieve Trow whistled for her son. Jellica's gaze was cast down, and her dress was wrinkled from where it had perhaps been pushed around her hips.

Across from Canning, a fair-skinned woman with cropped black hair swaggered into the ring. A thin man with a pallid face and a silver collar followed her.

Briony didn't know exactly what was coming, but she knew that it was how Cordelia had been husked. Canning and the woman stood at opposite ends of the arena, their heartsprings standing behind them.

When it began, Briony didn't understand. They were battling. The woman and Canning fought each other almost playfully. Canning laughed as he shielded against an attack, and the woman dodged a slashing cut with a grin. They went round and round, and the crowd screamed for them as the attacks became ever more elaborate, the sparks from each feint and counterattack lighting the skies in vivid color.

Toven wrapped an arm around Briony's hip and watched without interest. A man came around taking bets, and Toven lazily put fifty gold pieces on the woman.

Barely five minutes later, Briony saw a change. The woman's heartspring at first wobbled, then skittered to his knees, as though faint. The crowd screamed, but Jellica wasn't far behind. Soon, both heartsprings had to sit down on the floor, unable to stand.

"What—what is the purpose?" she whispered to Toven. "Do they fight until one of them is husked?"

Toven leaned into her and pointed out the edges of the arena lined in black sand. "If either of them steps out, the other wins. The fighters have to decide if it's worth it to husk their heartsprings."

Tears filled Briony's eyes as she imagined Cordelia, draining in front of a crowd. There was no telling if she would access her magic again. Some people never did.

Jellica Reeve began to sob, and Briony could see her mouthing Canning's name, begging him. It was all for show. With the collars, the heartsprings didn't need to be physically near the Bomardi when they fought. Jellica and the man were in the arena just so Bomard could enjoy watching them drain.

Canning and the woman were locked into position, each of them pushing against the other from across the circle. Canning's hands were outstretched, his fingers curling. The woman was snarling.

Both fighters began to slide backward in the sand, the other's power pushing them close to the edge of the ring. The woman's heartspring fainted, and suddenly the woman dropped her hands in defeat, sliding backward and out of the ring.

The crowd went wild, and Canning threw his hands up in the air. Jellica was pale, crumpled to the floor, but she wasn't husked. Neither was the man. The woman had stopped in time, but Jellica and the man would have to rest now, possibly for days.

The crowd pressed in on her, jostling her shoulders as tears fell down Briony's face.

All of this for sport. A display of power that meant nothing. No war was fought tonight. No heartspring served their master for a greater purpose.

Briony shivered; all they were to these people were hearts to drain.

She found Ilana moving through the crowd with a tray of hors d'oeuvres and fruit, another woman following her with drinks. Mr. Vein called for any other competitors.

Somewhere in her mind's eye, there was a lake. A clear lake, the water still and unmoving.

Briony's stomach squeezed, and vomit pumped into her throat. She swallowed it down and stared across the arena at Phoebe, who was smiling softly at everything Carvin said to the man next to him.

Toven whispered to her that they would leave shortly, and she blinked slowly at the sandy floor of the place she used to come to for a connection to her people's culture.

A pair of champagne heels attached to tan legs crossed into her view. Ilana with the tray. She offered to fetch Toven a drink, and he declined, saying they were leaving soon.

Briony barely heard them, slightly swaying on her feet. An overwhelming exhaustion pushed at her eyelids. How was she to move forward from this? How were any of them to move forward from this?

"Miss Rosewood?"

Looking up to find Ilana still hovering, her vision cleared when she blinked. She frowned, confused to be directly addressed. Toven had turned away slightly, in response to a greeting from a passing friend.

"Anything to eat?" Ilana asked, long lashes batting slowly at her, her arm lowering to offer Briony the basket of fruit. "Grapes, perhaps?"

Briony stared down, finding a vine of thick, burgundy grapes calling to her from another lifetime. Something that used to mean something when spelled out on a dungeon floor.

Her mind cleared like a shock. She looked up with wide eyes. Ilana plucked one singular grape and extended it to her with a soft smile.

Briony took it, tucking it away quickly in her hand as though hiding a stolen good. Her heart hammered against her ribs.

She searched for Ilana again, but she'd moved away.

Could she possibly know what grapes meant to her? Could she know what had transpired in a dungeon where Briony had no voice, only fruit, but she'd needed to tell the women that they weren't alone. That others would rise.

Could Ilana know?

In the center of the stadium, another pair of fighters were preparing. Another pair of heartsprings stood waiting to be drained.

Briony sought out Phoebe across the arena and jumped at the shock of meeting her eyes for the first time since the dungeon. Phoebe's arms were wound around Carvin's shoulders as he kissed her neck, but she no longer smiled contently.

Staring into Briony's heart, Phoebe released Carvin with one hand, opening her palm to reveal a plump, ripe grape. She pushed it between her painted lips, her eyes burning with the fire of a revolution.

CHAPTER 29

Five Years Ago

IN THE YEAR FOLLOWING GIN PULVEY'S ASSASSINATION and Veronika Mallow's ascension to the Seat of Bomard, the tension between the Bomardi students and Eversun students increased tenfold.

Collin Twindle started spitting on Eversuns as they passed, calling them "mind freaks." Lorne Vult crowded Eversun girls in the hallway, asking them to read his mind for what he'd like to do to them. Liam Quill started fistfights with Eversuns, and Larissa Gains began interrupting and sabotaging any tutor lessons that included any references to mind magic.

And Toven Hearst had shifted into an ice sculpture. Where he used to tease and smirk and even send heated gazes her way to make her uncomfortable, now he refused to look at her.

There had been no ring on Larissa's finger when they came back from the summer solstice break, and Briony watched Toven and Larissa's courtship die a slow death over the next year.

At the end of the Bomardi school year in the winter, Mallow had announced that the use of mind magic in Bomard was banned and liable for punishment.

"How in the waters is she going to do that?" Cordelia had said as she walked with Katrina and Briony to dinner that day.

"They don't study mind magic as it is," Briony said. "I'm sure everyone will be all too happy to have an excuse to not expand their knowledge.

Most Bomardi stop learning anything about mind magic once they all choose their specialties in year four. Next year, it probably won't matter."

Katrina snorted. "Probably. But it's hard enough to concentrate as it is with half the Bomardi arguing with the tutors."

A few weeks later, a Bomardi in a border town had been put to death for using mind magic.

At the winter solstice, Finola had spent hours teaching Briony advanced mind magic techniques like cloaking and blending, all while Rory was invited to shadow their father in meetings with General Meers. There was something in the tension of Finola's shoulders during those lessons that made Briony quite aware of how bad things were getting between the two countries.

When they had arrived back at school for their fourth year, the Evermore year, Toven Hearst was paler than usual. He took little pleasure in social activities the way he once had. The only one of his friends who was still stuck to his side like glue was Finn Raquin, and even he had stopped flirting with everything that moved.

One summer night after curfew, Briony was sneaking back to the heir's suite that she shared with Rory when she saw light bouncing off a far wall down a long hall.

After looking for any signs that a tutor might catch her, she moved silently toward the light.

When she rounded the corner, she found Toven Hearst in an abandoned hallway with a conjured flame to cast light. He held a page in his hand, and she wondered what he was reading before realizing . . .

He was *writing*. The pen was zipping over the paper, by itself. The fingers of his right hand were stretched, casting a complicated spell to send the words directly from his mind onto the page.

He was using mind magic.

Briony gasped, and a second too late she slapped a hand over her mouth.

Toven jumped up and his eyes were wide for a moment before they turned cold on her.

"You saw nothing."

Briony stared at him, and then glanced down at the page—a garbled mess of every thought in his head.

"You need to meditate first," she said. "That will clear your head of tangents."

She'd just learned these techniques from Finola herself, and Briony itched to share them with *someone*.

Something flickered in Toven's eyes, and a slow smirk spread across his face.

"That would be very helpful if it wasn't forbidden to practice mind magic."

"In Bomard," Briony said, finishing his sentence. "It's forbidden in Bomard. You're in Evermore."

"Ah, that explains the smell."

She narrowed her gaze at him. "You'll get better at it. It's a shame you can't practice anywhere—"

"I have no idea what you're talking about, Rosewood." His expression was cool.

She pressed her lips together and nodded. "I see. You know, Toven, I used to think you were different. But I see you're just the same as the rest of them."

He smiled and moved forward. "And what is that?"

"Ignorant."

Air puffed out of him on a laugh, and she felt it from a foot away. "That *would* be your best insult, wouldn't it? Eversuns are enlightened, and Bomardi are primitive? Is that right, Rosewood?"

"Your words, not mine."

"Well, our 'primitive' magic has been doing just fine for us. Heart magic has more sheer power than mind magic ever will. Why should we 'evolve'?"

She felt the full weight of his attention for the first time in a year, and it made her reckless.

"You tell me," she said. "You're the one transcribing nonsense onto a page after hours, using your mind."

"You're mistaken," he said simply.

Briony's volume lifted, a provocation. "Oh, no? I didn't see TOVEN HEARST PRACTICING MIND MAGIC?" she yelled down the hall, taunting him.

Toven grabbed her, his hand covering her mouth as her back slammed against the stone wall. Once he'd looked down the hall for signs that anyone had heard her, his hand shifted—his thumb and forefinger holding either side of her jaw. He could choke her with barely a slip of his hand.

Her eyes were wide, but his angry face enraged her.

"Don't speak on things you don't understand," he hissed.

"I know *exactly* what I'm talking about."

His breath was on her, and she could smell the peppermint of his skin. His fingers tightened, and she gasped.

"Your brother will be a head on a spike one day, and your body will be dragged through the street once Mallow has her way," he said softly. Briony's muscles locked in fear. He let his eyes drift down her neck. "And such a shame for such a fine body."

He was vile and she hated the thrill of him looking at her again—looking at her as a *woman* instead of an Eversun. She disgusted herself, so she turned her bile outward.

She spat in his face.

He glared down at her in shock. And then a smile crept across his features, curving and unfurling. Briony's breath was hot, but his hand was cool against her cheek. His body pressed up against her, pinning her in place. Her eyes widened to feel the long lines of him as he towered over her.

"If you insist on forgetting your manners, Rosewood, then maybe I'll be tempted to forget mine," he whispered against her mouth.

There were no words in her head as Toven Hearst's lips grew so close to hers.

"What manners?" she said weakly. "You're no gentleman, Toven Hearst."

He hummed. "If you wanted a gentleman, you'd already be betrothed to Winchester."

Her breath stuck in her throat. His eyes seemed to sparkle as he tilted her jaw up.

"Tell me, Princess," he said, sliding his knee between hers, just as she'd seen him do to Larissa when they were being intimate in the corridors.

She gasped, shock and thrill and longing singing in her blood.

Briony's hands braced on his waist, ready to push him away or pull him closer—she couldn't decide.

He smiled, and even though it was cruel, her gaze traced the lines of it.

"Do you want a gentleman?" he asked, his voice a low hum that sent waves through her.

She held her breath, overwhelmed with want, desperately trying to figure out if this was what it felt like to be wanted back. Wondering if that *thing* her body searched for with Didion under the willow would finally open to her. Wondering if she could keep his attention just long enough to let her find it.

The response fell from her lips, unbidden. "No."

Something flickered in his eyes. His gaze softened as it slid down to her mouth.

"Briony?"

Briony jerked her head toward the end of the hallway. Cordelia stood in her dressing gown, hands splayed to fight.

Toven stepped away, and there was a rush of cool air against her front. She tried to catch her breath.

"What's happening?" Cordelia asked harshly.

Toven smirked in response.

Briony quickly moved toward Cordelia, her legs unsteady. "Nothing," she said. Briony linked arms and walked back to the dormitories with her, saying loudly, "Toven Hearst simply forgot his manners again."

She sent a withering look behind her and found him watching her darkly as she walked away.

"What manners?" he called after her, echoing her own words. "I'm no gentleman, I've been told."

She ignored him, pulling Cordelia closer.

Briony sometimes wondered if she'd dreamed the entire thing, especially when Toven Hearst refused to look at her for the rest of the school year.

CHAPTER 30

 IRE WAS IN HER BLOOD as Toven finally excused them from the arena. Her feet wobbled under her, and there was a ringing in her ears.

Briony quickly ate the grape Ilana had given her, as if it were a forbidden correspondence that needed to be destroyed. The sweet juice of it slid down her throat as she searched for Phoebe's eyes again, but she wouldn't look back at her.

Toven's fingers wrapped around her elbow as he led them to the small section of the garden overlooking the sea that had allowed portaling in her father's reign. Her mind was elsewhere as he sliced open the tip of his finger and cast his hand for a portal. Her body was squeezed and pressed, and then she was suddenly in the Hearst drawing room.

Breathing heavily, Briony still felt the atmosphere of that arena hanging off her body like a beaded gown. She could still hear the crowd, taste the smoke in the air. And she could feel Toven's eyes on her, waiting.

She turned away from him, feeling simultaneously exhausted and energized. She tucked Phoebe and Ilana and grapes into a book on the shelf in her mind, and refocused on the questions she could get answers to.

She would begin where she needed the most clarification.

"Sacral Magic," she said slowly. "Am I correct that it has to do with sex?"

She could hear him swallow from across the room.

"Heartspring magic is meant for love matches," he began. She nodded, already aware of this. "When heartsprings are properly used . . . lovemaking strengthens the bond."

"You heart magicians love your metaphors. Not *all* romantic relationships include sex." Briony sighed. "So you're telling me that when Canning has sex with Jellica, against her will, she strengthens him." Acid dripped from her words.

"No," he said. "Sacral Magic is still sacred between willing parties . . . But . . ."

She turned her eyes on him for the first time since they'd arrived back. His lips were twisted as if he'd tasted something sour.

"But Canning's elixir has made things interesting," she finished for him, remembering Katrina's explanation.

He nodded.

"What lovely friends you have, Toven," she muttered. "I'm so glad to know it's not just rape. It's rape for magical power." Her molars ground together. He remained silent. "Who were all of those heartsprings?"

He slipped his hands into his pockets. "Most are from Eversun families who still flew the Eversun banner after Bomard had taken their lands. Some were part of your court on the day of Bomard's triumph, as you know," he said. Briony nodded. "Some were found assisting Sammy Meers."

She blinked at him but soldiered on. "And who are the Barlowes?"

"An Eversun family from near the border who flipped allegiance the moment your brother died. They have been assigned Biltmore Palace." His voice was clinical.

She swayed on her feet at the mention of Rory.

"And the silver-collared heartsprings are owned by the Barlowes?"

Toven's eyes flickered over her. "You should sleep."

"Later. The collars? Gold and silver."

"Gold collars are for the heartsprings who are privately owned—the ones who were auctioned, I mean." His eyes dropped to the floor. "And yes, the ones wearing silver collars are owned by the Barlowes. They can be . . . borrowed on Friday evenings, but they live at Biltmore. Some of them are also non-magical, to be rented for company."

Briony remembered the strawberry-blonde and nodded. She crossed her arms in front of her, hating that she was still in this stupid dress.

"The private dinner party. Those were all the successors of the line, minus the women," she said. Toven lifted his brows in agreement. "So every man at that dinner table owns a heartspring?"

"Canning owns Jellica Reeve, Lorne owns his girl——"

"Octavia," she snapped. "Her name is Octavia."

He dipped his head in a nod. "Octavia. And Collin has a heartspring at home, but if you'll remember, he was quite taken with Cecily in school. He has spent a lot of gold renting her from the Barlowes every Friday."

"Renting her," she muttered to herself, shaking her head. The bile in her throat bubbled again, and whenever she closed her eyes, she saw Cecily's hands shaking as she opened Collin's trousers. A slow chill spread over her shoulders, like an ice cube sliding down her spine. "And Finn? He was named a successor?"

"Cal Gidrey's daughter defected last month, leaving him without a successor as tenth in line. Finn was of great assistance to Gidrey during the last few months. As a reward, Finn was offered the position as successor to the tenth in line, superseding his own father as fourteenth."

"What did he do?" Briony asked.

Toven tilted his head at her. "You'll have to ask him."

She huffed. "Last I heard, Lorne Vult was still vying for a successor position. Looks like he got one."

"He is to replace Burkin as Cohle's successor."

Briony's mind spun with all the names and positions of the line. She needed to write herself a list.

"But it hasn't been made official yet? Is that why Lorne didn't have a gemstone on his ring?"

He blinked at her, brows lifting slightly. "Yes. Good catch."

At his impressed look, her chest warmed without her permission. Briony had to focus, even as her thoughts tumbled through tangents.

"What is required to make it official?" she asked.

"An oath to the Seat, signed in blood."

She paced away from him, longing to take off the heels. "Is that generally the *tone* of those dinners?" she asked, remembering how Jellica was humiliated and Cecily was forced to her knees.

"Things were maybe a bit heightened with your presence, but generally, yes. Canning brings his elixir around to small gatherings like that."

She glared at him as the heat and anger unfurled in her chest. The men had acted out more than usual that evening simply because she was there? And in the past, when she was hidden away, did Toven have another woman at his side?

Suddenly her blood felt white-hot again.

"And how did you manage when your heartspring had the pox?"

"Vesper came with me. The pox made you 'too weak to pull from,' so it was an easy excuse—"

"No, not magically," she said. "I assume you still had a girl on your arm."

His throat clicked, and his eye twitched infinitesimally as he said, "I used a Barlowe Girl. Or I borrowed from someone."

She wanted to breathe fire.

" 'Borrowed.' Like a cup of sugar," she hissed. She watched it land on him, like an arrow finding the center ring.

"It's late, Rosewood. I'll send up an elixir—"

"I don't need an elixir—"

"—and we can talk in the morning."

"I want to know who you pulled in your lap and groped while I had the pox—"

His eyes flashed. "You want an itemized list? What does it matter!"

"It matters because you're telling me that my presence alone tonight made it worse for those women. It matters because while I've been locked away in Hearst Hall, other women had to suffer through that—that vile display—"

She choked, her throat closing as a single tear betrayed her by rolling down her cheek. She slapped it away, furious with herself.

There was silence for a few moments as he studied her. She glared back, lifting her chin. He watched her carefully.

"Your experiences this evening have been traumatic," he said simply. "You should sleep and regroup your thoughts."

Scanning his perfectly impassive features, she wondered if he used mind barriers. His face was like a mask. Was he the one who used the meditation chamber in Hearst Hall? She pressed her lips together. "I have more questions."

"They can wait."

"You'll answer any question I have tomorrow?"

He stared at her blankly and said, "Yes."

"Eight in the morning," she demanded.

"Noon."

"Nine."

"Rosewood, it is after one. You will be up for another two hours writing a list of things to ask, and you will spend your morning meditating," he said, his eyes gray and empty. "You need sleep."

She narrowed her eyes at him, feeling her heart pound with anger at his assumptions, and irritation that those assumptions were correct.

"Is that an order from 'Master Toven'?" she snarled.

He didn't react. Some switch had flipped inside of him. He was no longer rile-able.

"It can be, if it needs to be," he said calmly.

She wanted to scream.

"You better clear your afternoon, Hearst," she hissed, and stomped toward the staircase.

*　*　*

The next day, as the clock ticked toward twelve, Briony was certain Toven was going to avoid her.

But at noon on the dot, there was a knock on her bedroom door. She stood from the chair in front of the window and said, "Come in."

Toven strolled in, wearing a pale gray sweater. As she prepared to ask questions, she realized that he'd managed to strengthen his mask overnight. He stared at her, a slight tilt to his head, with eyes cool and gray.

That's just fine. I've strengthened mine as well.

"General Tremelo's presence last night," she said, jumping in without greeting. "What does that say for Bomard and Daward?"

Toven twisted his ring around his middle finger, and her eye caught on the muscles in his hands, before she remembered to focus.

"Biltmore has hosted several officials from across the sea. I can only say that Mallow is 'courting' them, in a way. There are countries who are adamantly against her, fearing that she will try to cross the sea, but she has her ways of keeping them in line."

Briony turned her head to gaze out her window, thinking, noting these answers down on her mental checklist, stowing them into a tight corner of her library of shelves.

"You touched my tattoo as we crossed the threshold at Biltmore, just as you do here at the hall. Is it the same magic?"

"To my knowledge. The barrier keeps out undesirables and . . . keeps in the heartsprings."

She tucked the information away for a future escape plan. Taking a deep breath and centering herself, she prepared to ask the one question she knew she didn't want to hear the answer to.

"And Cordelia?" she said, and the words floated to him like a feather. "Tell me."

She watched him swallow and turn his eyes over her shoulder again.

"A few weeks ago, she broke a champagne glass and sliced the neck of a guard, killing him."

Briony scarcely breathed, the words like a bucket of water over her head.

"Cohle decided to enter the arena. He and Carvin battled, and Cohle didn't stop until Cordelia was husked."

"And so what happens to her now?"

"She is alive, but . . . no longer a heartspring."

Briony reached between the words he wasn't saying. "Now she's just a woman, held captive in a man's estate."

Toven met her eyes. "That may be true."

She spun away from him, blinking until her eyes stopped burning and she could see clearly again.

"Will she ever have magic again?" Briony's voice cracked on the words.

"It depends. Her heart magic is gone, but she could possibly use mind magic . . . if that option were ever returned to her."

She nodded to herself, slapping back her tears. There would be another time to process what had happened to Cordelia. But for now she had a role to play. She'd convinced him she could handle the truth, and that's exactly what she intended to do. Ignoring the buzzing in her ears and the tightness in her chest, she forced her shoulders to relax.

She'd been given signs of hope by women who had no business hoping. A grape. Her hand grabbed under the table by seven others with glass in their knees.

And Phoebe was waiting for her. She *had* to talk to her.

"Now that I know what to expect," she said, her voice clear and strong, "I will play my part better. The next time we go, I will be better prepared to—"

"We're not going again."

It took a moment for the words to sink in. She spun to him, eyes wide. "What?"

He stood with his hands in his trouser pockets, eyes dead and empty.

"We've made our appearances. You've been seen." He swallowed. "You won't go again. Not for a long time, at least."

Her heart pounded. These parties were her only chance to communicate with her friends—her only connection to what was happening outside Hearst Hall.

"So I'll just contract the pox again?" she sniped.

"I'll speak to my father, and we'll come up with something—"

"They'll see through you in an instant. It will be far too suspicious—"

"Listen," he said quietly. "If we go back, Canning will make you take the elixir."

She rolled her eyes, feeling the fire burn in her belly again. "Who do I belong to? You or Canning?"

"We can't go to Biltmore and not participate in those private dinners. If I refuse, they will suspect something is off about our relationship." His eyes flickered up to her. "Canning already suspects."

"And whose fault is that?" she said. "If you hadn't told all your friends about the wonderful amounts of consensual sex we've been having, we wouldn't be in this position, Toven, but you did——"

"You underestimate how desirable you were to those men back in school," Toven said softly. Something about his voice silenced her. Her cheeks flushed as he continued. "If I hadn't implied our relationship had progessed and therefore taken you off the market—so to speak—their interest would be tenfold what it is now. The only mistake I made was dancing with you at the estate dinner after the first school year. You were marked in their eyes from that moment forward."

Briony narrowed her eyes at him. She wanted to argue it, but she also remembered the way Liam and Canning had cut in. All of them strutting around, trying to get one over on each other.

But she wouldn't trade the memory of waltzing with Toven Hearst for the world.

She shook her head, trying to refocus on the problem. Canning's elixir.

Briony thought of Jellica, how she'd thrown herself at Canning the moment she could. The way her body swayed to him.

"I've seen the elixir in action now. Was Jellica's behavior standard?"

He breathed heavily through his nose. "Rosewood, if you mean to mimic this elixir——"

"We can figure out how to get around the actual drinking of it," she said, beginning to pace. "Perhaps we say you gave it to me ahead of time."

"I've already said we're not going back!"

"Toven, I don't know how you expect to keep me hidden for the rest of our lives. Something drastic will have to happen to me to keep you from bringing me along."

He clenched his jaw, gaze lingering on her face before looking away.

"Every eye will be on you the more often you come to Biltmore. Not just Lorne and Canning and the others. And it's not just at Biltmore Palace. There are other, very secret gatherings where it's more encouraged to . . . partake in your heartspring."

Her lips curled in disgust, but she refocused.

"I see," she said, voice dripping with disdain. "Do you all have sex in front of each other often then?"

He rolled his eyes. "They don't want to watch us have sex, Rosewood. They want to see you humiliated."

She swallowed, listening to her throat click loudly in the small room. Her cheeks were hot, and her fingers shook as she clasped her hands.

"That's a sacrifice I'm willing to make as long as you and I are on the same page," she said, more confidently than she felt.

Toven stared at her. "You must be joking."

"I watched Jellica tonight. I understand the basics—"

" 'The basics,' " he said, laughing. He crossed to her window, and she tracked him, indignation burning in her gut.

"Are you suggesting that because I haven't had sex, I've never lusted after someone? That I wouldn't understand those urges?"

He tilted his head, cracking his neck with his back to her.

"I'm sure you have an idea of it, but this elixir is no joke, Rosewood."

Briony glared daggers at him. She remembered the simpering smiles Phoebe gave Carvin. The flirty laugh from Ilana to Canning. Those women were capable of playing the game just fine without an elixir confusing their senses. She needed to prove to him that she could do it, too, or else he wouldn't take her back.

Briony released the tension in her body from their argument and focused on a different kind of tension. Her gaze swept over his back, remembering the skin she'd seen when Vesper had attacked her. Her lips parted, imagining what it would be like to have him all to herself, with no reason to stay apart.

Toven turned from the window, ready to give her another excuse.

Briony bit her lip, running her eyes over the front of him, remembering how Jellica seemed to press her thighs together, desperate for relief.

Words caught in his throat as he met her hot gaze. She stepped forward. "Toven . . ."

His mouth opened in understanding, and then he closed his eyes. "You're out of your mind, Rosewood, if you think—"

"Please touch me," she begged, voice breathy.

She reached for him.

His quick reflexes caught her, hands coming up to her elbows. She imagined the heady feeling of having his skin on hers after *hours* of begging, and she moaned softly, leaning her forehead onto his chest.

"Rosewood," he said, voice firm.

She couldn't hear him over the want pounding in her body. She pressed her mouth to his sternum, kissing his chest over his clothing.

He grabbed her shoulders and shoved her back. His eyes were wide and hot, almost scared.

"What are you doing?"

She panted and let her eyes glaze over. "Toven, please. Don't make me wait any longer."

His eyes widened, and she caught a glimpse of black pupils before he backed away. She stumbled forward, reaching up to pull his head down to her, but before she could connect their lips he pushed away again.

"That's enough—"

"I need you. Please, Toven." Her fingers wound into his hair, and she rose up on her toes, aiming for his lips and murmuring, "Touch me."

Quick as lightning, her hands were off him and her body was pushed against the windows. He was across the room in three strides, heading for the door.

"So?" she asked, breaking character and letting the wild look fade from her expression. "Was I convincing?"

His eyes hardened on her, and then he swept from the room, leaving her alone with lips tingling from where she'd touched him.

*   *   *

Toven diligently ignored her for the next six days. The first few days, she told herself that it was a good thing, but by Wednesday night, she started to get nervous. She had to go back. Regardless of how they might feel about each other at the moment.

She finally sought him out on Friday morning, finding him in the kitchens taking an apple from the basket.

She placed her hands on her hips and said, "I assume we'll be leaving at ten tonight?"

He turned, and his eyes scanned her before replying, "No. No party tonight."

She lifted a doubtful brow. "Why?"

"It's been postponed." He tossed the apple between his hands, keeping his eyes away from her.

"You can't avoid me forever, Hearst. We're in this together whether you like it or not, and the sooner you—"

"Did you hear a word I just said? It's not happening tonight." He brushed past her without another word.

Briony huffed at the empty kitchen, fists clenched. He was clearly lying.

So at ten o'clock that night, she cracked her door open, waiting to hear the sounds of him leaving the hall. After half an hour with her eye on the door, she moved to her windows and looked for the light coming from his bedroom.

It was dark.

She glared and stomped into her bathroom, deciding on a bath while she waited for him to return. As she relaxed into the warm water and bubbles, she tried to think of ways to convince Toven to bring her back to Biltmore. He didn't think she was capable of the sexual challenges they would face, but she could convince him. She had to.

She had to get back to Phoebe. She needed to figure out who Ilana was and whether that grape meant what she thought it did. She'd been stuck inside Hearst Hall for more than six weeks now, and Biltmore was the closest she'd gotten to her people.

Briony had to prove to him that she could handle herself. Whatever it took.

After midnight, she dragged an armchair to her window and read a book with one eye on Toven's windows, waiting for a sign of life from inside the room.

At a quarter past two, her bleary eyes drifted up from her pages. Light was pouring from inside his room. She jumped up, wide awake, the book tumbling onto the carpet. Without a thought to her pajamas, she marched out her door and to his.

She rapped on his door and waited, anger unfurling in her belly.

When no response came, she knocked louder, more insistently.

She was just raising her fist to pound against the wood again when it swung open. Toven stared down at her, leaning forward on the doorframe with one hand still on the door.

"Why are you still up?" he demanded.

She glared at him, lifting her chin. "I should be asking you the same thing. You haven't been out, have you, Hearst?"

He swallowed and said, "I have, but not to Biltmore."

"Then why do you smell like cigars and whiskey?" she hissed.

"I was at a private party, if you must know. I convinced the boys to play cards this evening instead."

Something about his posture made her doubt him. Who had he pulled into his lap this evening? Which poor woman had to sit through that vile dinner party this week? She would have this out with him and would demand that he take her next week.

Briony stepped forward to push past him into his bedroom, but Toven stood in the way, blocking her. She blinked up at him, scowling. After lying egregiously to her, the least he could do was let her in his damned room.

She stepped to the side and he moved with her, obscuring her vision. She stared up at him, a pale horror cracking over her skin.

He had a guest.

Her mind conjured a rapid-fire sequence of images of a Barlowe Girl sprawled across his sheets—the activities she'd just interrupted.

"Is there someone here?" she whispered.

He stared down at her, shook his head once, and said, "No. Just in the middle of something."

"My goodness," a familiar girlish voice called from inside the room. "Does she often visit your bedroom at two in the morning? How fascinatingly desperate of her."

Briony's mind whirred, struggling to place the voice that sounded like—that sounded like . . .

Toven closed his eyes in resignation.

And then the door was pulled open wider by a well-manicured hand that she knew so well—the same hand that she used to watch running fingers through Toven's hair, dancing pathways over his ribs, and squeezing quickly at his backside.

Briony's breath left her as a woman stepped into view.

Larissa Gains joined Toven in the doorway, her self-satisfied smirk firmly in place and her eyes running over Briony's body like a predator's.

CHAPTER 31

L ARISSA GAINS STOOD IN FRONT OF HER, and Briony had a sudden inexplicable urge to grab ahold of Larissa and make sure she was real. But before her body could actually try to *hug* Larissa, her brain caught up.

It was two in the morning. And Larissa Gains was in Toven's bedroom.

Her eyes slid to Toven, searching for any sign of rumpled clothing, black irises, lipstick on his neck—the things she used to see in the school hallways once Larissa was done with him. There was nothing to indicate that they'd been in the middle of something when she'd knocked. But as if reading her mind, Larissa chose that moment to link her arm around Toven's elbow and slide her hand up his left biceps.

"Briony. Captivity looks good on you." Larissa smiled.

"Death looks even better on you," she said.

Larissa laughed and tossed her hair over her shoulder. Toven cleared his throat and pulled his arm from Larissa's grasp.

"I was going to speak with you in the morning," Toven said, "but since you're here . . ."

He stepped back and gestured for Briony to enter.

Briony glanced at Larissa, who was watching her calculatingly, and then squeezed between the two of them to enter Toven's bedroom.

She quickly glanced to his bed, finding it perfectly made, no creases or rumples. Moving to stand near his desk, she turned to face the two of them. Larissa strutted to the fireplace and dropped into his wingback chair, crossing her legs sensuously and taking up the glass of wine on the table that had her exact shade of lipstick smudged on the rim.

Toven ran a hand through his hair and seemed to steel himself. He waited near the door, and if he had looked anything less than nervous, Briony would have thought he was blocking the exit.

"Larissa has a proposition for you," he said.

Briony glanced at the blond girl, who was grinning up at her.

"I've heard from multiple sources now that you were a spectacular disaster at Biltmore," Larissa said, sipping from her glass. Briony narrowed her eyes at her. "You looked a mess, and you fooled no one into thinking that Toven Hearst has been having his way with you."

Briony crossed her arms. "*That* was hardly my fault." She pointed at Toven. "*He* improperly prepared me. And he had no interest in—in being *cozy* with me, either."

Toven glared at her. Larissa waved her hand as if she were shooing a fly.

"Irrelevant. You need to step it up, Rosewood," she said. "Luckily for you, you're speaking with someone who knows exactly what it's like to be fucking Toven Hearst."

A knot grew in Briony's throat, and she tried not to flinch.

"Larissa," Toven warned. "That's enough."

Larissa examined her nails. "Apologies. To be fucking *anyone*. Full stop." She grinned at Briony.

As much as Larissa was trying to rile her up, Briony couldn't help but remember that Larissa had been among those taken from the dungeon by Canning Trow to try his elixir. And Larissa was right. She *knew* Toven intimately. She knew his heart better than Briony did. And hadn't Larissa said in the Trow dungeon that she was envious of what Briony's life would be? Did Larissa know that Toven wasn't using Briony as a heartspring, too?

Suddenly, Briony was more than a little interested in whatever Larissa had to offer if it gave Briony access to the things that Larissa knew about Toven and why owning the "golden heartspring" was so important to him.

"All right," Briony said. "You want to help me in some way with the ruse. And what is it you want in return?"

Larissa hesitated. Briony looked at Toven. The three of them were in a perfect triangle, equidistant from one another like players in a game about to begin.

Toven's throat bobbed. "Larissa would like lessons in mind cloaking."

Briony's brow furrowed. "Mind cloaking." She glanced at Larissa. Mind cloaking was a technique only practiced by advanced mind magicians. The tutors touched on it in school, but it had taken Briony many years with Finola as a guide to learn how to cloak. "You want to practice transparency and invisibility?"

Larissa pressed her lips together. "That, and also transmogrification."

The ability to change one's appearance, from as little as hiding a blemish to as much as becoming another person. It had less to do with changing yourself, as to do with manipulating the mind of the person viewing you.

Something told Briony that Larissa wasn't interested in hiding a few pimples.

"You'd like to change your appearance," she said. "To go into hiding?"

Larissa lifted her brows. "The opposite, in fact. I'd like to be hiding in plain sight."

Briony glanced at Toven. He was watching her shrewdly, waiting for her response. He wanted her to say yes.

"It's terribly difficult work," Briony said. "Particularly for someone who did not pick up the basics of mind magic in school."

Larissa smiled ruefully. "Well, thankfully, I have plenty of time at my disposal these days. We can start tomorrow."

Briony tilted her head at her. "So soon? Are you in a hurry?" She glanced at Toven. He was watching her, unmoving.

Larissa looked between the two of them, then sucked her teeth. "I need to start going to the Biltmore parties, clearly not as myself."

"Why?" Briony felt her forehead bunch.

"There's something I need access to there," Larissa said simply.

Briony knew she wouldn't get anything else out of her. Strangely, she had a moment to think about how nice it would be to have Larissa watching her back at these parties while Briony did the same.

Toven shifted and Briony looked at him. "I can give you space to practice tomorrow. Nine in the morning?"

There was a tension in his posture. She stared at him, wondering again if he shielded his mind with barriers, and if she could get under them without him knowing.

"How soon do you want to start attending parties transmogrified?" Briony asked.

"Next week," Larissa said.

Briony laughed. "Seven days! You think you can become proficient in powerful mind magic in seven days? They devote entire years to the subject at certain universities!"

"What's wrong? Do you have plans this week, Rosewood?" Larissa said flatly. "We're both rather free."

Briony looked to Toven, waiting for him—the other person who had some experience in mind magic techniques—to chime in about how ridiculous the notion was.

He was watching her still.

It was important to him, this idea.

She stared back at him, a sinking feeling in her gut.

Looking at Toven intently, Briony said, "And who is it that you plan to transmogrify yourself as, Larissa?"

"There are several options," Toven said. "People who should not be at Biltmore, whom Larissa can relieve."

Shivers crested across her skin, and she wished she'd put on her robe before storming over. Briony stared at him, her anger and disgust boiling over in her gut.

"You want to take Larissa to Biltmore. In my body."

She heard his throat click from across the room. "There are other persons as well—"

"Stones, she's sooo bright," Larissa said. Briony could hear the smile in her voice, though she couldn't take her eyes off Toven.

"The president of Southern Camly?" Toven started speaking quickly. "Her daughter was captured last week by Bomard. She's eighteen. She was given to Finn as a gift, to be his heartspring, but this could mean she'd never have to visit Biltmore again if Larissa could take her place."

There was bile in Briony's throat even as she filed away the war crimes Bomard was committing. Her hands curled into fists.

"You won't even deny it?" she asked. "That you would prefer to force Larissa to take my place?"

"No one's forcing anyone," Larissa said. Briony looked at her with hot eyes. "I'm volunteering for anything that would keep the both of you from getting killed."

Briony turned back to Toven. He slipped his hands in his pockets.

"It will be the easiest of options," he said.

She scoffed, pacing toward him. "Easiest."

"Yes, easiest," he repeated, voice harsh. "For both of us. Larissa has experienced the effects of Canning's elixir. She knows what it does, so now she can mimic the effects."

Rage choked her, her breath growing shallow as she thought about her own body in Larissa Gains's hands, her own hips straddling his lap, her own lips moving over his mouth. She stood in front of him now, Larissa's presence forgotten.

"How many times do I have to say that I *want* to go back to Biltmore? I *want* to see my friends and stay informed about what's happening to them."

"This is for your own good, Rosewood."

"You want to violate my body—"

"Your body will be violated either way," he snarled, holding his ground. "This way, you don't have to be in it."

Her arm moved quickly, slicing through the air and slapping him across the face. His head scarcely moved despite the angry red handprint on his cheek.

His eyes were dark, the gray fading into black dilated centers. She felt his breath on her forehead and the heat from his chest just inches from her own. His throat bobbed as he stared down at her, something barely restrained beneath the surface of his mask.

"I will teach Larissa how to cloak," Briony said slowly. "She will teach me how to play a part. And you will never cut me out of decisions about my body again."

She tilted her chin up and watched his gaze drop to her mouth and back up to her eyes.

The silence sent shivers down her spine. She summoned whatever confidence she had left and said, "Do I make myself clear?"

She searched his expression, finding his cheeks stained with more than just her pink handprint.

"Well," said a voice from behind her, and she almost jumped when she remembered Larissa. "I'll leave you both to it." Larissa chuckled.

Briony refused to look away from Toven first, refused to admit defeat here.

"I'll see you tomorrow morning at nine," Larissa said and slipped out the door.

It shut with a click, and Briony and Toven were alone.

CHAPTER 32

THE SILENCE WAS DEAFENING.

Briony swallowed, and she watched his eyes catch on the movement.

He stepped back from her as if fortifying himself. "It's clear to me that you still don't fully understand the danger we're in."

She lifted her brows mockingly. "Explain it to me, Master Toven."

His eyes narrowed before he went on.

"I was able to maintain control over the situation at the dinner table last week, but I consider that luck," he said. "You may think I had a certain level of control over those boys in school, but you must remember that my father is only eighth in line."

She remembered the way he'd put a stop to things before Lorne could cut her dress off, the way the other men's hands would wander over every backside that passed them—all but hers.

"It's not just about what happens within that group of successors," he said. "I suggested the private party tonight as a way to keep you from attending another week, but Canning invited Carvin and Reighven."

Briony flinched at his name, then recovered. Toven paused, gaze narrowing, before continuing.

"Canning could see through my suggestion for tonight's card game, of course," Toven continued. "He made sure to tell everyone that the golden heartspring will be taking the elixir at Biltmore next week."

Briony crossed her arms. "So you plan to have sex with Larissa Gains while she wears my skin. In front of the entire Bomardi elite."

Shaking his head, he said, "I would never have sex in public, and they know that." Briony glanced at him curiously, but before she could ask, he continued, "If you teach Larissa how to cloak this week and let her go in your place on Friday, then I can give my word that Larissa will go to Biltmore as the president's daughter for all dates in the future."

Briony stared at his expressionless face. She wanted so desperately to get under that mask behind his eyes, to force him to open his mind to her.

"You can't possibly think that Larissa can learn how to cloak in one week," she said.

"Maybe not," he said. "But I will cross that bridge when I come to it."

"We," she corrected him. "*We* will cross that bridge. All three of us."

His gaze flickered. Briony shrugged.

"If you are so sure you can avoid penetrative sex, then I'm not sure I understand why you're adamant that I not attend as myself."

He seemed to stare at her as if deciding if she was joking or not. He scoffed and brought a hand up to rub his eyes. Briony pressed her lips together in agitation.

"There are . . . other aspects to sex, Rosewood—"

"Of course there are."

"—and you are supposedly giving me those aspects regularly," he said, meeting her eyes again.

"Ah." She grinned at him. "So you don't think I'd be any good at using my mouth on you. How embarrassing for Toven Hearst to have such an unaccomplished whore, is that right?"

She paced away from him to lean on the edge of his desk, where she crossed her arms.

"You know," she said, "that spell to detect my purity told them all that I was a virgin, but you're assuming I have absolutely no knowledge of those 'other aspects.'"

She tilted her head at him, feigning confidence.

Toven stood a room's length away, his body held perfectly still.

"I am," he agreed stiffly. "Is that not the case?"

"I know how to use my mouth on men, Toven," she said, voice burning with acid.

She didn't. The closest experience she'd had with anyone had been letting Didion guide her hand around him last year. He'd enjoyed himself apparently, but Briony wasn't sure she had much to do with that.

But she was sick of this condescension.

There was something flickering in Toven's eyes that she couldn't read.

"Is that so?" he said. "And whose cock have you had in your mouth, Rosewood?"

His vulgarity stirred her, but before she could primly request that he speak like a gentleman to her, he stepped forward, prowling toward her just as his familiar might.

Briony swallowed.

"You want names? I'll have to think to remember them all," she said.

His lips twitched as he moved closer, and though he must not believe her, she refused to back down from this.

He came to a stop in front of her. As she leaned on his desk and he stood tall over her, she was forced to tilt her head all the way back.

"I think you're bluffing. I don't think you've ever parted those lips for anyone."

She smiled up at him. "Believe what you want. Would you like to put me to the test? Show you exactly how much I learned as the Rosewood princess? I had plenty of guards around me, you know——"

Suddenly he was leaning down, placing his fists on either side of her hips, and bringing his eyes to her level.

"Guards," he said acidly.

She nodded, her heart racing at his nearness. And she felt the weightlessness of throwing herself off a cliff as she said, "Guards and friends. You remember Didion, of course."

He smiled at her then, his lips parting to show her his sharp canines. His tongue ran across them.

"Didion Winchester, of course. You were always so close to him," he whispered, "despite his inability to untie your laces."

The blood drained from her face. She forced herself not to pull away.

There was no way he could have known how Didion had tried and failed to get under her ties under the willow tree at school. How they'd laughed a bit before giving up. How disappointed Briony had been to stop just when she'd started to forget about Didion's brown eyes and dark hair and imagine gray in their places.

How could he know about that?

"Well, he certainly learned later," she said shakily.

He pressed his lips together, and the mirth dripped from his expression.

"Show me," he said softly. And before she could let herself think of what he meant—if he meant for her to go to her knees—if he wanted her to touch him—if she would expire on the spot if he touched her back—he said, "Show me the memory."

Briony blinked at him. And as she stared into his gray eyes, she felt the pinprick of a mind asking for entrance into her own.

Her lips parted on a silent gasp.

He wanted to use mind magic to see inside her head. He was knocking at the door.

Briony swallowed. There was no way he was advanced enough to read her mind, surely.

"A lady doesn't kiss and tell, Hearst."

"Oh but you're trying to tell me just how unladylike you've been, aren't you?" he whispered, his breath on her cheek. "Pull forward the memory of your lips around Winchester's cock. I want to see just how good you are with that mouth, Rosewood."

She felt the tapping inside her head again. The asking of permission to enter.

Her confidence was shaken, but she didn't dare admit defeat here.

"I'd hate for you to be embarrassed," she said to him. "What with the size of him. It's terribly hard to compare."

His lips curled at the corners. "That's kind of you, but I'd love to see your prowess for myself." He leaned closer, and she wondered if their skin would brush. "Open," he said.

His mind knocked at the entrance to hers again.

She stared back into his eyes. "You open," she said. He blinked once. "You clearly think I have a thing or two to learn. Why don't you show me?"

His eyes slipped to her lips before coming back to hers, poking at the doorway to her mind again.

"You want me to show you how to suck me off, Rosewood?"

"Yes," she breathed.

She pushed forward with her own mind, spread her fingers on the desk to cast, and knocked at his walls. There was a door made of mirrors lined in brass. She saw herself staring at her own reflection as she knocked, and for the first time she got a sense of the barricades that she suspected he worked so hard to maintain.

It was impenetrable.

His mind nudged her backward, sinking back into her own like he was pressing her down on a mattress of feathers.

"Why don't you get us started," he whispered against her mouth. "And I'll correct your form."

And then he was inside her.

Briony gasped and grabbed onto the thread of him, guiding him away from things she didn't want him to see.

The bookshelves in her mind trembled. He sailed smoothly across her lake with still waters, letting his fingers drift across the surface and make ripples.

She wasn't sure if he found the memory of Didion under the willow tree or if she provided it since it had just been at the forefront of her mind, but suddenly her back was against the bark, and lips were on her neck, and hands were sculpting her skin.

Inside her own memory, she opened her eyes and found Toven Hearst standing at the lake's edge, watching as a young man clumsily kissed her collarbones and began tugging at her laces.

"I want to kiss you here," the young man said, and the shadow of him clarified into Didion. Briony tore her eyes from the Toven inside her mind and smiled at Didion as he fumbled with the ties.

"We'll have to do that in private, don't you think?" she asked shakily.

A shadow fell over her shoulder, and she looked up to find Toven crouching down next to her. "Show me your mouth on his cock, Rose-wood. Show me you on your knees for your brother's soldiers."

She glared into his black eyes even as Didion began kissing her neck again, curving his hands over her breasts.

She wanted to craft it. To show her twisting to push Didion onto his back. To show her unbuttoning his trousers.

She wanted to call Toven's bluff as much as he was calling hers.

Inside Toven Hearst's bedroom at Hearst Hall, he was leaned over her, his fists on the desk and his eyes locked on hers.

Briony unfolded her arms even as the version of herself in her mind's eye threaded her fingers through Didion's hair—and in the present, she reached up and took Toven's jaw between her hands.

She pressed against his mind, cast to penetrate, and whispered, "Open."

She was in his bedroom, inside his mind and outside it. The curtains blew a summer breeze across her skin as she knelt on his bed, kissing down his bare chest.

Briony's body sang as she touched her lips to his skin. One of his arms was thrown over his face, and the other one held his cock, stroking softly.

In the present, against his desk, she felt the puff of his surprise across her face.

Briony grabbed hold tightly of the thread and watched as she kissed her way lower and lower, finally replacing his hand with her own.

The Toven lying naked on his bed uncovered his face and finally looked down at her.

She was naked, too, she realized. Her hair was unbound and free, her breasts were rosy, and her hips were perfectly curved into her waistline.

Her hand moved confidently yet gently on his cock, and he watched her intently.

She leaned down, and her lips slowly parted. The tip of him was pink and dripping as it disappeared inside her mouth. She could almost taste him.

His head stretched backward as his eyes fluttered closed, and she let her mouth slip down, down, down until his cock was fully inside her, impossibly inside her. She watched her cheeks hollow and her eyes stay on Toven's face as he groaned.

Her mouth slipped upward, and he reached down to curve his fingers around her head, pushing her back down softly.

His eyes opened and watched her as she took him again—the same eyes that were connected to her now, at his desk, blown black with lust—and Briony's head bobbed.

Her hands moved across his hips, his stomach, his thighs. And Toven watched her as she licked at him, sucking and kissing.

Her body was on fire with that power. The slow measure of her movements on him, and his soft grasp of her hair.

His stomach muscles tightened. And she watched herself take his cock again, her lips slipping down and her cheeks sucking.

He threw his head back, and his mouth parted. "Briony . . ."

And suddenly he was alone in his bed, naked, his hand around his cock, his hips starting to jerk—

The room went cold. The summer breeze was gone.

And Toven Hearst was standing across the room, facing away from her, his shoulders high and his body strung tightly.

Her mind felt the rip from his consciousness then—as if the thread had been snipped.

She was in the present, not in the memory—or the illusion, it seemed.

She took a gulp of air as if she hadn't breathed in days.

Her body was still against his desk, but her eyes strayed to the bed she'd just been in, naked and magnificent.

He'd crafted something for her? He'd shown her what to do? It had seemed awfully slow and languid for what would be expected at the dinner parties.

Toven reached a hand out and leaned on the wall, as if gathering himself.

Briony's body felt tight. She ached with the emptiness, wishing she could live in that fabrication a little bit longer.

"Well, that was instructive," her voice rasped. "Is that what you'll expect next week?"

Without looking at her, Toven wrenched open the door and flew through it, slamming it behind him and leaving her alone in his bedroom.

CHAPTER 33

I F YOU'RE NOT GOING TO TRY, then maybe we should just stop."

"Oh, please spare me, Rosewood." Larissa slouched in her chair with a harsh look. "Perhaps you're an awful instructor."

Briony crossed her arms. She couldn't believe she'd *worried* about Larissa in her absence—that she'd actually *wanted* to see her at one point.

They'd been at this for two hours already. Earlier this morning, Briony had been woken from a fitful dream, full of soft white sheets, long muscular thighs, and warm hands. Larissa had been pounding on her door, claiming that it was nine o'clock and she'd be down in the drawing room waiting for her.

Toven had yet to make an appearance, and Briony wondered if he would.

She had considered asking about the meditation chamber near the kitchen for their lessons, but Larissa was nowhere near ready to stare at blank walls all day. And Briony was in no hurry to return there.

Larissa let her head drop on the back of her chair and breathed deeply. "We have to go faster," she said. "This is taking too long."

"If you don't comprehend the basics, then how can you possibly expect to master the advanced?" Briony stood from her chair and walked to the window.

They'd been facing each other in armchairs on either side of the coffee table, meditating for hours. As someone who'd never even practiced it, Larissa needed to understand where mind magic was drawn from.

Briony couldn't just tell her to reach for *that thread* if Larissa didn't know which one.

And of course, it was possible Briony was a bit distracted herself.

Whenever she let her mind drift, she'd see her lips, pink and full, closing over the tip of Toven's cock.

And speaking of, he must have a much more powerful mastery of mind magic than she thought in order to conjure an image of himself that must have been . . . enlarged. Exaggerated, perhaps. The version of Toven that he had supplied for instructional purposes had been quite imposing. True, she had never seen a man's cock before, but she couldn't possibly imagine that he was quite so . . . stately.

"I'm tempted to learn mind magic just to know what's gotten you so upset over there, Rosewood."

She looked at Larissa, finding her with legs crossed, elbows draped across the arms of the chair, and a wide smirk on her face. Briony realized she was running her fingers over her lips, staring off at the Hearst grounds with a flush to her cheeks.

Shaking off her thoughts, she said, "Nothing. Are you ready to begin again?"

Briony returned to her chair, but Larissa just kept smirking at her.

"So," Larissa said, "how often do you and Toven get into it like that? I must admit, I'm surprised he allowed you to strike him, much less speak to him in that manner, seeing as you're supposed to be his captive."

"And you're supposed to be dead," Briony said with a shrug. "We're all playing roles, aren't we?"

Larissa sent her a catlike smile.

Briony tilted her head. "Why do you want to attend the Biltmore parties this badly, Larissa?"

Leveling her gaze on her, Larissa responded, "Revenge."

Briony stared back. While she still didn't know what had caused Larissa to be put up for auction with the rest of them, she'd certainly seen her beg her own father for her life. She'd witnessed Hap Gains claim he had no daughter.

Nodding at the answer, Briony took a deep breath. "Ready to begin again?"

"I'm curious how this whole thing works," Larissa said slyly.

"What whole thing?" Briony assumed she was talking about the mind magic.

"Toven Hearst and his golden heartspring." Larissa examined her. Briony waited, wanting Larissa to do the talking. "I mean, he clearly isn't interested in taking advantage of"—she lifted her brows—"all you have to offer."

Briony didn't know if she meant as a heartspring or as a woman, and she wasn't about to ask for clarification.

"So what does he do with you all day?" Larissa continued with a shrug.

"Generally, he ignores me," Briony said.

"Does he?" Something glinted in her blue eyes. "Yet you feel comfortable pounding on his door at two in the morning? Do you visit each other in the dark often, Rosewood?"

Briony's memory snapped to Toven standing in the middle of her room in nothing but pajama bottoms, Toven's eyes drifting over the front of her blood-soaked nightdress.

"No," she said. "I was just watching from my window for him to come home last night, that's all."

Larissa tilted her head. "Your window."

"Yes, I'm in the room next to his."

Larissa went very still, and for a moment, Briony wondered if she was supposed to be lying to her about sleeping in a dungeon. But then the corner of her mouth ticked, and she breathed a loose laugh.

"Right," Larissa said quietly, turning her head to look out the window.

Briony had just begun to wonder if she'd said something wrong when there came a knock on the drawing room door, then Toven stepped through. Seeing him again after last night was like a lightning strike through Briony's body.

He stood just this side of the entry, as if he wouldn't dare come closer. He wore black trousers and a black shirt, and his eyes were empty.

"Come to check on us?" Larissa said when it was clear he would not greet them.

"I have news."

Briony stared at him, thinking it odd that he kept himself so far away. She couldn't even tell if he was looking at Larissa or her when he next spoke.

"Canning Trow's elixir has been outlawed from Biltmore Palace, by order of Mistress Mallow," he said, and Briony struggled to hear him with how low his voice was. "It is also no longer allowed on any heartsprings who are being held as political collateral."

Briony and Larissa glanced at each other.

"What happened?" Briony asked.

He began fiddling with the ring around his middle finger.

"Finn and I just returned from an audience with Mallow that I requested, so I could speak to a guilty conscience I had for something that transpired last night."

His tone was cold and his volume low, and Briony watched his eyes— unblinking. Larissa sat at attention, hanging on his every word.

"I told her that while it was indeed my idea to host a smaller gathering away from Biltmore last night, it was not my intention to expose the president's daughter to such vulgar festivities. We knew it couldn't be Mallow's strategy to instill such fear in a woman who would be returned in one piece one day."

Briony lifted her brows, and Larissa sat back in her chair with a deep, satisfied breath.

"Of course," Larissa said melodically. "It hadn't been your intention at all."

There was something in the way Larissa emphasized "your" intention. Something in the way Toven had phrased everything so carefully to them. Because if it hadn't been Toven's or Finn's intention, then the blame lay somewhere.

Briony's lips parted, and she almost smiled.

Toven had found a way to get one over on Canning. Just as she'd told him he should.

He'd also found a way to keep Briony from ever taking the elixir. She was relieved: He had no reason to fight her about going back to Biltmore any longer.

She cleared her throat. "Were either you or Finn punished?"

"No," Toven said. "Mistress Mallow was extremely grateful for the update and appreciated our acknowledgment of guilt." He nodded at Larissa. "Finn will be allowed to continue bringing Juliana to Biltmore, but as his guest only."

Which meant, Briony inferred, that Larissa could still go to Biltmore in Juliana's place, *and* she wouldn't be forced into demeaning sexual situations in the process.

Political collateral. That's what Toven had called the president's daughter. Briony thought it over for a moment. Was that how the Hearsts saw Briony, too? Was that how General Tremelo of Daward saw her? Something to be kept healthy and unharmed until a safe return?

She tried refocusing, but something was niggling at her.

"Finn is trustworthy in all this?" she asked.

Both of them looked at her as if she had sprouted a third arm.

She hurried to explain. "I just mean, he knows quite a bit of information, such as Larissa's true fate and this plot with the president's daughter. Couldn't Mallow find these things in his head?"

Toven glanced at Larissa before responding. "Finn isn't important enough to Mallow for an interrogation like that."

Briony narrowed her eyes. "He had an audience with her just this morning," she pointed out. "And he's now a successor, so wouldn't more opportunities arise—"

"Finn's mind is safe," Toven said, finality in his tone. "Your concerns are warranted, but you'll have to trust me."

Briony looked over at Larissa. She was examining her nails. Briony would drop the subject for now.

Toven took his first steps forward into the room, and something about seeing his body move made Briony's mind conjure up the image of his naked chest, his muscular thighs, his head thrown back on a sigh.

"Making progress here?" he asked them, but he kept his gaze on Larissa.

"No," Briony said as Larissa said, "Of course."

They sent each other narrowed gazes.

"Rosewood is being needlessly thorough," Larissa said, flipping her hair for Toven's benefit.

"Good," Toven said. Briony's eyes went to him, but he was staring at Larissa and Larissa alone. "You need to plan for hours of deception. There may be no way to give you privacy at Biltmore for a break." Toven pulled up a chair across from the two of them and sat. "I won't be allowing you to go until you are proficient."

Larissa snorted. " 'Allowing' me."

"Yes," Toven said, without warmth. "Only when you're ready. The person to decide that will be Briony."

She blinked at him. The rare sound of her name on his tongue conjured the sounds from last night, the way he'd moaned her name as he finished, the way his lips had formed around the vowels, the way his throat had bobbed with the deep sound of it.

She stared, waiting for him to realize it, too. But he kept his gaze on Larissa as if they were in a staring match.

Larissa clicked her tongue, and Briony met her gaze. "Well," Larissa said. "Let us continue then."

Briony flicked her eyes to Toven, who seemed to be making himself comfortable in his chair, lifting his calf to rest on the other knee.

"Right." She cleared her throat. "We left off with the clearing of the mind."

"Can we skip forward?" Larissa said.

"No." Briony let her hands drop to her knees, pointing her toes forward. "First we come to a neutral posture, finding a place for our eyes to rest."

Just as she let her gaze relax a few feet beyond Larissa's chair, she saw from the corner of her eye that Toven was uncrossing his legs, mirroring her pose.

Her heart skipped. He wasn't just observing; he was here to learn.

From her.

She swallowed down her nerves and continued.

"There will be plenty of distractions in real-life situations, so now is the time to take in everything—every sense you have. What do you hear, what movement do you see, what do you smell?"

Briony smelled Toven's aftershave—but this was a familiar distraction to her at this point.

"Feel the chair beneath you. Feel your feet on the ground."

There was a symmetry here that hadn't been present earlier. And she wasn't sure if Larissa was taking it more seriously now that Toven was in the room, but Briony suddenly sensed, with perfect clarity, three people breathing in tandem.

"Move your toes in your shoes. Pay attention to your ankles and calves. What muscles move there?" Briony's voice had dropped low and smooth. "Feel where your calves connect to your knees, your knees to your thighs . . ."

Unbidden, Toven's thighs came into her mind. And the image of her bracing her weight on them as she used her mouth on him. She breathed deeply.

"Distractions are normal," she said to them, but mainly to herself. "Focus on your being. Your hips, waist, and chest. Feel your blood flow— the vein you tug when you use heart magic. Find that in your chest."

Before Toven arrived, she had been checking with Larissa every few seconds to make sure she was paying attention, but now she knew from the three layers of breathing in the room that they were all ready. This next part was key to the difference between heart magic and mind magic, and the first thing one learned in the study of mind magic.

"Imagine it as a thread that slithers through your veins. It connects your blood to your intentions. As that thread moves upward, into your shoulders, your neck, it rounds the back of your head and connects to your forehead. Right between your eyes. Because blood moves everywhere in the body.

"This thread, attached at the center of your forehead—imagine that it has the most power of anywhere in the body. It connects your mind to your blood. Let yourself find this thread. Become acquainted with it. If you lose it, start at your heart again and sew it through your neck and shoulders, around the back of your skull, to the place between your eyes."

Briony allowed her instruction to come to an end. This was the area on which mind magicians spent most of their education prior to school—the communion with the thread. She knew it was important to just let Larissa be in silence.

She lifted her eyes slowly from the floor. Larissa was sitting perfectly still, eyes unfocused and breath slow. Briony was careful not to twitch a muscle, so as not to pull Larissa's attention.

She flicked her gaze to Toven and flinched—he was watching her. She looked away, checking on Larissa again. Her attention was focused still.

Briony wondered if Toven would have ever come to prefer mind magic as a root source if he'd learned at a young age like she had. He clearly had some experience with mind reading and barriers, but he didn't use mind magic for casual casting. He still relied on his familiar daily, like most heart magicians.

Briony let Larissa meditate for another half hour before finally pulling her out of it with quiet instructions. When Larissa's eyes finally lifted and met hers, she looked exhausted.

"Were you able to connect with the thread?"

Larissa nodded. "It slips out of my grasp a lot."

"Yes, it will," Briony agreed. "There are two parts to it. You have to meditate to find that thread and keep it for hours on end. And then to cloak, you begin to tug on it when you cast. Only a meditated, clear mind can do it. Apologies that the beginning is so boring."

Toven cleared his throat, and Briony looked over at him. "Only a meditated, *clear* mind," he repeated. His brows were drawn together. "This is incongruous with mind barrier magic, is it not?"

"It is," Briony agreed. When his confusion didn't clear, she said, "There is no known mind magician who has been able to cloak while keeping up mind barriers. Not even Vindecci could do it."

Toven's lips tightened. "So if you are in the presence of a mind reader, such as Mallow . . ."

"You can either cloak your mind or barricade it," she said. "In our history texts, many spies were executed for transmogrifying into another person, only to have their thoughts read as their mental defenses were down."

"Invisibility is the only real power then," Larissa said shrewdly. "If they don't know you're there, they can't read your mind."

Briony shrugged. "Possibly. I suppose it depends on your intentions."

Larissa stared back at her, giving nothing away. When she glanced at Toven, he was staring out the window, looking displeased.

*   *   *

They kept at it for another hour before Larissa developed a nasty headache. Briony knew it wasn't fake. She'd had her own headaches back in school.

But when Briony released her for the day, and Larissa said, "I'm going to lie down. Maybe I'll try again in the afternoon," Briony realized something for the first time.

"You're . . ." She glanced at Toven, then back to Larissa as she rubbed her temple. "You're staying here?"

"Just for the week," Toven said quickly. "While she's under your tutelage."

Briony's throat was dry. "Ah. Well, that's helpful."

There were eels swimming in her gut as she thought about Larissa in Hearst Hall. Larissa accessing Toven. Larissa sharing meals with him, even.

Briony stood and put her chair back where she'd taken it from.

"Don't worry, Rosewood," Larissa said loftily from the doorway. "You'll still be the only one visiting him at two in the morning."

Briony snapped her eyes to her just as Larissa smirked and walked out. She glanced at Toven. He was in profile, twisting his ring around his finger, shoulders tense.

"Speaking of last night," Toven said softly, and Briony's chest clenched. "I apologize. Nothing like that will happen again."

He kept his gaze on his ring. Briony felt an emptiness in her stomach.

"All right," she said, uselessly. "I suppose I did ask for an example of what would be expected of me on the elixir. And you . . . provided an example."

His gaze lifted to her. " 'An example,' " he repeated.

"Yes," she said, fiddling with the teacup she'd let go cold on the side table. "You conjured a scenario, detailed though it was . . ." She coughed, feeling her cheeks heat. "It was . . . It was much softer than I expected, though I'm sure you were diluting the scenario for my benefit."

She should stop talking. She drank her cold tea to silence herself. When the teacup clinked back down on the saucer, she turned to face him.

He stared at her, his lips attempting to form words. Then his jaw closed with an audible click, and he cleared his throat.

"Right. It was . . . softer. If anything were to happen in that vein behind the locked door at Biltmore, it would be much different." He took a deep breath and stepped back to face her fully. "But we were playing a dangerous game last night, and I should never have entered your mind."

She snorted. "Please. You've been entering my mind for years without permission, Toven."

His brows twitched in surprise, but he stayed silent.

"How else would you know about Didion and me at the lake? And the *laces*," she said, crossing her arms in a way unbefitting a princess. "Not to mention the pains in my legs all throughout year three. You knew all about them without me supplying the information."

Toven stared at her from across the room. "Ah," he said slowly. "Yes, I suppose I did know all about that."

Briony narrowed her eyes at him. "But fine, yes. I accept your apology, and we shan't be entering each other's minds without permission again."

He nodded. "Fine."

Shifting on her feet, Briony said, "I don't think Larissa will be ready to cloak on Friday unless she gives it her full attention this week. What is it that you hoped Larissa would 'teach' me for Friday night?"

He looked away from her, over her shoulder. "We can worry about that later, now that Canning's elixir has been eliminated."

She lifted a brow. "Please don't tell me you intend to send me into the lion's den without any more knowledge than last time."

He sighed. "What do you want to know?"

She threw her hands up in the air. "You're so frustrating. You say I need help from Larissa, but when I ask you outright what that is, you refuse to tell me."

"Perhaps it is *awkward* to tell you—"

"This entire situation is *awkward*, Toven. Just *trust* me to be an adult in this," she said. "I have seen many examples of the heartsprings' behavior at Biltmore. Just tell me if I should be more like Cecily Weape or like Phoebe."

He ran a hand through his hair. "It's not as simple as that—"

"Tell me what's so complicated—"

"You must become adjusted but not comfortable," he said, raising his voice. "You can neither be a vixen nor a victim. A vixen will be more desirable to them, but a timid girl crying all night long like Cecily will only attract their attention in a different way." He paced away from her. "If we are to give the impression that I am fucking you often—daily, twice a day, whatever." He waved his hand in the air noncommittally and turned to face her, walking closer. "Then we need a passing understanding of each other's bodies."

He came to stop in front of her.

"And you . . . you think *Larissa* is the one to teach me a passing understanding of your body," she said acidly.

He narrowed his eyes at her, as if to say *of course.*

She put her hands on her hips. "And how often *have* you been fucking me, Toven?"

His eyes flickered before returning to gray. "What?"

"Shouldn't you know?" she said "You certainly had an active imagination at dinner last week. You were well acquainted with how to unravel me, how to use your tongue on me. So how often does that all happen? Daily? Twice a day? How often do you fuck me just for your own satisfaction, and how often do you make me quiver for you?"

His jaw ticked as he glared down at her.

"You see," she said, stepping closer to him until her head had to tilt backward to see him. "It seems to me I'm not the only one who needs to get all my details straight. Perhaps we should work on this together."

He scoffed, and the air puffed across her face. "How in the stones should we do that?"

She shrugged. "You tell me. But honestly, I don't know how introducing *your ex-girlfriend* into this mess is supposed to make it better."

He breathed deeply, as if bracing himself. "She can inform you of . . . things you have less experience with—"

"Why don't *you* inform me?" she said, with more bravery than she thought she contained. "Come on, Toven," she continued, goading him.

"Tell me how often I'm on my knees for you, and how often you're on your knees for me."

His gaze danced across her face, his pupils sinking into blackness, but she wasn't done.

"Candles lit or snuffed out?" she said, repeating things she'd heard the maids talk about. "Do you bother to take your shoes off——?"

"Where do you hear these things?" he whispered, breath across her face. "What sinful conversations have you been listening to, Rosewood?"

"Do you call me Briony when you finish?" she asked, voice loose and chest tight. "Like you did last night?"

His face seemed to freeze in a smirk. She could feel the heat of his body just inches from hers. He breathed in through his nose, as if he was memorizing a scent, and suddenly he was even taller, forcing her head to tilt further backward.

"Generally," he began, "I like to take you in the mornings. I'll wake you by climbing into your bed. I find that you're more pliable then."

His voice was gravelly, and his eyes were black. Briony stared up at him without blinking.

"I push you on your stomach, or I curl around your side, and make you take me slowly, softly. Where you can pretend I'm your lover. You always come in the mornings."

She swallowed, taking in the scene he was painting. Her heart pounded.

"I'm in only my pajama bottoms, you're in a soft silk nightdress that slips down low over your breasts. If I find you wearing underwear beneath it, I don't let you come."

She felt the rumble of his words straight to her core. His voice was steady, and his eyes were even.

"Then sometimes in the afternoons I'll find you in the library," he said. His voice took on a musical quality. "I'll remind you that it's forbidden, but I'll let you stay there and finish your book if you take off your dress."

Her mind flashed to the time when Canning and Liam were there, when she'd spilled the whiskey on herself. But his words were painting a different picture.

"I'll bend you over the table, or a chair, or just press you up against the window that overlooks the ponds, and I'll tell you to keep reading as I enter you. I'll make sure you get to finish the chapter you're on before I spend myself inside of you, then I'll slap your ass and call you a good girl. You collect your dress and leave."

Briony's stomach was swirling with things she'd only felt rarely. Usually when this man was involved. She focused on his eyes, letting the images and sensations wash over her.

"But at night," he said. A smirk graced his lips. "At night, that's when I kiss you between your legs for hours. No matter how devious you've been throughout the day, I make you come on my tongue three or four times. And when I'm done with you, I lie back on my bed and watch your mouth sink on my cock. And yes. When I come, I call you Briony. And you *love* it."

She shivered, and she knew he saw it. She felt her breasts pull into tight peaks, and her breath caught in her throat.

Could he possibly have these thoughts? Was he describing more than just a scene to her? A desire?

His head dipped down, and she thought he would kiss her. She thought she would let him.

"Does that make things clearer, Rosewood?" he whispered, breathing in her air.

She didn't know what her face looked like, what kind of emotions were on display for him. She had no shields to protect her from Toven Hearst's seduction.

"Crystal," she said, her throat tight and her skin buzzing.

She stepped back and around him, heading for the door on shaking legs.

CHAPTER 34

LARISSA STARTED PROGRESSING QUICKLY. By Monday afternoon, she could turn her hair brown, though only for two minutes at a time.

Larissa was actually practicing when she wasn't with Briony. It seemed that whatever it was that motivated her to get to Biltmore was strong.

Toven didn't attend Sunday's lesson, but when he walked into the drawing room on Monday to see Larissa with brown hair, he stopped in his tracks.

"Look!" Larissa said, jumping up to twirl for him, but almost as soon as she had, she lost her grasp on that thread and let her hair fade back to blond. "Ah, damn it all."

Toven slid his hands in his pockets and moved toward their chairs as Larissa closed her eyes and tried to find the concentration she needed.

"It's impressive, even if it needs work," he said softly.

"Be quiet," Larissa snapped, her eyes squeezed tightly.

Briony watched Toven, taking note that his gaze never left Larissa as they all stood in silence.

Slowly, Larissa's hair turned brown at the roots. With her face still squished in concentration, she said, "Am I doing it?"

"A little."

Larissa huffed and shook out her arms, letting her concentration go again.

Toven cleared his throat. "My mother would like to entertain us all for dinner this evening."

Briony's jaw dropped. What a happy dinner party.

Larissa's expression was wary for a moment. "I can't," she said. "I really need to be practicing this evening."

Briony's brows jumped. She couldn't imagine staying in someone's home and declining a dinner invitation.

"I'm afraid it's not optional," Toven said, looking down at his shoes.

Larissa glanced at Toven, chewing her lip—something Briony had never seen her do at school. She shook her head and grumbled, "What time?"

"Six."

Larissa nodded, and Toven left without Briony's response.

Briony crossed her arms as Larissa slumped back down in her chair. "You don't enjoy Serena Hearst's company?"

Larissa snorted. "Much the other way around." She rubbed her thumb across her lips, her mind drifting. "I tried for years to get that woman's approval. I'm sure you've noticed how she is. Sharing a meal with her is just a chance for her to evaluate and dismiss. You'll see."

Later, Larissa used the dinner as a practice session, and endeavored to cloak a beauty mark on her cheek for the entire evening.

Briony sat down next to Larissa and across from Toven, Orion's place opposite Serena at the head of the table not set.

"Thank you for having us to dine this evening, Mrs. Hearst," Larissa said in the voice she used to use on the tutors at school. "It's been far too long since I've enjoyed your kitchen's food."

Serena's lips curved in a smile that didn't reach her eyes. "Yes, I thought it was time to have a meal with *everyone* under my roof."

Briony paused in placing her napkin on her lap as a glance passed between Toven and his mother. Toven's lips pressed together.

"Larissa is with us for only a week, perhaps a bit longer. She needs to spend some time learning some valuable tools with Miss Rosewood."

"Ah," Serena said, lifting her wineglass. "I presume that is the reason I see a spot appearing and disappearing on Miss Gains's cheek."

Larissa blanched before blushing.

"It is, Mrs. Hearst."

"If I remember correctly, you were always well concerned with cosmetology," Serena said. "You are in need of further effects for your appearance?"

Briony blinked. It was so strange to hear Larissa call her "Mrs. Hearst" when Briony had been permitted to call her Serena.

"All is necessary, Mother," Toven said, readjusting his napkin. "I promise."

Briony cleared her throat. "Thank you for having us to dinner, Mrs. Hearst," Briony said, lifting her fork.

"I've told you to call me Serena, Briony."

Briony paused, her entire body flushing with secondhand embarrassment. Larissa was still as stone next to her.

Throughout the rest of the meal, Briony tried to make easy conversation while Serena ignored Larissa, Toven ignored Briony, and Larissa shrank into herself, ignoring everyone.

* * *

"Let's go again," Larissa said, gulping down her tea.

It was Friday morning, and Larissa could turn her eyes green for twenty minutes. It was truly impressive, but unfortunately, it wasn't enough. She'd need to cloak herself as another person for far longer than twenty minutes.

However, Larissa hadn't quite yet accepted that she would not be going to the Biltmore party that evening.

She slapped her own cheeks to perk up, having nearly passed out from exhaustion in the last session.

"Larissa," Briony started.

"No. We go again."

Briony stared at her. "You can try as often as you want today. It won't change the fact that you're not ready for this evening."

Larissa narrowed her eyes. "Don't tell me what I can and can't do, Rosewood."

"That's precisely what she can tell you," said a voice from the doorway. The two women turned to see Toven, observing them silently.

"Toven—"

"It won't be tonight, Larissa," he said softly. "Be all the more ready for next Friday."

Briony watched a fire burn behind Larissa's eyes as her lips pressed into a thin line.

"Finn will make an excuse why he can't attend, and you both will appear next week," Toven said.

Larissa stood with the petulance of a toddler and marched toward the door. As she passed him, Toven said, "And I assume you will hold up your end of the bargain with Rosewood this evening, as she has spent six days working with you."

His words went unanswered as Larissa's heavy footsteps echoed farther and farther away.

Without a glance in Briony's direction, Toven excused himself.

Later that evening, Briony was just stepping out of the bath and draping her robe around herself when Larissa barged into her suite.

Briony peered out of the bathroom door and sputtered, "It's polite to knock, you know."

Larissa waved her off and went directly to her vanity to open the bag she'd brought with her. She started taking out brushes and powders.

Briony blinked, remembering what she'd said last week. *I've heard from multiple sources now that you were a spectacular disaster at Biltmore. You looked a mess.*

Breathing deeply, Briony said, "You're here to make me look good?"

Larissa smiled condescendingly. "But of course. Looking good is my *only* talent," she said, as if repeating the words from someone. She patted the back of the vanity chair and gestured for Briony to sit.

Briony didn't know if she was supposed to disagree with Larissa or not. She followed instruction and sat.

As Larissa started organizing all the powders and rouges, Briony frowned at her in the mirror. "Not every girl is done up and dressed to the nines."

Larissa dragged the chair to face her with surprising strength. "Not every girl fetched sixty-five thousand gold," she said, leaning down to meet Briony on her level. Briony froze at the knowledge that Larissa had finally figured out how much Toven bought her for. "Not every girl is on the arm of the wealthiest heir in line. Trust me when I say that you need to look and act the part. If you can't maintain the lie, Rosewood," Larissa said, voice sharpening, "you'll endanger the entire Hearst family."

Briony pressed her lips together. "I'm well aware of that, thanks."

Larissa stood upright, a bright smile breaking across her lips. "Good." She pushed a tube of something into Briony's hands. "Now moisturize."

Brushing the cream over her skin, Briony turned her eyes to Larissa's left forearm. The flesh was mangled and silver-white from the acid that Finn had used. Briony realized that she now had access to someone who could possibly give her a clue about the tattoos.

"Did it hurt?" she asked quietly.

"Don't be an idiot, Rosewood. You heard me screaming. Now go ahead and ask the real question you want to ask."

Larissa came at her with a large brush at that point, promptly covering Briony's embarrassed flush with a beige goo.

"What do you know about the tattoos?" Briony asked, once the brush was away from her mouth.

"Absolutely nothing." Larissa dipped the brush again. "All I know is that I can come and go as I please."

"Because you're 'dead.'"

Larissa's lips twitched. "Well, yes. That does tend to be helpful."

"I woke up with my tattoo already on my arm. Do you remember anything about the spell they used?"

"I don't remember a spell," Larissa said. "Just the elixir."

Briony felt her skin prick as every hair on her arms stood on end.

"What kind of elixir?"

"Well, gee, Rosewood, when I was allowed to examine it, my findings were inconclusive—"

"You drank an elixir?" Briony grabbed her wrist, forcing Larissa to tug her brush back. "You're sure?"

She scowled at her. "I'm positive. I remember having my jaw pried open."

Briony's mind raced at breakneck speed. She'd thought that the tattoo was a spell cast upon a person, an external charm. Was Briony given this elixir while she was unconscious?

An elixir had an antidote. She tucked away this new information, excited to examine it later in the Hearst library.

Briony let Larissa continue in silent concentration, dabbing at her face and smudging powders onto her cheeks. She hadn't bothered with any of this since before her father died. If there was a state event, the palace hired a team to come in and tend to her, but that was all she knew other than where to swipe rouge. Larissa, on the other hand, had already perfected a powdered and contoured face when they started school at sixteen. The only time Briony had ever seen her without a face on was when they were held captive together.

"You said you envied me in the Trow dungeons." Briony's voice was soft, as if she were speaking to a skittish cat.

Larissa didn't look up from her palette.

"You said you were envious of 'what my life would be,'" Briony said. "What did you mean?"

Larissa laughed, a bark of glee that made Briony jump in her seat. Larissa looked around the bathroom suite, gesturing with her brush.

"You knew, even then, that Toven was going to buy me," Briony said.

Larissa stabbed a new brush into a powder and hummed in confirmation.

Briony took a breath, heart pounding. "Do you know why?"

Larissa turned to her, hair swaying delicately. Her eyes took in Briony's, studying her, before narrowing like a predator's.

"I do," said Larissa, with a twist to her lips. "Eyes closed, Rosewood."

Briony opened her mouth to protest, but Larissa was already coming at her with the brush. Briony closed her eyes, puffing out her breath in defeat.

She kept silent and still as Larissa finished her eyeshadow. After, she felt Larissa twisting her fingers through Briony's hair, letting magic drift through the curls, tightening and taming them. When she was finally finished, Larissa grabbed the back of the chair, wrenching her toward the mirror so she could see herself.

Briony was a shadow. A figment of someone's imagination. Her cheekbones shimmered and her eyes were enormous. Her brows were crisp and jaw sharp—just like Larissa's. Her curls danced around her face like a lion's mane.

"You hate it, I know," Larissa said, putting her things away with a flick of her fingers. "But you'll have to bear it."

Larissa started to clean up all the powders and brushes, and Briony felt the clock ticking closer to ten.

"Is there anything else I should know?" Briony asked, her stomach twisting in knots.

"Be sure to take all this off and wash your face afterward," Larissa muttered.

"No, I mean . . ." Briony hesitated. "Anything about how to act?"

Larissa met her eyes in the mirror and bit back a smile. "What do you want to know?"

Briony watched her organize the counter.

"What does Toven like?"

Larissa laughed. "Well, doing what Toven likes and doing what looks good at Biltmore are two different things."

Briony's brows furrowed. "Do you mean that Toven doesn't like conventional affection?"

"No, no. It's just that . . ." Larissa smiled. "Well, doing what he *likes* while trying to play a part? That's asking for a bit of trouble, don't you agree?"

Briony didn't follow. *Trouble for whom?*

Larissa shook her head and said, "You know what, why not?"

She bent over Briony's chair and ran her fingers through Briony's thick curls. Briony immediately thought of the evening woman Larissa had told her about.

"Toven tends to like soft touches to the back of his neck." Larissa demonstrated, letting her fingers tickle the back of Briony's head. She gave small tugs on the wispy hairs at the base of her skull.

Briony thought it felt quite nice, but it wasn't really a turn-on for herself.

"Especially when your fingers are cold," Larissa said, pulling her hand away.

"My fingers are always cold," Briony quipped.

Larissa snorted. "That's right," she said with a knowing smile. "Are you really still cold in Bomard? After all these years?"

Briony nodded.

Larissa leveled her gaze at her. "It's summer, for stones' sake, Rosewood."

Briony shrugged.

Next, they went to grab Briony's dress and heels from the wardrobe. Larissa cast a charm on the shoes to make them more comfortable and prevent Briony's ankles from rolling. It was life-changing.

"Have a good evening," Larissa said. "My goal is to have an hour of full transmogrification by Monday." She walked to the door with a sway to her steps. She would probably be up the entire night working on her studies.

"Do get some rest, Larissa. It's no good passing out during lessons."

At the threshold, she turned and smiled. "Oh, don't go getting attached to me now, Rosewood. It will make it so much harder to despise you."

She disappeared, and the door clicked closed behind her.

*   *   *

Briony's dress was black lace tonight, with a low neck. It was tight on her body, leaving very little to the imagination.

With shoes on and one last look in the mirror, Briony headed down the hallway. She'd found her footing by the time she descended the stairs, but the sight of Toven watching her from the ground almost sent her stumbling again. His eyes dripped over her face, dress, and legs before tearing away and staring down at the marble.

It was the first time he'd looked directly at her since Saturday, when he'd described in perfect detail all the ways in which he had her every day. He'd refused to look at her at dinner with his mother. Briony's heart raced and her skin tingled.

She clicked down the stairs in her heels, awkwardly listening to every step until she reached the bottom.

He didn't immediately cast the portal, so she asked, "Is it the same entry every time? Through the main gates?"

After a beat, he nodded, almost as if snapping out of a trance. "Yes." He cleared his throat and surprised her when he offered, "The dinner will be infinitely tamer tonight."

He sliced his finger and cast a portal. Briony paused before she offered her arm to him.

"The president of Southern Camly doesn't support Mallow, does she?" she asked. "That's why Juliana was taken and made a heartspring. To coerce him into changing his mind."

"That's about the short of it," he said.

He took her elbow, pulling her through a void to the path outside Biltmore.

She allowed the long walk up to the gates to center her mind, the breeze to cool her emotions, and the sound of her footsteps to confirm that it was truly happening again.

The wolves howled, the guards smacked their lips, and the crowd of Bomardi in the courtyard whistled. She ignored them all, hardly registering their jeers as she focused on a lake with still waters.

Toven was putting on a show of being quite relaxed. During their first walk into Biltmore, he was rushed and anxious. This time, he was shouting back at the crowd with a laugh, stopping to chat with someone at the top of the stairs, and teasing someone who was coughing on their cigar. But when the spectators vanished and it was only the two of them, his face fell, an empty expression in his eyes.

He led her through the doors to the grand hall, and Briony's breath caught to see Ilana turning to them with a tray of champagne.

"Master Hearst," she said with a flirty grin. "Good evening. I have Minister Bagis back again."

Toven declined a fact sheet, and Ilana's eyes met hers briefly before offering her champagne.

"Miss Rosewood, welcome."

Briony reached for her own glass this time, hoping to draw Ilana's eyes, but she was already pushing aside the curtain and letting them into the hall.

The music and the chatter hit her like a wall, stirring her memories of two weeks ago. She was flooded with terror for a freezing moment before feeling Toven's hand on her back, warm and steadying.

He stopped to talk with people as they sipped their champagne. Briony tried to catalog the guests and conversations more fastidiously this time. Two weeks ago, she was far more focused on the women. This time, she needed to listen to the whispered jokes and unspoken clues.

Toven greeted Carvin, who did not have Phoebe hanging off his elbow. Briony's eyes scanned for her as inconspicuously as possible, but with no luck.

"Toven," a slimy voice called out behind them. They turned and found Caspar Quill, Liam's father, approaching, one hand on his cane. There was a round man at his side. "I was just telling Minister Bagis from Starksen about the protections on our heartsprings."

Toven shook hands, and Briony finally matched the name with the face of Minister Bagis. He was one of the leaders of Starksen's government and had conveniently ignored the letter she'd written to him in urgency, asking for his support while Mallow marched on Rory's armies. He was portly with rheumy eyes and pink mottled skin.

Quill continued, sloshing his glass a bit as he spoke. "I assure you, these protections we have cannot be beat. These tattoos? Unbreakable."

Briony's ears pricked.

"Ah," said Toven. "So these 'tattoos' cannot be broken, but the portal boundary lines can?" His eyes glinted cruelly as he watched the insult land on Quill.

"Precisely," Quill growled. "The magic is impenetrable. We have gone further than anyone in history to secure our heartsprings!" Quill gestured to the whole room, sloshing his glass. "The ancient Dawards, the clans of Starksen. Not even the Durlings could succeed where we have!"

He was drawing attention. Several nearby heads turned to see the commotion.

And it all fell into place. Quill had created the tattoos.

Briony looked down, her mind working quickly.

The Durlings.

She'd seen the term before. She couldn't place where, but the group had appeared somewhere in her reading.

"Right you are, Caspar," Toven said silkily. "And I do hope my father's library was helpful to you in your efforts to secure the portal boundary line. We are happy to point you in the right direction, should you ever be lost again."

Briony's brows jumped before she could school her face. Quill looked murderous.

"Now, if you'll excuse us, we really should be going."

Toven's fingers curled tightly on the curve of her waist, unsteadying her until she had to step back, following him toward the stairs.

She was racking her brain so hard to remember who the Durlings were that she almost forgot that she was headed upstairs into another viper's pit.

"Not leaving already, Hearst?" a gravelly voice sounded from their right. "I haven't even had a chance to say hello."

Toven froze. Briony's chest rattled, her hair standing on end from the memory of eyes on her naked body, a hand between her legs, a scratchy voice whispering filthy things into her ear.

A tall man with a twisted nose and twisted smile stepped into their path, and Briony came face-to-face with Lag Reighven for the first time since he'd won her at the auction.

CHAPTER 35

OVEN'S ARM TIGHTENED AROUND HER WAIST, and Briony reminded herself to breathe.

"Lag," Toven greeted in a stilted voice. "Back from Southern Camly so soon?"

"Just today." His gaze skated over her chest, her waist, her legs. "I'd heard you'd been letting her out of her cage. Had to come see for myself."

There was a pounding in her blood, but she focused on holding her head high, meeting his eyes.

"And now you've seen," Toven replied curtly. "If you'll excuse us—"

"Not sharing her, either, I've heard," Reighven said, stepping subtly to the left, blocking the narrow path around him. "What a shame that is." He took a small step forward, cocking his head. His eyes hadn't left her once. "With me, you would have been treated like the princess of Biltmore once again. The grandest prize, presented and polished."

A chill passed along her shoulders, but she didn't move a muscle. Toven shifted, his shoulder passing into her sight line as he put himself in front of her.

"I think she got the better deal, Lag," Toven lilted, and she could hear the nasty smirk in his voice, so reminiscent of their school days.

Reighven sneered and stepped into him, nose-to-nose. "Your daddy's not here, Hearst. I'd be very careful what you say to me."

"Oh, I have nothing to say to you at all. We have a binding agreement,"

Toven said, his voice low. "Now kindly step away from me and my heart-spring. I'll only ask you once."

"You've been keeping her locked away for far too long. Careful," he warned. "Or someone might figure out how to pick the lock."

Toven's left arm was twisted behind him, squeezing her wrist so hard that she knew it would bruise. He breathed a humorless laugh and slapped Reighven's upper arm.

"Good to see you, Lag. I'll give my father your regards."

With a sharp tug, he pulled her around him, passing Reighven on the right with a shove to his shoulder. Briony didn't look back, only focused on putting one foot in front of the other.

She tried to find a lake with still waters in her mind, but seeing Reighven again had rattled her. Once they were up the stairs, she tugged on Toven, asking him to pause without saying a word.

Toven looked up and down the arcade while Briony took two deep breaths in.

She nodded, and they continued.

Toven led her to the room where they'd had dinner two weeks ago. The same Bomardi guard stood at the doorway and checked Toven's ring for entry.

Boisterous laughter and shouting assaulted her ears, and when they entered, the room cheered, getting to their feet in their imitation of chivalry.

Toven herded her to the head of the table, and Briony took her position behind Toven's chair. She found Cecily behind Collin, Octavia behind Lorne, and Jellica behind Canning. And when the strawberry-blonde took her place behind Liam as he sat, Briony realized the chair to Toven's left was empty.

Finn wasn't here, just as Toven had planned. She wondered what the excuse was for it.

As soon as the men were seated, the women stepped forward for the wine bottles. Briony followed, reaching beyond Toven's shoulder and pouring wine into his glass.

They repeated their toast—"To Mistress Mallow. May she reign forevermore"—and Briony watched as seven men drank deeply to Mallow's honor. There was less food on the table than two weeks ago. No opulent pig roast or decadent side dishes. As the men settled back into conversation, the strawberry-blonde and two other women started moving around with trays, serving light hors d'oeuvres and cheese.

Without dinner in the way, it didn't take long for the first woman to drop into a lap—a giggly waif in a silver collar who draped herself over Kleve without a fuss. As if he'd been waiting for the cue all evening, Collin directed Cecily to his lap, his arms wrapping around her stomach and his face inhaling deeply at her neck as she grimaced.

Briony was listening to the conversations and watching the men closely, so she saw the exact moment Canning pulled a small box out of his robes.

"What do we say, gentlemen," he called out over the noise. "Shall we lose some gold tonight?"

The young men laughed and jeered, ribbing one another about who had won and lost last time. Canning's long fingers opened the box and plucked out a deck of cards and three dice. He began shuffling the deck as some men groaned about the holes in their pockets, and others rubbed their greedy hands together in glee.

Briony had seen the guards at Biltmore play this game before. They'd agreed to teach Rory but had balked at the idea of the princess playing cards with them. Her rudimentary understanding was that it was similar to poker, but without numbered cards.

Lorne started divvying the chips, and the cards slid across the table with a magical push as Canning dealt them. She looked up and realized that over half of the women were otherwise occupied. Some sat in laps or draped themselves over the shoulders of their "dates." The other half refilled glasses and offered snacks. Only Briony was left standing at attention.

She stepped forward as Toven plucked up his cards. Grabbing the decanter of wine, she refilled his almost full glass to look busy, and as he rearranged his cards, she brushed her fingers over the back of his collar, near the base of his skull, as Larissa had taught her. "Do you have a good hand?" she murmured, doing her best to imitate Larissa's purr.

He went very still. "Excellent," he said with a confident flick of his eyes to meet Canning's.

Canning smirked, then turned his gaze on her. "How are those heels tonight, Rosewood?" His gaze ran over her. "If you need to sit, you know my lap's always free."

Before she could craft a response, Toven's hand was on her hip, pulling her downward without even looking up from his cards. The men laughed.

She landed across both his legs, the right side of her chest pressing against his left. With how short and tight her dress was, she was forced to shift herself until her legs crossed, her arm slung behind Toven's shoulder. Toven provided no assistance.

Lorne started by rolling the dice, grinning down at the result. The glyphs on the sides were different than on the dice she'd seen the guards play with, so she gave up trying to summon the little she remembered. Canning called for wagers.

"Let's make it good this time, gentlemen." He nodded at Kleve. "You first."

"I have the names of two defectors."

Canning rolled his eyes. "That's terribly dull, Kleve."

"Well, that's what I have," Kleve grumbled.

"Then think of something better. I'm not risking what I know for something my grandmother could have told me."

He turned his eyes on Lorne, who cleared his throat. "I have news on Starksen."

"I'll take that," Canning said. "I'll raise you a sighting of Punt."

Briony's mouth felt dry, and she resisted the urge to lean forward. They were wagering secrets instead of gold—sensitive topics about the war, the outside world.

She chanced a look around the table and found the strawberry-blonde meeting eyes with another Barlowe Girl before quickly glancing away and reaching for a slice of cheese off Liam's plate.

"Intriguing, Canning. Who's your source?" said Toven.

"Well, you'll have to beat my hand to find out, won't you?"

"Collin?" Lorne asked. "Are you in?"

But Collin was nuzzling into Cecily's neck, content to fold.

"I have news on Mallow's dragon. Spotted near the Tampet Mountains yesterday," said the man whose name Briony didn't know.

Toven scoffed. "What could possibly be interesting about the location of Mallow's dragon?"

"You'll have to beat my hand to find out."

"Toven?" Canning asked. "Are you in?"

Briony felt every pair of eyes turn to them. She glanced down to Toven's hand, unable to tell if what he had was sufficient to win. He plucked a card from the middle and replaced it on the end.

"I'm in." He tilted his head, and Briony felt his hair tickle her neck. "Anyone interested to know who it was that skipped through the boundary at Javis last month?"

A charge pulsed through the table. Canning lifted a brow; Lorne leaned closer. Someone set down his glass with a clink. Liam, on the other hand, stiffened.

"That's classified," he hissed from their left. "You can't give away that kind of information."

"I'm not giving it away," Toven drawled. "I'm planning to win my hand, thank you very much." He took a leisurely sip from his wineglass. "And you, Liam? Do you have anything of value?"

Liam sat up straight in his chair, jostling the arms of the strawberry-blonde hanging off his shoulders. "I can tell you which major government official plans to pay Biltmore a visit next month," he said.

"Tremelo already said he'd be back—"

"No," Liam snapped. He sneered at the interruption. "Not Tremelo."

A pause as the young men considered.

"Well, you have my interest," Canning said with a grin. "Shall we play, boys?"

Canning whispered into Jellica's ear, and with some reluctance, Jellica leaned forward and chose a card from the pile in front of him.

"High suit is . . ." Canning turned over the card Jellica chose, and his face split into a smile. His eyes slid to Briony. "Roses."

The men chuckled as Canning flipped the card onto the table. It had an ornate rose in the center.

"Wild card is . . ." Canning took the next card from Jellica's hand and barked out a laugh. "The Rose in Chains." His eyes glittered as he stared across the table at Toven and Briony. "Well, if that isn't just the perfect thing."

Toven was still as stone as the men laughed, making jokes about not betting against Toven this round—"The odds are with him!"

Briony barely understood the game, but she could understand the insinuation.

They started then. Briony watched cards exchange hands, watched the dice roll, watched the quick shuffling as the men laughed and drank. She still couldn't figure out how the game was played, but she was far more invested in the conversation. One by one, the men lost, spilling their secrets and, afterward, their gold. By the time they were down to their last few wine bottles, only Toven, Canning, and Liam had kept their secrets.

Lorne's news on Starksen—that Mallow had lost several hundred new recruits there—had helped Briony puzzle together that despite Minister Bagis's presence tonight, not all of Starksen was in support of Mallow.

Another two hands, and she found out the name of a suspected traitor in General Tremelo's army.

Canning finally lost his hand to a round of jeers. "All right," he said, tossing back his drink. "That bitch who lost an arm—what's-her-name."

"Velicity Punt," Jellica said softly, and then immediately flushed red and stared down at her lap.

Canning seemed entertained more than anything. "Yes, *thank you,* Jellica," he said patronizingly. "Velicity Punt was spotted in the north at a closed-down apothecary last week."

Briony's mind snapped in millions of directions. Now that she knew the tattoo was created with an elixir, it was possible that Velicity, as one of the only escapees, was determined to find the ingredients for the antidote. But it could be anything. If Velicity was on the run with Sammy, as she'd seen in the papers, they'd need plenty of supplies.

Liam folded next, but he didn't seem terribly put out when he smugly announced that Biltmore would be hosting the rest of Minister Bagis's cabinet.

Toven didn't lose, keeping his secret of who had escaped at Javis. Briony shoved aside her irritation that he hadn't told her before. She'd take it up with him later, but now was not the time.

By the end of the next round, Lorne, having lost his gold and secrets several rounds before, began kissing Octavia's neck as he listened to the game, only piping in every now and then. Collin was doing something similar, only it seemed he had completely disregarded the game to focus on sloppily kissing Cecily's mouth.

It was Kleve's turn to throw the dice. The Barlowe Girl in his lap giggled when he offered her the deck of cards.

Briony looked away from the scene as Liam called out the results of the roll. They played their first hand, exchanging chips and cards. And when it was time to bet their information, Liam offered another visitor to Biltmore in the next month.

"Don't waste our time with that," Toven drawled. "I want to know what you were researching for your father in my library." Liam opened his mouth. "And don't feed me any shit about the portal boundary line," Toven continued, cutting over him. "I saw you lurking in the other sections."

A stillness swept over the table. Liam flushed at being put on the spot, and clearly not in a way he enjoyed.

"I'll take that bet," Canning said with a glint in his eye. "Especially since Liam is panicking."

The table chuckled. The strawberry-blonde cooed into Liam's ear and rubbed his shoulders as he scowled. Briony's pulse spiked, feeding off the intrigue, and she quickly looked down at the table to hide her eagerness.

Liam drummed his fingers on the table. "Well, I'm only in if Toven tells us where Daddy Hearst has been."

Toven's ribs expanded against hers, and the corner of his mouth lifted. He made quite a show of looking down at his cards, weighing the options.

"What do you think, Rosewood?" he lilted. "Think my cards are good enough?"

She blinked at his hand, not sure how to answer, but knowing it didn't matter. He was only buying time. She ran her fingers over the fine hair at the back of his neck, right over the place where she'd once sewed his skin together, and watched him shiver.

Briony plucked a card from the middle of Toven's hand and replaced it on the end. She leaned closer and loudly whispered, "I think Liam's about to spill everything."

The men burst into laughter—more raucous than the quip warranted. It wasn't terribly witty, but perhaps they were amused that it was said by her. That she was playing along.

"Now the game can start!" Canning yelled over the din. "I wondered when you'd show up, Rosewood!"

Liam won his hand, allowed to keep his secrets for a bit longer. Toven spread his cards on the table, and Briony inferred from the Rose that he had won as well.

Her heart was pounding in her chest as she decided to try something else to celebrate his win. Pressing her forehead to his temple and painting on a coy smile, Briony tilted her face up, reaching for his mouth with hers.

The barest brush of her bottom lip across the corner of his mouth—

And Toven jerked his face back, the smallest movement of his neck, like he'd dodged the swing of a sword.

She froze, feeling his entire body seize up, his ribs no longer moving against hers.

Embarrassment flooded her chest and neck, working its way to her cheeks. She'd tried to kiss him, and he'd rejected her—and more important, flinched in front of watchful eyes. She didn't dare look at him, staring at her lap as her face burned. He continued shuffling his new hand as if nothing had happened.

Soon enough, her embarrassment gave way to a boiling fury. He was going to jeopardize them. He couldn't accept a kiss from the woman he was supposedly intimate with. What did that say?

Had anyone seen?

The sound in the room returned to her slowly as she lifted her head. The men were chatting and passing cards. No eyes were on them, but there was something malicious about the way Canning Trow grinned at the table, his teeth cutting into his lip.

Toven's ribs moved again, and he audibly swallowed. Briony stiffened at the reminder that he was there.

They needed to talk. They needed a discussion about what their behavior was to consist of. He'd condescended at her ability to playact last time, and then proceeded to sabotage her once she'd actually tried to play the game. She breathed deeply; she couldn't show how she felt with so many watchful eyes in the room.

"Your turn, Hearst."

Kleve slid the cards over to Toven, and his arm extended to reach for them.

"You gonna let her wish you luck?" Lorne teased.

Toven held the deck in front of her. She pushed her embarrassment down and slipped one card from the stack, flipping it over for the table.

"The Virgin and the Wolf," Liam read for the table.

Now, that one she *had* heard of. It was an old fairy story, with a wolf that could smell a virgin's blood.

The men were just offering their secrets as she relaxed back into Toven's hand.

"I have something with potential now that we're in the final round," Canning said with a smirk. His eyes locked on hers as he said, "I happen to know the location of one Cordelia Hardstark."

A cold wave of dread crashed through her. And she knew she hadn't been able to temper her expression. Canning's eyes gleamed. She felt the hand on her back tense as well.

"And how would you know that?" Liam sneered.

Canning shrugged. "My elixir is no longer available at Biltmore. Such a shame that someone tattled," he said, and his eyes seemed to narrow at Toven before flicking away. "But now, I get to make house calls."

Briony's heart thrummed. Cordelia wasn't at Cohle's estate any longer? And Canning knew where she was being kept?

"But it is a huge secret, you know," Canning said with a pout. "I feel like we should up the ante if I'm going to reveal this."

Canning looked directly at Toven. Toven responded in a level voice, "I can reveal no more than the country my father is in, I'm afraid."

"I don't care to know that. Truly." Canning shrugged, his eyes falling on Briony again. She had the sinking sensation that he was playing with them, like a cat batting a mouse. "But I will wager that secret against a kiss from the golden heartspring."

Briony held her breath. Toven's jaw clicked, and the weight in her stomach dropped. He would decline. And then she would have no idea what had happened to Cordelia.

Her lips parted before Toven could take a breath. "One measly kiss?" She lifted a brow imitating the man beneath her and said, "That's an easy bet to take. Hardly fair for you, though."

Canning winked at her. "You sell yourself short, Rosewood. Perhaps that's just how madly I desire you."

Toven tensed, about to jump in, about to end this.

"How could Master Toven refuse?" she quickly replied. "It costs him nothing if he loses."

The hand on her back lifted, and she heard the arm of the chair creak under the strain of a hand squeezing it.

The young men were silent, watching the unspoken duel between the two heads of the table. But the match was won, and Toven knew it. The anger radiated off him even as he said, "Of course. An excellent wager."

All eyes turned to the cards as Toven and Canning played, pulling new hands and rolling the dice. She judged Toven's success off Liam, who had no poker face. The more disappointed he looked, the better Toven was doing.

When they both finally laid out their cards, the entire table released a breath. Briony waited.

"Fuck," Lorne whispered, running a hand through his hair.

"It's a draw, sweetheart," Canning said to her from across the table, his lips twisted in an arrogant smile. "Such a shame. I would have liked to have tasted you just once." He made a show of licking his lips at her as the men laughed and Toven stoically cleaned up his cards. Canning leaned closer, schooling his features in a mock pout. "And I'm sure you desperately wanted to know about your dear friend. Such a pity."

Canning tapped his chin, as if deep in thought.

"I'll tell you what," he said, shifting Jellica off his lap. "I'll still reveal my secret if you give me that kiss. Good and proper, now."

She felt her pulse in her fingertips. Then Toven scoffed and plucked up his wineglass, draining the contents and preparing to excuse them from the room.

She thought of Cordelia withering away in a dark castle. Her blue eyes dim, and her magic gone.

Briony stood swiftly. The room was still. They watched her as she moved to Canning, who was smirking at her with hungry eyes. She didn't spare a glance at Toven as she sat in Canning's lap and pulled his neck down to kiss him squarely on the mouth.

The table erupted in cheers and groans. She felt Canning smile against her lips before returning her kiss with a vengeance, his mouth cold and rubbery against hers. She was just pulling back when his hand slipped into her hair, and his other dropped to her thigh, rubbing the skin. His lips moved under hers, his hand gripping her curls to hold her still, and then his tongue was against her mouth, pressing forward to get inside.

He'd barely managed it when she pushed back with all her might, breaking free of him and stumbling to her feet. The sound rushed back to the room as Canning grinned up at her, his thumb brushing over his lips. The men pounded the table and howled.

"Your secret, Trow?" Briony hissed under the din, staring down at him, resisting the urge to wipe her mouth.

Canning raised his hand to quiet the room, his teeth shining proudly. "Cordelia is moved quite frequently. She was at the Locklin estate last week, the Seat's Castle before that. She may not have magic anymore, but she *certainly* has some good fight left in her."

Briony felt the blood drain from her face. There was noise somewhere in the room, but she couldn't decipher the sounds.

The Seat's Castle and the Locklin estate. Moira Locklin was fifth in line to the Seat, but Briony had no idea where the Locklin estate was.

She tried to find the voice to ask, but her wrist was taken, there was an arm around her back, and then Toven was leading her out of the room.

Pushing her, really. The game was over. Several others followed them out, passing the guard, moving down the stairwell.

Toven was silent. His hand on her hip was rigid as he guided her through the door, but she couldn't spare his temper a passing thought. Her mind was spinning with all the information she'd learned and the images her imagination conjured of Cordelia hanging on by a thread, bleeding on some castle floor. She walked the corridor in a daze, shoving her memories of Cordelia back into a closed book on the shelf, where she belonged.

Her lips still felt strange and dry from Canning's, and her dress felt too tight.

Toven steered her outside and toward the sound of the crowd. Around another corner, Ilana waited with a tray of drinks. Briony snapped out of her exhaustion. She was going into the arena again. She needed her wits about her.

They ended up in the stands this week. Briony and Toven sat on a bench, and the strawberry-blond woman dropped down next to Toven, Liam on her other side. Briony eyed her as she smiled at them.

Toven rested his arm on the bench behind Briony's opposite hip, and she did her best to cross her legs in her short dress. She was just starting to dissociate from the events of the evening when she heard a voice with thick vowels to her right.

"Is it true your heartspring used to be a princess?"

Briony and Toven looked at the woman with strawberry-blond hair together. The same woman who'd lived at Claremore for months with her, tending to the linens of said princess.

"You're not supposed to talk to her," Liam said lazily from the other side of her, sipping a glass of whiskey.

"My apologies," Strawberry-Blonde said, eyes still hungry on Briony's face. "I haven't ever seen a princess before."

Briony stared at her as Toven mumbled something about her no longer being a princess. Was it not the same girl? It had to be.

The woman propped herself on her knees facing Toven and Briony. "You must be very rich to have purchased such a prize," she said coquettishly.

"He is, just ask him," Liam said.

Strawberry-Blonde giggled and flipped her hair. "She's absolutely beautiful, Master Toven." The woman shifted a shoulder, and as if by magic, one of her straps fell. "And the way you talked about her two weeks ago. About her being delicious..."

Toven brought his drink to his lips, tilting his head back to swallow it all.

And the strawberry-blond woman took that opportunity to lick her lips, reach forward for Briony's neck, and pull her mouth to hers.

Briony's brows shot up, eyes wide open. The girl's mouth moved over hers, her hand sliding around Briony's neck as she pulled their bodies together over Toven's lap.

Briony couldn't move with the shock of it. This was... What was this?

The woman brushed her fingers around Briony's neck and let her tongue slide out, tasting Briony's lips.

The woman pulled back, smiling brilliantly. "Delicious," she said. "I'd love to taste more of her sometime, Master Toven."

Briony's cheeks flushed bright red as the room came back to her. Liam's drink had frozen on the way to his lips.

And Toven was wound tight like a spring between them, his eyes hardening.

The woman giggled again and then slid back to sit on Liam's lap as if she'd never been speaking with them at all.

Briony pressed her fingers to her mouth, trying to make sense of the last minute.

"I think you should let them taste each other, Toven," Lorne said from one seat farther on. "What do you say?"

Toven smiled thinly and slid his hand over Briony's thighs. "I'd say that I'm inspired to do my own 'tasting.'" He stood from the bench and dragged her up with him. "Gentlemen," he said in goodbye.

Briony stumbled behind him, turning to watch the woman who used to be her maid kissing Liam's neck, not sparing her another glance.

"The fuck was that?"

Her eyes snapped up to find Toven scowling at her as they marched through to the exit.

Briony opened her mouth. Then closed it. "She was . . . very friendly," she finally landed on.

He took her out into the garden and before she realized that they were at the portal spot, he cut his thumb, made a portal home, and said, "Any other friends you'd like to make tonight, Rosewood?"

He dragged her through as Briony protested.

Once they were in the Hearst drawing room, he dropped her arm and stomped out the door to the stairs. Briony blinked after him for a moment before her anger found her.

"Why did we leave?" she demanded, running after him. "We weren't finished!"

"I think you had enough fun for one night," he hissed, starting to climb.

Her mouth fell open at his retreating back. "You're angry that I kissed Canning? You think that was fun for me?"

He spun back, several stairs above her. "I'm angry that you made me look weak."

She gaped at him. "Are you joking? Canning only made that bet because you refused to kiss me! You made us both look like idiots!"

His jaw snapped shut. Starting to ascend again, he bit out, "Kissing is too intimate."

Her temper boiled, bubbling over. Storming after him up the steps, she cried, "Too intimate? Everyone else was kissing! You've shown me *far* more intimate things that we are supposedly doing!"

"So tonight was revenge, then? For intruding on your mind?" He laughed humorlessly. "You're going to go around flirting with as many people as possible to get back at me?"

"Don't flatter yourself," Briony snapped. "That woman was—" She didn't know if she should mention the fact that she'd lied about knowing Briony. "Strange," she finished, "but Canning was a calculated move. He had information about Cordelia—"

"Oh yes," he snarled, turning back to her, his face pink. "I do wonder what your old friends would have to say about your method of information gathering, Rosewood."

She glowered at him. "I wouldn't have to kiss your disgusting friends if you would just tell me what the fuck is going on!"

His nostrils flared, and he wheeled around to storm up the rest of the staircase. "I answer every fucking question you ask me, Rosewood—"

"The waters forbid you offer anything else!" She sprinted after him in her heels. "Like any kind of game plan for these evenings. Or having the decency to tell me about your stupid No Kissing Rule!"

She followed him around the corner as he made for his bedroom.

"You want a rule, Rosewood?" he yelled down the hallway, shoving open his bedroom door. "Don't throw yourself at my friends!"

"Fuck off, Toven!"

He glared at her and disappeared into his room, slamming the door behind him. She followed suit, marching into her bedroom, fuming with the fire in her blood.

She ripped off her heels, chucking them at the wall connecting their rooms, hoping he heard.

She reached up for her collar, hating it and all it stood for. And it *itched*. She screamed in the back of her throat as her fingers tugged at it—

Until her fingers brushed something.

She pulled her hands away in shock as a thin scrap of paper fluttered down from her neck.

Briony stared at it, her entire body frozen.

A piece of parchment, torn off the edge of something, no wider than her little finger.

She bent down slowly, thinking of the way the woman with strawberry-blond hair had pulled her forward by the neck—it had caused quite a distraction.

To slide a thin slice of paper beneath the gold.

Briony's shaking fingers reached for the paper, turning it over. Her breath hitched.

no dragon, don't Worry

Her heart leapt at its cage.

The handwriting was familiar, but the word that truly took her breath away was "Worry" with a capital *W.*

That was what she'd called Rory as a child, when she couldn't pronounce his name.

There really were only four people alive who knew the nickname.

Herself, Cordelia, Didion, and Sammy.

And one of them had written this note to her.

CHAPTER 36

S HE WAS UP ALL NIGHT, mind running through possibilities and probabilities.

She examined the handwriting for hours, trying to remember the shape of Cordelia's *R*'s, attempting to recall some of the notes Didion had written her before she'd thrown them away, wondering if she'd ever seen Sammy's handwriting.

But the letters were cramped and shaky, as if making those four words fit on a small enough paper had affected the entire shape of them.

Instead she considered how the note had gotten to her. The strawberry-blonde must have very limited interaction with the world outside of Biltmore, but Briony remembered the way Ilana had passed her a grape two weeks ago. Ilana had access to everyone who walked through the door at Biltmore Palace.

So who could have gotten a note to Ilana? Sammy and Didion were on the outside. Either of them could have remembered her pet name for Rory. Cordelia was moved frequently, if Canning was to be believed, but she had intimate knowledge of the Biltmore parties. Would Cordelia know how to coordinate with Ilana?

Briony sat on her bed, watching the first rays of sun over the grounds, holding the scrap of paper between her fingertips. She was still in her black dress. She knew Larissa would be upset if she didn't clean off her powders and creams. After putting the note inside the jewelry box on her bedside table, she heaved herself up and went into the bathroom.

With a clean face, she sat in the tub, thinking through a bigger issue.

no dragon, don't Worry

What a fascinating series of words. "No dragon" could mean many things. Briony wondered when the last time she'd heard about the dragon was. One of the men had said last night that the dragon had been spotted in the Tampet Mountains. That was where the Bomardi school had been located and where the Quill estate was.

But how long ago was the sighting?

Could the note possibly be telling her that the dragon was dead?

Don't worry about the dragon, it's dead.

Could that be it?

So then who could know such a thing?

Briony got out of the bath, wrapped herself in a robe, and returned to her seat at the window.

She needed to know more. She needed to return a message, to show that she was open to communication.

One thing was clear. She needed to get back to Biltmore. And that would only happen if she and Toven could keep from killing each other.

Briony took a long sip of tea, considering. Three things had seemed to upset Toven last night: kissing Canning, trying to play the part in the dining room, and letting the strawberry-blonde get close to her. Briony could see his perspective about Canning, but she'd do it again in a heartbeat. Surely he had to understand why.

The rest of his anger made no sense.

She closed her eyes, fighting back her irritation at the impossible riddle that was Toven Hearst. Perhaps understanding the root cause of his anger wasn't as important as making sure it wouldn't happen again. She needed to know what she could and couldn't do. Or else he might try taking Larissa in her body.

Briony frowned into her teacup.

That couldn't happen. She needed to make amends with him.

Even though he was in the wrong.

* * *

After collecting her thoughts, she searched the hall for him. She found him in a study on the first floor, the door slightly cracked. There was no response after a few knocks, so she pushed the door open with her fingertips, holding her breath as it swung backward. He was bent over a desk, sealing an envelope with the Hearst wax seal with an impassive expression on his face.

She swallowed and lifted her chin. "Can we have a discussion?"

"A discussion." He sighed and sat back.

The anger that only he stirred in her started to boil before she refocused.

Staying put in the doorway, almost blocking his exit, she said, "I'd like to talk about the fact that we haven't had a successful evening at Biltmore yet."

His eyes flickered up to her. "Successful." She nodded, and the corner of his mouth twitched. "And what would that look like?"

"You tell me," she said quietly. "I've been twice, and both times I've felt like I'm drowning."

There was a flash of something in his face—guilt, perhaps. She pushed forward, holding his gaze.

"I want to continue going to the Biltmore parties. I don't want you to take someone else in my body."

He inhaled sharply. "Rosewood—"

"As terrifying and disgusting as it is, Biltmore is the one place I get to see my old friends and feel a little less alone," she continued, rushing over him. "And hear a bit about the world outside."

She paused, biting her lip. She wouldn't tell him about the note or the communication channels. Though she had her suspicions about the Hearsts' allegiances—though the phrase "political collateral" still rang in her ears—she had no reason yet to trust Toven with her information.

"We need to be on the same page at these parties," she added.

"And how do you propose we do that?"

"Well, for starters, if I must refrain from kissing Canning Trow in the future, I suppose I can make the sacrifice," she said dryly.

He rolled his eyes. "How magnanimous of you."

"I think we need to be more comfortable with each other," she said, jumping right to the point.

His eyes snapped to hers, unreadable.

"I'm too stiff, you're too . . . skittish." He opened his mouth as if to argue with her. "Against 'intimacy,' whatever," she said with a flippant gesture. His mouth closed, and she looked away from his intense gaze. "I like to go into situations with all the necessary information. I didn't know you had an aversion to kissing." She tore her gaze from his desk and found his eyes staring at a point over her shoulder. She swallowed. "I believe Canning read my discomfort."

"And capitalized on it," he finished.

She nodded. Taking a deep breath and remembering the note, Briony voiced the request that had brought her down here to begin with.

"Have dinner with me tonight," she said. "Just the two of us."

His eyes jumped to her face. He was still, except for the muscle in his jaw.

"Have . . ."

"Dinner." She nodded. "I want to discuss what a successful evening at Biltmore looks like to you. What it would take on my part to convince your friends of the kind of relationship we are supposed to have."

He scratched his neck, and she saw pinpricks of pink under his collar. "I'm out this evening."

The response was swift, and it made Briony's eyes narrow.

"Tomorrow then," she said. He shifted on his feet, and she cut off the excuse she knew was coming. "Or any day, really. My schedule is wide open."

He stared a hole into his desk as he responded, "Tomorrow."

"Wonderful. Just the two of us." She paused. "Larissa isn't still in the house, is she?"

He shook his head.

She ached to ask where it was Larissa stayed while she was "dead," but she continued, "I'll arrange everything with the kitchen."

He lifted a brow and, with a tinge of reluctance, said, "It's a date."

Her pulse pounded and her cheeks grew hot. She mumbled something in the affirmative before disappearing from the doorway and racing up the stairs back to her room.

* * *

The word "date" stuck in her head like glue, flustering her as she tried to prepare the following evening. Briony changed dresses several times, back and forth between two of them, finding fault with each. When her hands had reached for the powders and creams in her vanity, she busied them with tying her hair into a braid to rest on her shoulder instead, chastising herself for considering something as silly as dressing up for Toven Hearst.

This wasn't "a date." This was preparation for another outing to Biltmore. She needed to get back to Cordelia or Sammy or Didion, and Toven needed to ward off suspicion.

At a quarter till eight, she headed down to the dining room to check on preparations. The house had set two places, just as she'd asked—one at the head of the table, and one just to the left. A bottle of red wine had been decanted, and the serving dishes were full of vegetables and roast beef.

She awkwardly took her seat at the side of the table and had to wait only five minutes before Toven's footsteps drew her gaze to the door. She stood swiftly as he entered, her gaze lingering on his dark-blue button-up shirt. His eyes skimmed the wine and food on the table before landing back on her, quickly assessing her braided hair.

"Rosewood," he greeted before sweeping to his chair at the head of the table, with the confidence of someone who enjoyed dinner with his captive as a matter of course.

She managed a quick nod. Retaking her seat, she focused on placing her napkin across her lap as she asked, "How was your day?"

He cleared his throat. "Fine. And yours?"

"Lovely, thank you."

She reached for her wineglass and drank deeply, trying, but failing, to think of something to break the silence. Toven filled his plate with food before pushing the serving plate in her direction, his lips in a thin line. Briony played with her utensils, heat creeping up her neck.

They ate in silence for thirty-six seconds before she could bear it no longer.

"Clearly neither of us is one for small talk, but I don't intend to sit for two hours in silence." He lifted a brow at her, and she felt the flush spread to her cheeks. "I have more questions. But I know you hate questions——"

"I don't hate questions——"

"They put you into a 'mood'——"

"They do not. *You* put me into a mood."

She scowled at him and speared her vegetables with a forceful clink.

He sipped his wine, studying her. She took a large, defiant bite of food and held his gaze.

"What are your questions, Rosewood?"

She swallowed thickly. "Who is Ilana?"

"Her mother is Bomardi but was disowned for marrying an Eversun. She was raised across the sea, and she lived there until after the fall of Evermore, when her father started organizing against Mallow, at which time she was taken and given to the Barlowes."

Briony's mind whirred, taking it all in. "And why has she been given so much authority at Biltmore? She seems to have more freedom than any other Barlowe Girl."

"I couldn't say, really." He sliced into his roast with small, precise cuts. "I suppose it's because she's . . . quite good at what she does."

A cold suspicion crashed over her. "And what exactly does she do?"

Toven's fork stopped halfway to his mouth. "Host. With a smile. Flirt and joke. Be seen when she needs to be seen, be invisible when she needs to be invisible."

Briony pursed her lips as she cut her roast. The arrogance of the Bomardi was astounding. It seemed like an awful oversight to give a woman with a background like Ilana's the keys to the Biltmore, allowing her to move from room to room largely at will.

"The tattoos. How did you and Finn find a way around them for Larissa?"

"We didn't." She narrowed her eyes at him, and he shrugged. "A blood-purifying spell and pure luck. We weren't sure if it would work. It's my understanding that if Larissa had crossed the estate line, it would have been all but impossible to remove it."

"And you have no idea how to find a way around these tattoos."

"It's not exactly the kind of question I go around asking other Bomardi, no," he said dryly. A muscle in his cheek twitched. "Making your grand escape plan, Rosewood?"

"Hmm," she said innocently, ignoring his question. "You were willing to divulge information on who escaped at Castle Javis during the card game. Care to share?"

She watched him chew, lips pressed tight with small bites, just like his mother, his aristocratic jaw moving quickly.

"Billium Meers made it out."

Briony blinked, pulling her gaze from his lips. "He's alive? I thought he died on the battlefield."

"He lived, apparently, and portaled out of Javis. The *Journal* page wouldn't have said anything about it. They wouldn't publicize a weakness like that."

Briony squeezed her napkin in both palms, letting out a shaky breath of relief. She had never gotten on with Sammy's father, but he had been her father's trusted general. It was a major loss for Mallow that he'd escaped.

"Do you know where he went?"

"Starksen." He drank his wine, and she watched him swallow. "They're causing quite a few problems for Mallow there."

Briony smirked into her napkin. *Good.* When she glanced back up at him, the smile still fading on her lips, he was still looking away from her.

She took a deep breath and braced herself for the second half of her plans for the evening. Grabbing her wineglass and taking two huge gulps, she stood.

His eyes snapped to her. "What are you doing?"

"I think"—she swallowed, hating the reedy sound in her voice—"I think we should practice."

His fork and knife hovered over his plate. His eye twitched. "Practice."

"To get more comfortable around each other." She moved to the other side of him, reaching for the wine bottle. He didn't move an inch while she filled his glass, as she usually did at Biltmore. Standing just to his side, she pressed her lips together when he didn't look up at her, still frozen in his chair. "I think you should pull me into your lap now."

He placed his utensils down and sucked in a sharp breath. "This is your master plan, Rosewood?"

"Yes. We need to be more comfortable to put on a convincing show." She twisted her fingers around each other. "We could both use a bit of rehearsal—"

"That won't be necessary."

"I disagree. You saw that stunt Canning pulled, and he'll try it again if we keep giving him reasons to—"

"This whole idea is just childish."

"What's childish is that you can't bear to touch me!"

"I touch you enough, it's absurd you're asking for more—"

"—and although it's quite obvious that I physically repulse you—"

A dry laugh burst from him.

Her nostrils flared. "I don't know how you behave toward women you're sleeping with, Hearst, but if this is your idea of intimacy, then you clearly need more help than I could ever offer—"

His hand darted out and grabbed her opposite hip, tugging her into his lap. She swallowed her squeak and steadied herself on the table, heart pounding. In an attempt to save her dignity, she lifted her chin, shifting until she could sit properly. It seemed it was no less difficult to find a balanced position in her long wool dress than it was in silk and heels.

"What now, Rosewood?" he rumbled, and she felt it vibrate through her rib cage.

The tips of her ears burned. "Just...behave normally. Like this is... normal." She cleared her throat and reached for her wine, stretching back to her table setting. "Eat dinner as if I'm not even here."

Toven seemed to take a long, slow breath before picking up his fork again. He pushed his vegetables around, staring at his peas intently.

She had a few choices of where to focus her gaze. She could awkwardly stare at his face. She could watch him play with his food. Or the safest option: She could stare at his neck, studying the way the pink blush spread under her gaze.

"How often do they play cards at dinner?" she asked softly, and she watched his throat bob as he swallowed.

"They play maybe every other week. There's no schedule," he said.

"And that's not dangerous? To have the women as witnesses?"

"Quite."

Briony frowned. She thought of the strawberry-blonde and her intent eyes during the game, listening to every detail. The Barlowe Girls might be on a tight leash, but they had access to a wealth of knowledge.

"Find me a book to teach me how to play the game. I can use mind magic to see everyone's cards."

"How do you think I keep winning, Rosewood."

She glanced at him, bringing their faces impossibly close. As he sipped from his wineglass, she realized that Toven Hearst was an endless vault of secrets.

"Oh, how could I forget," she said at last. "You have a habit of getting into people's heads, don't you?" She shook her head and sighed into her glass.

His fingers drummed on the tablecloth. "Contrary to your memory of events, Rosewood, I never entered your mind until last week."

She narrowed her gaze at him. That couldn't be. The leg tingles from year three. The knowledge of Didion fumbling with her corset laces. He had to be lying.

She steadied her heartbeat and asked the question she'd been fearing.

"So what do I do?" she continued. "How do we get . . . comfortable?"

He heaved a great, laboring sigh. "Your behavior on Friday was fine. We can keep doing that—"

"All right then." She reached up and ran her fingers through the hair on the back of his head. Brushing her fingers along his scalp, letting the smooth locks thread through her knuckles.

His head jerked away. "What are you doing—?"

"Oh, you have a No Hair Touching Rule as well?" She rolled her eyes. "Relax."

He let out a ragged breath as her fingers dragged through the hair over his ear. She saw him pick up his fork again but do nothing with it. Brushing through his hair as if it were silk, she curved over his ear, her fingertips rounding the shell.

She'd dreamed of running her fingers through his hair like this. So many nights.

Remembering Larissa's advice, she drifted soft fingers across the back of his neck, where his hairline ended.

As he shivered, she thought of the way Collin and Lorne held their women close and just watched the card game. The way the strawberry-blonde had massaged Liam's neck and kissed his cheek for luck. The way she'd seen other Barlowe Girls smile and whisper into men's ears or nuzzle into their necks.

"Relax," she repeated quietly. She brushed his hair over his ear again, her fingers trailing around and down to his neck, flushed pink with the wine. She leaned forward and pressed her lips to the skin below his ear.

The earth ceased to spin in the heartbeat it took for his arm to curl tighter around her waist, his hand splayed on her ribs. She parted her lips and kissed him again. His skin was clean and minty, and she felt his throat bob under her mouth as he swallowed.

And then in quick movements, she was pushed to her feet, and he was up out of his chair.

"The fuck are you doing?" he hissed.

She steadied herself on the table as he touched his neck, where her lips had just been. His mouth moved wordlessly as he stared at her. Maybe he felt like she'd contaminated him.

"I'm doing what I'm supposed to," she snarled. "If you'd just calm down—"

"You can't just sit in a man's lap and kiss his neck, Rosewood!"

She blinked at him, breathing quickly as he dragged a hand through his hair.

"And why not? That is precisely what happens at Biltmore—"

"That's *Biltmore*!" he snapped. "This is *here*, in my house!"

Her eyes were wide as she watched him move toward the exit.

"What is your problem? We're practicing—!"

"You cannot be this dense," he muttered, striding out of the dining room.

She stormed after him, stopping at the doorway.

"We're not done, Hearst! I expect you at dinner tomorrow evening!"

He disappeared around a corner, and Briony cursed under her breath.

She stomped to the table, drained her glass of wine, and finished her plate—and his, too, in case he planned to ask the house for it later.

*   *   *

After sending Toven a formal invitation to supper, Briony spent the rest of her Monday creating mind barriers.

She was perfectly prepared to spend another meal in his lap, and she'd work harder to convince him of the necessity. Pushing away her stray thoughts about the scent of his skin and the warmth of his chest against her side, she focused on how to stay focused.

At a quarter till eight, she made her way downstairs. She sat on a chaise longue at the side of the room and wondered if they should also practice being comfortable away from a dining table. As images flooded her mind of Toven Hearst and the *versatility* of a chaise, she quickly dismissed the idea.

She was still waiting for him to arrive at eight oh five, glaring into her wineglass despite her self-assurance that she'd be less reactive this time. At eight twelve, she finally heard footsteps scuffing across the stones. When she turned to lift a brow at him, he looked very much like a child who had been dragged to a dinner party with adults, scowling with bored eyes, resigned to having a terrible time.

"Good evening," she lilted.

He took his place at the table without a word. Once he was seated, she stood, poured his wine, and sat determinedly in his lap, as if daring him to object. His expression didn't change as she tugged her plate of food closer, sipped her wine, and munched on the canapés that the kitchen had sent as their first course.

"I have another question," she said primly, breaking the silence. He didn't respond, ignoring her gaze boring into him as he drank deeply from his wine. "Where is your father?"

That earned her a scowl, and he plunked his glass back on the table. "You know I can't tell you that."

"You were about to gamble that information away on Friday."

"I knew I was going to win."

"You tied. That was hardly winning." She felt his ribs expand against hers with a deep breath. "You were only going to name the country," she continued, in a gentler tone. "You can't even give me that?"

The expression that flashed through his eyes momentarily stunned her. A softness that told her maybe she could ask anything of him. She blinked at him over her wineglass, and it was gone.

Perhaps she'd imagined it.

"Southern Camly." His long fingers toyed with the white tablecloth. "That's all I know."

Juliana was the daughter of Southern Camly's president. It was also where Finola had trained in strategy and espionage—where many of Finola's contacts and acquaintances were.

"He's gone indefinitely?" she asked.

Toven nodded. "He's not to be disturbed unless strictly necessary."

She frowned, knowing she had nothing but pure speculation.

Not wanting to push him too much after the previous evening, she refrained from asking more questions. She sat quietly in his lap as he finished his wine and ate his meal, her mind sorting through all she'd learned.

She was disappointed by how much he didn't know—how much *she* still didn't know—but at least it was a start. She didn't have the sense that he'd lied or withheld information from her. More important, they seemed to be making progress on an interpersonal level. Despite the evening's rocky start, they hadn't fought, which was a significant improvement.

The next night, she ate early and finished her wine quickly, giving her the courage she needed to push their boundaries a bit farther. She spent the meal curled into his side, running her fingers through his hair as he poked at his vegetables. She noticed that he held her eye longer than usual, and she tried her best to ignore the fluttering in her chest each time it happened.

"Will things get out of hand again at the private dinners, do you think?" she asked. "I know the atmosphere seemed calmer, but—"

"This is fine," he cut in. "What we're doing here"—his hand gestured between them—"will be fine for Friday."

She lifted a brow but kept her reservations to herself. They'd cross that bridge later. For now, she didn't want to upset their progress. It was still too fragile.

As the week progressed, Toven began to distract her thoughts even more than usual. She woke in the mornings with the memory of what it felt like to be curled against his body. The scent of it. She had to increase the amount of time she spent meditating in the morning so she could stay on task the rest of the day while she scoured the news and continued researching.

But at night, when it was just the two of them, she pulled his shelf forward, letting his volumes flutter open to vibrant colors and patterns.

It was dangerous, she knew, given her history of feelings for him, but she couldn't see a way around the need to build trust. A solid connection with him, if not a friendship. She ignored the voice in her head that told her she didn't want to find another way.

On Wednesday, she picked food off his plate while sitting against his chest. He fought her for the last of his potatoes, his fork jabbing at her fingers when she reached for them. Her heartbeat thrummed as she smiled and tried to offer him the potato, pressing it to his lips. He rolled his eyes and turned his face away.

That's how Serena Hearst found the two of them—with Briony in her son's lap, his arm wrapped around her waist, and her trying to feed him as he dramatically twisted his head from side to side.

"Oh," Serena said.

Briony gasped, tumbling out of Toven's lap. Toven jumped up, knocking over his wineglass.

"We weren't—"

"This isn't what it looks—"

"It's only that—"

"Couldn't you have knocked, Mother?"

"My," Serena hummed, and Briony felt her face turn beet red at the barely concealed grin spreading across her features. "Don't let me interrupt."

"You're not interrupting anything," Toven said quickly, almost shouting the words. He started to push his chair in, shoving it roughly after it skidded noisily on the floor.

"No, no." Serena waved her hands. "Please finish your meal. I insist."

Briony stared at her shoes, pulse pounding in her ears. Her skin itched with guilt and embarrassment in every place that had just been in contact with Toven's body.

"Enjoy the rest of your dinner." Serena glided out of the room, and Briony thought she could hear a light laugh echo in the corridor.

Briony dropped her head into her hands as soon as Serena turned the corner. "Oh *waters*," she groaned.

Toven shifted on his feet before excusing himself with an unintelligible mumble, leaving her alone in the dining room with only her burning skin and guilty conscience.

CHAPTER 37

ON FRIDAY, THEY FOLLOWED THE NOW-FAMILIAR PATH to the courtyard, though she fell in step with him easily this time. She refrained
from playing with her collar as best she could, but she felt the note burning her skin.

That day, after a lot of trial and error to get words to fit on a paper so
small, Briony landed on something that was at least an opening of communication.

safe, Biney

Only Sammy, Didion, or Cordelia would know that "Biney" was what
Rory had called her when he couldn't pronounce Briony. She promised
herself that the next time she had an opportunity to pass a note, she would
have something solid from her research to pass on.

Caspar Quill had mentioned the Durlings, and try as she might, she
hadn't found a thing about them in the Hearst library.

They moved through the gardens with the reflection ponds and headed
toward the entry hall.

Briony was in tight blue lace tonight, something that almost would have
been reminiscent of Bomardi fashion if it hadn't been so short.

Larissa had come by to get her ready again, but she'd transmogrified
herself into Juliana, the president's daughter, for the entire hour. Briony
and Toven both agreed she could attend the party tonight.

As olive hands had spread powder on Briony's face, she asked Larissa,

"Was Toven averse to physical touch at some point before he was comfortable with you?"

Larissa, in Juliana's face, stopped what she was doing and raised a brow at her. "What?"

"He doesn't like it when I play with the hair on the back of his head. And I tried kissing his neck and he pushed me off him."

Larissa stared down at her from someone else's eyes, but that same look of disbelief was there.

"So I guess, I wonder if he just doesn't like physical touch, or—"

"I can't with this." Larissa had thrown down the brushes and left Briony to fend for herself.

They reached the doors, but Ilana wasn't the one to greet them. A red-head with a large chest smiled at Toven and didn't give Briony a glance.

She gave them champagne and that was it. She opened the curtain without giving Toven a guest sheet.

Briony found Phoebe hanging off Carvin's arm across the entry hall, smiling as his hand drifted lower on her back. But Briony's interest was elsewhere, her eyes wide and alert for any sign of the strawberry-blonde. Before she could get a decent look around the room, Toven was leading her up the twisting steps, through the guard's check, and into the dining room. Briony swallowed her disappointment, wondering if she'd made a mistake by not telling him about the note she needed to pass.

The first thing she noticed was Finn Raquin laughing jovially at something Liam had said, and Larissa disguised as Juliana standing against the wall behind him. Her eyes darted behind Liam's chair and found a different Barlowe Girl waiting quietly to pour the wine. She scanned, but there was still not a trace of Strawberry-Blonde in the room. The disappointment in her stomach twisted more heavily.

"Be still my heart," a voice called out as the door shut behind them, and Briony turned to find Canning Trow bowing dramatically at her. "My lady approaches."

She cast her eyes down, ready to play her part.

"Oh, love," Canning crooned, "did Toven whomp you good and proper after last week? Never one to share, our boy. Why don't you bend over my lap so I can kiss it better?"

The young men laughed as Toven took his seat, his jaw barely tensing before it loosened in a grin. As she assumed her position in front of the window, she glanced to the left at Larissa behind Finn's chair.

The young woman Larissa was pretending to be was so small and young. Her eyes were staring down at her shoes, her wrists thin and crossed submissively in front of her stomach. Briony didn't know how much was an act and how much was sheer concentration on the magic on Larissa's part.

Briony tore her eyes from her, determined not to attract suspicion.

The eight women stepped forward, pouring wine into crystal glasses, and before Briony could return to the wall, Toven's arm was around her waist, guiding her to his lap. Other than Finn lifting a theatrical brow at them, no one else said a word about it. Briony was quite pleased with their "practicing" paying off, but she did have a moment of guilt for the extra minutes Cecily had to spend against Collin's chest when he quickly followed Toven's lead.

She crossed her legs in her little lace dress, tilting her knees toward Toven's waist. His left arm slipped over her hip, holding her to him instead of clenching his fingers tight around the arm of the chair. When she shifted in his lap, nuzzling into his neck and letting her fingers play with the hair on the back of his head, he didn't flinch. She felt giddy with success. Their time together had been worth it, just as she'd predicted.

Nothing noteworthy had caught her ear in the table's conversation after the first half hour. But then Liam's voice rang out above the others.

"There's a Summer Cannon tonight," he said, lazily twirling his fork in the air.

A collective murmur of interest swept over the table. Briony narrowed her eyes at Liam, wondering what that meant. The Summer Cannon usually went off at noon.

Toven's thighs tensed beneath hers. She dragged her fingers through his hair, rubbing circles in his scalp.

"I love dinner and a show," Canning said, and the table erupted into laughter.

Toven's hand squeezed her hip, shivering her skin pleasantly. She caught herself, refocusing. She had more pressing concerns, like whether this new event would cut into her time to find the strawberry-blonde.

It was a rather uneventful evening in the dining room, despite the hours they sat there talking and laughing.

Then a chiming sounded, amplified throughout the dining room, cutting off the music and silencing the voices in surprise. Briony looked up, searching for the source. The clock on the wall read quarter till midnight.

The men cheered, grabbing their drinks and gripping their women close, rubbing their hands together.

Toven peeled her off him, all tension returning to his body. Finn shared a look with Juliana—Larissa.

"What is it?" Briony whispered to Toven.

He shook his head at her in warning and followed the others as they descended the staircase into the entrance hall. She kept her eyes open for the strawberry-blonde, searching the crowd of people as they headed to the exits into the courtyard.

Her hand reached for her collar to adjust it, and she caught herself.

"I'll get us drinks," Toven announced to Finn and Larissa. "See you outside."

Briony turned up to Toven as he steered them toward the hallway. Her mouth opened to ask—

"Don't," he hissed. "Just trust me on this."

Her heart pounded in her ears as Toven led them around the crowd, suddenly cutting left to the gardens where they could portal from.

"Not leaving already, Toven?"

Briony's blood chilled. Toven stilled next to her. When he turned them around, she already knew who would be standing there.

Veronika Mallow wore flowing deep purple. Her hair was pulled back tightly, lifting her features into youthful surprise. She was flanked by two Bomardi guards.

Toven dropped into a deep bow, and Briony followed, taking a moment to grasp her meditations.

In her mind, she stuck the note she'd received under her collar in between the pages of a worn book and shoved it deep on a shelf. She wrote Larissa's name on a blank page and closed it, locking it tight.

Once she'd risen, she met Mallow's black eyes.

"Apologies, Mistress," Toven said. "I was a bit zealous in my attempts to . . . get somewhere private." His voice dropped seductively.

Mallow smiled, her gaze still on Briony.

"You can't go just yet," she said firmly. "You must join me for the show."

Toven inclined his head. "It would be an honor, Mistress."

Mallow whispered something to her guard as she turned, not even checking that they were following her.

Briony's head spun as she fought back all the things she couldn't let Mallow see inside her mind.

Toven wrapped an arm around her waist and pulled her forward with him.

They moved into the chill of the courtyard, and she chanced a look to Toven's face—stony, impassive. A cold horror began building in her chest as they walked into the crowd gathering at the base of the hill. The courtyard looked out over the horizon and was filled with blue cloaks and shivering heartsprings.

Toven walked her behind Mallow and her guards, and the crowd parted for them, watching them pass with reverence. Briony checked the skies, wondering about the "no dragon" portion of the note. There was no sign of the beast. The note under her collar tonight was itching, and she considered abandoning her plan. Was it too dangerous to pass notes under Mallow's nose?

Mallow's purple cloak followed her up three steps to a platform, and Toven and Briony did the same. Cohle, Gains, and Quill were there. They bowed deeply to Mallow, yet their eyes cast over Briony hungrily.

She was the only heartspring on the platform.

But while they were the ones elevated, she realized the platform was not the set scene. To Briony's left she saw light being directed toward the front of the crowd at the palace ledge.

Briony's heart jumped in her throat. The strawberry-blonde stood at the front of the crowd, standing against the ledge overlooking the city.

She gasped breathlessly, stunned into silence. Sound disappeared in a vacuum.

The woman stood in a ragged slip, her hands magically bound in front of her. Her chin was lifted, and she was murmuring something, lips moving quickly. To her left, a boy with the same color of curls on top of his head stood shaking. He couldn't have been more than eighteen—Strawberry-Blonde's brother. He'd joined Rory's army. The only non-magical person to do so.

Briony thought of the note stuck between her skin and the gold collar. Had the girl been caught? Did someone know what she was doing with the collars? Briony tensed—was someone coming for her as well?—and flinched under Toven's hand, squeezing her tightly in warning.

A man stepped into view, and the cheering hit her in full force. It was Mr. Vein, from the auction. Vein smiled toothily and amplified his voice, greeting the crowd.

"To Mistress Mallow," he boomed, lifting his hand to the platform.

The crowd responded, "May she reign forevermore."

Mallow stood stoically with her hands folded in front of herself.

"A traitor to Mistress Mallow's reign stands before you," said Vein. "She and her brother—two servants *without* magic"—the masses snarled—"find themselves ungrateful for everything we've given them here, at the center of our mistress's power."

The booing and spitting rang in her ears. Toven stood behind her, a hand still on her elbow.

Briony knew what was to come. The girl and her brother were going to be executed, here in front of them all, as an example. Briony searched the crowd for someone, anyone. Her knees buckled as she tried to turn about, and Toven's hand tightened on her again.

Her eyes finally landed on Ilana, passing drinks around on a tray, smiling tightly. Ilana glanced to the front, a stab of sadness in her eyes that couldn't be masked quickly enough. Briony brought her fingers to her collar again, without thinking, and when she looked back to the strawberry-blonde, the woman met her eyes.

Briony dropped her hand quickly, her heart splintering at the edges.

"This non-magical filth," Vein continued, "showed no appreciation for what we've given her. We allowed her and her brother into our world. Allowed them to serve us. And how does she repay us?"

Briony held her breath, watching the strawberry-blonde flicker her gaze between herself and Ilana. She could feel Mallow's presence to her right, like oil.

"She was communicating with the rebels!"

The crowd hissed. Briony turned her gaze to Mallow quickly. Her lips were curved in a satisfied smile.

"She was caught at the gate! Not only speaking to the enemy, but also arranging for her brother's escape!"

The sea of people jeered. The note Briony had tucked beneath her collar burned against her skin. This woman and her brother were about to die, all because she'd helped the rebels communicate. Would Briony be next? Was she on this platform next to Mallow so she could be killed on a stage?

"Mistress Mallow!" Vein called. "How do you sentence this slut and her brother?"

Mallow's pale skin shone in the moonlight. Her jaw was sharp as Briony watched it move.

"Death. Painful death."

The Bomardi screamed and cheered.

Briony's world tilted on its axis, and it took her several long seconds to realize that Toven was steadying her lower back, pushing her upright.

Through the pounding of her blood, a thought clarified: If Mallow suspected that she had a note under her collar—if anyone knew that the collars were being used this way—every heartspring would be searched on their way in. The parties at Biltmore would cease.

This woman's sentencing had nothing to do with the note she'd passed to Briony. Glancing back to Strawberry-Blonde, Briony watched her eyes move back and forth between Ilana and Briony, the intensity in them burning as her brother sobbed next to her.

Ilana moved to the base of the platform on which Briony stood.

The strawberry-blonde turned to her brother, speaking quickly, too low to overhear. He nodded solemnly, his shiny eyes never leaving his sister's.

They were servants. Non-magical. They had no business getting involved in any of this horror. And yet, this was the woman who'd grasped her hand under the table with glass digging into her knees. A woman who had risked everything to get that note to her. Just as she'd risked everything to protect her little brother.

Briony looked away, blinking rapidly to stop the tears from falling. Throughout the crowd, silver-collared women were frozen, many with silent tears trailing down their cheeks.

A wild cheering brought her attention back to the front. A cannon wheeled forward.

Terror gripped her as the old war cannon that announced the time every midday in summer spun slowly to face the two siblings.

"No!" she choked, but it was too loud everywhere—inside her mind and out.

A pair of hands landed on her waist. A firm chest against her shoulder blades.

Vein raised his voice again. "Let us prove how foolish it is for anyone to resist Mistress Mallow's will. We will take the boy first and make his sister watch."

Briony was frozen in place, heaving for air, Mallow watching her as she panicked. She looked away and a hand moved from her waist to turn her chin back, forcing her to face ahead as they aimed the cannon.

A sharp jaw pressed to her temple. Warm breath fanned across her cheekbones.

"There is a lake with still waters," Toven's voice whispered. "A mountain range surrounds it. The waters are deep with hidden secrets, but the water is still."

She blinked, legs swaying, feeling her breathing even out as she let his words wash over her. His hands slipped around her stomach, pressing her close to him.

They lit the cannon, and she started to feel her panic drift away, like a leaf on a lake.

The courtyard screamed and stomped while they counted down.

"Think of your mind as a library. Shelves upon shelves of novels and journals and biographies," the voice lulled. "Find an empty shelf for this moment."

She pulled a book forward, her mind dissociating from the moment in front of her.

An explosive boom rocked the stones beneath her feet. Briony watched with a slack jaw as the spot where the boy had been a moment before smoked and crumbled, his sister speckled with his blood. The cannon was reloaded.

"An empty book in your hands. Its blank pages between your fingers. Write this moment into the book. Give it a title."

The Strawberry-Blonde, her mind supplied.

"Fill the pages and close the book."

The cannon aimed at the woman. She shed tears slowly, mixing with her brother's blood, dripping pink down her neck.

"Push it into a corner. Lose it within the piles and piles of texts and novels."

A book's pages fluttered shut in her mind. It locked. And she breathed deeply, stretching to her tiptoes to push it onto a shelf that was just too tall for her to reach. She imagined a hand with long fingers helping her reach the top.

A cannon was lit.

There was a woman crying.

A crowd cheered and counted the seconds.

The woman tilted her head back to the sky and screamed.

She disappeared in a spray of smoke and blood and rage.

There were hands on Briony's waist, leading her backward, tugging her down the platform steps.

A beautiful woman with a silver collar and a tray of champagne glasses stood at the last step. Briony's mind was blank. She was nameless to her.

"Master Hearst, can I get you anything?"

"Thank you, Ilana. We're on our way out."

Ilana. The name was familiar to her, but there were books in her mind that refused to open.

Briony's body jerked forward, stomach flipping over, the ground coming up to meet her face.

"Oh!" the woman—Ilana—caught her just before she landed. "Miss Rosewood, do be careful."

Two fingers slid along Briony's neck. A piece of paper was removed.

How had it gotten there?

"Have a good evening, Master Hearst."

Arms around her again, moving her quickly past the screaming fanatics and wolves and other monsters. Pulling her to descend a sandy hill.

Reality ripped as a portal opened, and a man with pale hair pulled her into the void.

She stepped through and into a bedroom of grays and silvers, a bed of dark wood, and neatly organized trinkets.

She turned around, bookshelves swaying and buckling, and Toven Hearst stood before her in his bedroom.

His hands came to rest on her jaw, examining her eyes.

"Look at me."

She blinked, and her bookshelf crashed to the ground. Free.

Shivers came over her skin, gasping breaths from her chest, a flood of tears down her cheeks. She sobbed, her hands clutching his elbows, keeping him close.

And without knowing how, she pressed against his chest, her forehead pushing into his sternum. Her cries shook her body. He enclosed his arms around her back.

There was a hole in her stomach the shape of a cannonball, filled with grief and rage and despair.

Toven didn't say a word, simply holding her.

She pulled back when she'd finally exhausted herself, stepping away from him. She knew she was red and swollen and wet. But he looked down at her with such a raw emotion that she couldn't feel vulnerable.

"They're going to pay for what they did," she vowed, her voice hollow and misshapen.

His gray eyes stared down at her. He moved a curl behind her ear. And he nodded.

PART THREE

My beloved,

The court was delighted with your presentation. I can see the name Vindecci on every tongue soon—though sooner mine than theirs...

I believe I understand the concept, but some members of the court had questions about your phrasing. "It is the magician's own mind that can be his familiar." Stirring words, but perhaps revise this. Some have begun to wonder about all it will take to learn magic of the mind, and they grow lazy. Already Barden Trow has questions about humanizing "the familiar."

Do not present the idea with the human mind as a "familiar," dearest. Barden and others have misunderstood you. They question if the human heart can be the familiar as well...and I know that is not what you intended. When you present your theory again, be sure to exclude familiars from the presentation altogether.

Come back quickly. I fear when the court buzzes like this.

—LETTER, UNSIGNED, FOUND IN THE BELONGINGS OF
VINDECCI, CIRCA YEAR 1515 AFTER RECORD,
ALSO KNOWN AS YEAR 0 BV
(BEFORE VINDECCI)

CHAPTER 38

Four Years Ago

"THERE WAS A FIGHT AT BARTA. A villager died."

Briony looked up from her breakfast at Rory who was reading a *Journal* page. "Barta?" Her brows drew together. Barta was a mountain village on the border of the two realms. "Was it an Eversun or a Bomardi who died?"

"Eversun," he said.

Briony sat back in her chair. They were in their suite at the Bomardi school, just a few days before the break for summer solstice. It had been a rough few months since the start of the school year in the spring, as the Bomardi tutors refused to teach mind magic to the Eversun children under penalty of death.

Rory looked at her. "It was a Bomardi who killed him."

Briony tapped her fingers on the table, thinking hard.

"Do you think this will change things?" Rory asked.

Briony smiled at him. "No. I'm sure Father will send an emissary, and it will all be figured out." She glanced at the clock. It was time to head down the stairs to class, and while the year fives were educated on a higher floor than the previous years, it was still quite congested getting down there.

Rory and Briony filed into the classroom with two minutes to spare.

"Your militia is getting sloppy, Your Highness," Liam Quill said as he sat down. "I heard an Eversun soldier killed a civilian in Bomard today."

Briony turned around in her chair to face him. "It was an Eversun who died, actually. One of *your* people killed him."

"Not likely," Toven said as he took the seat next to Liam. "You know how unstable mind magic can be, Liam." His eyes stayed on her. "An Eversun was probably trying to warm their tea and set the village on fire."

"That's a gross exaggeration," Briony said, turning back around.

The tutor entered the room and was just about to start the lesson when a scratching sound came from the windows that overlooked the mountain range.

All eyes turned to see a large hawk scraping its talons at the glass pane, flapping its wings and cawing.

A chair scuffed loudly as Toven stood.

"Is that your father's familiar?" Larissa asked.

Toven took two steps to the window, and then the mountain shuddered and quaked. The glass shattered as the floor rocked beneath their feet.

Screams filled the room, and Briony's hand flew up to guard her face against the glass.

People were running. Rory covered Cordelia, diving with her out of the room.

Briony pushed her hands into a protection shield just as rocks began falling from the ceiling—as the year five classroom caved in.

She flattened herself against a wall, her shield keeping the dust and rubble away from her as students screamed in terror and pain. Her heart pounded as she tried to decipher what exactly was happening. Was it something natural, like an earthquake? Or was it more sinister?

She couldn't stay here. Briony dashed out into the hallway as more of the ceiling fell.

She needed to find Rory. Her father would never forgive her if something happened to him.

She began to move down the hallway but then stopped dead in her tracks. There were men and women in blue Bomardi cloaks engaging in combat. With the students.

A man—Riann Cohle, she thought his name was—grabbed one of the Eversun boys by the throat and portaled out with him.

She stumbled back, horrified, and fell into someone. She spun around to face a man with a crooked nose and thick black brows, smiling gleefully.

"Well, if it isn't the princess." His voice was like gravel.

He reached out with his hand to drag her to him, and she blocked him, shoving. He slid back two inches on his feet, then cast a binding spell. Her left arm snapped to her side, but her right arm sliced at him.

He released her and jumped back. There was a cut across his shoulder. He grinned at her. "Oh, I like you."

She twisted her hand as violently as she could, flipping him backward even as she turned and ran, stumbling over rubble and bodies. Where was Rory?

Briony ran down the hall, dodging several men she recognized as they tried to drag her toward a portal. Collin Twindle was pulling an Eversun out of a closet by her hair and tossing her to his father. Liam Quill was on the floor in the corner, rocking and crying. Briony's brain couldn't hold it all.

She reached the stairs and headed up, trying to figure out how these portals were opening. Portals couldn't just open anywhere. You needed the blood of the person who owned the property to open one into private land, like the school.

She tripped up the stairs and caught herself. Of course: The Trow family owned the school property.

Briony stared at the blood on her hands from scraping them. Had all of these Bomardi received drops of Trow blood for this? Was this coordinated?

She remembered Veronika Mallow talking about students as collateral . . .

She had to find Rory.

On the next landing, she threw herself against a wall as a woman with bright red hair screamed, "That's the princess!"

Briony shoved and the woman fell back, rolling down the stairs. She tugged on the thread in her mind, shifting her form to invisible. Finola had taught her the basics of things after Mallow assassinated Gin Pulvey, but she knew her magic wouldn't withstand all these distractions.

Briony ran up to the eighth floor and started opening every door. Students were hiding, Bomardi and Eversun alike. She looked at every face for Rory, Cordelia, Didion, before shutting the door and letting them stay hidden. They couldn't see her as she opened each door.

She came to the end of the hall as she heard a deep voice singsonging from the base of the stairs. "Oh, Priiincess."

She stopped. The man with the thick brows was climbing the stairs to her.

Briony ran the other way, then skidded to a halt. Liam Quill's father was pulling doors off their hinges and separating the Bomardi students from the Eversun.

She darted down another corridor, feeling her hold on the invisibility falter. She could see her shoes as she ran. She had to double back when she found staircases crumbled in after the rattling of the mountain.

What would happen if they found Rory? Would they really kill the heir to Evermore? What were they doing with the other Eversuns they took? Just portaling them away? Where?

Boots ran down the hall toward her. Her eyes were wide; she was trapped. Just before her pursuer turned and found her in the middle of the hall with nowhere to go, a hand shot out of an office door and dragged her inside.

She took a breath to scream before her back was against the door and Toven Hearst was in front of her, his hand clapped over her mouth.

They stared at each other as the boots clomped by. As soon as it was clear, he lifted his hand from her.

"What is happening?" she whispered, voice shaking.

"I don't know. Is your brother still here?"

Her throat was tight as she echoed him. "I don't know."

The mountain shook again, and the school rocked beneath her feet.

Toven grabbed her hand and led her to an arched opening in the wall between this room and the next. They braced themselves, and he built a protective boundary around them.

Briony tried to make a plan. How could they portal out if they didn't have Trow blood with them? And where would she go? She needed the king's approval to get to Evermore when she was in Bomard. Every person coming to the realm had to portal to a border town and be given permission to physically walk across the border, even Rory and herself.

When the ground stabilized, Briony opened her eyes from where she'd shut them tight. "I have to find my brother and I have to get to a border town. I have to get to Evermore."

"This seems planned," Toven said. "They will have guards at every town. Bomard will stop you from going home."

"You mean, *you* will have guards at every town," she hissed. " '*Bomard* will stop me,' " she repeated, "but are you not Bomardi?"

He glared at her. "Do you want to fight with me or do you want to fight with them?" He nodded to the men out in the hall.

She glared back. "Both."

He was less than amused. "Let's find your brother and worry about the border town later," he said, and turned to lead her into the next room.

Briony's heart felt the "let's" ringing in her blood. She followed him, just as the door to the study flew off its hinges.

Briony ducked behind the archway, and Toven stepped in front of her, squeezing himself close to her to hide the both of them.

They held their breath, waiting to see if someone would come farther in and find them.

"Toven," said a firm voice that Briony recognized.

Toven's brows pulled together, and he stepped to the side, revealing himself to the person in the next room.

"Father?" Toven said. "What's going on?"

Briony pressed her fingertips to her lips, trying to keep her breath even. Orion Hearst couldn't find out she was here.

"I sent my hawk for you, but he didn't get here soon enough," Orion said. "We have to go."

Orion's footsteps sounded in the other room. He seemed relieved to have found his son.

"What has happened?" Toven pressed.

"Mallow attacked Jacquel. He's been . . . incapacitated."

Every muscle in Briony's body tightened, as though her heart stopped, then started again. Her father. *Incapacitated.*

Toven was tense, a foot from her, standing in the archway she was hiding behind.

"The others are capturing Eversun children to ransom against Evermore," Orion continued, but Briony's ears were full of fluff. He was saying other things, but she only heard the end. ". . . come here for you, but I have to get back to the border." He paused, and then almost in surprise, he said, "Toven? Come."

Briony could imagine his hand extended for his son. And his son standing immobile in the doorway.

"Who is with you?" Orion said quietly.

"No one."

Briony squared her shoulders, focused her mind, and pulled on the thread between her eyes. She fixated on blond hair swaying down to her hips, a perfect nose, and manicured fingers. She turned the corner into the archway and stood next to Toven, projecting the image of Larissa Gains to the two Hearsts.

"Mr. Hearst," she said in Larissa's voice. "This is terrifying. Have they caught Rory Rosewood yet?"

Orion blinked at her, scanning her from head to toe before leaning back on his heels. "Larissa. I'm glad you're unharmed," he said. He pursed his lips and looked at Toven, then back to her. "General Meers was seen leaving with the heir to the Evermore line and the Hardstark girl a little over ten minutes ago."

Briony's expression froze on Larissa's face. They'd left her. They'd gone with General Meers and left her behind. Had Rory tried to argue at least? Did Cordelia even bring up her name?

She nodded at Orion Hearst, swallowing back the stab of pain. She'd been searching for her brother in a castle falling down around her feet, and no one had been searching for her.

"Larissa, you should find your father," Orion said slowly, intentionally. "He and the others have gathered on the first floor, intending to search every level for Briony Rosewood." He stared at her unblinking. "They won't make it up this far for another half hour, most likely."

Briony stared back at him.

He knew she wasn't Larissa. And he was giving her a head start.

"Thank you, Mr. Hearst," she said carefully. "I'll be sure to go down."

"Come, Toven," Orion said, sweeping to the door.

"Shouldn't Larissa come with us?"

Both Orion and Briony swung to look at Toven.

"Surely it's not safe in the school. We can bring her back to Hearst Hall—"

"No, Toven," Orion said, and something passed between them. "Larissa has to stay."

Briony swallowed. They needed to go, and then she needed to get as far upstairs as possible, hoping that someone—*anyone*—would think to come back for her. Hoping that someone was thinking of her safety half as much as Toven Hearst was at the moment.

Toven was frozen next to her. And slowly, with one foot in front of the other, he stepped forward, following his father to the door.

Briony released her breath, and Orion escorted Toven out. He paused in the doorway, and she held on to Larissa's likeness for one more second.

"Miss Gains?" Orion said. Briony lifted her chin to him. "Tell your father that Miss Rosewood might have already left the mountains." He paused, leveling his gaze on her. "She may have figured out that the borders are open . . . as Evermore is currently without a king."

Briony blinked at him. Her soul shivered in her chest.

Incapacitated.

Her father was dead.

Orion Hearst was nothing if not delicate.

He reached into his pocket and tossed her something. It was a small vial with a drop of blood in it. "From Genevieve Trow. In case you can't find your father, you'll need it to portal out."

Briony's breath caught. He nodded at her and let the door close.

She stood alone in an abandoned study, letting the disguise of Larissa Gains drip off her body.

Her father was dead, and Rory would soon be coronated. She had a handful of minutes before Evermore had a new king and the border boundaries went up again.

She stared at the rubble of the place she was told would be safe, then poured the drop of Trow blood onto her hand. She slit her thumb, reaching out to swirl open a portal to Biltmore with her own blood, if it would let her.

When it opened at her command, that was all she needed to know to affirm that Orion hadn't been lying to her.

The borders were open. The king was dead.

And she was expendable now, it seemed.

She stepped into the void and disappeared.

CHAPTER 39

WAKING ON SATURDAY MORNING was like pulling herself from a thick bramble that had settled over her in the night. Fighting her way back to consciousness, she struggled against aching muscles and a pounding behind her left eye.

She turned on her side and willed her body out of bed. But she couldn't move.

And then she remembered.

The cannon.

The strawberry-blonde's scream.

Mallow's eyes.

And Toven's voice in her ear, steadying her, guiding her through the night's horrors.

He'd let her sob, let her lean on him, holding her close. And then he'd nodded. Agreeing with her?

He'd taken her back to her room with an elixir for sleep, and her mind had shut down the moment her body slid in between the sheets.

Her eyes fluttered open as her mind sputtered to life, remembering all the things she needed to be doing. But such strong mind barriers against the nearness of Mallow had taken a toll on her body and mind. Despite her intentions, she found herself drifting back out to sea.

* * *

When she could finally sit up in bed, the clock next to her read four in the afternoon.

Briony groaned. She couldn't afford to lose any more time. She needed to build up her mind barrier endurance in case there were suspicions around her. She needed to set an alarm from now on. She needed the house to splash her with pails of cold water if she didn't move before nine.

Briony focused her thoughts, closing the books in her mind that held the horrors of the cannon and the grief for the nameless woman and her brother.

A fresh memory fluttered to the surface. Arms holding her close, long fingers tracing the shell of her ear. Gray eyes locked on hers as he'd nodded.

Toven. He'd helped her last night. And maybe he'd help her again. Her heart thumped with the possibilities.

Briony decided to dedicate the day to researching the Durlings. Caspar Quill had drunkenly implied that they had also used magical brands—that perhaps he was inspired by them.

She headed downstairs to the library and pushed open the doors, then stopped in her tracks. Texts were strewn across the chairs, the floor, the small end tables. A dozen books hovered in front of their shelves, waiting to be plucked by whoever had called upon them from the book finder.

Briony's lips parted at the sound of pages turning quickly from deep in the stacks.

"Still not hungry."

She blinked. She checked behind her to see if Serena was standing there with a tray. As she turned back to the stacks, Toven poked his head from around a shelf, glaring. When he saw it was her, his frown vanished, and he snapped his book shut. He pulled a pen from behind his ear and twisted it between his fingers.

"Rosewood," he said. "I thought you were Mother."

His eyes whipped around the room as if just taking in the disarray she'd walked into. She held her breath as she studied him, watching the flush creep up his neck. He dropped the arm holding the book and tilted it so slightly behind him, and her eyes followed the movement.

"What are you researching?"

"Just looking for a solution to a problem," he clipped. He swallowed and ran a hand through his hair.

She nodded slowly, glancing at the book finder. She had wanted to ask it for everything on the Durlings, but now she wasn't sure if Toven should hear her topic of research.

When he'd nodded in understanding last night, what was he agreeing to?

She moved a few steps closer to him. "I wanted to thank you for your kindness last night."

He stared at her stiffly as she gazed up at him. His eyes were different from the warm ones that had locked on hers last night, in his bedroom.

"You're welcome."

She waited for more, but nothing came. "And I wanted to—"

"Rosewood, I'm in the middle of something. Can this wait?"

She startled at the bite in his tone. There was a tension in his posture, a squaring of his shoulders that she recognized from school. Determination.

Suddenly she felt very silly. Thanking him for taking care of her while she cried. Thinking something had shifted. Her eyes prickled, and she snapped her mouth shut.

His face instantly softened. "How are you feeling?"

"Fine," she replied, and his shoulders dropped. The burning behind her eyes faded into a slow throb. "Exhausted." She stood surrounded by all his books and notes and messy piles. "Is this 'problem' anything I could help with?"

She inched toward the table filled with notes, eyeing an open book on the edge. Toven was there in the blink of an eye, slamming it closed. She managed to catch a glimpse of ancient translations scribbled on parchment before he swiftly stepped in front of her.

Her eyes flicked up to him, so close she had to tilt her head back. They'd been this close the night before, when he'd folded his arms around her as she sobbed. He'd pushed a curl over her ear and stared into her watering eyes like he'd been entranced.

She tucked the memories away. "I am pretty good at research, if you'll recall." She smiled, hoping he couldn't resist the chance to tease her. To let her in.

Instead he jerked his head. "No. I'm almost there." He swallowed tightly. "Thank you, though."

She blinked quickly, nodding her disappointment at her shoes. Maybe when he was done with his "problem," they could finally talk.

She lifted her chin, took a deep breath, and said, "I find that in most cases, the answer is right in front of you."

His lips parted on a silent inhale, as if her flippant remark had disturbed him. Pink spots appeared high on his cheeks as his eyes roved over her before returning to her gaze.

"Thank you, Rosewood. I'll keep an eye out for that," he murmured.

Nodding one last time, she excused herself, heading to the doorway. As she turned to close the library doors, she caught a glimpse of him sitting at the table, beginning to organize whatever he was researching.

She ate dinner alone in her bedroom that night, poring over a heavy book that contained a reference to magical tattoos somewhere inside. She made it three chapters before an overwhelming exhaustion pushed at her eyelids, beckoning her to sleep.

*   *   *

"Rosewood, wake up."

Her eyes snapped open, jolting with the presence of someone else in her room. It was pitch black.

A candle flamed next to her, revealing Serena leaning over her bedside table, shaking out a match.

"It's all right, dear," she whispered, but there was a quiver to her voice, and she wouldn't make eye contact. "It's all right," she repeated—more to herself.

"What—" Briony fell silent, lips parting at the sight of Toven on the other side of her bed with another candle. His fingers fumbled a match out of a box, dropping it next to the candle without lighting it.

"What's happened?" she asked, scrambling into a sitting position.

"Come." Serena peeled back the sheets over her legs, reaching for her. "Come with me."

Briony slipped out of bed, heart pounding in her ears. Serena led her into the bathroom suite as Toven moved to the center of the room, hand roving in circles—opening a portal.

Serena shut the door behind them, and Briony blinked, taking in the elegant Serena Hearst in her dressing gown, without makeup, without tailored clothing. A white silk nightgown hung limply from her elbow, and she had a pale expression to match.

"Remove your nightgown," Serena whispered.

Briony swallowed, her mind begging for answers. But something told her to obey. "Are we going somewhere?" she squeaked.

"No, dear. There's . . . someone is—"

She watched Serena struggle for words. Briony's eyes went wide with rising terror, her breath coming quick. Mallow?

"We're having visitors first thing in the morning," Serena finally managed. "I don't know why. We were told they need to do a medical examination."

Briony pulled up the plain cotton nightgown with shaking fingers, fear overriding her modesty as Serena bunched up the white silk and tossed it over her neck.

"All right," she rasped. Chills bursting along her skin as the silk slipped over her. A trade of cotton for silk? "And what are we doing?"

"There's an old spell. Something that they used to use on their daughters . . . A ritual."

Briony stood frozen in terror as she let Serena pull the gown down her legs. Fingers pushed her hair to the side. A cool chain draped over her shoulders as Serena placed a crystal necklace over her.

"What kind of ritual?" She didn't recognize the sound of her own voice. The crystal hummed against her skin. Magical. The silk was part of the ritual as well?

Serena's blue eyes met hers. They pierced her, studying her.

"They will be able to see that your virginity is intact," she said quietly. "So we're going to remove it."

Briony's skin tingled, feeling the weight of the silk gown on her shoulders. Waiting for the words to make sense to her.

A rattling knock at the bathroom door. "One fifty-eight," Toven's clipped tone rang out, announcing the time. Her body jerked, and Serena gripped her arms to guide her out.

Toven stood aside to let them pass, his eyes firmly planted on his timepiece. The portal was a gaping hole in the middle of the room. Serena guided her to the bed, pushing her to sit.

Her mind caught up to her circumstances as Serena knelt before her, produced a bowl of water, dipped her fingers, and brushed her fingertips over Briony's eyes and lips.

There was a ritual.

A ritual to trick the virginity spell. The one they'd cast on her to decide her starting price at the auction.

Serena whispered something into the water bowl—something in another language—before bringing it to her lips and swallowing half. Briony looked at Toven. He stood rooted to the carpets, muscles moving in his jaw.

This was what he'd been researching. Finding this ritual. He hadn't let her help him.

The clock chimed two in the morning, and Toven moved away from the portal and stared at her with gray eyes.

Serena pushed the bowl to her, bringing it to Briony's lips. Briony drank the rest of the water, watching Toven over the rim. He stared her down as she swallowed.

He knew yesterday that they were coming. He knew they'd find her untouched, and he'd ransacked the library for a solution to his problem.

Briony's breath hitched at the realization that he'd skipped over the easiest one.

Serena placed the bowl on the nightstand and crawled onto the bed, her long limbs gracefully folding under herself. She guided Briony to sit in front of her, both of them facing the portal. Toven paced to the end of the bed, hand against the bedpost, watching the clock.

She opened her mouth to break the silence, to ask about the spell and question the research, but the words died in her throat as the portal sizzled and Orion Hearst stepped through.

CHAPTER 40

H ER HEART THUMPED IN HER CHEST.

Orion glanced at her, dressed in white silk, waiting for him on a bed.

Toven stepped forward, pulling a book from his back pocket and flipping it open.

"Translated from the Starkish," Toven said. "I've checked the translation. It's accurate." He met his father at the portal as it hissed closed behind him. "I've outlined the steps. The candle, the blood, the incantation—"

Orion Hearst raised a hand, halting his son. "Let me see it, Toven." He took the book and peered down, turning the pages. The air around Toven seemed to buzz with twisting energy.

A page turned, and Orion paused. His brow arched. Briony watched his eyes move quickly over the same passage until he lifted them to her.

The book snapped shut. Orion assessed her and said, "And if it doesn't work?"

"It will." Toven's mouth was a hard line.

"And if it doesn't?"

"Then I'll think of something else."

But Orion wasn't looking at his son; he was looking at her. She blinked at him, feeling the question under her skin.

If this doesn't work, will you do this the easy way?

She swallowed and tilted her head into the tiniest of nods.

Orion's eyes returned to the text, browsing the words, casually, as one might window-shop. He was supposed to be in Southern Camly. He was only permitted to leave for emergencies. They'd brought him in for an illicit dark ritual, and he had the nerve to act as if they had all the time in the world.

As if all of their lives weren't at stake.

Toven's fingers twitched. Serena's breath stirred her hair.

Orion closed the book and handed it back to Toven. He looked at the mantel clock and turned to her. "Ready."

"Let me see the book," Briony said, voice too loud for the quiet room. "Let me read it first—"

"There's no time, Miss Rosewood," Orion said, and she could hear the finality in his voice as he crossed to the unlit candle by her bed.

"What does it do?" She turned to look up at Serena, then to Toven near the windows, watching silently.

"There's no need to worry, dear," Serena whispered into her ear.

Orion struck the match and the flames hissed as he lit the wick.

The only light in the room came from the two candles, casting shadows against their cheekbones.

Serena crossed her legs and guided Briony to lie with her head in her lap. She stared at the canopy as her mind raced.

Who was coming? Why were they checking her virginity? Why now?

And then all thoughts were swept from her mind as Orion Hearst climbed into her bed.

She jerked her legs, almost kicking him as his long limbs crawled like a panther to sit beside her. Serena grabbed her arms to calm her, to hold her still.

"What does this spell entail?" she repeated, her voice cracking in her dry throat.

Orion's calm features sharpened into a smirk. "Now, now. Don't fret, Miss Rosewood. Just lie back and think of Evermore."

"Orion," Serena warned.

Briony's heartbeat strained beneath Serena's fingers, pounding to get out of her. And before she could ask another question, Orion was pulling a knife from his robes, his impassive mask on once more. She gaped at the glint of the blade as he pressed one long hand firmly against her collarbone. The knife drew a quick, shallow slice against her heart, too quick for her to wince. Orion's lips formed a silent prayer, wisps of Starkish brushing across her forehead.

She looked at Toven, bathed in moonlight near the windows, watching with his hand clapped over his mouth. Their eyes met.

And the candles went out.

The darkness was like a cold plunge into water. If she hadn't had the pressure of Serena's fingers on her wrists, she'd have shrieked.

Orion's cool tones dripped ancient words across her face. He shifted back, hovering over her stomach and chanting.

Her limited Starkish caught words like "wolf" and "protection."

She jerked her head over to where Toven stood in the corner, and her dizzy mind imagined she could see the whites of his eyes reflecting the darkness back at her.

There was a sharp pull in her belly, like the worst kind of menstrual cramps. She gasped, jerking. Serena held her down, and Orion raised his voice as he continued chanting.

It felt like her intestines were fighting to twist in opposing directions. She squirmed, trying to stretch her body into positions that would alleviate the cramping, but there was a wrenching low in her stomach.

She groaned, and the floor creaked near the windows.

A tight pop, as if something inside of her had been dislocated. She scrunched her eyes shut in pain, blocking out the darkness.

And then a wash of peace. Like sunlight. Her stomach relaxed.

She opened her eyes, praying that it had worked, and found Orion Hearst's face boring over her in the candlelight.

No. Not candlelight. A ball the size of her fist hovered over her stomach. Just like the spell the nurses cast months ago, burning so white it looked blue.

It cast shadows across the pitch-black room, sparking warmth in Orion's gray gaze.

Serena's fingers threaded through her hair gently as every pair of eyes stared at the ball of energy, symbolizing what hadn't yet been taken from her. She watched the light fluctuate like fairy wings were holding it afloat.

A glass jar pushed into view, scooping slowly under the orb, capturing it, and closing a lid over the top. Toven screwed the lid on, watching the light breathe. His eyes danced with its glow, and his lips parted in wonder.

He held the jar in one hand and placed a bundle of branching white flowers over her belly with the other. He cast the Virginity Detection spell over her. The scan hummed over her head and toes, scanning toward the center. When the magic reached her abdomen, the four of them watched with bated breath.

The bundle didn't catch fire the way it had when she tested positive for purity.

She didn't know what was supposed to happen if she wasn't a virgin. She hadn't seen it.

No one moved. She heard Toven swallow.

"Did it work?" she whispered.

A pause. And then: "It seems so," Serena breathed into her hair.

Orion cast the charm again, and they watched as the results were the same.

Orion stood abruptly from the bed, looking down at her, and then up to Toven. "You won't be able to contact me if there's an issue until tomorrow afternoon."

The light from the glass jar in Toven's palm cast eerie shadows across Orion's face. He turned, slicing his hand and using the blood to make a portal out of the property. He entered the void without a backward glance.

With a wave, Serena lit the sconces low. She slid off the bed and gathered the ritual candles. "I apologize for all this fuss, Briony, dear," she said, still not looking at her. "Get some rest. We'll talk in the morning." She sent Toven a stern look before leaving, the door clicking softly.

Briony took a few breaths before she jolted upright. She sat in a bed in a white gown, blood from her chest dripping on the sheets, and stared at Toven Hearst, who held her virginity in his hands.

The relief on his face dissipated, and he paled as he looked at her. He placed the jar delicately on her bedside table.

"This should stay here." He swallowed. "Keep it safe. It would . . . it can catch quite a price on the black market, so it's best to keep it hidden in your room."

She blinked at the light, still the brightest source in the room, even with the sconces lit. She wondered if she should feel different.

"I apologize for the suddenness," he said, shifting his weight. "I was only notified yesterday afternoon. And the spell required my father, and I wasn't even sure if I could—"

"Why would it matter to Mallow if I was still a virgin?" she asked.

Toven pressed his lips together. "Liam tipped me off that Canning requested an audience with Mallow. I suspect it has something to do with getting revenge for outlawing his elixir."

Briony stared down at her bare feet. "But again . . . why would Mallow care? The pressure was on from your friends to be intimate with me, but surely not from Mallow."

Toven closed his eyes and seemed to take a fortifying breath. "Mallow has made clear to me that she supports any way in which to harvest the most power from you," he said carefully.

Briony's heart dropped. Sacral Magic.

Suddenly, Briony remembered when she'd been brought before Mallow the first time.

Have fun with her, Toven. I look forward to how powerful you'll become once bonded to her.

That was moments after Mallow had learned that Briony had feelings for Toven—moments after she learned that Toven might not even need to entice Briony to—

Briony felt sick. She couldn't believe there was a woman in the world who would wish such a thing on another woman.

But she refocused on the problem at hand.

"I want to see your research," Briony said. "I want to read up on the spell."

He nodded, eyes distant but directed at the jar. "Of course. Tomorrow, after they—"

She scowled. "Now. I'm awake. You're awake." She stumbled out of bed, the long silk nightdress twisting around her legs in an awkward constriction. Unraveling it brought her close to him.

He glanced quickly down to the cut on her chest. She wondered if he thought about the last time she was in a nightgown with blood trailing down her chest.

He swallowed. "You should get your rest."

"Give me the book," she demanded.

He was always keeping information from her, especially if it pertained to her directly. Irritation sharpened and bubbled in her chest.

But this time something must have been different. He extended the book to her, watching as she grabbed it and flipped to the marked pages.

It was still in Starkish.

She cast a translation spell and took deep breaths, focusing on the words as they arranged themselves. It was done. There was nothing she could do to change what had happened or how it had happened. She just needed the specifics.

It was a journal. A magician's entry from a thousand years ago, back before they started measuring time after Vindecci. It detailed a ritual to save his daughter's "purity" from "the wolf."

Two candles. Two parents. The mother cleanses, the father bleeds her.

She slammed the book closed, cheeks burning in anger and embarrassment. She pivoted to Toven, ready to release her pent-up rage.

A warm hand dropped on her shoulder. He was staring down at the blood dripping from the slice over her heart. He raised his hand and cast a spell to sew the skin back together. His eyes didn't leave her chest as she felt the cut heal.

"What if it hadn't worked?" she asked, voice thin.

He stepped back from her and ran his hand through his hair. "Then I would have thought of something else. A different spell."

She wondered at what point he would have come to her room, held her down on the bed, and penetrated her.

Minutes before the "visitors" arrived? Or perhaps he'd rather let them all die instead.

"And if you couldn't find another spell? When would you have consulted me and my opinion on the matter?"

He blinked at her before looking away to her bookshelves. "I was hoping I could find something like a glamour. Something cast to deceive the detection spell." He swallowed thickly. "I was hoping—"

"You were hoping I'd never have to know," she finished for him. Her skin buzzed with anger. "To cast a spell and brush it under the rug."

His lips pressed together tightly. "Do you not understand that we could be under investigation? By order of Mallow, you are being examined tomorrow morning, and we have no idea why—"

"I understand perfectly, thank you," she spat. "I also understand that you had twelve hours in which you could have told me what was going on"—he took a breath to interrupt—"to inform me of the problem so that we might be able to come up with a solution *together*, but instead you chose to surprise me—"

"My family is in jeopardy, Rosewood—"

"And you're blaming me for that?"

"Sometimes I have to act without your approval to do what's best for my family! Not just you, all four of us!"

Her lips opened in a silent gasp.

His eyes widened as he seemed to realize what he'd just said. His mouth snapped shut, horror dawning over his features. Before she could press him further, he turned on his heel, dashing for the door.

Briony gaped at the empty doorway for several long moments before sitting down on the corner of her bed. She stared at the fluttering light in a jar on her nightstand, listening to the echo in her ears of him calling her family.

* * *

384 ᵉ JULIE SOTO

At seven the next morning, Toven knocked on her bedroom door.

"They've arrived." His voice was flat. And his eyes were cold.

She had been dressed for hours, unable to sleep. It seemed the same for him. Both of them resigned to whatever fate awaited them.

Pulling her bedroom door closed behind her, she followed him down the stairs and to the drawing room.

As he pushed open the door, he took her elbow in a firm grip, tugging her across the threshold behind him.

She cataloged the room quickly. Serena. A man and a woman in nurse uniforms that she didn't recognize. Cohle. And turning to greet them, a smug leer on his face, was Reighven.

She stumbled, her stomach tight, before she cast her gaze down to the floor.

Toven's steps slowed, but he gave away no other reaction.

"Cohle. Reighven," he greeted.

"Apologies for being so early, Hearst," Cohle said without a hint of remorse. "But your mother tells me you're early risers here at Hearst Hall." He smirked at her and Toven.

"Yes. Thank you for your hospitality, Serena," Reighven said with a wink.

Serena stepped forward. "Of course, Lag." A thin smile pasted on her face. "And I'd prefer if you called me Mrs. Hearst."

Briony turned her eyes down to the stone floor. Her skin was cold, and her breath was shallow.

"What's this about?" Toven asked. He crossed his arms over his chest, shifting in front of her.

"Reighven and I have been tasked to check in on the heartsprings," Cohle said. "There've been a few issues, and Mallow has asked us to follow up." His voice scratched down her spine.

The male nurse conjured an examination table and silently gestured toward it. They'd been silenced, she realized.

She padded to the exam table, and all eyes were on her as she obediently slid up onto it.

"Looks like you learned how to play nice after all, Princess," Reighven said.

"I'll ask you not to speak to my heartspring," said Toven coldly. "You may address me if you have a direct order for her."

Briony lay back, her mind numb. She breathed deeply, pulling air into her empty lungs. *A lake with still waters.*

"What kind of issues?" Serena asked. "What's wrong with the other heartsprings?"

The nurses hovered over her, silently casting several scans.

"One of them wasn't properly sterilized," Reighven said.

And Briony felt the room shake, quivering before her eyes.

There was a thick silence as the nurses tested her.

The only other woman she'd heard was to be sterilized was Phoebe, the other surviving Rosewood. Had Phoebe become pregnant?

Her chest shook.

Her fertility would be ripped from her again. This possibility. This small chance of a future.

The male nurse tapped against her left hip bone. A dim red light appeared. He switched to Briony's other side, and with a tap, a bright green illuminated the man's face.

A pause, like skipping a step on the stairs. She felt every eye in the room on her waist. She didn't dare look at Toven.

And then a sharp, "Ha!" cracked from Reighven's throat. He chuckled, and the room shook with it. "Two months with a fertile slut and she's not knocked up? You check to see if your boys swim, Hearst? With me, you'd have triplets by now—"

"That's enough, Lag," Serena hissed. "Please remember your manners while you're in my house."

Reighven scoffed. He breathed as if he would say something else, then stopped himself. He turned back to the male nurse. "Scan for her virginity."

The room tensed. Cohle laughed.

"Toven, you've fucked her, of course," Cohle said.

"*Gentlemen,*" Serena warned.

"I want proof," Reighven said. "Do it."

The female nurse produced a bundle of branching white flowers. Briony held her breath as the familiar scan washed over her, centering on her abdomen, then stopped. It found nothing. Briony almost cried in relief.

"See, Lag? Stones..." Cohle sighed. "All right, carry on. Finish the sterilization."

The room went silent.

The male nurse stepped forward.

Briony braced herself for the wrenching pain she'd felt the last time her tubes had been severed. She looked past the arm of the nurse toward the ceiling and took a shuddering breath, focusing on anything but the image of children with her curls and gray eyes—

"Don't—" A throat cleared. "She's my property. Don't I get a say here?"

Briony swallowed, blinking rapidly. A thick silence fell like snow.

"Why, Hearst? You want pups?" Reighven chuckled.

Cohle hummed. "The Rosewood girl and all tied to her line must be sterilized. Clearly, you know why."

"Carvin's wasn't done right, either, and we took care of that yesterday."

Phoebe. Briony's pulse thudded.

Toven seemed to have come to the end of his arguments.

Briony saw the faint green light over her hip fading, winking out of existence.

Her limbs were heavy. She felt cold and useless. Pain pricked behind her eyelids.

It would all be over soon.

The male nurse lifted his hands and positioned them over her hip. Briony squeezed her eyes closed as he prepared to cast—

A crack of wind whipped by her. There was a sudden voiceless gasp and a whoosh of air.

Briony's eyes snapped open as a grunt sounded to her right, followed by a *crash!*

"Mother!"

Briony jolted, springing to her side off the table. Toven was next to her in a heartbeat.

The male nurse was on the floor several feet away, face dazed, as if not quite knowing what had sent him there.

Reighven lay crumpled against the far wall, head lolling and unconscious.

Serena Hearst's hands were outstretched, magic crackling between her fingers as she faced Cohle, who looked as shocked as Briony felt.

"I'm afraid I can't let you do this," Serena said, voice pitched low and dark, eyes intent on Cohle. "Miss Rosewood is under my protection."

CHAPTER 41

"WHAT THE HELL HAVE YOU DONE?" Cohle whispered.

Briony's heart thundered. She looked among the people in the room, taking stock.

Toven was next to her, his breath coming quickly in her ear. The female nurse was frozen on the other side of the table, with no indication that she'd raise her hands to cast. The male nurse lay still, unsure if coming to his feet was best. Reighven was unconscious.

And Cohle and Serena Hearst faced each other, magic sizzling.

"Watch the nurses, Toven," Serena said. And then her hands swung in a wide arc.

Cohle was quick to throw up a shield and sliced through the air.

Briony watched in awe as the two of them danced through the room. Serena moved fluidly, catching Cohle's magic and sending it back to him. Cohle was brutish and thick in his movements.

Toven grabbed the corner of the table and flipped it, dragging Briony down to her knees.

"Stay here."

He positioned her behind the table barricade, then jumped up and extended his hands toward both nurses. The woman slid to him with a gasp, but the man blocked the spell and came to his feet. Toven threw more spells at him, but he blocked them all.

The female nurse fell to her knees near Briony, and Toven kept her on the floor with one hand while the other swung wide circles to entrap the second nurse.

A window crashed from above, and Briony protected her head from the falling glass. The white seabird from the Hearst grounds sailed inside, swooping low to peck at Cohle just as he'd reached for Serena's heart. The albatross swerved through the air, dancing with Serena to battle Cohle.

Toven stumbled over a fallen chair, and before he could right himself, the female nurse took off. She wove through the hall and ran out the door.

Briony jumped to her feet in a panic, but Toven stepped in her path.

"Keep him here," he said, nodding to the male nurse, and then he was running out the door.

Briony glanced at Serena and Cohle, deflecting parry for parry and blasting through furniture, and then to the man on the floor, who was just coming to his feet again.

She ducked behind the table to hide and slapped the floor with her palms. The man fell, and she peeked around to see him tugging on his legs in confusion. She'd stuck his shoes to the floor. It was basic, but she was rusty and she shouldn't *be* doing magic.

Crawling to the other side of the overturned exam table, she peeked at Reighven—still out cold.

The nurse was just beginning to unstick his boots when Briony turned back around. She shoved her hands out and he tumbled forward. Uninventive, but she needed to stall.

Serena screamed, and Briony tried to focus—tried to remember everything she'd learned about close-quarters battle.

She glanced up to the portraits of Hearst family members past hanging high on the walls, then reached for one with her magic and tugged it off the wall. She sent it sailing toward Cohle where he stood over Serena as she writhed and the albatross scratched at him.

The portrait flew into his side, the corner catching him under the ribs, just as she'd intended.

Serena stumbled to her feet and assessed the players, searching for

Toven. Her eyes widened in alarm, and Briony turned just as the corner of the male nurse's uniform disappeared around the door.

Briony took off. She had to believe that Serena could handle Cohle. She had to believe that Reighven wouldn't wake up. Each slap of her feet against the marble floor held a new wish she needed to believe.

She skidded to a halt outside the drawing room and looked left then right, spotting the man running toward the front doors. Briony threw her arms out and tugged them into her chest: the man pulled and pulled on the doors to throw them open, but they wouldn't budge.

She ducked behind a corner as he turned and ran down the other hall, desperate to get out.

It had been clear from him fighting with Toven that he was not a field-trained medic. He had likely never seen battle. She would have felt bad for him if only their lives didn't depend on him not escaping.

If he got out and revealed what Serena had done . . .

If he told someone that she wasn't sterilized . . .

Briony ducked through a passage, knowing the shortcut. She skidded out into the opposite hall just steps in front of the man. He stopped so suddenly that he stumbled and fell on his backside, looking up at her in horror.

"I don't mean you any harm," she said breathlessly. "You won't be killed. You just can't leave."

Her heart pattered a rhythm in her chest. She hoped she was telling him the truth.

He scooted back from her, mouth flapping uselessly with words he couldn't voice. Briony brought her fingers to her throat, doing the same thing Serena had done for her when she first arrived. She gave him back his voice.

His hands moved to his throat in shock. He looked her over from head to heel.

"You have magic," he said. His voice was scratchy, as if it hadn't been used in months.

"Are you a prisoner?" she said. She fell to her knees so as not to stand over him. "Are they keeping you?"

He nodded. "My sister is . . . they have her." His eyes were wild. "Have you seen her? She is at Biltmore Palace."

Briony's brows jumped. There was no time for this, but she couldn't ignore his anguish. "What's her name?"

"Maggie. She has dark hair like me."

"I'll keep an eye out for her, but I don't know her, no." She reached out her hand. "Now, I'm sorry, but you'll need to come back with me——"

"We were both in your father's medical unit!" He seemed to gasp out the words. "W-we both served you!"

Briony blinked at him. "You're Eversun?"

He shook his head, tears in his eyes. "Is there such a thing anymore?"

Her mind worked quickly. This man was a prisoner like her. Would she really send him back to his captors? Before she knew what she was going to say, the words tumbled from her.

"If I let you go, you must tell no one what you saw today."

He shook his head, his eyes wide. "But I can't leave. They'll kill Maggie——"

"We'll tell them you're dead," she said quickly. "Whatever has to happen tonight . . . there will be a lot of cleanup. You'll be dead, I swear it."

Briony's hand reached out, offering him a deal.

His fingers trembled as he took her hand. "What do you want?"

"Nothing. You can find the rebels. Sammy Meers. A woman named Velicity Punt is traveling with him. She has one arm. They were last seen in the north."

"Because of the tattoo?" His brows furrowed.

Briony nodded. Her heart beat wildly with hope as she held on tightly to his hand.

"Tell Sammy . . ."

She paused. There was so much. She was nowhere close to knowing the answers to the tattoos.

"Tell Sammy that I'll be waiting for his signal."

She came to her feet, still holding his hand, and he followed her up. She opened her mouth to tell him where to go.

"Cordelia Hardstark is now at the Seat's Castle. The one in the mountains," he said, the words tumbling out of him.

Briony's hand squeezed his. "You're sure?"

He nodded. "She is Mallow's favorite. She . . . I'm not sure what she does to her, but I have healed her once."

Blood froze in her veins. Briony nodded stiffly.

"Go that way," she said, pointing. "Run to the tree line, then portal."

When his hand pulled from hers, the warmth left her body, and all of her decisions seemed bound for failure.

What if he was captured? What if he was lying?

He started to run, and Briony turned back toward the passage, her footsteps pattering the belief into her bones.

"Miss Rosewood?"

She turned. She hadn't been called that by anyone but Serena without sarcasm since she was a princess. Her hope burned bright.

"Something's not right with her," he said.

Briony felt her chest tighten with fear. "Cordelia?"

"Mallow," he corrected, and her brows drew together. "She's . . . She was furious to learn that Phoebe Rosewood was pregnant. I took the fetus out of her myself, but . . ."

Chills crested down Briony's spine, thinking of what Phoebe had been through.

"There's something she's not getting. She thinks there's a boy heir somewhere," he said.

He looked with purpose to her belly.

"It's not me," she whispered. "He hasn't . . . Toven and I . . ."

The nurse shrugged. "If she finds out you can conceive, she'll kill everyone in this house."

She stared at him. Realization dawned on her, hot as daylight.

Briony could still bear the heir twice over.

She was a Rosewood.

The Rosewood line was not ended with Rory.

A crash sounded from down the hall and they both jumped.

"Go!" Briony turned and ran as his footsteps did the same.

It wasn't until she was back through the passage that she realized she'd never learned his name. Just like the strawberry-blonde's.

She flew through the doors to the drawing room where Serena stood with her arms outstretched, Reighven's body in the center of the floor and the female nurse's just a few feet from his.

"What happened?" she said, panting.

Serena whipped her head around. "Where is he?"

There wasn't time to discuss her colossally impulsive decision.

"He's subdued." She looked around. "Where's Toven?"

"Reighven woke up," she said. "We had to engage. Toven brought back the girl"—Serena nodded to her body—"and then Cohle ran. I have to keep them both down."

Briony nodded, and she was running again before Serena could ask.

She burst through the front doors and stopped, deciding which way they could have possibly gone.

A screeching howl yipped from around the back of the property.

Vesper.

She ran, heading toward the tree-lined lane that opened to the property line.

There was a lump of gray fur on the path, and Briony dropped to Vesper's side.

She was alive, but only her eyes were moving. There was blood in her jowl, as if she'd sunk her teeth into someone. Briony ran a scan over her and found her back broken. She hissed in empathetic pain.

"We'll fix you. Just hold on." She ran her hand through Vesper's fur.

The fox looked like she would bite Briony's fingers off if only she could move.

Briony kept going, turning down the lane and stopping dead.

There were two figures standing silhouetted in the morning sun. One was on the ground, the other above him, and Briony's heart begged for Toven to be the one upright.

She breathed deeply, tugged on that string in the center of her mind. Her body disappeared, turning invisible. She hurried on.

She ran full-out without the need to sneak up on them.

When she saw it was Toven on the ground, his gray hair pale in the morning sun, her legs pumped faster. His body was convulsing, twitching in pain.

"Do you have any idea what kind of problems you have, boy?" Cohle's malicious voice reached her as she ran. "No. You have *no* idea what your father is up to in Southern Camly, or else his wife and son would never have been so reckless!"

Briony planted herself twenty feet from them and shoved with all her might. Cohle flew off his feet, sailing through the air and landing in the grass.

She realized her mistake too late.

He'd landed only five feet from the barrier line. The line he could cross and portal out.

Toven sucked in air, greedy with need, and pushed himself to his feet as Cohle did the same.

Briony ran closer, panic forcing her cloaking to give out. She saw her hands, visible, as she lifted them to drag Cohle back toward her and away from the line.

Cohle blocked, eyes on her. He smiled.

"Oh, I see. You're not an idiot, Toven Hearst," he said, looking between them. "You're a traitor to Bomard and to Mistress Mallow. Your bitch has her magic!"

Briony reached, ripping a tree out of its roots and toppling it to land on Cohle. He ducked and ran forward to avoid it, putting the fallen trunk between himself and the boundary line.

Toven's hands were shaking in exhaustion when he lifted them, and Briony knew that Vesper's injury must have cost him greatly in his magic wells.

She stepped in front of him and sliced her arms at Cohle.

He deflected and chuckled. "Is she going to fight your battles for you, Toven?" Cohle lifted his hands—and before Briony could block, a pain like thousands of knives sliding against her skin erupted in her body.

Briony screamed until it stopped, then she collapsed on the grass, staring at the sun.

Toven thumped to his knees next to her. She turned over. He was barely able to stay upright.

She pulled herself up. Cohle stood over them both, a slash across his face, as if a sword had caught him. Toven must have used his last ounces of heart magic.

Cohle stared down. "Enjoy your final moments with your Eversun whore, Toven. When Mallow finds out about what's been going on at Hearst Hall, it will be the end of your line."

Cohle turned, moving sluggishly over the tree trunk and heading for the property line.

He mustn't draw a portal. He mustn't get to Mallow.

That was all Briony heard as she stood, magic rushing through her blood.

And the nurse's words rang loud and clear—*If she finds out you can conceive, she'll kill everyone in this house.*

Briony reached her hand out, and with the spell she was unable to complete only two short months ago in the Trow dungeon, she imagined his heart in the center of her palm.

And she squeezed.

Cohle was two steps from the property line when he froze, clutching his chest.

A rush of power flooded her as he fell to his knees, gasping—and then the rush left her, taking a part of her with it.

Her hand was in a fist, and Cohle was dead on the grass, his body falling past the barrier line.

And inside of her, there was only darkness and death.

CHAPTER 42

One Year Ago

AFTER RORY'S HASTY CORONATION on the day of their father's death, Evermore's borders were safely locked again, but Bomardi militia and spies had already gotten inside the country in that hour Evermore spent without a king. Between the attacks from the inside and the daily losses at the border, Evermore's size grew smaller and smaller.

Briony had been confined to Biltmore Palace for three years while it was under siege, and even though it was her favorite place in the whole world, she almost sighed in relief when Anna came to tell her that it was time to pack and retreat to the lakeside castle, Claremore.

It was a fortnight's ride on horseback between the two palaces. Briony refused to ride in the carriage like a royal while five hundred people behind them traveled on foot, especially when Rory chose to ride his horse and greet the villagers they passed on the road. General Meers wanted the court to portal and leave the people in the areas surrounding Biltmore Palace to walk on foot, but Rory refused. Portaling them all was out of the question, not only because it would require Rory to bleed for hundreds of portals, but also because that many tears into the boundary line around Claremore would weaken it. The castle's fortifications would be gone before they walked through the front doors.

Finola slowed her horse to ride beside Briony's mare one afternoon in the second week.

"We have about two days left," she said, tying her blond hair up in a messy twist to keep it off her sweating neck. "The general and your brother have gone on ahead with a portal."

Briony gaped. "What? When?"

"Two hours ago. Rory is strengthening the boundary line for our arrival."

"Why wasn't I informed? I should be with him," said Briony.

Panic rose in her. Would Rory succeed in casting the protections if Briony wasn't pushing her magic to him?

"It had to be done quietly," Finola said. "There are defectors hiding in every corner these days. Eversuns who think they'll trade information for their freedom in Bomard."

"And do they think *I* am the liability?" Briony scoffed. She straightened the brooch at her clavicle.

"Oh, you know the general." Finola sighed. "It was privileged information."

Briony huffed. General Billium Meers did whatever he could to cut her out of the tactical meetings. There had been more than one occasion on this journey when she was barred from the tent used by the strategists' council. Over the last three years, Briony had pushed the general to negotiate a safe return of the four Eversun students who'd been taken from the school on the day of the attack, but her requests had fallen on deaf ears. Rory was hesitant to make the wrong move when it came to those captives, so he relied on General Meers's advice.

"When this is over," Briony said, "I want you to take me to Southern Camly like you said you would. I want to learn how to be useful to the court and council. I'm tired of being nothing more than a bargaining chip in this country."

Finola snorted. "Careful, you're speaking like a Bomardi now."

"I'm serious."

Briony turned to look at her cousin. Finola chewed on the inside of her cheek before replying.

"I think the time for that has passed," Finola said softly. "When this is over, there will be a new peace treaty signed. The countries will need to move forward under similar agreements—"

"And I will be nothing but collateral to a betrothal," Briony finished for her. "I see."

Briony looked straight ahead, clenching her jaw.

"It won't just be you. My sister, Phoebe, as well. The rest of your court, including some of the men, will all need to do their duty to hold the peace."

Briony's eyes landed on Cordelia as she rode with Katrina and Didion, fifty feet ahead. "Not Cordelia, though," Briony said, feeling jealousy flash in her blood before she could push it down.

"Well, if your brother was smart, he'd keep himself available to someone on the line, but that's a losing battle." Finola glanced at her. "There is another option for you."

Briony waited for her to say it, her eyes resting on the back of Didion's head. "Yes?"

"Didion Winchester would marry you without hesitation," Finola said. "And don't pretend you haven't been stoking that flame."

Briony eyed her uneasily. "And what is that supposed to mean?"

Finola lifted a brow at her. "Anna says you disappear to the docks at the end of every week."

Briony gasped and sent a glare behind her to where Anna was riding. Anna shrugged.

"It is *not* every week. And 'the docks' makes it sound tawdry. We walk together, that is all." Briony's cheeks were bright red.

"After midnight?" Finola prodded. "My, what a lovely time for a *walk*—"

"I'm twenty-four, you know," Briony said. "I'm not a child who needs to be watched and reported on."

"I didn't say that."

"You're an unmarried Rosewood woman, as well," Briony said, accusingly. "Are you going to tell me that you've been virtuous all this time? That you never sought comfort in Southern Camly?"

Finola gave her a soft smile. "I'm only pointing out that there is an easy route for you that your brother would happily grant." She lowered her voice so only Briony could hear. "Unless you were hoping still for something else?"

"No," Briony said quickly. Gray eyes flickered through her mind, like they often did. "No, I grew out of that fascination."

"Good." Finola breathed deeply, changing the subject. "You and I will set the shelter wards tonight in your brother's absence. It will have to be done quietly so no one suspects Rory is gone."

Briony nodded at her. The Rosewoods were known for their shielding magic. Rory had done it every night of their journey, with help from Briony, unbeknownst to him.

Finola kicked her heels against her stallion and urged him forward, leaving Briony to contemplate the lie she'd just told.

The name whispered in every meeting of the strategists' council was *Hearst*. Orion could perform Heartstop on two hearts at once—an unheard-of skill—and rumor was that his son was just as talented. Toven's name was next to his father's in every report from the front lines, though no reports had come through about his abilities with Heartstop yet. Briony wondered what had happened to the boy who'd tried to help her escape the Bomardi school—the boy who hesitated when his father told him to leave her there. She hadn't seen Toven since that day, but she'd heard stories of his deadliness on the battlefields.

When the caravan stopped to camp for the night, Briony shared a tent with Cordelia, as she usually did. As the cooks began dinner and the soldiers began building campfires, Briony and Finola met at the center of the camp and moved outward and away from each other, expanding a wall around all five hundred that traveled with them. Briony walked among the tents, pushing the shield to the edges.

Didion found her at the far end of the camp.

"Are you stuck doing Rory's shields in his absence?" he asked.

Swallowing back her annoyance that Didion was granted information on the king's movements, Briony nodded. "Finola and I both."

Didion cleared his throat and moved closer when she finished her casting. "I was wondering if maybe we could disappear for a bit ourselves," he suggested quietly.

Briony forced herself to match his shy smile.

She'd tried to fall in love with Didion. Every two weeks for the past year, Briony met him near the docks at midnight for conversation and sometimes more.

But even now, as she smiled softly at him, Briony couldn't shake the feeling that this wasn't her future husband, no matter how easy Finola made it seem.

"I was thinking," she began slowly, "that maybe we could pause our meetings until the war is over."

His face fell, but to his credit, he recovered quickly. "All right." He cleared his throat. "I understand. The retreat to Claremore must be very stressful."

"It is," she said, latching onto the suggestion. "Things are far too fragile now to be . . . indulging in frivolities." She winced at the words as soon as they were out of her mouth, but she wouldn't take them back, even as Didion swallowed and looked at the ground.

It did feel frivolous. Perhaps it felt like more to him, but to her, it was an unnecessary indulgence.

"The eclipse is in a year," he said with a sad grin. "Your brother shall prove he is the Heir Twice Over when 'the sun shines at night,' so we can revisit all of this then."

"Didion, you don't have to . . . to wait for me." She bit her lip. "I don't expect you to, I mean—"

"I would wait millennia for you, Briony Rosewood."

His eyes were clear and his voice soft. And though it was the most romantic thing anyone had ever said to her, she felt nothing.

Didion kissed her cheek and left her staring into the trees. She stood for a long moment, wondering why she couldn't just accept Didion's affections and live comfortably with him.

Briony shivered against the growing dusk. She'd turned to take the long walk through the camp back to the tent she shared with Cordelia when a light in the trees caught her eye.

It bounced like a fairy, slowly moving toward her. It was a navigator flame.

Briony held her hands splayed to cast, standing on the safe side of the shield. She would be undetectable to anyone on the outside of it.

As the flame came closer, she recognized the young woman wandering behind it. She was a merchant from outside Biltmore Palace. Her mother ran the fish market and always made comments about her daughter's indigo-dyed hair. Briony loved her rebelliousness.

She was alone in the woods, looking lost and worried.

Briony stepped forward so the blue-haired woman could find her. "Did you get separated?"

The woman jumped, grabbing her chest in shock. "Oh! Miss Rosewood!" Her eyes were wide and haunted. "My brother was sent for firewood and didn't return. My family and I went looking for him and couldn't find our way back."

Briony searched behind the woman, the glow of the navigator flame revealing no one with her. "Did you find him?"

She shook her head tearfully. "I don't know where any of them are. I lost them all."

Briony cast a shield around the two of them. It wouldn't make them undetectable like the one around the camp, but it would ward off magical attacks. "The woods can twist you around. I'll help you find them."

The woman sobbed grateful tears. "Thank you, Miss Rosewood!"

"You may call me Briony."

"I'm Delilah," the woman said and led them back the way she came. She moved fast, stumbling in the dark past the reach of Briony's shield and looking at the trees.

"It's your brother and who else? Your mother?" Briony sped up, trying to keep both of them under the bubble of protection.

"My mother, my father, and my uncle. We all spread out looking."

Briony was about to tell her they should form a search party if the family was spread in different directions, but the caw of a bird above her head stopped her.

She looked up, finding the beady eye of a black bird watching them.

Magic sizzled the air, and Briony felt something bounce off her shield. She flinched and spun in a circle.

The man from the attack on the Bomardi school stood ten paces away, yellow teeth smiling at her from under a crooked nose.

Reighven.

Briony's heart galloped. In the years since she'd seen him last, his name had become synonymous with terror and dark magic on the battlefields, and his face had taken up permanent residence in her nightmares.

"Stones, what luck we have tonight," Reighven said, his voice like gravel. "The princess herself."

Briony heard shifting in the trees. She reached for Delilah's wrist to bring her into Briony's protection shield, but before she could, Reighven cut his arm through the air. Blood blossomed across Delilah's chest.

Briony gasped and stretched her shield further to cover them both as Reighven and whoever else was in the trees began an assault on her shield. Briony lowered Delilah to the ground, pressing her fingers to the slice across her chest and trying to bring the skin back together as the magic ricocheted around them. Delilah's eyes were wide in panic.

Briony gripped the thread in her mind and pushed with all her might. Reighven and another man stumbled, their magic ceasing momentarily. She reached for a tree and brought it down on them, the crack of the trunk heavy in the dark night. As Reighven and the other man dove out of the way, she cast up purple sparks into the sky like a firecracker. A distress call for Finola.

She glanced at Reighven as he righted himself and saw the other man for the first time: Toven Hearst.

The world slowed and abruptly sped forward as his cold eyes met hers.

Briony refocused on her shield as they moved toward her, hoping she only had seconds until the Eversuns came to her aid. She turned back to Delilah as twigs snapped under hasty footsteps. Color was just returning to her cheeks now that her wounds had been sewn up.

A hand reached through the wall of Briony's shield and grabbed the front of her dress. She gasped, eyes wide, as Reighven slammed her up against the nearest tree.

She hadn't thought of physical violence, only magical. Her shield was useless against his hands.

"Princess, let's go have a little talk. See if we can't find out how to lure your brother out of that camp, huh?" Reighven grinned at her, and then cast a portal five feet to the left.

Briony panicked, her mind nothing but white noise and her skin trembling. Her eyes caught Toven's as Reighven tugged on the front of her dress, as though to pull her toward the portal. His lips were pressed into a thin line, but he made no move to stop Reighven.

Briony kicked and clawed, screaming for the camp to hear her.

"Hey!" a voice called from the trees behind them. Reighven paused.

A man in Eversun merchant clothes stood in a clearing of trees. The woman who ran the fish market stood next to him, as well as two brawny men who looked like them. Delilah's family. Briony thanked the waters for their timing.

"You can't just take her!" the man yelled. "She's coming with us!"

Briony had half a second to ponder his choice of words before Delilah came to her feet, hands raised to cast.

Delilah's body flew into the trunk of a tree, and her head cracked on the bark. She crumpled.

Behind her, Toven Hearst lowered his hand, his eyes still cold. "She's not going anywhere with you," he said.

The mother screamed, and Briony barely had time to put up a shield before the magic sizzled around her, like being thrust into the center of a bonfire.

She ducked as Reighven let go of her to cast. Pulling herself around a tree, she caught her bearings on which way was back to camp as the screams and grunts of a battle broke out behind her. She couldn't run back to the Eversun camp now. She couldn't lead them there, shields or not.

A pale hand with strong fingers grabbed her wrist and tugged. Briony fell forward against Toven's chest. She shoved him backward as he began to draw a portal.

"Don't," he warned her, voice deadly.

A spell flared over his shoulder, and he howled, curling over in pain and releasing her. One of Delilah's relatives stood twenty paces away with his hands outstretched.

"Thank you! Run!" Briony screamed at him.

She took off to the north, running through the trees, leaping over roots and fallen branches.

The zip of a spell flew past and into the tree in front of her, and she curled in on herself, veering right.

There should be a river half a mile ahead. If she could get there, she could channel the water's magic into a stronger shield.

A spell slammed into her back and she fell, cracking her chin on the ground. Stars spun in her head. She pulled herself up just as a knee pressed into her back, hot breath on her neck.

"This is fun, isn't it?" Reighven growled, taking her wrists and pushing them into her back. "I think I'll make you my new pet. We can chase each other for hours."

Briony focused her mind on the earth beneath her. The fear and adrenaline spiked her magic, and the forest floor began to split apart underneath her.

Reighven rolled, taking her with him. She struggled under him until he was straddling her, pinning her wrists down.

Then Reighven screamed. He grabbed for his head, his fingers scrabbling across his skull, then his chest as he screeched in excruciating pain.

She didn't delay. She slipped from under him and kept running, hoping she'd hear the river soon to help guide her direction.

She got her answer when one of the merchant men jumped into her path. She skidded to a halt.

"Miss Rosewood!" he said. "The camp is this way!"

Briony caught her breath, staring in the direction he was pointing. Was she really so turned around? If she had four guesses on which way was east, that would have been the last.

A spell sizzled past her ear, and the man was blown back off his feet. Briony ran for a nearby tree for cover. As she spun around it, Toven Hearst was advancing toward her.

She dragged her hands together, and two tall trees were pulled off their roots, crashing down in front of him. Toven jumped back, and she ran the way the man had pointed—toward camp.

By now Briony didn't care who else was alerted to her location. She needed Finola and the army to find her and the merchants. She started lighting trees on fire as she ran past them.

A bush caught on fire to her left. She hadn't lit it. Briony swerved around it, listening to a pair of heavy boots chasing behind her. A tree fell in her path, and she was forced to veer right.

Toven was running alongside her through the trees, twenty feet away, and Briony felt sick as she remembered how they used to race to the willow tree. How much faster he'd always been than her. How racing him used to thrill her. She shoved her magic at him to keep him away.

He brought another tree down in front of her, and she had to twist to avoid it.

He was playing with her. Herding her. Forcing her to go in the direction he chose.

She glanced over to him as he kept pace with her, and just before she could cast against him, a spell slammed into his shoulder, and he tripped and rolled.

The sounds of a magic fight hissed behind her as she kept running. She heard the merchant woman scream again, the same keening cry she'd made when Delilah's body had crumpled to the forest floor.

Briony wanted to go back for them—the merchant family who was fighting off Toven and Reighven with her when they could have just run—but she needed Finola and the army to find them first.

A large twisted tree trunk was dead ahead of her. It was actually two trees grown into each other, with a hole at the base. She slid against it and caught her breath, taking stock of who was chasing her and where exactly she was.

The three trees she'd lit on fire were starting to light up the area. She could see the illumination of them fifty feet away.

She watched through the undergrowth as spells zipped past one another. There were five figures scattered throughout the trees, moving and casting.

And then suddenly it was quiet, without so much as a scream.

Briony blinked into the growing light of the forest, waiting for movement. When nothing came, she rose to her feet, casting a shield to protect against all kinds of violence this time, and crept to the edge the clearing.

One of the merchant men lay on his back, twenty feet in front of her.

His eyes were open and glassy, and his hand was clenched over his heart. Heartstop.

Briony scanned the trees before moving forward again. In another ten feet, she found Delilah's mother and the other two men on the ground in similar positions. Tears pricked her eyes, and her stomach churned, hating how cowardly she'd been to hide and wait while they died.

Briony's hand covered her mouth as she knelt over the dead body of Delilah's mother, remembering how she'd always sighed about her daughter's blue hair.

She glanced through the trees. She had to get out of the forest.

A flare of purple sparks lit the sky to her left. Finola, guiding her in. Briony gasped to see just how close she was to the camp, wondering how she'd found her direction through the chaos.

She began to carve a path through the trees but stopped cold when she saw another body in the underbrush.

One with pale gray hair and long limbs.

Her feet moved to him before her brain could think.

Toven Hearst lay on his side, unmoving. Her ribs seized, and she choked on a gasp.

He'd hunted her, toyed with her, and still she shook as she approached, begging the waters for his heartbeat.

Coming around his body, she found his eyes open, staring straight ahead, past her.

When a breath rattled from his throat, and a tear slipped out of his eye, Briony almost sobbed in relief.

"Briony!" a voice called from a distance. Maybe half a mile away.

The Eversuns were coming for her, but Briony dropped to her knees at Toven's side.

He was too exposed. That was the only thing Briony thought as she levitated a few fallen branches to cover him from her army.

Toven's gaze was far away as she hid him. He fought for air, in intense pain.

She heard her name called again.

Briony took one last second to reach for his hand, pausing as she looked down.

Both of his hands were curled into fists. Both of his arms were out-stretched in the direction she'd come from. In the direction of the four dead bodies in the grass.

Heartstop.

And not just Heartstop. A split casting, like his father. No. Worse than his father.

Briony scrambled away from him, coming to her feet. He'd killed four innocent people because they were in his way—because they were between himself and her.

And four lives in one breath? He was shivering and struggling for air because the Heartstop had torn his heart open four times over. And she'd *coddled* him for it.

Killing four people with two hands was utterly unheard of. Not even Orion had such talent.

Her legs shook as she stared down at possibly the most dangerous man in all Bomard.

One day, he'd be able to do it without blinking. Without a gasp for air.

She wondered if she should kill him now, before he had a chance to do it again. Before he learned to take six lives. Eight.

Toven Hearst shuddered on the ground, his eyes beginning to flicker.

Briony hardened her heart and ran into the night, hoping Toven Hearst would rot there under those branches.

CHAPTER 43

THERE WAS A BODY IN THE GRASS, and her hand was in a fist.

Briony felt the cold seep into her chest, crawling up to her mind. Her breath shook, air shivering into her lungs and rattling out.

There was a body in the grass . . .

"Briony."

A man whispered her name.

Her mind was a library of books. She reached for a blank one and wrote *Cohle* across the spine. She filled it with a body in the grass and her hand in a fist, and she pushed it onto a low shelf where no one would see it.

"Briony."

There were hands on her face, tilting her head toward gray eyes.

Toven stood in front of her, his gaze wide and searching.

She placed her hands on his wrists.

"There's no time for this," she said, and she didn't recognize her voice. "Bring his body over the line so I can help you lift him."

Her mind ticked on, because her heart was torn open.

*　　*　　*

They levitated his body down the lane. When they came to Vesper's body, she looked so small.

Toven knelt down and whispered words over her. She was still blinking.

Briony watched with empty eyes as he looked up at her.

"I can't . . . I don't have enough strength to—"

With a thump, Briony lowered Cohle back to the earth—*there was a body in the grass*—and moved to Vesper's side.

She ran a scan over the fox's spine, finding the broken bones and the severed nerves. She'd never specialized in healing, but she knew Toven knew enough.

He pointed at the nerves. "You'll need to knit those back together. Put her under first."

Briony passed a hand over Vesper's eyes, and the fox was asleep.

Everything was much simpler when there wasn't anything else in her head to think of. She followed Toven's instructions, realigning the bones and clearing the pathways of nerves. At a certain point, when Vesper was no longer on the brink of death and her magic could flow to Toven again, he took over.

Briony stood over him, feeling hollow as he poked the fox's bones back together and knit her nerves into place.

Inside her mind, there were shelves upon shelves of books that begged to be opened and read—but it wasn't time for that. If she opened herself up to any of them, *Cohle* would tumble down first. And then she'd need to feel her heart rip open again. She'd have to understand what killing a person did. What murderers feel.

Because that's what she was.

Her pages shivered, and she silenced them.

Toven lifted Vesper into his arms. She was still asleep.

Without another word, Briony levitated the body in the grass, and they continued up to the house.

*   *   *

Serena stood vigil over Reighven and the female nurse. Her eyes turned wide on the two of them as they walked into the drawing room.

"You caught him. Good."

"I killed him."

She tested the words in her mouth. They didn't feel any different from other words.

Serena's lips opened in shock as the color drained from her face.

Toven laid Vesper on the sofa and looked around the room. "Where is the other nurse?"

"I let him go."

Both sets of eyes swung to her. She stood in the center of the drawing room, a shell of herself.

"He was Eversun. We will say he died and produce a body. I promised him."

Serena gazed at her with careful eyes. "I see. And he will tell no one about what he saw today?"

She shook her head. "They have his sister at Biltmore. She's a Barlowe Girl. Her name is Maggie."

She rattled off the details as if she were being quizzed in school.

"All right." Serena sprang into action. "I've sent my albatross for your father. We will deal with . . ." She gestured to Cohle's body and then wrung her hands, staring between the clock and the bodies. "Cohle attacked us. He intended to steal the golden heartspring for his own. Reighven was incapacitated early, as were the nurses. The male nurse was caught in the crossfire, and I killed Cohle as he tortured my son."

"No," Toven said. "I killed him. He was absconding with her——"

"You cannot kill for her, Toven," Serena said swiftly, eyes filled with something Briony couldn't read. "I can kill for my son. You cannot kill for her."

Briony thought Toven would argue again, but he seemed to hold his breath tightly.

"So that's the story," Briony said. "but that's not what Reighven saw. He will tell Mallow the truth."

Serena swallowed, pacing. "We will fix his memories. His and the nurse's."

"But that's highly advanced mind magic," Briony said. She glanced between Toven and Serena.

And then she remembered the meditation chamber near the kitchen. The way Toven could slip into her mind and fall into her memories. The way one glance from Orion Hearst felt like she was being sliced open and inspected.

Through the haze of her own mind barriers, blocking emotion from interacting with her brain, Briony felt a spark of horror as she wondered how many times her own mind had been invaded by Orion and Toven Hearst. But before she could let the panic seep in, Toven spoke.

"What do you need?" He stared at his mother, as if waiting for her cue.

Briony's eyes slid to Serena, suspicion bubbling in her chest.

Serena's gaze never left the clock. "If Mallow recognizes my techniques from my own mind—if my signature is apparent—we'll all be dead by sundown," Serena said, voice cold. "She is in my head too often to risk it. I need a second set of eyes, so we will wait for your father."

Realization dripped into Briony's mind like water from a loose faucet.

Serena Hearst was the advanced mind magician at Hearst Hall. For some reason, Mallow looked inside Serena Hearst's mind. Often. And Serena used mind magic to block her. No, not block her. To alter her own memories.

Briony stared, emotionless thoughts coming quickly.

There were no servants at Hearst Hall. They entertained no guests. They hosted no parties. There were secrets within these walls, and Briony had only scratched the surface of them.

"Let me do it," Briony said.

They looked at her.

"Let me do it," she repeated. "Toven just walked me through advanced healing techniques. I can be instructed on memory alteration."

Serena shook her head, her eyes still on the clock.

"They should have left by now," Briony argued, knowing that she was speaking Serena's exact thoughts. "They should be reporting back to Mallow by now. It could take Orion hours to return."

Toven strode forward. "We start with the nurse," he said. "Come on, Mother. With the three of us, we'll do it right."

Serena took one last look at the clock and then joined them at the nurse's feet.

Briony knelt next to her. "What is the technique?"

"We have to pull her out of stasis and keep her calm and still." She looked at Toven. "That will be you."

Toven nodded.

Briony felt the ticking of the mantel clock inside her chest. Her mind was focused and hollow. Was this what the inside of Toven's head felt like all the time—absence of panic, absence of pain?

"I will instruct you with the nurse, and we will hope that Orion will be back to take Reighven," Serena said.

Briony's waters rippled. There was a book in her mind that shook loose, and Reighven's dark eyes and acrid breath flooded her senses before she could shut it.

Briony closed her eyes and breathed deep.

Her shelves reorganized, and before she could even glance at one called *Cohle*, it shuffled to a distant shelf.

"Follow my thread," Serena said, and she nodded to Toven.

Toven dragged his hands upward, tugging the woman up out of her unconsciousness. Her eyes fluttered open, and Toven pushed back down, grounding her. One hand held her muscles still, the other fluttered slow rhythms—her heartbeat.

Serena took the woman's face between her hands, and Briony moved close to her shoulder. She focused on the energy emanating from Serena's mind. The thread of magic from her forehead.

When she found it, it was a silver shimmering tightrope from Serena's mind into the nurse's. Taut, it glinted in her head, a steel connection that pulsed with energy. Briony danced on it, like a circus performer, and then she slid down, down, until she was entering the woman's mind.

She stumbled inside, finding unfamiliar people and unfamiliar worries. A father who was worried about his daughter working for Mallow's medical team. A sister who ran away early, narrowly missing their village's sacking.

A warm hand seemed to drop on Briony's shoulder, and then she was turned to face the memory of that morning.

Serena stood next to her, and together they stared at the scene. Briony lay on the exam table. The male nurse stood near her, raising his hands.

"Don't—" Toven said. "She's my property. Don't I get a say here?"

Briony watched as all eyes turned toward him.

"Why, Hearst?" Reighven said. "You want pups?"

Cohle folded his hands in front of himself. "The Rosewood girl and all tied to her line must be sterilized." He gave Toven a patronizing look. "Clearly, you know why."

Reighven adjusted his belt with a grin. "Carvin's wasn't done right, either, and we took care of that yesterday."

Inside Briony's own mind, sorrow pulsed through her for Phoebe and her own losses.

She refocused as the male nurse began following orders, and she watched as the Serena from that morning reached out suddenly and ripped the nurse back, then shoved Reighven off his feet to smack into a wall. Serena turned to engage with Cohle just as Toven ran for the exam table, covering Briony with his body.

Inside her heart, something fluttered. But there was no connection from her brain to her chest. She was empty still.

The scene slowed, and the Serena next to her inside the nurse's mind walked them backward a step. Reighven was upright. The male nurse's hands were extended.

"Don't—" Toven said.

Serena turned to her as the moment froze. "We start here," her voice whispered, though her mouth didn't move.

The scene rearranged. The male nurse's hands were extended.

And a thread seemed to weave over the scene, sewing up holes and knitting together moments.

The nurse's hands tugged, and Briony's body flinched as her fallopian tube was severed.

Serena showed her how, and then Briony took the thread.

Briony spent what felt like hours on those movements. She first focused on the nurse and his arms. The way they tugged. The thread moved over them until they were seamless. Serena instructed her to make Briony—the one on the exam table—jerk in pain.

They knitted over Toven's reaction. Toven stood stoically now. He didn't protest. He just watched as Briony's chance at childbirth was taken from her.

They spent less time on Serena's past self's reactions than Briony would have thought, but Serena Hearst only winced when the male nurse tugged and severed Briony's fallopian tube.

Once it was done, Serena guided the thread to stitch, writing new moments into existence. Briony followed her lead.

"That wasn't so hard, was it?" Reighven said with a leer.

Cohle stepped forward. "Now that that's been seen to, I'm afraid I have some bad news, Toven." Cohle smiled. "Mallow has decreed that the golden heartspring should belong to her most loyal. Her second in command."

Toven's brow furrowed.

Serena pressed her fingers to her lips.

And then things began moving swiftly, some of it taken from reality.

Only, Toven was the one thrown against the wall, not Reighven, and Cohle was the one causing a ruckus.

The nurses were scared. Briony hid under the exam table. And Reighven hesitated for a moment and then began to engage.

Serena knocked Reighven out.

A stray curse caught the male nurse.

Cohle tortured Toven.

And then Serena killed Cohle.

It all happened quickly. But then they went over the scene again and again, until it was perfect. Serena instructed Briony to tailor everyone's reactions. She hemmed here; she let out seams there.

At the end, Serena from that morning turned and knocked out the female nurse, and the scene went dark.

Briony felt the thread of Serena's mind tugging on her, beckoning her backward.

They were in the drawing room. They were kneeling over the female nurse.

Toven's hands were outstretched over her, shaking.

"Put her back under," Serena said.

Toven flipped his hands and the nurse's eyes closed, sliding back into stasis.

Serena looked at the clock, and Briony followed her gaze. It had been half an hour that they'd been inside her mind. And Orion still wasn't home.

Serena rubbed her hands together and rolled her neck, summoning more energy. She looked pale.

"Are you ready?" she asked.

Briony nodded, feeling nowhere near ready to enter Reighven's mind.

Toven moved to hover his hands over Reighven. He dragged his hands upward, and as soon as Reighven's eyelids fluttered he pressed down again.

Eyes black as tar pits looked up at Briony. Though he wasn't fully there, though he wasn't leering at her, she still felt his eyes on her naked body, his hand between her thighs.

"I'm with you. Begin," Serena instructed kindly.

Briony took hold of the thread in the middle of her eyes and connected it to Reighven. She slid down, falling deep into his eyes.

His consciousness was oily and suffocating. Briony wanted to pull out and ask if they could just kill him, too.

Images flooded up, moments that she recognized.

Her naked body.

The auction—herself in a slip in the spotlight.

A hand landed on her shoulder, and Serena pulled her close, leading her away from Reighven's older memories and into the scene they needed to adjust.

That morning unfurled from a different angle, and it took Briony a moment to grasp it.

"Don't—" Toven said. "She's my property. Don't I get a say here?"

From Reighven's point of view, Briony saw Toven swallow.

"Why, Hearst? You want pups?" Reighven chuckled from right next to her.

And Briony began.

She stitched over the scene. She threaded through the moments that needed to be forgotten. And if she was ever sloppy, Serena was there with an extra eye, pointing out an extra stitch.

She thanked her broken heart for staying away from her head. She didn't know if she would have been able to work like this if she hadn't buried everything that had happened after she lay on that exam table deep inside her bookshelves.

Serena made her wind through the scene again, examining it from every angle.

Something shivered outside of their consciousness. Serena nudged her to refocus, but Briony was just about done.

They slid backward on that thread, up, up. The oil of Reighven's mind dripped off her.

When Briony arrived back inside her own consciousness again, she stared down at Reighven, his eyes open and on her. Toven put him back under again.

"Well," said a slick voice from behind them. "It seems like my family has been quite busy this morning."

She twisted around slowly. Orion Hearst stood in the middle of his drawing room, staring down at her, looking murderous.

CHAPTER 44

ORION TOWERED OVER THE SCENE—three bodies laid out in his drawing room, two loved ones exhausted from earlier heart magic, and one problem in the shape of Briony Rosewood.

Serena came to her feet, reaching for her albatross, who'd come back with Orion. The bird landed on her arm and nuzzled her cheek.

"It's almost done," Serena said.

Orion looked between Reighven and Cohle. "Tell me."

"Cohle is dead." Serena's voice was tired but firm.

Orion lifted a brow, his mind seeming to run through several scenarios at once.

"So, he attempted to abscond with Miss Rosewood, I presume," Orion said, and Briony was shocked how quickly he chose the same path as Serena.

"He tortured Toven," Serena said. "And I killed him."

Orion still stared down at Cohle's body as he nodded slowly.

Briony looked up at Toven. He was swaying on his feet, clearly needing rest. He'd been using heart magic to subdue Reighven and the nurse, depleting himself further.

"And Reighven?" Orion asked, turning his attention to the other man.

"He was knocked out early on," Serena said.

"And the nurse?"

"She saw it all, and then was knocked out."

Orion lowered himself next to Reighven. "You should have waited for me. If she recognizes your needle—"

"It was Briony," Serena said. "I guided her."

Orion closed his eyes in exasperation and then opened them on Briony. His mouth was set in a grim line.

"Well then, Miss Rosewood," Orion said silkily. "Show me your work."

Like he was one of the tutors at school.

Briony swallowed, and then nodded to Toven to bring Reighven back up from unconsciousness.

Sliding back inside Reighven's mind was even less appealing the second time. She stumbled through several terrible images and memories she didn't wish to see before Orion firmly guided her to that morning—much less gently than Serena had.

Orion stood at her shoulder as they watched the scene. He made her go over every second, positioning them in different places in the room. His technique wasn't with a thread but with a pen, rewriting instead of sewing over. Where Serena was a needle sliding past minuscule holes in fabric, Orion was a well-inked pen, gliding and meeting no resistance.

When he pulled them out, he stared at Briony with displeasure.

"Sloppy, but serviceable. Take her upstairs, Toven."

Briony narrowed her eyes at him. Her bookshelves shook with the first emotion that threatened to break her walls—irritation.

"We'll need a dead body, too," she said. "I let the second nurse go."

She stood and turned her back on Orion Hearst, walking away before he could say another word to her that wasn't *Thank you.*

*   *   *

A pair of footsteps followed her up the stairs.

She didn't say a word to him all the way up to her room. When he followed her inside, she turned to face him.

Toven quietly shut the door behind him, his eyes carefully on her the entire time.

"I'm fine," she said.

He slid his hands into his pockets and rocked back on his heels. He watched her, waiting for something.

"I won't release my mind barriers until after Mallow has come and gone, if that's what you're worried about."

There would be too much too suddenly. It could take too long to build up her mental defenses again, and there was no telling how long they had until Mallow arrived.

"I'm worried about the opposite, actually," Toven said. She stared at him blankly. "You should let go. You're holding back too much. Maintaining this level of barrier for this level of circumstances won't help you in the long run."

He spoke as if he knew. He spoke as if he knew this level of barrier intimately.

"How——" She stuttered. "How long have you been practicing mind barriers?" she asked.

His face was impassive as he said, "A long time."

She nodded slowly. It explained so much that she'd suspected.

"And your parents?" she said. "All three of the Hearsts are talented mind magicians?"

He betrayed nothing. He moved forward toward her. "You need to release, rest, and replenish."

"Mallow could be here any moment——"

"You've erected shields in stressful circumstances before. You can do it again." He stood before her. "You need to deal with Cohle, so that he can live in the library of your mind undisturbed."

The book named *Cohle* slid forward inside her mind. She swallowed thickly. "I don't want to."

"Briony," he whispered, and she swayed toward him like the tide. "Your heart was ripped today. Let your mind heal it."

A tremor whispered across her skin. His eyes were unguarded on her, and she forced herself to meet them.

There was a body in the grass.

And her hand was in a fist.

The book named *Cohle* dropped to the floor, and a wind shushed the pages open.

The cold emptiness rushed up, the howl of death surrounded her, and the piece of her heart that had ripped open cawed like a moon-black raven.

Her lips parted, and the final sigh of innocence slithered out of her.

He blurred in her vision.

"I killed someone," she said, voice trembling in a way she hadn't let it in hours.

Toven nodded. "You took a life. It was your first?"

Her chest shook, and she slapped a palm over her mouth. "What did I do?" Her eyes were wide and bright and full of unshed tears.

He stepped forward and placed his hands on her arms. "You did what was necessary to protect yourself."

She leaned into his weight, and at last her tears spilled over, streaming down her cheeks. "To protect you." Her throat clicked as she hurried to add, "Your mother. All of us."

There was a body in the grass and her hand was in a fist.

She had squeezed the life out of him with his back turned. He hadn't seen her coming.

Briony gasped soundlessly on a sob, trying to draw air into her lungs, but failing.

She was in Toven's arms, her forehead pressed against his collar. His shirt was wet with her grief.

"My heart will never be the same," she whispered, voice reedy.

"You did what was necessary," he rumbled, words she felt as much as heard. "You did what I didn't have the power to do."

She let his voice wash over her. She remembered that day in the Trow dungeon—how she had Reighven's heart in her palm for one moment. She could have finished him then and maybe escaped with Katrina. She hadn't had the strength that day, but today was different, and she couldn't help but think that having Toven's life in the balance was the difference.

Her legs gave out as her heart beat a rhythm over and over—*killer, killer, killer.*

Toven lifted her in his arms, and as she sobbed and gulped for air, she wished she wasn't so weak about this. She wished she had never let her emotions rise past her throat and into her mind. She wished he wasn't seeing her like this.

He laid her on her bed, and she curled into herself, bawling in pain.

The missing piece of her heart ached.

And it wasn't just the act of killing Cohle.

It was the oil on her skin from Reighven's mind, his memories of her naked body.

It was the nameless nurse who she'd given the chance she couldn't have—the way her heart needed to hope that he could find Sammy.

It was Phoebe—knowing that she'd lost a child she couldn't have wanted and her chance at one she did, all in the same day.

It was Cordelia, husked. The note about the dragon that Briony wished had been from her, so that she knew Cordelia was still in there, still fighting.

And it was Rory. Rory whom she hadn't said goodbye to because she was so confident in a prophecy that was nothing but nursery rhymes. Rory who marched into battle over and over because Briony knew it was right. She knew he was the one. And he believed her, the fool.

Briony's throat was raw, and she realized she'd been howling through the pain inside her heart. Her face was hot with tears and her muscles were sore with shaking.

And two arms were still around her.

She sucked in a shaking breath as she came back into her body. Toven was wrapped around her, holding her back against his chest. His thighs were flush with the backs of hers, and she could finally recognize the breath on her neck, disturbing her hair.

Briony's eyes dropped, and she found a muscular hand wrapped around her fist, the black gem ring winking at her.

As her grief and panic and sorrow ebbed away with each shaky breath, she grounded herself with the feeling of his chest pressed to her back. His heartbeat thumped against her spine, slow and steady. She breathed in deeply, finding comfort in the press of her ribs into his.

As her tears dried up and her breathing returned to normal, she waited for him to pull away—for him to excuse himself—for his duty to be complete.

It didn't come.

Briony watched the sun inch down the sky and traced the veins in Toven's hands with her eyes.

If he wasn't worried about what could be happening downstairs, then she wasn't, either. Mallow herself could burst into the room, her dragon could breathe fire on all of Hearst Hall, and Briony would still hold on to this moment for a second longer.

Quietly, half hoping he was sleeping, she said, "Did it feel like this after your first kill?"

For a moment, she wondered if he wouldn't respond, but then his voice rumbled into her chest, his air puffing across her neck. "Yes."

She used to hold him in a separate box in her heart after she'd seen him kill that Eversun family. He was a *murderer*, and what business did he have inside her chest, where her yearning and care resided. She belonged in that same box now.

"Did someone hold you like this when your heart ripped?" she asked.

Her pulse seemed to hang on a cliff, waiting.

"Someone helped, yes." His voice was far away.

A pang of jealousy flared hot in her. She wished she could have been that person for him.

She shifted, turning in his embrace, and his arms readjusted around her back as her knees tangled with his.

His eyes were a soft gray. She wanted to run her fingers over his skin, through his hair, under his shirt. She held her fists against her chest, but she couldn't help herself. She reached up and brushed the fine hairs that had fallen over his eyes. She ran her fingers down his cheekbone, carving the path to his jaw.

"Why did you buy me, Toven?" she whispered against him.

His eyes flickered between hers. "I can't answer that."

She blinked at him, and though he was erecting a boundary, she didn't feel him pulling away. It was as if he was inching closer, his eyes softening, his mind opening.

She feathered her fingers over his lips, and she moved forward.

Toven's head shifted back, just slightly out of reach. His eyes closed, and his brows furrowed.

Briony ran her fingers over his chin. "Ah yes," she whispered. "Your No Kissing Rule."

His eyes fluttered open, and one eyebrow lifted. "I don't have a No Kissing Rule."

The corners of her mouth curved upward. She trailed her fingers down his throat, and he swallowed.

"A No Kissing Me Rule, then," she teased.

His lips parted, and his tongue was quick to wet them.

"Exactly," he breathed.

Her eyes flicked back up to his, and then he was kissing her.

Briony's breath caught. He'd stolen it, locked it away inside his chest.

Her mouth grew soft against his, and her eyelashes fluttered closed.

He moved his lips luxuriously, slowly, so gently that Briony thought he might pull away at any second, but he just kept kissing her.

She gulped in air against his lips and curled her fist around his collar. One of his hands splayed across her back, pulling her closer until her breasts pushed against his warm chest, but still his mouth was soft and unhurried.

Her heart pounded so fast, pulsing life and *want* into every inch of her body. She wanted his hands on her skin. She wanted his tongue. She wanted her hips against his.

But Toven Hearst took his time. She'd seen him kiss Larissa Gains plenty of times. She'd seen his hands rove over her.

She'd never seen him like this. She'd never felt *anything* like this.

When his lips finally parted, and she felt the smooth glide of his tongue, a moan poured from the back of her throat. She clenched her thighs, and she brought her hips closer to him.

That was when Toven finally rolled her onto her back, slotting his body between her open legs.

Her arms wrapped around his neck, pulling him closer, and her right knee moved up to his waist.

His lips were still slow and languid, like she was something to handle with care. But as his tongue brushed against hers, and as she learned to open her mouth the way he wanted her to, she didn't want to be touched like glass.

She wanted the weight of him. She wanted his sweat. She wanted him groaning for her.

He shifted and pushed his hips against hers. She could feel *everything*.

Briony's mouth fell open in a sigh, her eyes fluttering in pleasure.

"Toven, please," she murmured into his mouth.

His lips were firm on hers as the kiss started again. She arched against him, trying to feel more of him.

As he kissed her more deeply, his tongue hotter, his lips more direct, Briony slid her fingers around his neck to the place where his fine hair ended at the base of his skull. Her fingers drifted in soft movements, finding a raised scar where she'd sewn his skin back together all those years ago.

His chest rumbled—*finally*—a moan pouring into her mouth. His hips snapped forward, pinning her into the mattress, and his hand grabbed for her other leg, tucking her knee up to his waist until her hips cradled his.

She gasped at the feeling of him pressing against her. Her eyes flew open as his hips rolled over and over. She could feel him right where she needed him. He was unspeakably hard against her softness, and his mouth attached to her jaw, her neck, her pulse, as he groaned into her skin. She kept running her fingers through his hair softly, and his pace became frenzied.

She memorized every gasp, every moan, every sigh. She prayed he was leaving marks on her as his mouth sucked.

It felt decadent. Indulgent. There was an ocean inside of her, the waves gathering.

And then he shifted his hips just a bit lower, and through all their fabric, Briony felt his erection press against her center—

Her breath caught, and her mind went white. She whimpered, feeling closer to something than she'd ever felt before.

He lifted his lips to the shell of her ear, and as he rocked against her again, he moaned her name. "Briony."

Her eyes rolled back in bliss.

It sounded exactly like it had before. Inside his mind. In the fabricated fantasy where she'd put her mouth on him.

If she could hear one sound for the rest of her life, she wanted it to be Toven Hearst moaning her name.

A knock rapped on her door, shocking her system.

They froze. The pleasure drained rapidly from her body.

Toven's gaze was black as he pulled back to look down at her. His cheeks pink, his hair falling forward in a mess, and his lips red from her kisses. He sprang back, and Briony felt the absence of his body like a fire doused.

She bit her lip, wishing the knock had come either two minutes earlier or twenty minutes later.

She sat up and watched as Toven pushed a hand through his hair, adjusted his trousers, and breathed deep.

Like a reptilian blink—he was composed again. His shields were up.

When he answered the door, Serena's voice whispered, "How is she?"

"Better."

Briony pulled herself off the bed and quickly tugged at the bedsheets to straighten them.

"Reighven and the nurse were sent off. Your father's hawk has returned from Mallow. She will be here after nightfall."

Cold ice trailed down Briony's spine. She glanced out the window. The sun would set in a few hours. At least she had time to build her barriers again.

"And is everything going smoothly?" Toven asked.

"To the best of our knowledge," Serena said. "We won't know for sure until she's here. Your father would like to see you."

Toven nodded. He glanced at Briony once, and she found those familiar cold eyes again, as if he hadn't just been cradled between her hips or inside her mouth.

He left, leaving the door open.

Briony took a deep breath. "Come in, Serena."

Serena moved through the door and closed it behind her, folding her hands in front of her. Briony stepped away from the bed, taking the memories of Toven's hands and tongue and lips and closing them away in a book as she faced his mother.

"Thank you for what you did today," Briony said.

Serena tilted her head. "I was about to say the same." She glanced down. "You've had a very hard twenty-four hours, and I know that taking a life twists your heart, but I want you to know that you have never been more brave to me than now."

Briony nodded her head, forcing herself to believe it. "Please know that I wasn't hiding my ability to bear children from you."

"I understand. It wasn't my business to know," she said simply.

Briony steeled herself and broached the topic on her mind.

"You said Mallow searches your mind often. Why?"

Serena lifted her chin and gazed past Briony's shoulder. She thought the woman might not answer her until Serena spoke.

"I've been given the gift of sight. Three large visions and a handful of small images that all came to be," she said. Briony blinked at her. "I used to report my dreams weekly to her, but she has become suspicious of everyone around her and even doubts that I understand my own subconscious. Now I report daily to Mallow for inspection of my mind."

Briony's brows drew together as she struggled to understand.

"You're a seer," Briony said.

"It's a generational trait in my family. It appears every hundred years or so."

The gift of visions was rarer and rarer these days. The only seers Briony knew of were from over half a millennium ago, the ones who had foreseen the heir twice over. Most seers wouldn't flaunt their gift. It was too easy to become a target.

Briony shifted on her feet, thinking. "Why does Mallow even know about it?" she asked.

Serena looked at Briony. "I saw her coming," she said simply. "I saw her on the Seat. And Orion and I acted quickly to become . . . favored."

Briony remembered how the Hearsts had been the ones to introduce Mallow into society the first time Briony had met her.

"You'll forgive me if I've been absent. Cold," Serena said with a rare smile. "Until you'd begun learning mind barriers, I couldn't risk much conversation with you. And there is already so much I cut out and set aside in my own memories."

Briony tried to imagine Mallow in her mind every day, digging into dreams of her subconscious that she had no control over.

"There is a meditation chamber downstairs," Briony said. "It's yours?"

Serena nodded once. "As you progress with mind barriers, you are welcome to it."

Briony wanted to ask Serena about her visions. She wanted to know the future so badly. She wanted to know the things that Serena had seen that she'd given over to Mallow. But she also knew that it wasn't hers to know. Most seers lived in isolation to avoid these types of conversations with friends and family.

"I won't ask you about your dreams, but when you stopped them today . . ." Briony paused and rephrased, finding the words that had echoed in her mind since she'd let the nurse go. "I have reason to believe that Mallow thinks the Heir Twice Over could still exist. When you saved the Rosewood line today . . ." She sighed, diving in. "Do you have reason to believe your son will one day father that heir?"

Serena's brows lifted clear off her head. "Oh. Oh, I see." Her thumb tapped against her opposite wrist. "No. My intention today was only to give you a choice in your future."

Briony felt the weight of those words cascading down on her. "You're a seer," Briony said with a small smile. "You speak as if all futures are possible, when you already know certain outcomes."

Serena nodded. "I have not yet seen the future that I most wish for, but I am hopeful. I think a world where we both have choice again is possible."

Briony swallowed around a lump in her throat. Her heart beat fast, and with the knowledge that Serena Hearst was under this roof with her, she felt suddenly less alone.

Serena inclined her head in goodbye. "Take care, Briony. I'm sorry for giving you another conversation to tuck away as you prepare your mind."

She excused herself, and Briony focused inward.

CHAPTER 45

MALLOW DIDN'T COME AT NIGHTFALL.

Briony stood at the window that faced the front gates, watching the horizon for the sizzle of a portal, but it never came.

The Hearsts didn't come up to check on her, either.

Briony focused her energy on her mind barriers, pulling together everything she needed to hide from Mallow and finding a place for it all on her mental shelves. She went over everything with a needle and thread, just as Serena had done inside the female nurse's mind, until Briony wasn't even sure if Cohle *hadn't* tried to take her that morning. She wrote over her own memories of her fist squeezing, threading over them with the image of a paler, more delicate wrist until it was Serena whose hand had contracted in Heartstop.

If she concentrated, she could find the truth in her mind, but it was also easy to think of that morning and have the fabricated scenario pull forward.

At four in the morning, there was a thunder of wings in the sky.

Briony looked up just in time to see the belly of the last dragon in the world skating over Hearst Hall, wings long and spindly.

Briony narrowed her eyes at the beast. So the dragon was not dead.

no dragon, don't Worry

She puzzled over the words again as the dragon fluttered—almost elegantly—over the forest where Vesper lived, settling gently in the field next to it. In the beginnings of the dawn sun, Briony could just make out a rider sliding off its wing, her long black hair shimmering down her back.

Deep inside Briony's mind, beneath the shields and behind the bookshelves, she wondered at the necessity of bringing the dragon, much less riding it. Surely a portal was quicker.

The figure glided through the gates and down the lane. Once Mallow disappeared inside the front door, Briony returned to her chair to wait. Either the plan had worked, or it hadn't.

Twenty minutes later, her door opened and Toven stepped inside.

"Mistress Mallow wishes to see you."

His face betrayed nothing. She could be walking into anything.

Briony followed him down the stairs and into the drawing room. Her memories shivered on the bookshelves in her mind, but she was pleased to note they were the fabricated ones.

Mallow stood near the fireplace, the glow illuminating her silhouette, with Orion and Serena at her side. Though Briony had only seen her two nights ago at Biltmore Palace, it felt like it had been months. When she turned, Briony noted that her eyes were exhausted. Again, she wondered what Mallow's true age was.

Cohle's body lay in between the couches, like a coffee table.

"Briony," Mallow hummed with a soft smile. "I hear you had a little procedure yesterday morning."

Briony said nothing. Toven stood just off to her left.

Mallow slid forward, her long dress moving around her like oil.

"Did you know all along that you could still have children?" Mallow asked.

Briony hadn't prepared her memories of the nurses who severed her first fallopian tube, so there was no reason to lie.

"I suspected it."

"You will address her as Mistress," Orion said firmly.

Her eyes flicked to him. Briony added, "Mistress."

Mallow's lips curled. "What else are you hiding, Briony?"

Her heart skipped, but her mind remained focused.

"What do you mean, Mistress?"

Mallow stood in front of her, her gaze black and her mind brushing up against Briony's.

"Your country is Nevermore," Mallow said. "Your people have lost, but still you find ways to rebel against my authority, don't you?"

Briony's mind shook, every volume she'd tucked away threatened to fall to her feet. Collars and notes and grapes. She focused on Mallow's gaze.

"You must tell me what you know, Briony," Mallow said.

And then the knives were in her mind.

Briony gasped as her memories were flayed. Mallow's technique was blunt. Where Serena endeavored to get in and out without notice, Mallow wanted to be felt for days later.

She prepared herself to fight the knives, but Mallow swirled around a familiar scene.

General Meers was standing in her father's study. "I really must object to so many ears in a confidential meeting—"

"You're a fool if you think Briony's ears to be the least useful of the five of us here," Rory said.

Briony waited as Mallow slithered through the scene like a serrated blade, leaving her mark everywhere.

There was little she could do to hide anything. She had no idea *what* to hide.

Mallow flew through her mind, circling memories of Rory like a serpent. She spent ages in family gatherings from fifteen years ago with aunts and uncles who had been dead for years. She slithered through any memories Briony had of her father, winding around the difficult lessons he would dole out and the requests he made that Briony be less of who she was so Rory could be more.

Her body shook, knees weak. Mallow held her upright in the center of the room. Her mind could just barely recognize the scene—the shape of Mallow in front of her with wild black eyes, and the pale gray of Orion out of focus, twenty feet back.

She had no idea what Mallow was after. Briony kept from hyperventilating even through the pain, knowing that she needed the secrets she had to remain secret. At odd moments, she felt another presence in her own memories. Where Mallow was cutting and opening with wrenching slices, there was also a smooth glide, like that of a pen. Careful to remain hidden.

After what felt like hours, Briony simply followed Mallow through her own mind like a guest.

Mallow was determined and laser-focused in her quest, leaving Briony suspicious of what exactly Mallow was looking for. The pain exhausted her, making Briony reckless. An idea slithered into her head while Mallow was elsewhere. If Briony could only know precisely what Mallow wanted . . .

The knives in her mind were attached to Mallow's thread of mind magic.

And just as she had slid down the thread into Toven's mind weeks ago . . .

Just as she had joined Serena on a single thread that morning into the nurse's mind . . .

Briony waited until Mallow was focused on a memory with Rory and Sammy Meers, and then she walked that thread like a spider, sliding down, down, down, and into Veronika Mallow's mind.

She balanced on a needle, like Serena had taught her, careful not to disturb anything.

But she needn't look long. There was a question tattooed on the back of Mallow's eyelids, living at the front of her mind without any barriers to fight it.

Where is he?

Briony felt her consciousness floating. Her heart hung suspended. And before she could fully process what she'd found, she climbed up the thread, surfacing out of Mallow's mind.

A mind that Mallow didn't bother to barricade. Arrogance? Or stupidity?

As Briony latched back onto the path Mallow was taking through her memories, she focused on maintaining her heartbeat, unwilling to feel anything other than confusion and pain.

Because there was one *he* Mallow was examining in her mind.

Something's not right with her.

The male nurse said Briony would be killed if she could conceive.

And the only thing Briony could focus on while her mind was flayed was the dragon outside the gates. The unnecessary shows of power. The exhaustion in Mallow's face.

no dragon, don't Worry

The dragon that had refused to bond to any magician for six hundred years until Mallow.

A magician with a dragon familiar wouldn't bother with any mortal problems. They would be all-powerful.

Unless the dragon wasn't her familiar.

no dragon

Briony felt herself outside her body. She could see the scene in the drawing room.

Orion and Serena at the fireplace, having prepared to be interrogated over Cohle's body.

Toven standing to her left, waiting for his heartspring to be returned to him.

And Mallow—not caring at all about the dynamics of the Ten or the death of her second in command. Mallow not concerned with the way things happened yesterday, only caring to search Briony's mind for something she was missing—*again*.

Perhaps the nurse was close to the truth, but not quite.

Mallow was concerned about an heir to the Rosewood line who would stand to defeat her—the Heir Twice Over.

Only it was the same one she'd been battling with for four years, since their father's death.

don't Worry

Briony thought it was strange that she didn't feel it when her brother died.

And maybe that was because he hadn't.

The collar didn't work on Briony because she had given her heart magic away to her brother. What if she still was giving it?

Magic freely given couldn't be taken.

The room was silent except for her gasps of pain, but she was separate from herself now, in a world where Rory might still live.

Her mind was elsewhere as Mallow flew through her memories.

The sun was up.

And Briony had work to do.

She reached inside herself, finding a moment, fabricating it quickly. Sewing over it the way Serena would, then inking it clean like Orion.

She and Rory sitting on the cliffside at Biltmore. Briony asked him what he would do if he wasn't their father's heir.

I don't know, Rory said. *Maybe I'd be a sailor. I've always loved the harbors at Daward.*

Briony took the moment—the fabrication—and slipped it inside a box in her mind.

When Mallow was ready to move on from a solstice gathering from years ago, Briony dropped it in her path, like a stolen bracelet, fallen out of her dress.

Mallow was quick to grab it up. The box opened for her.

And sooner than Briony expected, she was alone in her mind, and her body was dropped on the floor of the Hearst drawing room.

She was barely conscious as Mallow turned and moved to the window overlooking the grounds. The window that faced the dragon in the field.

Briony fought to hold on to the present, panting on the floor.

Orion stepped forward. His movements smooth . . . like a well-inked pen.

"Mistress, how can I be of service?"

Mallow seemed to watch her dragon through the window. "Serena," she said. "I'm sorry to say you'll have to live without your husband again for the foreseeable future."

Serena cleared her throat. "Anything for Bomard."

Mallow turned over her shoulder and nodded at Briony's body. "That will be all. Please excuse Orion and me."

Toven began to collect her from the floor. Serena was at her side quickly, assisting.

But Briony was focused on the conversation at the window.

"I appreciate your discretion, as ever, Orion."

"Of course, Mistress."

She watched Mallow slip Cohle's ring off his finger.

"It seems the position of first in line to the seat is open, since Cohle

failed to name a successor after Burkin's death. And while succession dic-
tates differently, I'd be happy to offer it to you, Orion."

Serena and Toven froze. Briony's head was lolling on Toven's shoulder.
Her eyes fluttered, watching Orion.

Orion took only a heartbeat to think. "You are kind, Mistress. But the
Ten means a great deal to me. It always has. I do not wish to upset the natural order of things. I happily accept the advancement to seventh in line,
with the death of Riann Cohle."

The room held its breath. Mallow assessed him. "I appreciate men who
understand power but do not covet it."

Orion inclined his head.

Briony felt her body shift as Serena and Toven moved her along again.

"Toven?"

They stopped at Mallow's voice. Briony's body slumped against Toven,
all her energy being used to stay awake for this.

Toven stepped forward. "Yes, Mistress Mallow."

"It's been suggested to me that you have not been using Miss Rosewood
as a heartspring. You told me just weeks ago that you were fully bonded
and reaping the benefits."

The room fell silent, and Briony wondered if she'd passed out with the
lack of sound.

"Apologies, Mistress. I recently severed the bond. The connection
was terribly powerful. Apparently, it's true what they say—the golden
blood makes the heartspring that much more potent." He chuckled. "I
find I was a bit overwhelmed by the magic. I had to siphon so much of it
elsewhere."

Mallow stood at the window, eyes on her dragon. "Too much power?
Well, if that's the case," she said, "perhaps we'll need to find more for you
to do, Toven."

Serena's arm tensed around Briony's body. Orion's lips tightened. The
back of Toven's neck stiffened.

"I would appreciate any opportunity to further your cause, Mistress,"
Toven said.

Briony's heart raced, and she finally gave over to the dark.

*　　*　　*

Briony woke up the next day. Her mind still felt sluggish.

There was a pot of tea waiting for her on her side table, and she dragged herself up to fix a cup.

There was too much to do.

She reached into the jewelry box on her table and pulled out the note.

no dragon, don't Worry

She traced the shape of the *a*. The curve of the *r*'s.

Could it be Rory?

Her chest ached with the certainty that she felt. Her brother, her piece of herself, wasn't lost after all. Her eyes pricked with tears.

The simplest explanation was likely correct. Mallow certainly thought Rory was alive—that much Briony had gathered.

So somehow, Rory had found a line to the Barlowe Girls at the Biltmore.

Briony ran her fingers over the note. Rory had touched this. She was closer to him than ever in the last two months, but still so far away.

Looking around her room, Briony felt the weight of it on her. It was a nice cage, but it was still a cage. She needed to find a way around the tattoos, not just for herself, but for Cordelia and Phoebe and Katrina.

And after that . . . she supposed it was time to look into how to kill Mallow.

Now that Briony was questioning whether the dragon would fully bond to her, Mallow didn't seem so terribly powerful. She was just a clever, enigmatic liar.

Briony chuckled to herself as she remembered how feared Mallow was because the dragon's bond gave her the ability to read minds. It wasn't a dragon; it was a poor study at mind magic, sloppy and painful.

Briony thought of Finola, and how Mallow had searched for her in Briony's head. Maybe that had nothing to do with her strategies and connections. Maybe it was because she was a Rosewood woman who hadn't been sterilized.

There was a knock on her door.

"Come in," she said.

Toven slipped inside, and Briony's heart skipped at the sight of him. His face was set, distant.

"What is it?" she said.

"I wanted to see how you are." His voice was clipped.

"Fine. Why do you look so strange?"

"Strange?" he said.

"Cold. You look cold."

He pressed his lips together. "Once you are healed, we will do the bonding ceremony. I will make sure the collar doesn't take away your ability to harness your magic."

"But you will have access to it," Briony said.

He nodded. Her breath was tight, thinking of giving a part of herself to Toven with nothing in return. She didn't know what other options there were. They'd gotten around this heartspring bond for this long.

They were quiet for a moment. His fingers played with the black ring as he looked around the room.

"I suspect Canning suggested to Mallow that we weren't bonded, in retaliation for getting his elixir banned. She will expect me to remedy that soon."

Briony nodded. "And your father? He's left again?"

"Tomorrow. I don't know where to."

Briony did. To the port at Daward first, then to the home of every sailor in town.

"But once we are bonded," he said slowly, not looking at her. He seemed to rephrase his words. "There is something to be said for Sacral Magic . . . and its effects."

Briony lifted her brows as a blush rose on her cheeks. "Yes?"

"So nothing like the other night will happen again." He looked meaningfully at her bed. "It shouldn't have happened in the first place. It was inappropriate."

"Inappropriate," she repeated, narrowing her eyes.

"You were emotionally very raw," he said. "It never would have happened had you been yourself."

Briony felt a sharp sting, as if she'd been slapped. Did he consider it her fault? Did he not remember leaning in first?

"Is it your habit to tend to emotionally raw women by lying in bed with them?" she bit back.

His jaw twitched. "I'm just here to inform you that nothing of the sort will happen again."

"And I've been informed." Her tone was acidic. "Is there anything else?"

His exterior cracked. "What has crawled up your skirt, Rosewood?" he hissed. "I said I was sorry—"

"You *did*?" She laughed. "I didn't hear it!"

"Yes! I'm *sorry*. It won't happen again!"

"And why is that?" She stepped closer to him, crossing her arms. "When plenty other Bomardi are happy to take what they own, what *moral superiority* does Toven Hearst have?"

He gaped at her. "Am I hearing you correctly? You're asking why I haven't had my way with you?"

"Yes," she said simply. "Why is it that I'm here? Why am I so well taken care of at Hearst Hall? I get to keep my virginity *and* my fertility. My goodness, what hospitality!"

He pressed his eyes closed and paced away from her. "You are . . . so infuriating."

"You know, I was on that stage, Toven. I was there when you bid on me. I didn't just *fall* into your lap. You gave Reighven something to get me, and I want to know what it is."

He spun back to her, advancing on her. "You don't *get* to know, Rosewood! You are not *entitled* to know these things, contrary to what you believe!"

"Oh, *finally*!" She threw her arms wide. "Finally, I'm treated like a second-class citizen in this house!"

"Is that what you want?" he said, arching a brow. His voice dropped an octave. "Is that what you want? Are you so starved for righteous indignation that you'd like for me to take away your magic and your books and your privacy?"

"I want to know why I have those things," she said. His face was so close to hers, she could feel his harsh breath. "I want to know the Hearst end-game. Is it because I am the Princess of Evermore?"

His eyes flashed at her. His breath hitched, as if the words were ready to tumble out of him. And then he said simply, "Yes."

Briony watched his face harden. She felt it in her heart, when he failed to say what she wanted to hear——that she wasn't special, but that she was special *to him*. But instead she was a gold-blooded bargaining chip to him and his family.

She nodded, swallowing back her emotions. "That makes sense," she said weakly. "Your family is clearly prepared to play both sides."

He said nothing, just watched her.

She tilted up her chin, preparing herself to play both sides as well. "Are you ready to begin the game against Mallow, Toven? Or are you content to stand on the sidelines while your father does all the work?"

He narrowed his eyes at her. "What does that mean?"

She licked her lips, and when his eyes dropped to her mouth, she pushed back the hope that he would ever kiss her again.

This wasn't a love story.

"It means," she said, "that I am more certain every day that my brother is alive." She watched his eyes slowly widen. "And I'm wondering if you're going to help me or stand in my way."

EPILOGUE

THE DRAGON LANDED ON THE turret of the castle that had belonged to her first human. The woman who lived here now slid down her wing and into the window, and the dragon resisted the urge to shake her off.

The black-haired demon turned to her.

"When I call you, you come. That's how this works."

The dragon turned her snout toward the magician who had made her too many promises to count. She huffed hot air at the woman, but she didn't budge.

The woman—Mallow—tilted her head at the dragon and met her stare. "You doubt me, but I'll be rid of this prophecy soon. I am close to eliminating the heir. Then you'll complete the bond with me."

Maybe, the dragon thought. *Maybe I just don't like you that much.*

Mallow narrowed her black eyes. "I can only complete my promise to you if you bond with me. *You're* the one prohibiting that."

The dragon huffed again, sending a harsh wind into Mallow's chamber, disturbing papers and blowing paintings off the walls.

Mallow just stared her down.

The dragon pushed off from the tower, flying away. She hated humans.

She beat her wings against the air and coasted around the mountains to the rocky terrain on the other side of the cliff, to the nest where that demon had found her in the first place.

For over five hundred years she'd lived in peace, unless she was disturbed by a human. Humans had a way of mucking things up for her.

Case in point . . .

The dragon landed lightly on the ledge of her cave, smelling more humans than she liked to have around.

The man with the rust hair and the woman missing half an arm were back. The dragon snarled.

The man turned and held his hands up in peace, bowing deeply. The woman followed.

"We just need a moment. And if you won't allow anything else, we'll leave."

Humans had a habit of multiplying that the dragon hated. She folded her wings and settled herself on the ledge, staring them down.

The rusty-haired man nodded in thanks. He was nicer than his father at least.

From the back of the cave, her boy came into the light. He hugged the other two, and the dragon listened as the rust-haired one showed him a slip of paper too small to see.

"So you've made contact?" her boy said.

He was excited. And the dragon knew what came next. She sighed, staring at the lonely mountainside. She knew she couldn't keep him. He wasn't hers in the way a dragon child could be. But something about him had called to her, begging her to save him.

But saving him meant dealing with all his . . . *friends*. She snarled at the word.

"Dragon," her boy called anxiously. "It's time. If you'll allow me to go, I need to."

The dragon huffed, refusing to look at him.

When these two had come for him the last time, they'd all decided that it was safer for her boy to stay here. Foolishly, the dragon thought he'd chosen her that day. That he would have preferred to stay.

She wished she'd never taken him with her two months ago. That day near the lake as the dust billowed up into a cloud and the battle sizzled under her talons.

She'd grown fond of him. And now he wanted to go.

"Thank you for healing me and keeping me safe," he said. "But I have to get to my sister. I know you had one once. And I hope you remember what that bond means."

Bond, the dragon thought derisively. She thought she'd known a bond again. When the demon woman climbed up this mountain and promised to make her a dragon mate, the dragon had agreed to a bond. But from the moment she opened her magic up to the demon, she'd known it wasn't right. She'd felt Mallow's power and had mistaken that for the right partner. But the boy had more of what the dragon yearned for in his blood than Mallow could begin to dream of.

And now he wanted to leave. Fine.

The dragon turned her snout back to him, pressed her nose to his side, and moved her tail out of his path.

"Thank you. I hope we meet again," the boy said. "I want to introduce you to my sister. If anyone can figure out how a magician can make a dragon's mate, it's her."

The dragon rolled her eyes, sick of hearing about this sister already.

"Come on, Rory," the woman with one arm said. "We'll get you caught up."

Rory reached his hand out for the dragon's snout, and she huffed, pushing him back.

She took off into the sky, determined to forget about the rose prince and the itch she had to belong to him.

ACKNOWLEDGMENTS

If I truly took the space to list all the people who had a profound impact on the journey of this book, the acknowledgments would be as long as the book itself (and she's thicc). If I could, I would list every AO3 username who left comments and kudos, every person on Discord and Facebook who interacted with me while writing, and every fan artist and not-for-profit bookbinder who made something beautiful out of my words.

To Mar and Cat—who were my rock for eighteen months, committing to a project with me before and during a pandemic—thank you to my bbs for getting me to where I am today. They are still the girls whose hands I clutch under the table when the world gets too rough.

To my coach, Anna, who champions me through anything and talks out all kinds of nonsensical ideas, thank you for pushing me. Claire, you looked at this first, and you yammered about climate and building materials and historical context, and I really probably took none of it but I just gazed lovingly at you. Thank you for having such a pretty face.

Gaia Banks, you are the greatest agent in the world, and I'm so lucky to have you in my corner. Thank you for the (what feels like) hourly phone calls and endless support of my mental health.

Thank you to my editors who worked tirelessly on this book and encouraged me to stretch myself with it. Junessa Viloria at Forever and Martha Ashby and Rachel Winterbottom at HarperCollins UK, all three of you are amazing and took a wonderful chance on this. Thank you to the entire team at Forever, especially Mama Estelle, Cousin Dan, Caroline Green, Leah Hultenschmidt, and Sabrina Flemming. Thank you to the entire team at HarperCollins UK.

I want to thank my foreign editors and publishers, who at the time of writing this include: Maria Runge at Goldmann, Elena Paganelli at Newton Compton, Sonia Mennour at Bragelonne, Julia Barreto at HarperCollins Brazil, and the entire Crossbooks/Planeta team in Spain, especially Paula Hernández.

Thank you to my parents, who hardly saw me for eleven months. Thank you to my dog, Charlie, because why not?

My writer friends, my vampire coven, my group chats—thank you. Especially to Christina and Lauren, Susan Lee, Rosie Danan, and Ali Hazelwood, who experienced *throws glitter* the joy of this book with me. Thank you, Kate Goldbeck, Kate Golden, Margaret Wiggins, Amanda Jewell, and Thea Guanzon. Thank you, Lauren Goldgrub, Shaye Lefkowitz, and Tatyana for your enthusiasm and endless emotional support. Thank you, Nikita Jobson for the art you've bestowed upon me over the years. I was unworthy of "The Golden Girl" and I remain unworthy of this gorgeous cover.

And most important, thank you to my readers who follow me across genres. To my longtime readers and my new readers, to the content creators and the book reviewers, to the meme makers and the sock enthusiasts, you are why I do this.

Briony and Toven's spellbinding story continues in

the next Evermore book . . .

Coming in Summer 2026

About the Author

JULIE SOTO is a *USA Today* bestselling author, playwright, and actress originally from Sacramento, California. Her musical *Generation Me* won the 2017 New York Musical Festival's Best Musical award, as well as Best Book for her script. She is a musical theater geek, fandom nerd, and the author of many spicy fan fictions as Lovesbitca8. Julie now lives in Fort Bragg, California, with her dog, Charlie. She is probably drinking coffee as you read this.

Find out more at:

juliesotowrites.com
X: @JulieSotoWrites
Facebook.com/JulieSotoWrites
Instagram: @juliesotowrites
Pinterest.com/juliesotowrites
TikTok: @juliesotowrites